From quiet beginnings, without any
'discovery' except by the great reading public
itself, Frances Parkinson Keyes grew to be
one of the most popular and best-loved
women writers in the world. Her books
appeared simultaneously in half a dozen
languages and she appeals to those millions of
people who demand a good story with a rich
and varied background.

JOY STREET is a story of the old aristocracy
of Boston—of a young woman carefully reared
against a background of wealth and tradition
who finds herself catapulted into a world that
is strange to her—a world where breeding and
family count for little against vigour, brains,
and hard work. Against her own beliefs and
breeding, Emily Thayer comes to know the
true worth of friendship, and the real meaning
of love . . .

Frances Parkinson Keyes

Joy Street

CORGI BOOKS
A DIVISION OF TRANSWORLD PUBLISHERS LTD
A NATIONAL GENERAL COMPANY

JOY STREET

A CORGI BOOK 0 552 09220 7

Originally published in Great Britain
by Eyre & Spottiswoode Ltd.

PRINTING HISTORY

Eyre & Spottiswoode edition published 1951
Cedric Chivers Ltd. edition published 1965
Cedric Chivers edition reissued 1972
Corgi edition published 1973

This book is set in Plantin 9/10 pt.

Corgi Books are published by Transworld Publishers Ltd.,
Cavendish House, 57–59 Uxbridge Road, Ealing,
London, W.5.

Made and printed in Great Britain by
Richard Clay (The Chaucer Press), Ltd., Bungay, Suffolk.

**NOTE: The Australian price appearing on the
back cover is the recommended retail price**

TO
LEBARON BARKER
WHO KEPT INSISTING THIS BOOK MUST BE WRITTEN
UNTIL I GAVE IN AND DID IT
AND TO THE MEMORY OF

ELIZABETH SOULE SWEETSER
WHO LONG BEFORE LEBARON BARKER WAS BORN
AND ALSO
LONG BEFORE HE OR ANYONE ELSE THOUGHT OF ME AS AN
AUTHOR WAS CONFIDENT THAT SOME DAY I WOULD WRITE BOOKS
WHICH WOULD BE A CREDIT TO BOSTON OF WHICH SHE WAS
THE FINE FLOWER

CONTENTS

PART ONE

CHRISTMAS EVE 1936 TO JUNE 1938

ROGER

CHAPTER I

Emily Thayer stood beside the Christmas tree in the drawing-room of the old Forbes house on Louisburg Square, looking out at the candle-lighted windows across the park and listening to the carollers who came stamping through the snow. At least, this was what she appeared to be doing. As a matter of fact, she was hardly conscious of the illuminations or of the hearty songs; she was watching for Roger Field, who had promised to drop in at her grandmother's house some time during the course of the evening, and who was later than she expected.

He was very dependable; if he were late, something must have happened to detain him. She could not help visualizing all the different kinds of accidents which could occur when the streets were slippery and the traffic heavy between Cambridge and Boston; besides, there was a great deal of 'flu going around and sometimes it struck very suddenly. She thought the world of Roger, and the mere supposition that he might be injured or ill was painful to her. Moreover, she was almost sure that he meant to propose to her that night and she had made up her mind to accept him, though she knew that such a decision would be far from pleasing to her parents, her grandmother and Homer Lathrop, the old family friend who acted as trustee for the substantial fund her grandfather had left her.

Not that her parents and Homer Lathrop disliked or disapproved of Roger Field; they could not very well help admitting that socially the Fields' standing was equal to that of the Forbeses and the Thayers, even though financially it was not; and they had already told her, separately and collectively, that they 'had nothing against Roger'. But this, Emily knew, was damning with faint praise. Her elders, every now and then, made some allusion to the fact that his father had never set the world on fire, implying that the ability to do this was more or less requisite in a suitor, and that there was a strong family

10

resemblance between the late Mr. Field and his only son. Less casually—in fact, as emphatically as was consistent with good breeding—they expressed their very real dislike for Roger's sister Caroline, who was ten years his senior, still unmarried, and very pronounced in her views, with few of which Mr. and Mrs. Sumner Thayer, Old Mrs. Forbes and Mr. Homer Lathrop were in agreement.

Unconsciously, Emily shook her head and sighed. She was by nature a peace-loving girl and she dreaded arguments. Moreover, she could not argue about Caroline with any degree of conviction, because she herself intensely disliked Roger's sister. She was determined not to admit, even to herself, that she was 'in love' with Roger until after he had proposed; but she certainly was very fond of him, so fond that she was prepared to put up with the arguments, and even with Caroline, in order to become engaged to him. . . .

A band of carollers slackened their pace as they neared the old Forbes house; then came to a stop and grouped themselves around the doorstep. The light from a street-lamp shone brightly upon their leader as he stationed himself directly in front of the house. He had on a heavy overcoat, but his head and hands were bare. A few snowflakes glistened on his thick curly hair, intensifying its blackness, and his black brows gave his handsome face a forceful look which it might otherwise have lacked. He had one arm around a girl who was wearing a shabby shawl draped over her forehead and around her shoulders, which she held closely in place under her chin with tightly clenched fingers. Her face, thus framed, was very beautiful. The other carollers had formed a semicircle with their backs to the steps, and Emily had only a general impression of dark figures— bareheaded men and girls with shawls or scarves over their hair. But the two persons facing her were unmistakably striking. The leader released the girl at his side and raised both hands. Instantly the carollers began to sing, the sound of their vigorous young voices ringing out through the frosty air.

'Those must be some of the worthless Italians from St. Leonard's, that Roman Catholic church down on Prince Street. I must admit they sing better than most of the young hoodlums who are out making a night of it. Don't you think so, my dear?'

Emily turned quickly. She had been so absorbed in the singers that she had not been aware of Homer Lathrop coming up behind her and she was startled when she felt his hand on her

11

shoulder—startled and a little disappointed. For a moment she had thought that perhaps Roger ... not that Roger had ever given her a casual caress like that, or indeed any caress at all. But she had been hoping that, tonight, if he did propose ... And instead of Roger, who was rather awkward and apologetic and did not wear his clothes particulary well, here stood Homer Lathrop, who was the personification of both assurance and polish. His linen was glazed and immaculate and he patronized the best tailor in town. To be sure, his fine clothes fitted him just a shade too snugly and his laundered look did not prevent him from suggesting the *bon-vivant*; in another city, gossip would have had it that he might be a bachelor, but that nothing about him indicated the celibate. In Boston—that is, in Homer Lathrop's Boston—no such unkind comment was ever made or, at any rate, circulated. Privately, Emily thought his personality much more engaging than that of her handsome, defeated father, though she had never voiced such an opinion and did her best to suppress it, as disloyal. After all, though she had always called Homer Lathrop 'Uncle Homer', he was not even distantly related to either the Forbeses or the Thayers.

'You must agree with me about the singing,' Homer Lathrop went on, as she did not instantly answer his question about the carollers' talent. 'You seemed completely spellbound when I came up to you. I'm sorry if I frightened you.'

'You didn't frighten me, Uncle Homer—that is, not exactly. It was just ... Yes, I do think they sing wonderfully. And aren't they wonderful looking too—the man and the girl who are facing us, I mean?'

Homer Lathrop shrugged his shoulders slightly. 'I suppose so, if you care for that type. Personally, I've always thought the Italians were just one notch below the Irish—and you know where that would place them, in my opinion. The Hill's fairly swarming with them too—the other side, of course. But the next thing we know, they'll be over the top of it—right on top of *us*. They'll be grabbing for power and getting it, just the way the Irish have done.'

'They're not—well, quite so aggressive, are they?' Emily inquired, less because she was interested in the comparative qualities of the Irish and the Italians than because she realized she was expected to say something.

'They're just as violent—and they fight with knives instead of with their fists when they're aroused. They never should have

12

been admitted to this country. I've asked Russell again and again why something wasn't done, years and years ago, to curb immigration.'

'Something *has* been done now, hasn't it?—I mean, since Uncle Russell was in the Senate.'

'Oh, something! But nothing anywhere nearly drastic enough. I've told Russell so.'

When Homer Lathrop announced that he had made a statement, he meant that this was conclusive and that it should be convincing. Russell Forbes, who had been Governor of Massachusetts and was now the junior United States Senator from that commonwealth, was generally regarded as the most distinguished living member of his clan; moreover, he was the only one who had actively and successfully opposed the control of those Irish politicians so misprized by the rest of his family. But when Emily's grandfather had established the trust fund for her, both Russell and Homer had felt entitled to manage it. Russell because he was really her uncle and Homer because his outstanding success as an investment broker qualified him, to an exceptional degree, for the task. Emily's father, Sumner Thayer, was not entitled to any such responsibility, in the opinion of old Mr. Forbes. Sumner had been very extravagant in his college days, and though he had committed no further financial follies, his father-in-law never trusted him again where money was concerned. Russell was already preoccupied with politics when the fund was established and old Mr. Forbes had finally agreed that Homer's position was the stronger of the two; there had been hard feeling between him and Russell ever since. It was this feeling which Homer was now obliquely voicing. . . .

The Italian carollers had finished their song and their leader was motioning to them to be on their way. He had slipped his arm around his companion's waist again and, as he did so, she looked up at him with loving eyes. He bent his head and kissed her. She raised her hand to stroke his cheek and, in doing so, inevitably released her shawl, which fell to the ground. Her parted hair, roped around her head, was heavy and black, like the leader's; but it was straight and smooth where his was wavy and unruly. The young man picked up the shawl, shook it free from snow and replaced it caressingly over her head and shoulders. Then, once more holding her embraced, he started down the Square, followed by his little band.

'That was what Caroline Field would have called "disgust-

13

ing" and for once I should have agreed with her,' Homer Lathrop remarked, with visible repugnance.

'Did you really think that was disgusting, Uncle Homer?'

'Why, yes! Didn't you?'

'No-o-o. It seemed so natural. So—so instinctive. I thought it was rather sweet.'

'You *did*?'

'Yes, I did. Truly, Uncle Homer.'

Homer Lathrop gazed at Emily, his astonishment tinged with displeasure. He had always been greatly attached to her, and this attachment was largely based on the fact that she had never disappointed him, but had fitted perfectly into his most approved pattern: the Windsor School, the Petite École Française, the Junior League, the Vincent Club; the traditional coming-out tea on Louisburg Square and the ultra-smart coming-out ball at the Ritz Carlton; no nonsense about going off to college for several years, but a few special courses in English literature at Radcliffe and in Romance languages at the Sorbonne; a transitory interest in nursing, which, fortunately, had not progressed beyond a Nurse's Aide course at Massachusetts General; a reasonable interest in sports and the ability to sit a horse well, and play a good game of tennis, but no tweedy, doggy tastes; charm and vivacity enough to hold her own at a Hasty Pudding Club dance or a Beck spread, but no predilection for parked cars, road-houses or night-clubs; the possession of sufficient emotional stability to cope pleasantly but conclusively with her numerous suitors, none of whom had apparently made much impression upon her, which was all to the good, since, so far, strangely enough, there had been no definite prospect of a really advantageous alliance....

All in all, her standards, her intellect, her behaviour and her appearance had consistently pleased him from the time she was a very little girl. Her manner was still deferential and he had never seen her look prettier. Usually she was rather pale, but tonight there was a little colour in her cheeks, which was very becoming, and he liked the new way she was doing her hair—parted in the middle and drawn down over her ears into a large, smooth coil at the nape of her neck. Her dress of golden-brown velvet suited her perfectly. So did the topaz ear-rings and necklace she wore with it. She never went in for extremes, but she had a certain style of her own and knew enough to adhere to it; and certainly she would have a faultless figure as soon as it had

14

filled out a little more.

'Well, let's forget about the carollers,' he said leniently. 'I didn't come here to discuss street roisterers. I——'

'But, Uncle Homer, they aren't any more roisterous than Mrs. Shurcliff's bell-ringers! You said yourself that they sang beautifully. I had almost the same feeling, while I was listening to them, that I have when I hear the nuns singing in the chapel of St. Margaret's Convent.'

'I didn't know you were in the habit of going to the chapel in St. Margaret's Convent.'

'It's not a habit exactly. But I do go there sometimes for "meditation and prayer". The nuns have always made me feel very welcome.'

'I wish you wouldn't refer to those Episcopal nursing sisters as nuns,' Homer Lathrop interposed irritably. 'Besides——'

'Those Episcopal nursing sisters call themselves nuns, so I don't see why I shouldn't, too,' Emily remarked placidly. 'Look, Uncle Homer! Some of them are at the windows of their Convent right now! Don't they look lovely, standing there like that?'

'Look here, Emily, I hope you're not seriously interested in religion. If you are, let me tell you that it's just a phase—a phase that passes very quickly. Almost every girl, and not a few boys, briefly imagine, sooner or later, that——'

Her laugh interrupted him. 'I'm not imagining I want to be a nun, if that's what you're worrying about,' she said merrily. 'Rather the contrary. Do you feel better now?'

'I'm not sure that I do. You don't sound like yourself tonight. Emily. But this discussion doesn't seem to be very productive and I don't think we ought to prolong it, in any case, because I came to fetch you. We've missed you. In fact, your grandmother's asked for you twice now. If you're really interested in the Christmas illuminations you can see those even better from upstairs. But I don't see why you should be. They're no novelty to you.'

'No, but I think they're even more beautiful than usual. And it's such a perfect night! Just look at those stars!' As she spoke, she thought inconsequentially of the snowflakes on the young Italian's black hair. He must have been outdoors for a long time. Little flurries of snow had passed briefly over the city several hours earlier; obviously, he had been wandering through the streets ever since then, for otherwise the snowflakes would have melted; it was the cold which had kept them intact. Emily wondered if all the time the dark young man had been leading his carollers he had kept his arm around that beautiful girl's waist, holding her warm. . . .

'You can see the stars from the library too, Emily. As for the lighted windows with the shades all up—don't you ever feel, on Christmas Eve, that we're permitting the public to share our privacy a little too freely, even if we don't actually open our doors to them indiscriminately, as so many persons do?'

'No—just that we're inviting them to share our privileges. Besides, I wasn't just listening to the carollers and looking at the lighted windows and the stars,' she went on, courage coming to her as she spoke, 'I was watching for Roger. I hope nothing's happened. I thought he'd be here long before this.'

'*Watching* for Roger? Roger Field? But my dear Emily, why should you watch for him? Naturally he will ring the doorbell when he arrives and naturally Pearson will let him in if your grandmother has invited him to come here this evening.'

'She didn't. But she said I might. I asked her if I could.'

'I'm rather sorry you did that, Emily. I thought your grandmother was so wise in deciding that the Christmas gathering this year should be limited to a family group—a family group and a poor lonely bachelor like myself who happens to be a close friend. It's a relief to me that she's declined to keep open house or to go in for a big, rowdy party like Mrs. Putnam's.'

'I've been to one or two of Mrs. Putnam's parties,' Emily announced surprisingly.

'You have!'

'Yes. They're fun, sort of. I think you'd like her, Uncle Homer, really I do, if you got acquainted with her.'

'I doubt if the occasion for me to find out will arise,' Homer Lathrop said, rather coldly. 'And now, my dear, as I've already reminded you, your grandmother——'

'I think Grandmamma will understand if you just tell her I'm waiting for Roger. We'll come up together, by and by.'

She raised her eyes and met his steadily. Again he realized that he had never seen her look as lovely as she did tonight. Like her hair, her eyes had warm lights in them. The gaze and the smile with which she regarded him were not only sparkling, they were definitely determined and definitely charming.

'I think you're making a great mistake, Emily.'

'I'm sorry, Uncle Homer, very sorry.'

'Then, why not——'

'I meant I'm sorry you felt that way about what I'm doing. I didn't mean I was sorry I was doing it.'

'You haven't come to some sort of an understanding with Roger Field, without consulting any of us, have you, Emily?' he said, grasping at straws. 'Because I think I should tell you——'

'I haven't yet, but I'm hoping to. And there isn't anything you could tell me, Uncle Homer, that would change my mind.'

She turned away and went closer to the window, drawing the draperies more widely apart. Then she stood motionless, gazing out into the Square. She did not look at Homer Lathrop again, or move when he finally left the room.

Emily's trustee had hardly left the drawing-room when she saw her suitor coming up the front steps. The street light which had illuminated the young Italian's strong head and vigorous form now shone on Roger Field's earnest face and thin figure. When he caught sight of Emily he removed his hat, so he, too, was uncovered as he approached; but his well-cut hair was without lustre and was brushed back in a way that made his fine forehead appear too high. His movements, without being exactly clumsy, lacked distinguishing grace and, as usual, his clothes did not seem to suit him, though there was nothing particularly wrong about them. The refinement and intelligence of his countenance redeemed it from mediocrity; and, as Emily threw open the door for him, the smile with which he greeted her gave his expression sudden animation and elusive charm.

'How nice of you to let me in yourself! How did you guess exactly when I'd get here?'

'I didn't. I've been watching for you.'

'Why, that's nicer still! It's wonderful. Only I'm afraid you've had a long wait. I'd no idea I'd be so late. I'm awfully sorry.'

'It didn't matter. That is, I enjoyed looking at the lights and listening to the carollers while I waited. But I began to be afraid there'd been an accident.'

'No—I ought to have telephoned. Caroline was alone and I didn't like to leave her on Christmas Eve. I thought she'd go to her room right after dinner. Usually she does. But tonight she started talking and—well, there just didn't seem to be any good place to interrupt, for quite a while. You didn't think I wasn't coming, did you?'

17

'Oh, no! I knew you would, as soon as you could. You always keep your word. It's just that I was a little anxious.'

While they were talking, Roger had taken off his overcoat, folded it carefully, and placed it on a chair in the hall with his hat and gloves neatly laid on top of it. Then, smoothing down his unruffled hair, he followed Emily into the drawing-room.

'Do we really have this all to ourselves? How did you manage?'

'The others are in the library. Uncle Homer was here until a moment ago, trying to get me up there too. He said Grandmamma sent him for me. But I don't feel so sure.'

'I suppose he didn't want you to stay down here and wait for me. Or didn't you tell him that's what you were doing?'

'Yes, I told him.'

Emily had walked back to the bay window. Now, instead of standing beside it, close to the Christmas tree, as she had before, she sat down on a love seat which she had previously moved from its traditional position by the fireplace.

'Uncle Homer says we can see the illuminations just as well from the library,' she went on. 'I don't agree with him. I think you can see them much better from here. Look at the Della Robbia plaques at the Drummonds' next door—one in almost every window-pane. You must have noticed those as you came by.'

'I'm afraid I didn't. The truth is, I was hurrying so fast, trying to make up for lost time, that I didn't see much of anything. I bumped right into one group of carollers.'

'What sort of a looking group?'

'Why—I don't know. They looked just like any other group to me. What makes you ask?'

'Because some Italians stopped here that didn't look just like all the others. There was a young man who made me think of Michelangelo's David—except that this man was ever so much more striking because of his colouring. And the girl with him made me think of a Botticelli Madonna.'

'You did your sight-seeing thoroughly when you were in Florence, didn't you, Emily?'

'Of course I did. But nobody made me. I wanted to.'

'I was only teasing you—well, so this living art gallery stopped in front of the house and——'

'And sang divinely. Even Uncle Homer admitted that. And you know how he despises Italians. But after he had admired their singing, the leaders kissed each other, and you can imagine the effect that had on him.'

'Yes, I can. I'm sure he denounced them unsparingly. But don't you think that was partly because he enjoys denunciation on general principles? I can't believe he never felt like kissing anyone himself, though. Or that he didn't do it, either.'

'Not in the street!'

'No, I suppose not. But he must have had a sweetheart some-time, somewhere, even if it was "long ago and far away".' Privately, Roger was of the opinion that Homer Lathrop had kissed a good many women in his day and even suspected that such embraces were not entirely delights of the past. Now an unwonted bitterness crept into his voice. 'Probably Lathrop didn't marry because he discovered no one completely suitable.'

'Who's critical now? You're not fair to Uncle Homer, Roger!'

'Perhaps I'm not. And I don't claim for a minute that two wrongs make a right. But do you think he's fair to me?'

He had seated himself beside her, and now, very quietly, he took her hand.

'He knows I'm in love with you, Emily, and he knows there isn't any real reason why I shouldn't tell you so. But he's done everything he could to convince you that you shouldn't listen to me when I did, hasn't he?'

'Yes, but——'

'He thinks I'm not good enough for you. Of course I'm not —no man could be. But when he says "good enough", he isn't thinking of character, the way you and I would be. He's think-ing of money and power and prestige. And he hasn't any confi-dence in my future as a lawyer. He's asked me over and over again whether I'd made the *Review* and he knows perfectly well I haven't. He's also asked me over and over again whether Fiske, Ford and Gibbons had approached me any time during the fall. He also knows perfectly well that no one from the firm has. And, if a senior at the Harvard Law School hasn't been ap-proached by Fiske, Ford and Gibbons, or some firm just like it, he's bound to be a failure at the Massachusetts bar, as far as Homer Lathrop's concerned!'

'Yes, but——' Emily began again.

'And, of course, all your family agrees with him,' Roger went on, speaking with a vehemence as unwonted as the bitterness a few moments earlier. 'Your father and mother and your grand-mother and Senator Forbes. I don't know about the others; I suppose most of them never heard of me. But I know about those four and it's a pretty powerful combination, added to Homer Lathrop.'

This time Emily did not try to break in; she waited for Roger to go on. In all the years she had known him, she had never before heard him make such a long speech, and still he had not said quite what she wanted to hear, and she thought he might if she let him alone, now that he seemed headed in the right direction.

'They don't think it matters that I've loved you all my life,' Roger went on. 'Ever since we first went to dancing school at the Somerset and riding on the swan boats in the Public Garden and I bought you balloons and pinwheels—remember? They must know I have, even if I couldn't do showy things to prove it to them or to you. But, thank God, I've had a break at last! I've finally had a chance to ask you to marry me!'

He jumped up, pulling her to her feet with him. Then he drew her towards him and looked searchingly down at her. To his amazement, he saw that she was gazing at him not only tenderly but laughingly.

'I kept trying to tell you,' she said, 'that it didn't make any difference who tried to convince me I shouldn't listen to you. I meant to, right along. Only I thought you'd never say anything I *could* listen to. I mean anything that mattered. Of course, that's why I waited for you here tonight, Roger—because I thought that, perhaps, at last you would!'

They reluctantly agreed, half an hour later, that it might be better if they went to the library on their own initiative than if they remained downstairs until someone came to fetch them.

'We can't keep them from suspecting, especially if we stay down here much longer,' Emily said. 'But if we go up to the library, not holding hands or anything, they won't actually demand an explanation. That is, I don't believe they will. I think we ought to try the casual approach, because the result is bound to be at least the lesser of the two evils. . . . I do hate to, though,' she confessed.

'So do I. Don't let's, just yet,' Roger said, in a voice that did not sound quite natural. He had been wondering whether he should talk to her a little about his prospects, since these were not quite as gloomy as she had hitherto been given to understand, both by himself and by others. He thought it might be

20

fairer if he did, because of course he would have to tell her father and her trustee about them very shortly, and he felt Emily was entitled to hear the encouraging news first. It did seem as if this one time, at least, he and she might have been spared the discussion of any intrusive subject. Yet, on the other hand ... as always, his conscience prevailed against his desire.

'There's something else I want to tell you before we go upstairs,' he added slowly.

'It can't be as important as what you've told me already.'

'It isn't. But it might be pretty important at that. I have a prospect—just a slight one—of a job.'

'You *do*! Oh, Roger, how marvellous! Why didn't you tell me so before?'

'Well, as you said yourself, the other was more important.' He bent his head and brushed his lips over her hair and forehead, drawing her a little closer to him as he did so. Then, realizing that a more fervent embrace would automatically postpone the telling of his great news, he went on, 'There's nothing definite about it yet, but I honestly think there may be, a little later.... You know Mr. Harold Swan, don't you?—Marion Swan's father?'

'I know Marion, just slightly. She went to Miss May's.'

'So she did. And of course she's an older girl too—about half-way between you and Caroline, I should think. But Caroline happens to know her quite well and I've been to the Swan's house a few times with her, when I knew you were tied up with something else, like last night.'

'Was it just last night that——'

'That's right. Mr. Swan asked me if I'd made any special plans for next year. Only he didn't put the question the way Homer Lathrop always does, as if he were perfectly sure that I hadn't. He sounded as if he thought I might have. And he seemed quite pleased when I said no.'

'Is Mr. Swan a lawyer?'

'Yes. I've never heard much about his firm either—Cutter, Mills and Swan. But it's in one of the best buildings on Devonshire Street.'

'Well, of course, that counts for a lot. What did Mr. Swan say after you told him you didn't have any plans for next year?'

'He asked me to drop by and see him at his office some day soon. He said he'd like to talk to me about an experiment his firm was making.'

21

'Did he give you any idea what kind of experiment it was?'

'Yes. He said Mr. Cutter, the head of the firm, had very progressive ideas about its development. Mr. Mills doesn't always agree with him, but Mr. Swan thinks he's on the right track. At first they always picked their juniors from Harvard, like Fiske, Ford. For instance, they took in Elliot Berkeley and Cyrus Fletcher. You know them, don't you?'

'Not very well. Of course they're both older. I have met Elliot Berkeley at one or two hunt balls and ridden in the same horse shows that he has. But I've never been to his house in Hamilton and I don't think Grandmamma ever asked him here. Isn't he—doesn't he——'

'Yes. He's a little on the thirsty side. But he is a wonderful horseman. And, of course, very, very social register. More so than Fletcher. And I think he has more brains, of a sort. Fletcher really hasn't much between the ears and he's almost as much of a sissy as Berkeley is of a he-man. But then Fletcher's family owns most of the shipyards and practically all the granite quarries in Quincy. Not that those amount to as much as they used to, but I suppose they help to give him a semblance of intellect and masculinity.'

'I suppose so,' Emily said rather doubtfully. 'Well, you were telling me——'

'I was saying that Cutter, Mills and Swan followed the standard practice of picking their juniors from Harvard at first. And, as far as I know, Berkeley and Fletcher have been perfectly satisfactory. It would look that way, because they're about to be taken into the firm. But Cutter isn't sticking entirely to Harvard any longer. He's picking graduates from other law schools—men with all sorts of different backgrounds.'

'Why, you're at Harvard!'

'I know. But Mr. Swan thought there might be a place, next year, for one Harvard graduate, if he qualified in other ways. You see, Mr. Cutter has been carrying this experiment of his so far that Mr. Mills is getting pretty disagreeable about it. An Irishman who graduated from Holy Cross and an Italian who graduated from Boston College were taken in. Both Roman Catholics, of course. The Irishman, Brian Collins, is a South Boston product. Mr. Mills accepted him without too much fuss. It seems his father's a very successful contractor and he was sure to bring lots of new clients into the firm. He's brought in quite a few wealthy ones already and he's only been there two years. Law firms have to be practical about things like that.'

'Yes, I suppose so.'

'But Mr. Mills raised a row over the Italian,' Roger went on rather hurriedly. He could tell from Emily's tone that the word 'practical' in connection with the experiment troubled her a little. It troubled him too. 'Mr. Swan didn't say where he lives and I can't remember his name. But I gathered he wasn't as well fixed as Collins.'

'You know how Uncle Homer feels about Italians, Roger.'

'Yes, I certainly do. I've heard him enlarge on the subject often enough! He and Mr. Mills ought to get together. Well, to finish the story, Mr. Cutter added insult to injury by taking in a fellow named David Something-or-Other, who'd been an honour student at Columbia.'

'But then he must be awfully bright!'

'He is. Phi Beta Kappa, *summa cum laude*, the whole works. He's also a Jew.'

'Oh! And Mr. Mills——'

'That's right. Mr. Mills is even more allergic to Jews than he is to Roman Catholics. He threatened to leave the firm if Mr. Cutter went on with his experiment. Well, I guess things got pretty hot around the office for a while. But finally, Mr. Cutter promised that the next man they took in would be—well, some-one more like me. And he asked Mr. Swan to keep on the lookout.'

'You like Mr. Swan, don't you, Roger?'

'Yes, very much. He reminds me of my father. He's got very high ideals.'

'And this experiment the firm's making—you think that's based on high ideals?'

'I'm sure it is, as far as Mr. Swan's concerned. It was really very moving, the way he talked—about bringing together differ-ent racial groups that had never mixed very well in Boston before. He made me feel it would be a privilege to have a part in an undertaking like that. And, if I had you to help me——'

Again he drew her closer to him. If it had not been for the contemptuous attitude of her family, his only words that night could have been of love. He would always feel that the radiance of betrothal had been dimmed by the intrusion of material things, and that this intrusion might have been avoided if he had not needed to justify himself in his beloved's eyes. Well, he had told her now that his future was not altogether without

23

some promise of those things by which her elders set such store; perhaps, in so doing, he had made things easier for her, since, reassured, she might find ways to reassure the others. But having told her, he had the right to be the lover again.

'You know I'll help you, dearest, in every way I can!' Emily was murmuring. But she could say no more, before he sealed her lips.

CHAPTER II

When Emily and Roger entered the library, having discreetly unclasped hands before reaching the threshold, they were not immediately observed by the girl's parents and Homer Lathrop. These three greatly resented the amount of bell ringing and horn blowing which now resounded through the Square. The bay window offered a vantage point from which to identify the miscreants—doubtless intoxicated—and the indignant trio, while attempting to do this, stood with their backs to the room, exchanging vexed remarks.

'We should really be thankful that Major Higginson did not live to see such a perversion of his plan,' Mrs. Thayer was saying. 'Christmas Eve on Beacon Hill was truly beautiful, as he visualized it. But now, instead of an atmosphere of goodwill, there is all this frightful rowdyism.'

'I agree with you, Eleanor. And I think the worst of that noise is coming from across the park, near Mrs. Putnam's house.'

'I'm afraid you're right, and in that case her guests are probably making most of it. We can't very well complain to the police, under those circumstances.'

'I don't see why not. It's regrettable that Mrs. Putnam was ever permitted to acquire property in Louisburg Square. Any action that makes her feel unwelcome here would have my complete approval.'

'We're lucky,' Emily whispered to Roger. 'If they'd only been concentrating on the street hoodlums, they'd have turned around in a minute. But now that they've got started on Mrs. Putnam too, their righteous wrath will have no bounds. Come on, we'll say Merry Christmas to Grandmamma.'

Old Mrs. Forbes, as she was invariably called, was enthroned in a great carved chair by the fireplace, under the splendid portrait of her which Sargent had painted when she was in her prime. Except for this one portrait, the high walls of the immense room were lined with books; and it had none of the drawing-room's forbidding qualities. Old Mrs. Forbes also appeared to be deep in conversation. But the animated discussion in which she was engaged with her son, Russell, had not prevented her from observing the approach of her granddaughter and Roger Field. Emily was quick to sense this; she knew that her grandmother still had the use of all her faculties and that these were acute. Old Mrs. Forbes had put on a great deal of weight with advancing years and she moved about with difficulty, using a cane when she did so; but mentally she was even more nimble than when her sumptuous figure had been conspicuous for its perfection in exclusive ballrooms from Boston to Budapest.

'Good evening, Roger,' she said agreeably if a little condescendingly. 'I had been wondering what had become of you. I didn't hear you ring.'

She extended a hand that was still comely in spite of its fleshiness and which set off its superb rings well. Old Mrs. Forbes had always been fond of jewellery and she wore a great deal of it—much more than her daughter, Mrs. Thayer, approved. In addition to the rings, she was now wearing a diamond necklace, a diamond bar pin, a diamond wrist watch and diamond-studded combs in her iron-grey hair, which was sleek and abundant and elaborately dressed; and all these diamonds served as accessories to the magnificent black-and-silver brocade which was her latest Worth importation. 'Mamma—just for a family party too!' Mrs. Thayer had said rebukingly, when she arrived that evening; and as she spoke, she glanced fleetingly but approvingly at the reflection in a nearby mirror of a trim, middle-aged woman who had kept her figure and who was appropriately turned out in dark *crêpe* marocain and medium-sized pearls. But Old Mrs. Forbes did not care a whit what Eleanor Thayer thought of her taste, or anyone else either. She intended to go on wearing her diamonds and her brocades till the day of her death—in fact, she intended to be buried wearing large quantities of both.

Roger kissed the extended hand, which was what he was expected to do. Old Mrs. Forbes had spent a great deal of time in foreign courts when her husband was alive, and there were some who said she had been the better diplomat of the two; there was no doubt that she had left the more lasting mark or that she still enjoyed being treated like an ambassadress.

'Roger couldn't very well leave Caroline alone on Christmas Eve. So he had dinner with her and stayed with her until she went to her room. We ought to have invited her tonight too, Grandmamma.'

'What an exemplary brother! Of course, I should have been pleased to invite Caroline too, my dear, if you had suggested it, and any number of other young people, as far as that goes. But when you mentioned only Roger, I naturally concluded that, for some strange reason, you wished to see him alone.'

'Oh—Uncle Russell, I'm so sorry! You remember my friend Roger Field, don't you? You should! He's always been one of your greatest admirers.'

Old Mrs. Forbes looked at her granddaughter with a glint of pride in her shrewd old eyes as the senator, with something of his mother's condescension and less of her grand manner, tardily permitted himself to be drawn into the conversation. So the girl had had the gumption to take the bit in her teeth after all! Old Mrs. Forbes looked at Emily still more closely, recognizing the girl's new radiance, and knew exactly what had happened during that hour in the drawing-room, before the newly engaged pair had come up to the library. It took a very special kind of kissing to make a girl look like that. Involuntarily, Old Mrs. Forbes sighed. It was many, many years since she ... And no matter what anyone said, there was nothing to equal it, nothing in the whole world. ...

'Besides, I have every reason to believe——' Mrs. Thayer said, turning from the window. Then she caught sight of Roger and Emily, standing by the fireplace. 'Oh—how do you do, Roger?' she went on, as coolly as was consistent with her ideas of courtesy. 'This is quite a surprise. I didn't expect to see you here this evening.'

'I did,' Old Mrs. Forbes said tersely. 'I invited him. I suppose I don't have to tell you beforehand, Eleanor, every time I invite someone to my own house.'

'Of course not, Mamma. But you did say this was just a family party, so I thought——'

'We agreed a long time ago that Homer was one of the family, that he should always be included—that is, if he cares to be—he's showing very little sign of it tonight.' Old Mrs. Forbes glanced in the direction of the window, where Sumner and Homer were still standing and, as if galvanized into action by

27

this piercing look, they both tardily turned and came forward, Sumner giving Roger a limp hand and Homer merely nodding in his direction. 'I decided it was time to expand the circle again,' Old Mrs. Forbes went on. 'Unfortunately, it is not as large as most family groups in Boston and we were growing rather static. . . . Eleanor, will you please ring for Pearson? I don't see what we are waiting for, now that we are all here. I wish to have the punch and cakes brought up at once. I have been growing steadily hungrier and thirstier for nearly two hours now—ever since Emily so mysteriously disappeared. Perhaps it is all this talk about tariff that has made me feel the need of more sustenance. Do you always talk about tariff, Russell? No wonder your wife left you!'

And no wonder everyone within the orbit of Old Mrs. Forbes was afraid of her, Roger said to himself, as he went down the front steps into Louisburg Square about two hours later; no one was safe from her eyes and her ears and her tongue, unless they escaped from her completely. Roger had already been made to feel the force of it; though Old Mrs. Forbes had spoken and acted in his defence, he knew she would expect—and exact—tribute in payment of her largess; and unless he were very careful, that payment might well take the form of loss in independent thought and action.

Of course, there were a few who had escaped from her, which explained why her family circle was smaller than that of most prominent Bostonians. She had not been powerful enough to cow Letitia, though the girl had looked so frail and flowerlike when she married Russell. Letitia had divorced Russell on grounds of cruelty—allegedly his, but undoubtedly really his mother's! She had not only given up her proud position as a senator's wife and a Boston Brahmin; she had further flown in the face of Providence by marrying an Austrian violinist who had refugeed to the Riviera—to some funny little town no one had ever heard of before!

When Roger had come in from Cambridge most of the streets not barred to traffic were already lined with closely parked cars; he had been obliged to leave his dilapidated Ford on Beacon, beyond the State House. Now, as he turned from Louisburg Square into Mount Vernon and began the climb that led steeply towards the Hill's summit, he scarcely noticed the carollers who were making a night of it or the candles which continued to burn brightly in the windows. He was still thinking about Letitia, living meagrely in an obscure little French town, and he wondered whether she did not sometimes long for the fleshpots she had abandoned. As to the others who had eluded Old Mrs. Forbes, there was her younger son, Sherman, who lived on the Cape all the year round, and said he couldn't take time to come to Boston—though everyone knew that his manager, Jarvis Compton, was perfectly capable of looking after the cranberry bogs from which he derived the ample income that, added to his wife's fortune, made him entirely independent of his mother. Old Mrs. Forbes hated Sue, Sherman's wife, because she made no proper use of her fortune. Even as a débutante, Sue had looked better in a cardigan sweater and a tweed skirt than she did in sequins and tulle, and now she lived in shorts or slacks, according to the season. It was doubtful if she spent a hundred dollars a year on clothes; and she liked to do her own housework, so she spent almost nothing on servants either. And she let her children run wild. Sherman encouraged her to share in the sports which he enjoyed himself, such as hunting, fishing and sailing. Of course, it was sheer nonsense for him to pretend that he spent all his time in the cranberry bogs—far more often he was out in a marsh, shooting ducks, or out in a boat trolling for 'blues' off the coast or salmon fishing in Long Pond. And Sue went with him.

In short, everything about Sue Forbes' tastes and her mother-in-law's was so antagonistic that they never voluntarily sat in the same room. Besides, Old Mrs. Forbes hated the Cape as much as she hated Sue. She owned a house at Manchester-by-the-Sea and another at Dublin, New Hampshire; but, except when the world war had interrupted her schedule, she had spent at least part of every year in Europe.

Her separation from Sherman automatically separated her from all her grandchildren except Emily, for Russell and Letitia had been childless and her younger daughter, Elizabeth, had never married. Undoubtedly, Old Mrs. Forbes would have enjoyed having Serman's big brood about her, partly because children were more easily dominated than grown persons, and partly because she could not play the matriarch as effectively as she might have wished in a circle so regrettably small as that made up of Russell—who was in Washington most of the time —Sumner, Eleanor, Emily and Homer Lathrop. But in this instance, neither Mahomet nor the mountain yielded; Sherman remained stubbornly among his cranberries, and his mother, with equal stubbornness, on Louisburg Square. . . .

The crowds on Mount Vernon Street were not quite as dense as they had been on Louisburg Square, but they were even more hilarious. A solitary pedestrian who plodded along, neither singing nor blowing a horn nor jingling bells, looked strangely out of place among the merrymakers; more than once, Roger felt that he was the butt of some jeering comment as he forged past a boisterous group. Other carollers, more convivially inclined, caught hold of him and urged him to join them. One of these was so insistent and so obviously drunk that a burly policeman intervened, and Roger lost no time in taking advantage of his welcome release.

When he was at a safe distance, however, feeling that he had been rude and abrupt, he called back a Merry Christmas, adding that he was sorry that he hadn't been able to join in the song. As a matter of fact, conviviality was far from his mood; he had succeeded in dismissing Sherman and Sue from his mind, only to find himself dwelling on the subject of Old Mrs. Forbes' younger daughter, Elizabeth, who had also eluded her.

Elizabeth taught chemistry at Bryn Mawr and spent her vacations in northern Vermont, where she lived in a brick farmhouse, which she had remodelled with intelligence and affection.

Old Mrs. Forbes was graciously willing to concede that there might be a few persons of background and culture in the Vermont village which Elizabeth used as a post-office address. But the remodelled farmhouse was two miles back in the hills; and though Emily and her friends greatly enjoyed using it for headquarters during the midwinter period when the special 'snow trains' were running, the accommodations it offered were certainly not calculated to cater for the comfort or appeal to the taste of a lame and luxury-loving old lady. Moreover, there was a conspicuous lack of good hotels within a radius of miles. It was never feasible for Old Mrs. Forbes to visit Elizabeth and she suspected—as others did—that there was method in her daughter's choice of a home, just as there was method in her choice of profession and of her conversational topics. . . .

As Roger trudged along through the snow, finding the going harder and harder all the time, he kept on thinking anxiously of those persons who had taken desperate measures to escape Old Mrs. Forbes, instead of thinking only of Emily, as he expected he would and as he still wanted to do. He also thought of the two other Forbes children who had died, one during a bitter winter in St. Petersburg and the other during a torrid summer in Rome. In both instances, Old Mrs. Forbes—who was then young and beautiful and the American Ambassadress—had been warned that the climatic conditions were unhealthful for her children—or so her enemies had said, and like most other women who are beautiful and rich and powerful, she had never lacked enemies.

It began to appear certain to Roger that, short of dying, the only way to find escape from Old Mrs. Forbes was to move away from Boston—as far away as was humanly possible, even if that meant the Pacific Coast or the Deep South. But he feared he would not fit into either of these regions. Besides, Emily had left Boston very little, except for brief visits to Washington, made under the highest official auspices, and for the sojourns in Europe which her grandmother had supervised. Even in Boston, she had moved almost entirely in a small, circumscribed circle; why, she had said, 'Marion Swan went to Miss May's,' as if that explained why she did not know Marion well! And if he took Emily to Seattle or San Francisco or Birmingham or New Orleans, she would meet many young women who had attended public high schools and had never been to Europe; she would be baffled in her attempts to talk with them because they would not think about the same things or do the same things that she did.

Moreover, if he took the desperate step of moving away from Boston, he would lose the one possible opportunity for suitable employment which had presented itself to him so far. He knew that the firm of Cutter, Mills and Swan did not have the prestige of Fiske, Ford and Gibbons and other firms of long-established standing. But it must be sound financially, or it could not have had offices in a highly reputed Devonshire Street building; perhaps it might even pay its juniors better than the old firms, some of which were niggardly when it came to money, on the principle that any young man fortunate enough to be connected with them, in any capacity, should be so sensible of his privileges as to be above considerations of filthy lucre.

He did not know how much it would cost to support a wife, but he had heard the sum of five thousand dollars mentioned as a minimum, with the qualifying remark that, of course, this meant a very small house and only one maid and that it was to be hoped there would be no children. Roger hoped nothing of the sort; he wanted very much to have children and—though of course he had never spoken to her on such a subject—he would have been bitterly disappointed to discover that Emily did not feel the same way. He and Caroline were managing on a good deal less than five thousand, because they had to; he had given up living in a dormitory, which he had greatly enjoyed, and they did not have a house at all, only a very small apartment in an unfashionable section of Cambridge and only a part-time maid. He could not expect Emily to live like that. Naturally, she would never have to; her family would see to it that she did not, even if it weren't for the trust fund, which Roger, like everyone else, was aware of. But he shrank from the idea of having Emily accept more than was absolutely necessary from the Forbeses and the Thayers. It was the irony of fate that his own straitened circumstances made it doubly humiliating to accept bounty from others. If he had been wealthy enough to give Emily everything she really needed, he would not have minded letting her family supply her with luxuries; and he would have been glad to see her in possession of an allowance from a trust fund.

If he could only have taken her to the house in Brookline where he and Caroline had grown up, that had been very pleasant and comfortable and sunny, even if a little shabby and graceless and located in a neighbourhood which was fast going downhill. But that house had been sold to settle his father's estate, and if it had not been, probably Caroline would have felt she had a right to live with him and Emily, which would never have worked out either. Poor Caroline, she would be terribly alone after he was married! And she would be no more pleased with the engagement than the Forbeses and the Thayers, though for different reasons. She did not hesitate to say that Old Mrs. Forbes was a termagant, Russell an opportunist, Eleanor a snob, Sumner a weakling and Homer—whom she bracketed with the others—a wolf in sheep's clothing. She had never said anything really derogatory about Emily; but she had not failed to imply that there was not much hope for a girl brought up under such unfortunate influences.

As Roger finally turned from Mount Vernon into Joy and began to walk downhill, he became aware of a large, squarely built brick house, looming up across the street. It stood on a corner and it had the substantial massive look of a place which had been built to endure. But only one window in it was lighted and this solitary illumination was electrical and altogether out of harmony with seasonal festivities. It served only the better to display a large placard which read:

FOR SALE
TO SETTLE ESTATE
APPLY TO BROOKS, BRIMMER AND SHAW

For some moments he stood still, gazing at the sign; then his eyes wandered away from the window where it was displayed and he surveyed the entire structure. It had none of the architectural beauty which distinguished so many houses on the Hill; but it bespoke solidity and spaciousness and cultured, orderly living. He could visualize double parlours, with an ample dining-room leading out of them; an upstairs library, comparable in size and comfort to the one he had just left; a master's bedroom and dressing-room, guest chambers, day and night nurseries. This was the sort of house to which he might bring Emily with pride, where they could live happily together and welcome their friends and bring up their children in a way which even her family would be bound to approve and actually to admire. Slowly he unbuttoned his overcoat and felt for the small pad, with infinitesimal pencil attached to it, which he always carried in his waistcoat pocket. When he had extracted it, he jotted down the number of the house and the name of the real estate agents. Probably that house cost more than he could earn in a lifetime. Still it did no harm to dream. . . .

'Hey! Look out where you're going! What are you doing anyway? Sleep-walking?'

'Oh, I'm sorry—terribly sorry! I don't see how I could have . . .'

For the second time that night he had collided with a band of carollers, this time with such force that one of them would have slipped and fallen if her companion had not quickly caught her up. Roger's distress was so obvious and his own inept attempts at helpfulness so kindly that the other man's anger died down as quickly as it had flared.

'Skip it! We ought to have yelled at you. But we thought you'd be bound to see us before you started knocking us over. . . . You're all right, aren't you, *carissima*?'

The bareheaded young man with the glistening black hair had

turned from Roger to his companion. She smiled up at him tenderly.

'*Si, si!* I didn't fall—you wouldn't have let me.' Then, looking towards Roger, she said, reassuringly, 'Don't feel bad, please, sir. It wasn't anything at all. Just gives us the chance to wish you Merry Christmas!'

'That's right! Merry Christmas to you, whoever you are!' Her companion smiled suddenly, revealing teeth that were startlingly white in his dark face.

With no further trace of ill-feeling and with no self-consciousness, the carollers grouped themselves around their leader. Roger could not very well continue abruptly on his lonely and troubled way in the face of such friendliness; it would have been too ungracious. Besides, something that Emily had said, earlier in the evening, began forcing itself to the forefront of his mind. 'A young man that made me think of Michelangelo's David, except that this man was ever so much more striking because of his colouring—and a girl with him who looked like a Botticelli Madonna. . . .'

'These *must* be the same carollers,' he said to himself. 'I'll call Emily and tell her about this the first thing in the morning.' He would have liked to shake hands with the leader, to say that he was Roger Field and learn the names of the young Italian and of the girl addressed only as *carissima*. But innate shyness prevented such a gesture. Besides, the group was already singing and presently, without any pause in the song, it broke ranks and went on up the hill.

After Emily had bade Roger a lingering good night and returned to the library, she found, as she had expected, that her family was awaiting explanations; and, exhilarated by her first experience with declared and released love, she acted and spoke on the impetus this had given her.

'I'm sorry if you're annoyed because I didn't come upstairs right after you sent Uncle Homer to fetch me, Grandmamma,' she said, almost casually. 'You see, Roger was telling me about his new job and I got so interested that I didn't realize the flight of time.'

'His new job! What job?' the family asked, almost in unison.

'He's just been offered one—that is, practically. By Mr. Harold Swan. You know his firm, of course—Cutter, Mills and Swan.'

'Know his firm? Who doesn't?'

'Well, of course I realized it was a very important one, but——'

'*Important!* It's notorious! What your father meant, Emily, was that it's a firm headed by a bounder, a renegade and a dreamer.'

'Sumner is quite welcome to call Roscoe Cutter anything he likes, as far as I am concerned,' remarked Old Mrs. Forbes,' but I think Emily had started to tell us something when she was so rudely interrupted.'

'Really, Mamma!'

'If you please, Eleanor! As you were saying, Emily——?'

'I was saying that this firm is trying a very interesting experiment. Two of the original juniors are going to be taken into partnership pretty soon and——'

'Are you referring to that horsy inebriate, Elliot Berkeley, and that inbred moron, Cyrus Fletcher?'

'If that's the way you want to characterize them. As I was saying, the firm's now taking in juniors from several different groups that haven't been represented in the leading law firms here in Boston before and——'

'Dagos! Shanty Irish! Sheenies!'

'Wops is the more modern term, I think, Lathrop. And the Shanty Irish are the ones who keep pigs in their parlours, not the ones who send their sons to law schools. Those are locally known as Castle Irish. And now that Mr. Brandeis is a respected member of the Supreme Court——'

It was Emily's turn to take the initiative in exchanging glances with her grandmother. Even her new-found daring had not emboldened her to look for any help from this all-powerful quarter. She continued her recital with increasing assurance.

'I think the Brian Collins Roger mentioned must be Castle Irish. His father's a very wealthy contractor. He's brought lots of clients to the firm already and he's only been there two years. Roger says Mr. Cutter is very practical about such things.'

'*Practical!*'

'If you groan like that again, Sumner, I shall certainly have Pearson call a physician. As I said before, go on, Emily!'

'And the firm has another junior who was Phi Beta Kappa at Columbia and graduated from there *summa cum laude*.'

'The Jew, no doubt,' interposed Homer Lathrop.

'Yes. Roger couldn't remember his last name, but his Christian name's David.'

'I suppose you mean his *first* name. Your Uncle Homer just reminded you that he isn't a Christian. And to hear you talk, Emily, anyone would think you were quite prepared to call him by his *first* name, in the course of a nice, friendly chat in your own house.'

'Why, I am, Mamma! You see, Roger——'

'I do wish you'd stop quoting Roger Field as if he were the Law and the Prophets.'

'I suppose you didn't mean to make a poor pun, Eleanor. But I think we may as well reconcile ourselves to the fact that Roger Field is the *law*, as far as Emily is concerned. Isn't that what you were gradually leading up to, Emily?'

Once again Emily met her grandmother's direct gaze. The look she saw there was all she needed.

'Yes,' she said. 'That is, I didn't mean to tell until after Christmas, but from the way you're all acting and talking, I think I might as well. Roger Field proposed to me tonight and I accepted him. That's really why I was downstairs so long.'

Sumner Thayer groaned again and Eleanor gave a small, shocked cry. But neither of them had time to interrupt their daughter before she went on.

'I know everything you're going to say. You're going to tell me, in a minute, if I give you the chance, that Roger can't support me and I know he can't. He knows it too. But if you'll give him a chance, he'll prove he can hold down a job and that he can get better and better at it all the time. We're both willing to have a long engagement—we won't even call it an engagement if you'd rather we didn't, for the present. We'll just call it an "understanding". We won't even see each other. I'll join the Frontier Nursing Service. So I'll go to Kentucky. Of course I'll have to go as a courier, but at that, what I learned in my Nurse's Aide course might come in handy. And Roger will start working for Cutter, Mills and Swan as soon as he's graduated and save his money all next winter. But a year from next June I'll be twenty-two, and after that I can have half the income from my trust fund. When I'm twenty-five I can have the whole income and, in the meantime, I can just run up bills if Uncle Homer won't be a good sport and let me have what I need—everyone knows I'm going to get the money some time. I'm not going to wait around for ever to marry a man I'm in love with and I'm not going to live in a tenement when I do marry him.

I'm going to have a nice big house and invite all the people he knows to come to it—those Sheenies and Dagos you were talking about, Uncle Homer, and the *Castle Irish* too! You're going to tell me Roger'll never set the world on fire. Well, I don't *want* the world to be on fire. I want it to be peaceful and pleasant and safe. I want to share my place in it with Roger Field. And I'm going to!'

Emily walked over to Old Mrs. Forbes' chair and threw her arms around her grandmother's neck. Then, defiantly, she faced the others. Old Mrs. Forbes heaved her great weight from her throne-like chair and reached for her stick.

'Well,' she said, 'that all sounds pretty conclusive to me. I don't know that we'll gain anything by arguing about it at this hour. Why don't you spend the night here, Emily? I can send Doris over to get your things. I'd like to have a little talk with you, alone, in the morning. What I mean is just a pleasant conference about trousseaux and things like that. I'm afraid diamonds and brocade wouldn't ever suit you, but I think possibly sapphires and satin—well, we'll settle all that later when we don't have so many antagonistic onlookers. Come along, I'm going to put you in the Chippendale guest room. Good night, the rest of you. Don't blame either Emily or me if you don't have a Merry Christmas.'

Old Mrs. Forbes was right about the futility of further argument. Homer Lathrop and both Eleanor and Sumner Thayer attempted it, but vainly. According to Emily, who departed promptly for Kentucky, her mail reached her very irregularly there; and she had no time to answer letters even when she did get them. Her angry trustee and her distracted parents were thwarted by her tactics. Roger graduated creditably from the law school, passed his written examinations for the Massachusetts bar and immediately thereafter went to work for Cutter, Mills and Swan. It was understood from the beginning that, since he had no vacation that summer, but stayed on the job while all the other juniors were having theirs, he should take double time off the following year. He worked early and late at the office and saved every penny he could possibly spare, including his Christmas bonus. By spring of the following year he had put by five hundred dollars. Insignificant though this sum appeared to Homer Lathrop, he could not deny that, in a rather plodding way, Roger was making good; and when he announced his first raise, Homer threw up his hands and wired Emily to come home. On her twenty-second birthday, she and Roger were married in Trinity Church and the wedding reception was held on Louisburg Square.

The ostensible reason for this arrangement was the spaciousness of Old Mrs. Forbes' house. The residence of Mr. and Mrs. Sumner Thayer on Gloucester Street belonged to a later period and had obviously been designed with an eye to keeping the width of a building lot within economical limits. But the real reason that the wedding reception was held at Old Mrs. Forbes' house, whatever was generally circulated to the contrary, was because she was willing to invite Roger's new associates to it and her daughter was not. Though this reception was very large, Emily had known nearly all the guests from childhood; therefore, she had no difficulty in immediately identifying the few who were strangers and in giving them an especially gracious greeting, despite the relatives and close friends who came crowding in upon them as they went down the line. Roger did not fail to voice his appreciation of this when he and Emily were settled in their drawing-room on the train for New York, with their handsome new baggage piled up all around them. The baggage was liberally labelled, for though Roger's commitment to Cutter, Mills and Swan did not give the bridal couple enough leeway for a trip around the world, they were going briefly to Europe, and were to sail that same night, going direct from the Grand Central Station to the pier. Roger counted the suitcases, hatboxes and overnight bags to be sure nothing was missing, and shifted the position of several pieces to make them more orderly, before he pulled down the shades, and seating himself beside Emily, clasped her in a fond embrace.

'You looked like an angel, darling,' he told her after an interlude. 'Really, I never saw such a beautiful bride! I'm not telling you that because I love you so much. I'm saying it because it's true. And you acted like an angel too—making everyone feel welcome and at home and giving them the idea you were really glad to see them.'

'But I *was* really glad to see them! I liked all your friends, Roger, ever and ever so much.'

'Truly? Not just the ushers and the rest of my old crowd? Of course, you knew them already. But the juniors in the firm— could you get any idea what they were like, seeing them so hurriedly?'

'Of course I could. I'll describe them to you. Then you'll know I'm not pretending.' She locked her fingers a little more firmly in his and went on, 'David Salomont was almost the first person who came down the line. I thought he was very arresting. And very—very virile. There is such a word, isn't there?'

Roger laughed. 'There certainly is—also such a quality. Yes, David has it all right. And arresting describes him too. I can see how you'd remember him. He does stand out in a crowd, not just because of his size or his good looks or his wonderful clothes either. He's a born spellbinder, too. It doesn't matter much what he says, because he says anything and everything so darned well. I'll never be able to argue cases the way he does, Emily.'

A slight wistfulness had crept into his happy voice. Emily tightened the clasp of her fingers again and leaned over to kiss him.

'Of course you will. Or if you aren't, you'll do something else better than he does. He might make the mistake of being a little too forceful and insistent. That doesn't appeal to everyone. It doesn't especially appeal to me.'

'Doesn't it really?'

'No. And I thought of it when he came back in the line a second time. He made me feel as if he were determined to talk with me. I was glad to, because I do think he's very attractive— very intriguing. But there were lots of other people I had to talk to and he didn't seem to be taking them into consideration at all. And somehow, I was glad I'd thanked him for his wedding present right away and that I'd remembered exactly what it was—you know, the punch set in the scroll design.'

'All right, that'll do for Dave. What about Brian Collins?'

'Well, I didn't like him quite so much. He isn't forceful; he's almost impudent. Of course, he wasn't impudent to me. I don't mean that. But I felt he could be. He drank a good deal of champagne. Then he went over to the window and shouted to one of the policemen he caught sight of outside—evidently a crony of his, and afterwards I overhead him making two or three jokes that were—well, they weren't nice at all. I'm not used to men that make jokes like that.'

'But you said you liked all my new friends!'

'I did. I do. But I like them in different ways. I liked David instinctively and I liked Brian in spite of myself! And if it hadn't been that I fell in love with you before I ever met him, I'm sure I'd have fallen in love with Pellegrino de Lucca at first sight!'

It was her turn to laugh, joyously and spontaneously, as if she knew Roger would understand how silly it was to suppose for one moment that she could possibly have fallen in love with anyone but him. He smiled pleasantly and kissed her again, but he did not laugh with her, and after a little while she went on again in the same light and lilting way that she had spoken a moment earlier.

'Besides, I had the funniest feeling this *wasn't* the first time I'd ever seen him. Do you think I could possibly have met him anywhere else?'

'No, I'm almost certain you couldn't have. Pell's *really* poor. I'm sure everything he had on was hired for the occasion and that even renting clothes cost more than he could afford. Brian isn't poor at all and I imagine David's better fixed than he'd admit. But Pell lives somewhere on the north side of the Hill and never talks about his family or asks anyone to come and see him. He doesn't go much of anywhere himself, either. I was surprised that he came today.' *And I'm afraid he was sorry he did,* Roger added mentally. *Pell can't forge ahead for himself the way Dave and Brian can. He was a lot more hurt than they were at being treated like an outsider.*

'I'm glad he did come though, aren't you?' Emily said quickly, again divining his unspoken thought. 'Because I think there's really something very fine about him. How did Mr. Cutter happen to run across him?'

'I haven't the slightest idea.'

Suddenly Roger felt very tired and did not want to talk at all. It had been hard work, keeping up with the endless requirements of the office during the same period that he was expected to attend the innumerable parties given in Emily's honour. Very often he had been obliged to sit up all night in order to do both, though he had never told her so. And the night before, his bachelor dinner had seemed interminable to him, and he had not been able to forget that, in order to give it, he had been obliged to sell certain securities.

Here it was again, this hideous question of money, raising itself to torment him even on his wedding day. His starting salary with Cutter, Mills and Swan had been fixed at fifteen hundred dollars a year and this was more, he learned, than the

40

other juniors, who had been taken on earlier in the Depression, had been given to begin with; his first raise gave him an extra three hundred and his Christmas bonus had come to one hundred dollars more; meanwhile, his annual income from his father's estate was a little less than two thousand. If a well-to-do uncle, who had hitherto shown himself very stingy, had not unexpectedly come forward with the startling suggestion that he wanted to give the young couple their trip abroad for a wedding present, they would have been almost forced to accept Elizabeth Forbes' offer of her remodelled farmhouse for a honeymoon home.

During the final days of their engagement, when he and Emily were taking one of their frequent walks together, he had steered her in the direction of Joy Street and paused before the house which he had already eyed surreptitiously several times since the Christmas Eve when he had first seen it. The 'For Sale' sign was still in the window and, as Emily did not immediately notice this, he called it to her attention and, for a few moments, they talked in a desultory way about the potentialities of the house. A week or so later, she telephoned him and asked if he would go with her to see it the following Sunday. Their inspection of it revealed an interior which fulfilled the promise of his imagination; but, after the ubiquitous agent, who insisted on accompanying them to every nook and corner of it, casually mentioned its 'bargain price', Roger recoiled from his dream with something approaching horror. He had been right in the first place; it was doubtful whether his life earnings would equal the cost of purchasing, renovating and maintaining this house. He never spoke of it to Emily again and she did not mention it to him either. Reluctantly, he suggested the Cambridge apartment as a temporary abiding place 'while they looked around'; and Emily had agreed, rather vaguely for her, but still very pleasantly, that this arrangement would be all right 'unless they unexpectedly found something better'; at all events, she did not think they should spoil their wonderful summer abroad by worrying about what they were going to do next.

Homer Lathrop had, of course, talked to Roger about Emily's financial status and Roger still winced at the memory of this conversation. Homer had, he said, reluctantly given his consent to an allowance from the trust fund which would preclude Emily from being noticeably shabby, or going hungry, or working her fingers to the bone. He did not divulge the sum which he

41

thought would do this, and Roger was too proud and by that time too wretched to ask; his only thought was to bring the humiliating interview to an end and, when he went to see Emily that night, it was with the purpose of telling her that he thought he could not inflict a life of want upon her or endure one of almstaking for himself. But she had received him so confidently and so lovingly that he had not been able to speak the words which would have chilled her happiness and separated him from her, perhaps for ever.

In the days before their marriage, he and Emily had sometimes sat quietly side by side for long periods, so content in the communion of their minds and spirits that they needed neither words nor caresses to complete their consciousness of harmony. It did not seem strange to him that they should do so now, enclosed in the privacy of their drawing-room, while the train sped on its way through the twilight; after the turmoil of their wedding day, before the ecstasies of their wedding night, this silence, this deepening dusk, were balm to his weariness. Emily, sensitive to his mood, did not break in upon it; she was not tired herself, but she understood his exhaustion. Roger had not been sustained by the exhilaration which had never lessened, for her, since she learned that Old Mrs. Forbes was her ally. She had known from that moment that she and her grandmother were somehow kindred spirits; but she had also known that the elderly woman and the young man misprized each other and that perhaps they always would. Roger had never told her about his feeling in the matter; but she was so close to him, that without words, she had divined his antipathy. Old Mrs. Forbes had expressed hers with her usual brutal frankness one cool afternoon late in May when she and Emily were sitting by the fire together.

'Of course, I've nothing against that Field boy,' she told Emily. 'He's agreeable, he's intelligent, he's well born and well educated, he's got good principles—in short, he's a gentleman. That's the trouble—it isn't what he's done or may do that worries me; it's what he hasn't done and never will do.'

'That doesn't worry me at all,' Emily said serenely.

'I know it doesn't. Well, I think your life will be pleasant and peaceful and safe with Roger and I think you'll be reasonably happy with him too—so long as you don't want the world set on fire and as long as someone doesn't set it on fire for you.

Right now, you imagine you're in love with Roger Field and——'

'Of course I'm in love with Roger.' Emily did not hesitate to say it to herself or anyone else now. She said it proudly and confidently.

'My dear, if you had been, in the sense I mean it, you never would have voluntarily gone off to Kentucky and postponed your marriage for over a year, to prove your point. You'd have eloped, in the face of family opposition, within a week after Roger's proposal of marriage.'

'Well, if you didn't think I was in love with Roger, why have you made it easier for me to marry him?'

'Because I knew you had to get this pseudo love affair out of your system. If you hadn't, there's no telling what might have happened. You'd have gone on and on building it up into a shining tower. And when it toppled over with a crash, it would have hurt you terribly. As it is, I think it may be just what you need, in the way of preparation.'

'Preparation for what?'

'For life. Real life. Life in a world that *is* on fire. Your private world. If ever there was a girl who needed to learn by experience, it's you. I think Roger can help you to get it, without hurting you too much in the process. I'm afraid he may not hurt you quite enough for your own good. He'll always be "considerate" and I don't mean just one thing by that either. But some other man will come along who hasn't the least idea of being considerate, in any way. He'll want you and sooner or later he'll try to get you. But not as soon as you'll want him to. Because, that time, the pain will be real.'

Old Mrs. Forbes leaned over from her throne-like chair and patted her granddaughter's cheek. Then, even more surprisingly, she bent still farther and kissed her.

'Don't be angry with me for telling you all this, Emily,' she said with a gentleness that came as another shock. 'And don't take anything I've said to mean I don't like that Field boy. I like him very much. In fact, I can't think of anyone I'd rather trust you to. I don't want you to be hurt. I only think you'll have to be some day—in childbirth and in love too. And, unless I'm very much mistaken, you'll feel, in the end, that the agony was worth while in both cases.... Now, let's talk about something else. What about that house on Joy Street you dragged me out to see? Would you like to have it for a wedding present? If you would, I'll buy it for you and have it all ready for you to move into when you get back from Europe. Only, don't tell Roger. Let's keep it for our secret and give him a nice surprise, shall we? And of course Homer Lathrop's got to give you more than three thousand a year to run it on. I never heard such nonsense in all my life. That wouldn't pay for your clothes—at least, it shouldn't. There, there, my dear!'

Unwillingly, Emily's mind kept reverting to this conversation as she sat silently in the dark beside Roger, while the train sped on towards New York. At last, determined to change the tenor of her thoughts, she called him by name and pressed his hand. He did not answer her or return her caress and, after a moment, she realized that he had fallen asleep from sheer exhaustion. Then, afraid that her least movement would disturb him, she sat still more quietly, thinking about the house on Joy Street and wondering where it was that she had seen Pellegrino de Lucca before her wedding day.

PART TWO

JUNE 1938 TO NOVEMBER 1938

ROGER AND DAVID

CHAPTER III

As far back as she could remember, Emily had gone to Europe every other summer, and she had also spent several winters on the Continent, in schools which encouraged their pupils to take trips during the Christmas and Easter holidays and assisted them in making their excursions illuminating and enjoyable. During the course of their long friendship, Roger had mentioned to her his own lack of opportunities for travel; but it was naturally not a subject on which he cared to enlarge and his brief, reluctant references to it had slipped Emily's mind. When he told her about the gift from his Uncle Nathaniel, which would make their European honeymoon possible, the intensity of his pleasure was so evident that she tardily realized how greatly he had missed the advantages which she had taken for granted.

'It's wonderful, darling, wonderful,' she said. 'Let's see—you say you don't have to go back to work at the office till the Tuesday after Labour Day. That means we can have two whole months abroad, besides the time we're at sea, if we go on the new *Normandie*. Why, we can do a lot in that length of time! And Roger, what would you think of taking my new car, so that we can be perfectly independent? I mean, about travelling wherever we like, whenever we like. We wouldn't have to go straight to Paris from Le Havre on the boat train; we could work our way slowly down through the Norman towns and along the coast of Brittany to La Vendée and Le Bordelais and then to Auch or Avignon. Afterwards, we could go on to either Italy or Spain, whichever we'd prefer. We could——'

She stopped, aware that she was saying the wrong thing. Roger had not interrupted her, but she could tell, from his expression, that he did not want to seek out remote, exotic places of which he had hardly heard; he wanted to take the beaten track which had long since ceased to enthral her, because it was so familiar to her, but which he had vainly yearned, for years, to follow. Later, she confessed her mistake to her grandmother.

'I smoothed it over right away,' she said. 'I don't think I hurt his feelings—not really. I said of course that what I'd suggested was just one way of spending our time. I got the atlas and asked Roger to map out an entirely different kind of a trip.'

'Very sensible of you, Emily. And I suppose his plan was to take a Cunarder, because he's always heard Cunarders have such a wonderful record of reliability. Then, of course, you'd go straight to London, and after you'd been to the Tower and Westminster Abbey and the British Museum, he thought you might do a little touring—say to Stratford-on-Avon and Oxford and two or three of the cathedral towns. And that afterwards you'd go to the Scottish Lakes, via Edinburgh. You'd travel to Edinburgh on the Flying Scot—such an excellent train, always on time to the minute.'

'How did you guess, Grandmamma?'

'If I'd never had anything harder than that to figure out, I certainly would have had an easy life—and a very dull one. Roger wasn't thinking in terms of Honfleur and Quimper and Carcassonne and Urbino and Burgos—and you were. But you'll be very wise for more reasons than one to take the route Roger's mapped out—this time. Places don't really matter very much anyway to a girl when she's on her honeymoon. It's the man that counts.'

'That's the way I feel about it,' Emily said contentedly. 'So we're sailing on a Cunarder and we're going to stay at Brown's Hotel in London. And we're leaving my car behind.'

In answering her grandmother, Emily had focused her attention on the old lady's final remark; but later, she could have agreed quite as sincerely with everything that had been said. Her honeymoon was a very happy one; and it was not until Roger himself confessed that he would welcome a change from brussels sprouts and drizzly weather, that Emily realized these had begun to pall on her too. By then, there was not time enough left to do much on the Continent; but a rapid change of plan enabled them to have a whirl in Paris and an interlude of sheer enchantment at Ravello before taking the *Vulcania* home; and it was while they were stretched out, at ease, in the sunlit privacy of the little veranda leading off their cabin, that Emily told Roger the secret she had kept so well until then.

'I've got a wonderful surprise for you, darling. We don't have to bother Caroline or start a more or less hopeless search for an apartment. We've got a house of our own.'

'A house of our own! What are you talking about? Where? What kind of a house?'

'That house on Joy Street you liked. Grandmamma's giving it to us for a wedding present. She's been having it fixed up for us while we've been gone and we're to stay in her house while we supervise the final papering and painting and that sort of thing. She's going to stay late at Manchester-by-the-Sea this fall, so we'll be by ourselves on Louisburg Square.'

'Emily, you must be joking. It couldn't be true. It's too—it's too——'

He was unable to go on. Emily moved closer to him and put her arms around him.

'It is true. I wouldn't joke about a thing like that. Oh, Roger, we've been awfully happy this summer, haven't we? It's been perfect—in its way. But after all, it was just a prelude to our real life together. Now we're going to have that—on Joy Street. And it'll get better and better all the time.'

He held her to his heart, believing her.

After everything was in order, Roger recognized that, in its realization, the house on Joy Street had far surpassed his vision of its potentialities, when he had first become aware of it, on Christmas Eve. It had dignity and spaciousness and beauty; but it contained no rigid chairs, no sombre hangings and no over-powering family portraits. Through care and taste, Oriental rugs, Italian furniture, Russian ornaments and a heterogeneous collection of books had been assembled to create a surprising degree of harmony; and if Emily's decisions in regard to these had now and then been influenced by her frequent conferences with her grandmother, the expert hand of Old Mrs. Forbes had never been obtrusive. Sunlight streamed in on freshly polished floors, pleasant wallpapers and glistening white paint; and the perfect cleanliness of the house did not detract from its easy cheer. In the evening, when the curtains were drawn, there were always open fires burning behind shining brasses; and dinner came hot and hearty and abundant to the polished table in the candle-lighted dining-room.

The gloom of the Gloucester Street house had been peren-nially deepened by 'servant troubles', and Emily had not been without secret misgivings lest she should fare no better than her mother when it came to a question of domestic help. Old Mrs. Forbes' impeccable staff had been assembled during her years of foreign sojourn and every member of it had relatives who would gladly have augmented its numbers. But the immigration laws which Homer Lathrop found so deplorably lax were still sufficiently restrictive to make such additions complicated. A niece of Pearson, the butler, did succeed in penetrating to New England, but her calm assumption, when Emily approached her, that she would have at least two scullery maids at her disposal and a sitting-room to which the humbler domestics would have access only through her condescension, put an end to the interview; the allowance which Emily had finally wrested from Homer Lathrop, while much ampler than he had originally intended to give her, was not elastic enough to provide for scullery maids; and, on this occasion, Old Mrs. Forbes merely snorted with indignation when Emily referred the matter to her.

Unfortunately, there were no other prospects on the horizon when Roger and Emily prepared to move into their house on Joy Street. Emily, who was facing the thought of her first interview at an employment agency in much the same spirit of mingled fortitude and fear which would have marked her delayed approach to a dental chair, confessed her apprehension to Roger.

'Why, perhaps I could help you find someone,' he said, speaking with the pleased surprise which always marked his train of thought when he discovered that he actually had, or could, contribute something tangible to their design for living. 'I don't know what Deirdre's doing now, but I could find out.'

'Deirdre?'

'Yes. She was our general maid for years. She left us after Father died, when we sold the Brookline house. Of course Caroline and I couldn't really afford to keep a maid, so I suppose it was just as well. But Deirdre'd been with us ever since I can remember and I took it for granted she always would be. It's never seemed the same to me without her. She and Caroline kept having arguments, though. I ought to tell you that.'

'What kind of arguments?'

'Oh—about going to Mass. Deirdre's very devout. And how many pounds of butter we used per week—she's rather extravagant. And whether she ought to have so much company—she's got an enormous family. So one day she left—just like that—

49

and Caroline said it was good riddance to bad rubbish. I'm not so sure. Deirdre's a good plain cook and she can turn off a lot of laundry work too—never acts as if that weren't part of her job. Besides, I think she must feel something the way I do—that she really belongs to the Fields. She's never stayed in any one place long since she left us. I know, because we've been asked so many times to give her a reference. But I don't think she's ever been discharged. I think she's left all those other families because she's been restless.'

Deirdre came to see Emily the following evening and their mutual understanding and admiration were immediate. Deirdre —stocky, vigorous and collected—was not working; she hadn't liked her last job so well, she said, implying that this would not be the case with the next one. Sure, she could start in right away—in the morning if Mrs. Field wanted her to. And sure, she had a niece who could help out too. Maybe the niece, Ellie her name was, couldn't come till the next week, but Deirdre could manage all right alone until then. With just two in family and a fine new kitchen and all, it would be nothing but child's play.

She left without mentioning the subject of wages and Emily did not bring it up either; somehow it seemed out of harmony with the tenor of their talk, and both instinctively felt it could be quietly and satisfactorily settled later. But as Deirdre reached the door she turned and, with one rough, capable hand on the knob, delivered herself of a single pregnant remark.

'And can I ever wait to see the look on Miss Caroline's face when she finds me, that she turned out, in this grand house of yours!'

As it happened, Deirdre was denied this satisfaction, for Caroline learned of the unwelcome presence indirectly. She told herself that it was her duty to see that her brother's life was not completely wrecked, if she could help it; with this end in view, she made frequent visits to the house on Joy Street during its organization. When the bridal couple was actually installed there, she appeared promptly at tea-time, and was chagrined to be admitted by a neat, rosy-cheeked maid in a spotless uniform, who beamed upon her with great goodwill and ushered her competently into the library, announcing that Mrs. Field would be down right away. A shining samovar was already singing beside the pleasant hearth; and almost immediately Emily appeared on the circular stairway, humming a gay little tune.

'How nice of you to drop in!' Emily said pleasantly, as she submitted to Caroline's solid kiss and returned it lightly. Emily did not care for stereotyped kisses as a form of greeting between women, but she had quickly discovered that Caroline, though she derived no pleasure from such caresses, considered them an essential part of correct family ritual. 'Roger isn't home yet, but I think he will be, any minute. Let's have some tea right away, shall we? And then some more, made fresh, when he does come. That'll give us an excuse for second cups.'

She seated herself beside the samovar, lighted a cigarette and leaned back luxuriously in her chair. Caroline did not smoke and had impressed on Emily her opinion of this 'filthy habit' so forcefully that the latter did not proffer her the cloisonné box from which she helped herself casually. She crossed her knees and Caroline observed that Emily's hostess gown, though very long, was 'suggestively' cut. It was not actually too low or too tight; but it revealed Emily's lovely white neck and emphasized the lines of her figure in the artful way which only a skilful dressmaker could effect. Emily, apparently quite unaware that her costume was an affront to her sister-in-law's sense of decorum, began to chat pleasantly and inconsequently. Caroline interrupted her.

'Where did you get that maid?' she demanded.

'Ellie? She's cute, isn't she? Roger found her for me.'

'You don't mean to tell me that with everything else he has to do you're sending Roger out to employment agencies?'

Emily laid aside her cigarette and rearranged the folds of her crimson robe. 'I don't "send" Roger anywhere, Caroline,' she said quietly. 'He goes wherever he likes, whenever he likes, as far as I'm concerned. But he hasn't gone to any employment agencies yet—at least to my knowledge. He knew Ellie before we were married. Or rather, he knew her aunt very well, and he knew Ellie in a vague way, as one of Deirdre's nieces. You must have seen her around sometimes too.'

'You don't mean to tell me that the maid who opened the door for me was one of that gang of grimy runny-nosed children that Deirdre had around all the time?'

'I suppose she must have been. Hush—here she is now with the tea.'

Beaming more proudly than ever, Ellie entered with the tray and set it down on the small mahogany table beside Emily.

51

'Thank you very much, Ellie. I'll ring if I want anything more,' Emily said, nodding in easy dismissal. 'How many lumps of sugar, Caroline? And I forget whether you like a spot of brandy.'

'Then you haven't a very good memory. I never touch alcohol in any form. And I've told you over and over again that I consider it the ruination of good China tea to put anything in it.'

'I'm sorry. Will you have a scone? Or did you tell me something about those that I've forgotten too?'

'I prefer toast, but I don't suppose it's convenient——'

'Of course it's convenient. That's here too.' Emily reached to a lower shelf of the muffin stand and uncovered a deep dish. 'There's plum cake too, if you like that. I thought of the scones first because Deirdre makes such good ones.'

Caroline set down her cup so quickly that it made a sharp, clicking sound against the saucer. 'You don't mean to tell me——' she began. But this time Emily interrupted.

'Yes I do. Deirdre's here too. I think she's wonderful.'

'Just wait until the newness wears off,' Caroline said warningly. 'After all, you've only just started.' Then she had another harrowing thought. 'No doubt, you're paying Deirdre perfectly fantastic wages?' she added accusingly.

'No doubt.'

'What do you mean, "no doubt", Emily?'

'Why, probably the same thing you did! I haven't discussed wages with her yet. I haven't had time.'

'*You haven't had time!* You lie in bed half the morning and then you say you haven't had time to settle a vital point like a servant's wages! Doesn't Roger have a key?' she inquired, cutting short her own words as she heard a step in the hallway and saw Ellie hurrying towards the front door.

'Yes, of course. Apparently, I have another visitor.'

'But surely you wouldn't be "at home" yet.'

'Of course I would be. I haven't had any callers before. But evidently——'

'I couldn't help overhearing what you were saying. And I'm delighted to learn that you *are* "at home". Your grandmother thought you might be. I've just been making my party-call on her. I'm sorry it was so long delayed, because I really appreciated her invitation to your wedding reception, also her suggestion that I might try my luck at finding you in too.'

52

At the sound of a strange voice, Emily had instinctively risen. Caroline sat still, watching her, as she moved gracefully across the room and held out her hand to David Salomont.

He came forward with all the assurance of a welcome guest, the freshness of his face and the breeziness of his bearing in no way suggesting that he had been through a gruelling day; Emily could not help noticing the contrast to the tell-tale signs of fatigue which Roger failed to conceal when returning from the office.

As she greeted him with cordiality, Caroline stiffened in her chair. Matters were at a pretty pass indeed if a presumptuous Jew could come, uninvited, to her brother's house—in her brother's absence—and be made welcome.

'I'm sure you wouldn't remember me, Miss Field,' he said. 'I was only one of the wedding guests who belong in the category of those brought in from "the highways and byways".' Having made this announcement, he appeared to forget her entirely and, after accepting a cup of tea from Emily, looked about him with obvious appreciation. 'What a delightful room! Roger's been bragging all over the office about his bride's accomplishments as a domestic organizer. But I didn't realize that she'd have so many museum pieces at her disposal. That's as fine a Gaugengigl as I ever saw, over there, and I don't know that I ever saw one more advantageously placed. And this is the "missing" tea service from the Winter Palace, isn't it? Where did you get all these treasures—and learn what to do with them?'

'My grandmother helped me,' Emily replied steadily. 'At least, the etchings came from Roger's family. But it was Grandmamma who suggested hanging "The Intruder" on that particular wall space and lighting it the way I have. And she's loaned me lots of the other things—among them the tea service. It was given her when Grandpapa was Ambassador to Russia, about thirty-five years ago. I never knew before it was supposed to be "missing".'

'Oh, yes, it's had an interesting history. I'll have to tell it to you sometime. I must tell my stepfather I've seen it. He'll be terribly jealous of me.'

'Is your stepfather especially interested in such things?' Emily inquired, offering the scones.

'Well he's an antique dealer, catering to the luxury trade. So he keeps himself informed. He certainly would give anything to

53

see this room,' David added. 'I'd like to bring him here some time.'

'I'd be very pleased if you would. If you let me know beforehand when to expect him, I'll see if Grandmamma wouldn't join us for tea.'

'And of course he'd given his eyeteeth to meet her,' David said enthusiastically. 'He could go to her house if her lameness makes it difficult for her to come here—and come here himself, of course, beforehand or afterwards. I'll wire him tonight about your kind suggestion. I know he'll come right over from New York unless he's tied up with a sale or something.'

'Perhaps it would be just as well, Emily, if you would find out when your grandmother is free and whether she feels equal to making new acquaintances at this time.'

Caroline spoke freezingly. Only her sense of duty constrained her to stay in the same room with this common, pushing person. But she did not feel she should leave Emily alone with such an obnoxious creature. There was no telling what might happen.

'I'll telephone and ask her. It won't take me but a minute.'

'Miss Field and I've been discussing the drama,' David said when Emily returned. 'I have found her viewpoint extremely illuminating. . . . I hope you have a good report for me about your talk with your grandmother?'

'She'd like very much to meet your stepfather. In fact, she thinks she may have met him already. Is his name Morris Brucker?'

'It certainly is! Did she say when and where——'

'Budapest first. St. Petersburg afterwards. I gathered that was another interesting story, though she wasn't too definite as to time. But apparently they didn't lose touch with each other until '14, when the war broke out. They haven't met since he settled in New York and married. But anyway, she'd be glad to have him come in for a cocktail, after he's been to tea here, any day next week except Friday.'

'So that's still sacred to the Symphony! Well, more power to her! I'll get in touch with the old man and drop by again to give you his answer. . . . Well—sorry I can't wait to see Roger. I'm having an early dinner with the Stockbridges in Chestnut Hill. Probably Roger's told you that Ellery Stockbridge's slated to be president of the Third National Bank next January. No? He's one of our most promising clients. But he's a little on the stiff side. Just the sort of man that outsiders seem to feel is typical of Boston. Good night, Miss Field. I really think you ought to reconsider and go to see that play.'

Roger arrived barely five minutes after David had left, so there was not much chance, during the interval, for Caroline to impress Emily with her disapproval—especially as Emily seemed wilfully bent on being pleasant and was, moreover, preoccupied with the prospect of Roger's impending arrival. She heard his key turn in the latch before Caroline detected any such sound and ran out into the hall to meet him. The next sounds were easily identified, even by Caroline, and there was a considerable delay before Roger and Emily came into the library. Roger was smoothing his hair and Emily's pretty colour was heightened.

'Hello, Caroline,' Roger said and kissed her too. 'How are you? Emily says David's been here. Sorry to have missed him. But I'm usually later leaving the office than he is. He has his own secretary who polishes off all his odd jobs and I have to wait for poor old Miss Riley to finish everything Mr. Mills gives her before she does my work. Half the time, when I ring for her, she just appears in the doorway long enough to say, "I can't come in now, I have eight more pages to do for Mr. Mills." That happens even when Mr. Mills is riding me for a memo. But of course I don't rate anything better and David does.'

'I haven't the slightest doubt that David Salomont would gladly leave some poor, overworked girl to "polish off his odd jobs" while he goes out on the town,' Caroline rejoined. 'He seems at liberty to make any number of engagements. He's about to get in touch with his stepfather—a New York antique dealer —about coming over here for tea any day next week except Friday, and as soon as he gets the answer, he's going to "drop in" and report to Emily—presumably also at tea-time.'

'Well, that's fine,' Roger replied. 'I hope I won't miss him again. I think he's about the most brilliant man I ever met—and one of the most versatile.'

Caroline rose, buttoning the jacket of her severe and rather shabby suit. 'You look very tired to me, Roger. And you seem to be coming down with a cold. Don't forget that your colds always settle in your chest. One of these days you'll be having pneumonia, if you're not more careful. Good night, Emily. I suppose it's useless to tell you that Roger ought to go to bed at once and keep *completely quiet* until he's better.'

Unfortunately, Caroline's predictions about the symptoms of

a cold proved to be correct, and by the time he did take to his bed he was really ill for several days. Therefore, to his great regret, he missed both David's second call and Morris Brucker's visit. However, Emily's detailed accounts of these served to while away some of the tedium of his illness, though they did not compensate for her temporary absences from his side.

'David has only just left,' she told him, returning a little breathlessly to his sickroom an hour or so after Ellie had announced that Mr. Salomont was in the library. 'Mr. Brucker's coming over from New York next Saturday. I called Grandmamma and she said that would be fine. Most of the time David and I were talking about Morris Brucker—not just about his visit, but about what he'd meant to David and David's mother. One subject seemed to lead to another. David's father must have been a very cultured man.'

'Was he?' Roger inquired, without much interest.

'Yes. And his mother married above her, as the saying is. She was very proud that Rafael Salomont wanted her for his wife. And she really cared very greatly for him. But she found it hard to live up to his intellectual standards. He knew seven or eight languages, several of them dead ones—read all the Greek plays and poems in the original for pleasure. He had any number of degrees and corresponded with scholars all over the world. David respects his father's memory very highly; but I think, in a way, his stepfather means more to him—not just because he's had a much more comfortable, happy life himself since his mother married again, but because he believes his mother's been happier too. Morris Brucker's given her everything in the world she could possibly want. He thinks the sun rises and sets on her head and he lets her see he feels that way. Besides, he's more her kind anyhow than her first husband was.'

Roger, who failed to find any of this especially intriguing, made no immediate answer. Emily did not seem to notice the omission; she was pursuing a train of thought that was new to her.

'It's nice, isn't it, that David should be so fond of his stepfather? I didn't think people were, usually. And it's nice, too, that his mother should be so happy in her second marriage. I never supposed, either, that there was much romance in those. But the way David talked, I could see that a woman might sincerely love two men, in entirely different ways, at different periods of her life—enough to marry them both, I mean. And that she might find life more exciting all the time, in spite of growing older, if she had the kind of husband who told her how much he loved her, and how beautiful she looked to him. David says his mother really is very beautiful still. He made me feel I'd like to see her. I'm sorry she isn't coming over to Boston with Mr. Brucker.'

'Did you suggest it?'

'No, because I didn't know how Grandmamma would feel about it. I thought perhaps she'd rather see Mr. Brucker without his wife. You see, Grandmamma . . .'

Emily left her remark unfinished and Roger did not urge her to continue. He had become more interested in her observations as she went along, but they were vaguely disquieting to him, and he did not feel that a discussion of her grandmother's characteristics would be any less so. To be sure, Old Mrs. Forbes had married only once; there was nothing in her history which would help to develop a train of thought about second marriages. On the other hand, no one supposed, for a moment, that her husband had been the one love of her life. Indeed it was common knowledge that she had not lacked opportunities to remarry, even recently, and also that she had fascinated any number of admirers while her husband was still living. Though she had never caused an open scandal. Roger could not help believing that this was due partly to adroit management. Altogether, it was better to let the subject of romance drop.

It was inevitably revived, however, after Morris Brucker's visit. According to plan, the antique dealer came to Joy Street with his stepson, and snatches of animated conversation and echoes of hearty laughter from the library below reached Roger in his sickroom. The voices became clearer as Emily and her visitors came out into the front hall. She called up to Roger and he could tell she was enjoying herself very much.

'We're off to Grandmamma's, Roger. . . . Anything I can do for you before we leave?'

'No, thanks. Tell Mr. Brucker again how sorry I am to miss him. David too. Have a good time, all of you.'

He was very hoarse, it hurt him to raise his voice and a fit of coughing followed the effort. But the others were already outside by that time, so he was not self-conscious about the racket he made, and presently the sound of their footsteps on the brick pavement died away in the distance as they went on up the Hill. He tried to read, but his eyes smarted and watered, so he gave up the attempt and lay in the dark, listening for Emily's return. This was so long delayed that he began to fear something untoward had happened and it took real will-power on his part not to pick up the bedside telephone and call Old Mrs. Forbes' house. . . .

He had almost dozed off when he was suddenly aware of her presence and sat up with a start, to see her standing beside him, her eyes shining, her dimples deepened as they always were when she was especially pleased about something. She put her arms around him and hugged him ecstatically.

'I've had such a good time!' she exclaimed. 'Morris Brucker is the greatest fun! Not especially good looking, in fact, sort of shrivelled, but the best company, amusing and lively and very, very witty. You should have heard him and Grandmamma sparring! He said that when she was first in St. Petersburg, she used to go to his shop very often and that they had wonderful talks together, while she made selections from his stock.'

'Did anyone tell the story of the missing tea-service?'

'No one told the story, but Grandmamma and Mr. Brucker both referred to it in a cryptic way. And finally, he took a little package out of his pocket and told her that, since there were no more grand dukes, he'd venture to bring her a present himself. She undid the package and there was a signet ring in it—a man's ring with a great carved emerald; I think the carving was the Russian double eagle, though I couldn't see very clearly. She didn't say a word, just sat and turned the ring over and over, and then she put it on and looked at him—and Roger, there were tears in her eyes!'

'But you never heard the history of the ring either?'

'No. There was something mysterious about the whole meeting, something a little uncanny, even though everyone joked so much. Grandmamma still had that ring on when I left and she told Mr. Brucker she thought he'd better stay to dinner, it was getting so late. I think she must have meant all along to ask him, because she said they would have borsch, and I haven't known her to do that in a long time. But she didn't ask David and me to stay.'

'So David brought you home?'

'Yes. We had a good time walking up the Hill and trying to figure out the story about the ring. Of course, David does know the one about the tea set. He said there wasn't time to tell me between Louisburg Square and Joy Street—it wasn't as if this

58

were a warm summer evening when we could loiter along. I thought of asking him to stay to dinner here, so that he couldn't use lack of time as an excuse. I think he half expected I would.'

'I'm rather glad you didn't. Not that I want you to be tantalized indefinitely by curiosity. We'll ask David some other time. But I've missed you a lot, darling.'

He did not say he hoped she would not leave him again while he was ill or that she would not entertain any more visitors until they could do this together. But she realized this was how he felt and, fearful lest her own excellent health might have made her insensitive, she reproached herself for having been lacking in tenderness and devotion towards him. During the next few days she redoubled her efforts to keep him comfortable and to divert his mind, remaining with him constantly; and eventually, on his own initiative, he again brought up the subject of company.

'What would you think of giving a little dinner, darling?' he asked.

'Why, I'd like to! As a matter of fact, I'd been meaning to suggest it myself, as soon as you were well enough.'

'I'm well enough now to plan.... David seems to feel welcome here already. I'd like to have Brian and Pell feel the same way. Incidentally, do you remember asking me, the day we were married, how Mr. Cutter happened to run across Pell?'

'Yes, and you told me you hadn't the least idea.'

'I didn't have then. But since, I've found out. Well, when he got through studying law at Northeastern, he opened a little office with his shingle in the window, on the ground floor of the same house where he has a room on the third storey.... I've told you he lives on Joy Street, too, haven't I?'

'Why no, you haven't! How nice that he's a neighbour!'

'Well, you couldn't really call him a neighbour. He lives on the other side of the Hill, opposite the police station. It's way down near Cambridge Street. I don't believe you've ever been that far.'

Emily, who took a walk every day as a matter of course, admitted that this was true. 'I'll go down there tomorrow morning though,' she added.

'Good idea—you'll be amazed to see how the street changes once you're over the crest of the Hill. Of course, Pell isn't in that spare little office any more. There was a sign in the window with the words, ATTORNEY AT LAW, NOTARY PUBLIC, after his name. And the office had just a few pieces of beat-up, old, second-hand furniture and Pell's diplomas on the wall—the one from the parochial high school and the one from Boston College and the one from Northeastern. I'm sure he couldn't have afforded to keep a secretary all day, but he'd probably have had one part-time and she might have been one of the relatives he lives with. That third-floor room of his is in their tenement.'

'He hasn't moved then? I mean his living quarters?'

'I don't think so, but that's not the point. The big shot who owned this tenement wanted to get Pell's relatives out for a tenant who would pay higher rent, and since the lease still had some time to run, he needed an excuse for breaking it. Well, on some saint's day or other, the Italians had a nice, comfortable family party and in the course of it they put away quite a lot of Dago Red along with their *pizza* and made a lot of happy noise. So the realtor brought eviction proceedings, claiming that the party was a lot wilder than it really had been. He gave the case to Cutter, Mills and Swan.'

'Whereupon Pell defended the Italians, I suppose.'

'And how! He won their case for them hands down and Mr. Cutter decided then and there that he was exactly the sort of chap they wanted for the group of juniors. But to get back to where we started: I thought we might invite Brian and David and Pell here all together, so none of them would think we were singling him out from the others, and we'd better ask three girls too—Caroline and Marion Swan and anyone else you'd like, and maybe another couple, too.'

'Caroline was pretty rude to David Salomont the other day,' Emily said doubtfully. 'Do you think we ought to risk having her snub him like that again?'

Roger laughed, and though the laugh ended in a cough it was an untroubled one. 'Don't worry about that. David's more than a match for Caroline. He can tell her off any time he likes.'

'Well, there's Caroline to think of, too. Do you believe she'd consider it a compliment to be asked to dinner with David Salomont?'

'She'd be very much hurt if we didn't ask her to our first dinner, no matter who the other guests were.'

He began to cough again and Emily said they mustn't talk any more about the dinner just then, but that she would speak to Deirdre about it the first thing in the morning. She was sure, if

Uncle Sherman knew they were going to have their first dinner, he would send them some game from the Cape. And there was Uncle Homer's famous cellar on which he had told her to draw at any time. He knew all about vintages, and she didn't yet. But she intended to learn. When it came to the way the table ought to look, she was on firmer ground; she was sure that nothing could be more suitable than her *point de Venice* cloth and her Sèvres service.

Roger agreed to Emily's every suggestion in regard to the dinner. There were several reasons why the choice of her cousin, Priscilla, for the third girl seemed to him wise; it would have indicated a lack of delicacy to ask Uncle Sherman for game if no member of his immediate family were invited to share it; as it was, Sherman could bring Priscilla and the ducks to Joy Street at the same time and he would, of course, be urged to remain for tea. Then there was another consideration : if Priscilla, who was now seventeen, were to come out the following year, it was high time for her to have a little preliminary social training; she and her brothers and sisters had run wild among the cranberry bogs far, far too long. Roger had noticed her trapped look at the wedding and he also recalled that, strangely enough, this had been less marked when David Salomont tried to engage her briefly in conversation. In response to Emily's suggestion, he mentioned this, and said he thought it would be a good plan to put David and Priscilla side by side at table. Emily agreed and from that point they went on to discuss the table plan.

'I think we ought to put Mrs. Putnam at your right and Mr. Putnam at mine, don't you, Roger? After all, they're older people. We ought to pay them a compliment.'

Inwardly, Roger had been less enthusiastic about Emily's selection of the Putnams than over her choice of Priscilla. Mr. Putnam was a third husband who had appeared tardily on the scene; Roger had nothing against him, and was indeed rather sorry for him; but he did not seem likely to provide stimulating conversation at a dinner-table. Mrs. Putnam, on the other hand, always talked too much and sometimes drank too much. But her family background, like her husband's, was 'good', and on this account much had been forgiven her by people who had forgotten the details of her earlier marital adventures.

'Well, we've got that far. Mr. Putnam at your right and Mrs. Putnam at mine. Who goes on our left?'

'I thought I'd put Pell on mine. He's been with Cutter, Mills and Swan longer than the others, hasn't he?' Then, as Roger nodded his assent, obviously feeling that this seniority entitled Pell to a certain precedence, she went on, a little hurriedly, 'And Marion on yours, I should think. After all, if it hadn't been for her, you probably wouldn't be connected with the firm at all.'

'No, I suppose I wouldn't—that is, not if Caroline and Marion hadn't got so chummy. And of course I can't have Caroline beside me.'

'I thought I'd put her between Pell and Brian. It couldn't possibly be any worse than putting her beside David and there's just a chance it might be better.'

'I guess you're right again.... Yes, that seems to work out very nicely. But since the party's all planned now, can't we take a little time off? It's a long while since you've given me a kiss.'

CHAPTER IV

Everything continued to go propitiously with the preparations for the dinner-party and all the prospective guests accepted their invitations. Moreover, when Sherman Forbes arrived with Priscilla and the ducks, he was in such rare good humour that Emily derived more enjoyment from their brief chat, over the teacups than she had ever experienced in previous contacts with him.

He departed in great good humour, leaving his niece in equally high spirits. She took one last look at the perfectly prepared dinner-table, assured herself that the pantry was equally well ordered and started upstairs. Priscilla had gone straight to her room, declining her cousin's offer of tea and saying she wanted to unpack. Emily had assured her that Ellie would do the unpacking, but Priscilla had looked so frightened at the suggestion that Emily had not insisted; now she decided to see how the poor girl was getting along before she herself began to dress.

There was no immediate answer when she knocked at the door of the little guest room where Roger's spool furniture had been installed. She opened the door part way, to be confronted by the sight of Priscilla, struggling into her bridesmaid's dress. Her tight red curls were uncombed and the dress, which had been so suitable for an elaborate June wedding, would have looked entirely out of place for a small autumn dinner, even if it had retained its first freshness. But the tulle was now limp and the lace torn in several places. Evidently, the dress had been carelessly put away after the wedding and not even inspected again before it was tossed into a suitcase and brought back to Boston that day.

Emily experienced a momentary feeling of irritation because Priscilla had not been provided with something smart and seasonable in satin or velvet. This would not have necessitated so much as a special trip to town, for, with her figure, Priscilla could have stepped straight into any standard-sized model; an earlier start that morning would have been all that was necessary. And certainly expense was no object; if Priscilla had bought out a speciality shop, either Sherman or Sue could have paid the bill without wincing. Really, it was time somebody else in the family took hold and Emily was quite prepared to do so. But she knew she must proceed cautiously. She would have liked to offer Priscilla one of her own dresses, then and there, but this would hurt the girl's feelings and anyway, they would have been far too long, for Emily was the taller of the two. She did not even dare offer to mend the torn lace. Priscilla looked at her cousin with miserable eyes and put a piteous question to her.

'Emily, do I have to go down to dinner? Couldn't I have it up here on a tray, the way I had my tea?'

'My dear child, you've come on purpose for the party!'

'I know. But I didn't want to. I wouldn't have, if it hadn't been for keeping Daddy company when he brought the ducks. I don't like parties any better than he and Mummy do.'

'Isn't it too soon to decide? You haven't been to many parties yet, have you? I really believe you'll like this one. And David Salomont would be terribly disappointed if he didn't see you again.'

Instead of appearing pleased at this information, Priscilla's expression became more terrified than ever. Emily was afraid that if she left her, the girl might actually lock herself in her room and decline to come out.

'Listen, Priscilla, it would help me a lot if you'd go down to the library right now. You're dressed already and I haven't so much as started to change. What's more, Roger isn't even in the house yet. If one of the guests happened to come early——'

'You mean I'd be all alone down there with some perfect stranger? Oh, Emily, I couldn't! Please——'

'It would only be for a few minutes. And one of us has got to be downstairs.'

With less gentleness than she habitually showed, Emily propelled Priscilla, still protesting, down the stairs, installed her in the library and fairly fled to her own room. She was really short of time now. Roger was still absent and she knew the doorbell would be ringing any moment. Presently it did ring. If that were only David.... But it was not David. It was Caroline, who had come with Marion. Caroline's harsh voice penetrated to the second storey.

'We're not to take our wraps upstairs? Are you *sure*? You look like a new maid. Probably you don't know. I *always* go upstairs.'

'Please, ma'am, I'm Deirdre's niece, Dolly, accommodating for the dinner. And Mrs. Field said, ladies in the powder room, the gentlemen in the cloakroom.'

Marion said something that was evidently conciliatory, though just what it was Emily could not hear, for Marion's tones were more subdued. Then the two guests were apparently ushered into the library and Emily's heart smote her, thinking of poor Priscilla. Emily had pulled on her dress hastily and now she snapped on her bracelets and was screwing on the second ear-ring when the doorbell rang again and Mrs. Putnam's hearty laugh sounded through the hallway.

'Who'da thunk it? Little Em'ly blossoming out like this, givin' dinners n'everything. Are you there, Em'ly? Oh—she hasn't come down yet. Why, hello, Roger—are you invited to this party too? So's Jasper, so's Jasper. You remember Jasper, don't you? He's my husband and he comes to my parties, just like you're coming to Little Em'ly's. Only I make *him* come on time!'

If Mrs. Putnam's greeting to the returning master of the house were a sample of what could be expected of her throughout the evening, it had certainly been a mistake to invite her. But, thank heaven, Roger was home at last, and evidently one of his fellow juniors had arrived at the same moment, for Emily could hear another male voice. Then there was a slight delay, suggesting that the host was apologetically introducing guests to each other before he came racing up the stairs. He and Emily met on the threshold of their room.

'I'm terribly sorry, darling. It's the same old story. There was a draft of a will that simply had to be finished tonight. But I thought of course *you'd* be ready.'

'I would have been, except for Priscilla. . . . Who besides the Putnams came in at the same time you did?'

'Pell.'

'Oh—I hoped it might be David. Well—hurry, won't you, Roger?' .

'Of course.'

He had unbuttoned his waistcoat and undone his tie while they were talking and now he went hastily along, pulling off his coat. For the first time since their marriage, they had not even exchanged a kiss after a day's separation. Emily flew on down the stairs, reaching the bottom step just as Dolly opened the front door to admit David.

'Oh—I *am* glad to see you! Now everything will be all right.'

'Of course everything will be all right. What do you mean?'

'I can't stop to explain now. Come on in with me!'

She had intended to greet her guests, rather formally, in the drawing-room, where she had arranged the flowers and studied the lighting with the greatest care. But Priscilla had not stirred from her place by the radio and everyone else had naturally drifted out to the library. As Emily welcomed them all in turn, she noticed that the company had that expectant and slightly thwarted look, suggesting that drinks have been too long delayed. Leaving David, who had competently made the rounds with her, to cope with the situation, she hurried to the pantry.

'You may begin serving the cocktails right away, Ellie. You'll have to manage alone. Dolly can't leave the door. Mr. Collins isn't here yet.'

Strange that Ellie, who had been so cheerful and capable up to that night, had apparently sensed that everything was not going as it should and had caught the prevailing malaise. Well, it could not be helped, and when Dolly was released, probably the two cousins would manage very well together.

Roger and the cocktails arrived almost simultaneously, and when he had taken charge of the mixer, and begun to dispense drinks with a hospitable hand, the strain in the atmosphere slackened. The Martinis were very good; so were the canapés which Ellie brought in their wake—the small square of toast thickly overlaid with caviar, the beaten biscuits stuffed with Virginia ham, the piping hot sausages wrapped in crisp bacon. David had successfully eluded Mrs. Putnam and reached Priscilla in her corner. Mr. Putnam had wandered over towards Caroline and said something about the weather to which she took no exception, and Marion and Pell seemed increasingly at ease with each other. Emily sat down on the sofa beside Mrs. Putnam, allowing the lively lady to rattle on, while she continued to glance from Roger, making his welcome rounds with the mixer, to the clock, whose hands now pointed to eight-fifteen.

She had told Deirdre she was sure they could count on getting to the table promptly at eight, with the guests invited for

66

seven-thirty; and here was Brian Collins three-quarters of an hour late already! What was worse, when he did come, he would want a drink—two or three of them, to judge by the way he had guzzled champagne at the wedding! The ducks would be utterly ruined, those beautiful ducks which Sherman had brought to her with such pride and which Deirdre by this time would have cooked to a turn! As for the *soufflé*, that would have to be omitted altogether. Deirdre had told Emily that she could keep one from falling for fifteen minutes, by putting a little tapioca in the mixture; but no one could keep a *soufflé* from falling for half an hour. . . .

'I wouldn't worry about Brian if I were you,' David said reassuringly. 'He'll turn up all right.'

'Roger's worrying about him, I expect. I'm not. I'm worrying about my dinner.'

'Then I wouldn't worry about that, any longer.'

'Evidently I don't have to. Dolly's opening the front door right now.'

Her voice betrayed her relief; but this was short lived. When the *portières* parted, Brian Collins was revealed wearing a salt-and-pepper suit and red tie. However, this was not the worst; below his disordered hair, his face was flushed and his normally keen eyes were glazed. He looked about him and laughed loudly.

'Well now, a real party, is it? I thought it was going to be just us boys, getting together for a fine poker game, or the like of that. I've got glad rags myself at home, believe it or not, but I never bothered putting them on.'

'We were getting worried about you, Brian,' Roger said, still speaking in a troubled voice. 'Did you have an accident?'

'Accident? Accident? Never had an accident in my life. You did say seven-thirty. I remember that now. But then I knew you were always late getting home yourself, so I just stopped in to chew the rag and drink a drop with my cousin, Tim Tupperty, around the corner from the station. You ought to get to know Tim yourself, might come in handy some time. Matter of fact, he does know you, half-way, seeing as he was one of the traffic cops at your wedding.'

'Unless you'd like another drink, Mr. Collins, we'll go out to dinner now. You're taking in my sister-in-law, Miss Field. David, will you take Priscilla? And Mr. de Lucca, I have to separate you and Miss Swan after we get to the dining-room, but you can have the pleasure of each other's company that far.

67

Mrs. Putnam, you lead off with Roger, of course, and Mr. Putnam, you and I'll bring up the rear.'

It was inexcusable to have said 'another', Emily knew that. But she was angry, so angry that she had been obliged to give the conventional directions. Only that one word had come out spontaneously. She hoped that Brian Collins had realized its significance—and that Roger had not heard it. But anyway, she was not sorry for it. She did not blame Caroline for sitting so rigidly beside him, turning her head away. Emily would have done the same in her sister-in-law's place. But Brian Collins appeared quite undisturbed by Caroline's avoidance; indeed, he seemed to have found such a kindred spirit in Mrs. Putnam that he had promptly dismissed Caroline from his mind. During the long wait for his arrival, Mrs. Putnam had consumed a number of drinks herself; she was now in top form.

Nothing had happened to the soup; Deirdre had not been defeated there by Brian Collins. The clear green turtle was strong and hot, perfectly seasoned—and perfectly served. Emily looked down towards the other end of the table, beyond the flowers and the silver birds and the tall epergne with its overhanging fruit, and saw that Roger and Marion were chatting quietly and contentedly. Priscilla and David were also getting on very well. When the *vol-au-vent* of sea-food came in, as unspoiled as the soup and complemented by Homer Lathrop's excellent Chablis, Emily relaxed a little and turned to Pell, giving voice to the bewilderment which had plagued her for so long.

'I'm ever so glad you could come tonight. And do you know, I have the strangest feeling that I've seen you before.'

'But you did. At your wedding.'

'No, I mean before that. It puzzled me when I saw you that day too. I've kept wondering about it. I'm annoyed with myself because I can't remember when and where it was.'

'Then I must put an end to your annoyance. It is not suitable that lovely ladies should be annoyed, especially without reason. You saw me Christmas Eve, on Louisburg Square. I saw you too.'

'Christmas Eve——'

'Yes. You were waiting for someone, I imagine—was it perhaps Roger? I think it must have been, for I saw him later too—on Joy Street, near this very house. At all events, you were standing in the bay window of your grandmother's drawing-room, beside a big Christmas tree. You had on a golden-brown velvet dress and you looked very beautiful. But then I am sure you always look very beautiful.'

'Why, I *was* standing in Grandmamma's window waiting for Roger!' she said, tasting the duck which, unfortunately, so far fulfilled her worst fears that even the Pommard could not redeem it. She decided that perhaps it would be better to make no direct rejoinder to Pellegrino's final remark, much as she wished that she could have spoken in the same natural way that he did about her looks. Besides, her curiosity was still only half satisfied. 'But where in the world were *you*?' she asked impulsively.

'Outside, in the street. With a group of my friends. We stopped beside the steps of your grandmother's house to sing.'

'Of course! Then *you* were——' She checked herself suddenly. She could not say, 'You were the man who made me think of Michelangelo's David, because you were so strikingly handsome.' Yet the statement would have been no more candid and direct than the one he had just made about her beauty. Then, perhaps the girl who had been with him on Christmas Eve, that lovely, lovely girl whom he had kissed, was just a relative, someone he took for granted, though it certainly had not looked that way. 'You were the song leader,' Emily continued, rather lamely and tardily. 'And your singing was marvellous. I remember it all perfectly.'

'Well then, you do not need to keep searching your memory or to be perplexed any longer. The puzzle is solved.'

He smiled and half turned towards Caroline on his other side. Evidently he considered the reminiscence closed. Emily was not yet ready to do so, however. The salad had come in and there was no soufflé with it. Deirdre had shown great presence of mind. She had substituted *pâté de foie gras* and it was excellent. But that in no way exonerated Brian Collins.

'I remember both you and your son very well now,' she said. 'It was terribly stupid of me not to place you before. I don't see why I didn't.'

Pellegrino turned towards her again. 'But there's no reason why you should have,' he said quietly. 'After all, you saw dozens—probably hundreds—of street singers that night. It was different in my case. I did not see dozens of beautiful girls dressed in golden-brown velvet, standing in bay windows beside Christmas trees. The vision of you was unique.'

'But you had a very beautiful girl with you! I remember her perfectly too!'

Even before she finished speaking, Emily realized that Pellegrino's pleasant expression was becoming vague. He shook his head slightly, as if it were his memory which was now playing tricks.

'There were five or six girls in our group that night, as I recall it, and probably they were all pretty. It seems to be quite a habit with young Italian girls. I wouldn't know which one you mean.'

'Why, you must! She was a great deal more than pretty! And besides——'

Again Emily checked herself. She could not say, 'And besides, you had your arm around her all the time. Besides, you and she kissed each other.' As a matter of fact, she could not say anything, for the simple reason that Pellegrino had put a conclusive stop to their unfinished conversation by turning wholly away from her and beginning one with Caroline, who was no longer able to remain withdrawn in the face of his quiet persistence. But Mr. Putnam was hopeless. Across the void created by his silence, Emily listened to David and Priscilla.

'I don't know the first thing about raising cranberries. I'd like very much to come and see your bogs.'

'Oh, would you really? You mean, when we're harvesting next fall? It *is* something of a sight then. . . .'

'Do I really have to wait until next fall for an invitation? I thought maybe you'd ask me down for Thanksgiving dinner this year and let me help make the cranberry sauce.'

Well, that combination at least was working out better than Emily had even dared to hope. The champagne was bubbling up in the glasses now and the 'rock-ice' with hot raspberry sauce, a super ice-cream which was one of Deirdre's own inventions, was being passed. In another ten minutes, Emily would be able to give the signal to leave the table. But now Mrs. Putnam's booming tones sounded through the pleasant, expectant hush which had followed the complimentary reception of Deirdre's *pièce de résistance*.

'Who do you suppose I ran into on the Square the other night. Em'ly? That scoundrelly antique dealer, Morris Brucker! And what do you think he had the nerve to tell me? That he'd just been having dinner with your grandmother?'

'But he had. They're old friends. He came over from New York on purpose to see her.'

Emily spoke with a calmness that was no less effective because it was forced. David, who had looked up at the mention of his

70

stepfather's name, now turned quietly back to Priscilla. But the pleasant hush had suddenly become a strained silence. Then Mrs. Putnam laughed.

'Well, do excuse me! Of course I didn't know. I used to spend a lot of money with Brucker myself, when he first opened up that fancy shop of his in New York—not that I ever knew him socially. I stopped going to him because I found out he was a faker—claiming all that loot he had came right out of the Tzar's palace! Some of it may have, but if it did, I bet he stole it, and there was a lot of junk in with the good stuff. Besides, he was getting away with murder, the prices he asked.'

'My grandmother has some of the things that came out of the Winter Palace too, Mrs. Putnam, and I can assure you——'

'Oh, I know she didn't steal! She had other ways of getting what she wanted—and how! And maybe Brucker didn't *exactly* steal either. After all, I guess he's a reasonably honest—for a Jew.'

Emily had precipitately risen and with her everyone else at the table, except Mrs. Putnam and Brian. David was still talking quietly to Priscilla when Caroline, with a frozen expression, accepted Pell's arm and Roger offered his to Marion. Mr. Putnam, oblivious of his hostess, plunged in the direction of his wife, reaching her side just as Brian seized her by the shoulder.

'Shut your trap!' he shouted. 'You think I'm going to let you sit there and insult my friends? I can tell you that old Forbes gal may have had her moments, but she never was the bitch you are. Something else: David's dad is as straight as they come and his money's a lot cleaner than yours. I know, see? You'd better take my word for it and say you're sorry!'

With a dexterity which suggested previous practice, Mr. Putnam had managed to get his wife out of the house before Brian's outburst could result in a serious altercation; Pell was similarly successful in dealing with Brian. Immediately after their removal, Caroline remarked cuttingly to Roger that of course it would be unthinkable for her and Marion to remain when such a scene had taken place; and though Marion tried to soften the statement with gentler excuses, it was obvious that she was also glad to escape. Neither Roger nor Emily made any effort to detain them; and with the group reduced to David, Priscilla and their hosts, the tension in the atmosphere slackened. David glanced at his watch.

'It seems to be a little on the late side for a show,' he said, as

71

casually as if there had been some previous question of going to one. 'But what about dancing for a while? We'd hit it just about right at the Copley.'

The suggestion proved a godsend. The festive atmosphere of the ballroom at the Copley Plaza precluded any sort of serious conversation; and, by the time they finally started home, they were all much too tired for any. David said good night at the door of the Joy Street house, after suggesting to Priscilla that he might take her to a matinée the following afternoon and drive her back to the Cape afterwards, with dinner along the way—an invitation which she accepted with mingled shyness and astonishment, not untinged with delight. When Roger and Emily reached the threshold of their bedroom, they paused, by mutual impulse, and put their arms around each other, saying almost the same thing at almost the same time.

'Let's try not to talk about it until morning, darling.'

But, as each had secretly hoped, morning was not a good time either. Roger had to hurry off to the office, and, after he had left, Emily lay quietly thinking for some time. She told herself that if Brian Collins had been possessed of a single saving grace, he would have sent her some token of apology. But eventually she settled down to hard thinking along more objective lines. Obviously, dinner-parties were not the best means of bringing alien elements harmoniously together; it would be folly to attempt anything more along the same lines. On the other hand, she could not admit herself beaten after her first attempt to make the house on Joy Street a centre of good feeling and a place where better understanding could be promoted. She must keep on trying until she had found the right solution for the problem, and she wanted to find it for herself, without help or advice from anybody.

The daily walks which she took as a matter of course seemed to furnish the best opportunities for reflection. During the beautiful days of Indian summer, she frequently cut across the Common to the Public Garden and, sitting down near the little lake, where she and Roger had ridden on the swan boats together when they were children, deliberated the questions which troubled her. She also went, occasionally, to see her grandmother; but though Emily could have confided in Old Mrs. Forbes more easily than in her mother, the fact that such a confidence would have been an admission of failure, instead of a revelation of success, kept her silent on the subject of her problems. She wanted to wait until she could speak not only candidly, but pridefully. More than once when she had started out with Old Mrs Forbes' house as her intended destination, she went instead to the chapel in St. Margaret's Convent; but somehow Homer Lathrop's cynical remark to the effect that he hoped she was not 'seriously interested in religion', that such an interest was 'just a passing phase', which almost every girl went through, kept coming, unbidden, to the forefront of her consciousness. If the sensation of peace and the seeming awareness of Divinity which came to her almost instantly after she entered the chapel, tranquillizing her and uplifting her as long as she remained there, were only part of a 'passing phase' she could not depend on them for succour and support. She wanted to believe in their permanence and reality; but her faith in them had been undermined and she could not. One morning, when she was leaving the chapel, she did so with the sorrowful knowledge that she was not going back there unless and until her doubts about the validity of her feeling for it had been stilled.

Since the one time when her curiosity about Pell had taken her over the crest of the Hill, Emily had never again surveyed the northern slope of Joy Street; she had felt afterwards as if she had been too inquisitive and was slightly ashamed of this. Pell's non-committal answers on the night of the dinner had increased her conviction that she should not pry into his private life, however much this intrigued her. But the day after her decision about the chapel, having hesitated for a moment as to the direction she should take for her constitutional, she started down the unfamiliar thoroughfare. The fire escapes were still cluttered with rubbish and the garbage cans still stood, unemptied, on the corners. Traffic was heavy and trucks, taxicabs and delivery wagons impeded each other's progress as they swarmed down the Hill, the drivers honking their horns and shouting and swearing at each other. The battered brick sidewalks were crowded, too, by pedestrians. But neither the drivers nor the pedestrians were really part of the locality; only the children playing with their rubber balls in the concrete courtyard which separated the Peter Faneuil School from the street seemed to belong there.

Emily had stopped by the iron railing which served as a fence for the yard and was watching these children when a ball skimmed over the iron railing, struck the uneven pavement and rebounded into the crowded street. Instantly a little boy rushed

73

through the gate after it, leaped from the kerb and darted directly in front of a plumber's truck.

Above the wail of locked brakes and screaming tyres, there was a loud shout, followed by lesser cries and by the honking of horns. Then the tumult ended abruptly in terrible silence.

'Don't touch that kid, any of you. We'll have First Aid here in a minute and it's for them to say what to do. Jim, get through a call for an ambulance on the double and put one of the other boys at the corner to untangle this traffic jam. And let's have less noise around here. Stand back there, every one of you, except the driver. Now, let's see your licence, bud.'

The driver thrust a shaking hand into his hip pocket and from this extracted a worn wallet which he opened with fumbling fingers. While the policemen inspected the proffered licence, the frightened truckman jabbered excitedly.

'Jeez, officer, I just turned into Joy from Myrtle, I was still in second. Brakes okay too, or I couldn't have stopped like I did. But that kid come out in front of me from nowhere.'

'That's true, officer. The little boy was running after his ball.'

Emily, who had knelt by the child, now looked up at the policeman. He answered her tersely.

'You saw it happen, did you, Mrs. Field?'

'Yes. I was standing by the fence, watching the children play,' she replied quickly, without even noticing that he had called her by name. 'This little boy ran right in front of me, so close that I tried to catch hold of him. I couldn't, he went so fast. But do you mind if I take a look at him? I've had some experience in nursing.'

'One of them Grey Ladies?' The question was contemptuous.

'No. Nurse's Aide and Frontier Service in Kentucky.'

'Okay. Go ahead. I guess you can't hurt him anyway.'

Emily turned back to the child and put her fingers on his thin wrist. Then she gave a little cry of gladness.

'I can feel his pulse. It's slow, but it's steady.'

Another shout went up from the crowd which, though it had retreated, had not dispersed and had, indeed, increased in size. The policeman raised his hand.

'I said less noise around here. On your way, everyone who doesn't live in these parts. I still don't want the kid moved. He may be alive all right, but that's not saying no bones are broken. And move along, the rest of you. Except you, Mrs. Field.... And you, Miss. Did you see this happen too?'

74

The officer was now addressing a second kneeling girl. With her hand still on the little boy's wrist, Emily turned again and gave a cry of surprise. She had been slow to identify Pell, but now recognition was immediate; the girl beside her was the same one who had been with him on Christmas Eve. There was no mistaking that rare, madonna-like beauty. . . .

'No, not everything from close by, like the lady here,' the Italian girl was saying, speaking rather haltingly. She had a sweet voice, but she spoke with a strong accent and it was evident that she had to grope for the right words. 'I was standing at the window. I live right there, across the street.' She motioned in the direction of a tenement house and once more Emily was struck with the grace of her movements. 'I know the driver is telling the truth. I saw Pietro run after his ball too. It was a new ball and——'

'You the kid's sister?'

'No, he's not a relation. But——'

'You went through the crowd like you'd been shot out of a gun. If I hadn't 'a thought you was his sister or something, I wouldn't 'a let you stay. What's the rest of his name?'

'Danielli. And please let me stay, even if he isn't a relation. I know him very well. His mother is our neighbour. She goes out to work, so we try to help her take care of him.'

'Who's "we"?'

'My mother and my brother and myself. Pietro's mother will think we did not take good care of him this time and ... couldn't I please put my shawl over him at least? It's so cold and he's so little.'

The girl's sweet voice ended in a slow sob. The officer spoke more gently.

'Sure, that's a good idea. And look, he ain't dead. He ain't even bleeding any more. And kids like him has got nine lives anyway. At that, I guess I'd better take your name as a witness of the accident. What is it? I know your address already.'

'Simonetta de Lucca.'

She was absorbed in arranging her shabby shawl so that it would cover Pietro as completely as possible. She did not even look at the officer as she answered.

'Would you need to use my name too?' Emily inquired as casually as possible.

'Could be. But of course I knew that already: Mrs. Roger Field, and I know your Joy Street address too. No reason why you should remember me. In case it would be handy for you to get in touch with me later on though, I'm Tupperty, Tim Tupperty.... Well, have a look here now, will you?'

Emily and Simonetta both followed the direction of the officer's pointing finger. The little boy whom they had, momentarily, ceased to watch with the same closeness that they had at first, was stirring uneasily, but with no indication of pain. Then he opened his eyes and looked up into Simonetta's face, putting his hand to his head as he did so.

'What happened?' he asked in a puzzled whisper.

'You ran after your ball, *caro*, and you forgot to take care. A truck was coming and it hit you.'

The shrill sound of a siren drowned out her final words and the crowd scattered as the ambulance tore down the Hill and came to an abrupt stop. Two policemen leaped from it, nodded to Tim Tupperty and, bending over Pietro, inspected the cut on the child's head.

'Just a surface wound,' one of them said encouragingly. 'A touch of Mercurochrome and a bit of Band-aid will fix that up in no time. Don't worry, sonny. It won't hurt you none. But we're going to take you along with us, see, just to make sure there's nothing else wrong.'

'Where to?'

'Over to M.G.H., right around the corner. You'll like it there.'

For the first time, Pietro's under lip quivered and again he looked appealingly at Simonetta.

'Can't I go home with you, Etta? You could take care of me.'

'I could try, *caro*. But I think perhaps this time I should go with you instead of taking you with me. You will let me go with Pietro to the hospital, will you not, *signori*?'

'The kid's mother works out,' Tim Tupperty said in an undertone. 'This girl and her family look after him.'

The officer, who had finished putting the Band-aid neatly into place and, with his companion's help, taken a stretcher from the ambulance, nodded again.

'Sure. She can go along. Now, if you'll just lie still, sonny, me and Ned'll roll you over on this nice little number and we'll get going.'

The ambulance shot off, making the same shrill sound with which it had approached, and less noisily, but almost as speedily, the plumber's repair truck followed down the Hill. As she walked away in the opposite direction, Emily was conscious of curious glances and whispered comments from the onlookers who still lingered in the street. However, nobody spoke to her and she went home feeling not only shaken but rebuffed. The following week she went to the tenement house where the de Luccas and the Daniellis lived, but the middle-aged woman who answered her ring at the de Luccas' either spoke practically no English or pretended that this was the case. Eventually, Simonetta appeared, apologetically. She was sorry she had not been able to come to the door immediately herself, she said, but she had just gone out on the fire escape to bring in the laundry. Yes, Pietro was doing very well—in fact, he had already left the hospital and was back in school. The X-rays had revealed no broken bones and the cut on his head was healing rapidly. It was very kind of the lady to inquire, but no, he needed nothing. She spoke with the utmost politeness, but she did not ask Emily to come in and there was a certain unmistakable finality in the way she said good-bye.

Emily continued to worry about Pietro and to wish she could do something to improve his lot. Moreover, Simonetta herself had become an increasingly enigmatic figure and as such, an increasingly provocative one. De Lucca was not a common name among the Italians of Boston and, in any event, Emily knew that Pell lived with relatives. Simonetta had spoken of a brother to Tupperty; but she could not have been referring to Pell when she did this—or at least, so Emily persistently told herself. Conceivably, he and Simonetta might be cousins, brought up like brother and sister, though there had been nothing to suggest such an unromantic relationship in their attitude towards each other. To be sure, marriages between cousins were by no means rare among the old Boston families; but such marriages did not occur, as far as Emily knew, either between young men and young girls who had lived all their lives under the same parental roof, or between young men and young girls who loved each other so passionately that they embraced, with abandon, on the street—and still went unwed, year after year. Yet Pell and Simonetta were doing both these things.

There remained Tim Tupperty, whom Emily could have dismissed easily enough from her mind if it had not been for his connection with Brian Collins. In that case, there was no question about the relationship; the two proudly proclaimed themselves cousins and they were boon companions to boot. Tim Tupperty doubtless owed his position on the police force to some form of political graft, or else profited by this position to practise graft himself. And what was true of Tim Tupperty must be correlatively true of Brian Collins. Emily despised him and she could not understand why she did not stop thinking about him.

It was all very different from what she and Roger had planned. She did not want Brian for a friend and Pell did not want to be hers. Only David was friendly and he did not need her friendship; she had never met anyone so self-assured and so self-satisfied. It was all very puzzling. She was sorry she had decided never to return to St. Margaret's Chapel. Whatever Homer Lathrop thought, she could not help feeling that if she had gone there long enough, she might have found understanding and wisdom as well as peace.

CHAPTER V

Only one person gauged the degree of Emily's distress or guessed some of the reasons for it. Old Mrs. Forbes, with a mercy she would have shown no one else, while making no direct allusion to the girl's perturbed state of mind, adroitly sought to divert Emily's thoughts.

'What are you doing about the first Waltz Evening?' she inquired when the two were lunching together, without guests, according to their not infrequent custom.

'I don't know. I hadn't thought about it. The invitation only came this morning.'

'Then you haven't made any plans for dinner beforehand?'

'No. I don't seem to be in just the right mood for giving dinners.'

'No one expects a bride to keep giving dinners all the time, or to devote herself exclusively to philanthropy. People in your own set ought to be giving dinners for you. Naturally, your father and mother can't do anything, as long as they unreasonably stay on in that horrible little Gloucester Street house; what's more, I don't want to foster the idea that I've got a monopoly on you. But Homer Lathrop gives very nice dinners at the Somerset Club, as you must remember.'

'I hope you won't suggest it to him if he doesn't come across of his own accord.'

'Why not? There isn't any special reason, is there, why you're not interested in dancing? A reason that you thought you might tell me two or three months from now when there wouldn't be any need of it? In other words, to quote Maurice Hewlett, I hope you'll proclaim your condition before your condition proclaims you.'

'I would, if there were anything to proclaim. But there isn't, I'm sorry to say. Roger and I want children—several children. And when husband and wife both feel like that, don't you think

79

it's—well, reassuring if—if——'

'If a girl begins to lose her breakfast before she's home from her wedding trip?' Old Mrs. Forbes inquired tartly, so that Emily would think she had not noticed her distress. 'Why yes, I suppose it is "reassuring". But it certainly doesn't add to the glamour of the situation.'

'I'd rather have the reassurance than the glamour. And some girls never lose their breakfast. Somehow, I don't believe you did, Grandmamma.'

She was speaking and acting naturally again, Old Mrs. Forbes observed with relief. She was distressed herself when Emily was troubled, though she would never have been able to make anyone believe it, and indeed would not have wished anyone to do so. Her relief increased as Emily went on talking more and more normally.

'I'll call up Uncle Homer myself. I was going to anyway. I need some more money. That's the worst of a spring trousseau —it doesn't provide for things like fur coats and my old one is a sight. It wouldn't ever do to wear for a Waltz Evening. Thanks, Grandmamma, for the lunch—and the good advice—all you gave me and all you didn't. I don't know which I appreciated more.'

Homer Lathrop put no obstacles in the way of a new fur coat, even when Emily told him she thought it had better be mink this time—mink was so practical, you could wear it for anything and everything. Moreover, he was most receptive to the suggestion of a dinner at the Somerset Club before the first Waltz Evening—his only regret was that he hadn't beaten her to the draw, as of course he should have done. They discussed a guest list, first over the telephone and then over a cup of tea. Roger, coming in even later than usual, found them deep in a conversation into which he entered himself without much spirit. If he had not felt so uneasy about his progress at the office, his mood might well have been different, or he might have been able to throw this off on his return to a comfortable home and a cheerful wife. But, day after day, he was dispatched on errands, charged with delivering or filing papers which he thought could just as well have been mailed, and sent to look up information which, in many instances, he could have obtained more easily and quickly by telephone. He could not escape the suspicion that some trips were more or less invented to occupy him. Most of his time in the office was spent in looking up doubtful points of law, and when he had finished with these, they appeared no less doubtful than when he had begun. He was allowed to write letters demanding the payment of overdue accounts, to draft simple contracts and to prepare briefs. But none of his drafts was accepted as a finished product and none of his work was creative.

On the afternoon before the first Waltz Evening, Roger found himself thinking enviously of Bradford Olcott, a classmate who —as he tardily discovered—had been offered the job which he now held himself. Brad had turned it down and struck off independently to a small city in Vermont where he had opened his own office. He had written Roger jokingly about his first case: a farmer's wife was suing her husband for divorce because he had spanked her. The spanking, so the farmer claimed, had been administered only after his stubborn spouse had declined to press his pants, and this was freely admitted; but it next transpired that the reason the man wanted his pants pressed was because he was taking the hired girl to a chicken-pie supper at Odd Fellows Hall!

Roger had smiled rather ruefully when he first read this letter and he had re-read it a number of times. Obviously, Brad's first case had been humorous rather than rewarding; but it was his own case and he had won it. He had not spent all his time acting as someone's errand boy or poring over old statutes in books which were, literally, as dry as dust. Roger, who was seeking to resolve an intricate point in a minor bankruptcy case for Mr. Mills, found his thoughts straying from the dull subject to dwell with increasing envy on Bradford Olcott's invigorating freedom.

'Mr. Mills wants to see you in his office,' the switchboard operator informed him.

Roger knew exactly what would happen next. He would be chided for 'devoting so much time to a simple matter of elementary practice' and asked how much longer he would require. He would then be reminded that he was not being asked to prepare a brief for the Supreme Court and told that, in Mr. Mills' day, it was presumed that a Harvard graduate could at least look up the Index in Corpus Juris. Probably he should have asked advice from David. Well, it was too late to think about help from that quarter now. Roger hastily gathered together such notes as he had assembled in the bankruptcy case and, papers in hand, entered Mr. Mills' commodious corner office.

'I'm afraid I'll need a little more time in going over this, sir,' he began. 'You see, I've found what may involve the receipt of technical preference by our client on at least one transaction.'

'Eh? Bankruptcy? What the devil ... Oh, yes, of course, to be sure,' Mills replied. 'Forget that for the time being. And don't labour it to death when you get back to it. Prepare a proof of claim and worry about the law when it comes up. Meantime, first things first.'

He pulled a bound folder from the litter of papers on his desk and extended it to Roger in the manner of one bestowing largess. His pale lips parted over his yellow teeth in an ingratiating smile.

'Got a real job for you, my boy. Want you to take over for me in a jury trial that comes up in Salem this very afternoon.'

'But, Mr. Mills——'

'I know, I know,' Mr. Mills admitted graciously. Having rid himself of the folder, he smoothed back his thinning hair, adjusted his costly tie, and went on with increasing fervour. 'Short notice and all that sort of thing. Reason for it, though. Expected to handle the matter myself. It's my own case, you see. Then, not ten minutes ago, Van Pick called me from Bennington and says he must see me up there at once.'

'But how can I argue a case before a jury this afternoon, when I've never even heard of it until this minute, Mr. Mills? Can't we get a continuance, under the circumstances?'

'Doubt it. Trouble is, it's been continued a couple of times already. 'S why I'm counting on you to step in for us. Know you'll give it all you've got. ... File right here. Study it on your way to Salem. Can't stop to explain. You've got one train to catch, I've got another. Let's get going!'

Again Roger smiled ruefully as he left Mr. Mills' office and strode along the corridor to his own last-and-least door. 'The Artful Dodger's a great one to give "pep-talks",' he muttered to himself. Then he realized, quite abruptly, that this was it. His first jury case. His real opportunity. Better than Brad's. The big chance. Well, he would show them. He would show them all. ...

'Hallo there! What are you throwing out your chest for?'

David, who had just emerged from the elevator, looking, as usual, fresh, complacent and unhurried, regarded Roger with a tolerant smile not untinged by condescension. He had noticed the same expression on David's face before and he had never resented it; David had a right to his feeling of superiority. But though Roger still felt no resentment, he was slightly embarrassed, for the first time, in his friend's presence; evidently he gave himself away too easily.

'Well, really, Dave, I wasn't ... I mean ...'

'Don't mind me. I'm only kidding. You did look rather on the exalted side, though. What's coming off? Anything special?'

'My first jury case.... This afternoon, too. Got to catch a train for Salem.'

'Oh, no, not that! Anything but that, Rog. Not the Hart thing, is it?'

Now the 'exaltation' was entirely gone, but Roger was still determined to 'show 'em' when he reached the North Station and boarded the cinder-grimed local for Salem. Then he buried himself in the file, finding, the further he went into it that he had more and more cause for concern. If Mr. Mills had neglected the case, as it became increasingly clear that he had, then the defendant, Hart—Roger's first client at a jury trial—might not even have been notified to appear in court. There would not be time to locate him in Beverly, where he had *his* place of business, and still be present when the case was reached. Momentarily, this handicap appeared to him insuperable. But, as he forced himself to study the faltering and inadequate list of payments, Roger caught what he hoped was an inspiration and scrawled a motion on ruled white paper, hurriedly finishing a duplicate as the train slowed down at his stop.

A few moments later he entered the grey stone courthouse and, following the signs pointing to 'Courtroom', hurried up the stairs. As he had feared, he was none too soon; the place was already sparsely occupied by scattered groups, and the clerk was already at his desk, fiddling with a little barrel-shaped drum. A grey-haired, poker-faced judge in a loose black robe entered briskly and everyone stood.

'Court is open. Be seated,' intoned a deputy sheriff.

After a gruelling hour in which Roger managed to stall and so hold over his case until morning, he watched his opponent out of sight with a mounting sensation of triumph. He was far too excited to feel fatigue and he was not even conscious of being hungry. Though all the cards had been stacked against

83

him, his first desperate efforts at trying a case had not ended disastrously; even David Salomont, even Roscoe Cutter himself could not have stalled more successfully than he had. His nervousness, his lack of self-confidence, his sense of inferiority were all gone. Never again would he feel intimidated by a nondescript jury; never again would some small-town lawyer be able to browbeat him. He had proved that he could hold his own against any and all of them. Of course, he must still find Hart, his missing client, but first he would take time out to get to a telephone and tell Emily....

Tell Emily? Tell her what? If he had suddenly been kicked in the stomach by a mule, the sense of shock would hardly have been greater. He could tell her about the jury trial, of course. But he would also have to tell her that he was delayed in Salem, for how much longer he had no idea. He had placed in jeopardy the Waltz Evening which was to make up for their own disastrous dinner.

He located a pay telephone in the basement, secured some nickels from a bored clerk, and called his house. The answer was so immediate as to suggest that Emily was already awaiting a call from him. He swallowed hard.

'Hallo, darling. I'm calling to say that I'm in Salem on a jury trial.'

'At last! That's what you've been hoping and hoping for, isn't it?'

'Yes. And things have gone pretty well, so far—a lot better than I expected. I'm feeling awfully good about that. The hitch is, I don't know just when I can get home.'

'Roger, it's terribly important that you shouldn't do anything to offend Uncle Homer.'

'I realize that. But this case is still more important. The job has to come first. You know that, don't you, dear?'

There was no immediate answer. 'Don't you?' he persisted.

'Yes, I suppose so, but——'

'Listen, Emily every minute we spend talking is going to make me that much later. You know I'll get there if I possibly can. Wish me luck. Good-bye.'

He hung up, looked in the telephone book for Hart's number and dialled again. There was no answer and, after a moment or two, his nickel was returned. His feeling of triumph was gone now. Suddenly he knew that he was inexpressibly empty and tired, that he wanted food and drink and rest. But he must keep on trying to locate his client. This being the case, the next step was to take a taxi and get to Hart's Lobster House in Beverly as rapidly as possible.

The drive to Beverly consumed far more time than he had anticipated and, when he reached the Lobster House, he was informed that Mr. Hart, though expected, seldom came in before six. Of course the gentleman was welcome to a seat in the restaurant whether he ordered dinner or not.

Roger hesitated. With a good meal inside him he probably would feel better. On the other hand, if he stayed in the restaurant, Mr. Hart might continue to elude him. He decided in favour of a dingy passageway outside the private office, where he reviewed the file in the feeble light that came from a solitary bulb. He had read it through several times when the outer door to the passageway opened, and a heavy man, wearing baggy trousers and a tight-fitting coat, came lumbering in Roger's direction. He glanced at his visitor in a surly way and without speaking. Roger stepped forward.

'Mr. Hart? I'm Roger Field. I've been trying that lobster case in Salem.'

'Who? Oh, that one! Well, what about it?'

'We were reached this afternoon and you weren't there. I had to stall—drag out my cross-examination to kill time—till you could get to Court. Didn't you hear from our office?'

'Oh,' Mr. Hart said again, without making any direct answer. Then, as if struck by a sudden thought, he added, 'You don't mean you expect me to go to Salem tomorrow?'

'Why, yes, Mr. Hart. This is your case. I'm trying to win it for you and you're my only witness.'

For the first time, Hart smiled. 'Shucks, boy! You're okay, but I can't spare the time. Lots coming up tomorrow. I'm about through for today, though. Here, come on into my office. Sit down. Have a cigar. Have a drink.'

'I'm sorry, sir, but I'm in rather a hurry. My wife and I are going to a dinner tonight. So, if you will just be kind enough to glance over this testimony with me——'

While Roger was speaking, Hart had leaned forward to push a button and he now interrupted his caller by giving an abrupt order for Scotch and soda to a waiter who appeared in the doorway. Then, tilting his chair back, he smiled more and more expansively.

'Don't worry about your dinner, boy. Never any harm being a

85

little late to shindigs women are mixed up in. And look, there don't have to be any testimony. I've hocked my house, and the bank's letting me have cash enough to hand those dopes half what I owe them. I'll just call Stan up and get him to drop the whole thing. He'll be glad enough to do it when he hears about the ready money.'

'But, Mr. Hart, I think with the case pending, this sort of thing ought to go through Mr. Fleeney, especially with the trial actually going on.'

'Maybe, maybe.'

Tardily seating himself on a dingy couch, Roger accepted the glass Mr. Hart handed him and slowly drank a little from it. Then he set it down on the floor beside him. It was unbelievable to him that his client, his very first client, whose standing as a substantial citizen and whose commercial salvation had been entrusted to him, Roger Field, when both were endangered, and who had now been temporarily rescued, should be shrugging aside everything that seemed of such vital importance. Yet that was what Hart seemed to be doing.

'Mr. Hart,' he said earnestly, 'I want to be sure you understand exactly what I did do in court. I had an entirely new idea. I got your answer amended to say that your last payment was in accord and satisfaction, so that it would settle the whole thing. It looked to me, from our file, as if that was what you intended, after they shipped you so many bad lobsters. If you could come and testify to that, we might be able to beat them.'

With a reproachful look, Mr. Hart poured more Scotch into Roger's glass and refilled his own, which was already empty.

'That's nice of you, boy, and don't think I can't appreciate all you're trying to do. But I don't like trials and I don't want to get up on the stand and give some smart-alec lawyer, like Fleeney, the chance to make a monkey out of me. You get hold of him right now, on the phone, and tell him he can have half his claim in cash, if that's your idea. It isn't a bad one either. If you clean this thing up tonight, then you and your little woman can go ahead and have all the fun you want, and I can forget about the whole damn business.'

Reluctantly, Roger fumbled through the directory and, reaching for the telephone on his client's desk, called Mr. Fleeney's house. A woman answered.

'Is Mr. Fleeney there?' asked Roger.

'No.'

'Is that Mrs. Fleeney?'

'Yes.' The voice was guarded.

'This is Roger Field, Mrs. Fleeney,' he explained. 'I've been trying a case against your husband in Salem and he wanted to discuss settlement with me this afternoon. I couldn't do so then, but I can now. Have you any idea when he'll be home?'

'Might be almost any minute.'

'Then I'll come right over to your house, if I may, and wait for him.'

'That's the way to talk,' Mr. Hart said approvingly. He opened the top drawer of the desk, took out a cheque-book and, breathing hard, began to write. Then, as he ripped out a cheque and handed it to Roger, who was already standing, hat in hand, he added, 'You just dangle this in front of Fleeney's nose and I bet he won't be able to resist it. But understand, he's got to take it or leave it, just as it's written. So long!'

Mrs. Fleeney, a somewhat slatternly and vaguely unpleasant woman, received him rather suspiciously. Then she disappeared, and Roger sat interminably on a stiff sofa trying, without much success, to focus his attention on the tinted enlargements of family photographs which hung on the walls. At last a key turned in the lock and the front door opened.

'Hi, Molly! Any supper left?'

The voice was unquestionably Mr. Fleeney's. Footsteps above hurried towards the stairway.

'Sure I have supper for you, warm on the kitchen stove,' Mrs. Fleeney called down. 'But there's a Mr. Field in the parlour, waiting to see you.'

A short silence, plainly indicative of displeasure, followed this announcement. Then Mr. Fleeney strode into the parlour, frowning.

'Well, what now?' he inquired abruptly.

'I'm sorry to bother you at home, Mr. Fleeney,' Roger began apologetically, 'but I thought you seemed interested in a settlement. So I talked to my client to see if we could avoid going forward tomorrow morning. I'm please to report that I have a cheque right here for half Mr. Edgerly's claim.'

'On account?' Fleeney inquired grimly.

'Why, no. In full settlement. I'm sorry, Mr. Fleeney. This cheque is all I can offer you. I hope very much you'll accept it. But Mr. Hart said you could take it or leave it.'

'Oh, he did, did he? Well, you can tell him I leave it. I'll get my judgment and put his joint into receivership.'

'Mr. Fleeney——'

'Look here, you're wasting your time and mine. You'd better get on back to Boston.'

There was no mistaking the finality of his words. Roger put the cheque slowly back into his pocket. 'May I use your telephone?' he asked tonelessly.

'Sure. There it is on the hall table. But, if you don't mind, I'm going in to supper. Good night.'

'Good night.'

Roger gave the number of the Lobster House and listened to the repeated ringing of the telephone. Finally, a gruff male voice answered.

'May I speak to Mr. Hart, please?'

'He's gone.'

'Listen, my name is Field, Roger Field. I'm Mr. Hart's attorney. Could you write down a message and leave it on Mr. Hart's desk? Say "Mr. Field called. Be in Court at ten." It's most important.'

'I got it.'

'Thanks. Good night.'

Outside drizzly rain was falling and again there was no taxi in sight. Turning up the collar of his coat and buttoning this more closely around him, he walked to the station, where he found that a train had just left; so he paced up and down the platform until another came along, nearly an hour later. Then he climbed aboard and sagged into a seat, utterly discouraged.

Mr. Mills had, no doubt, expected him to lose the case, but not to antagonize both his opponent and his client. Mr. Fleeney was ready to try the case to the end and seek a receivership; Mr. Hart would be angry at his failure to persuade Fleeney to settle. And as for Emily, whom he had not even tried to reach again. . . .

He became aware that the local, which had been lurching towards Boston, was slowing down. Then it stopped altogether. He rubbed the window near him with his hand, but could see no lights outside, except at a distance. He sat a few minutes, his concern growing, and finally went out on the platform. At the foot of the steps stood a brakeman.

'Better stay up there, mister,' he warned.

'Why, what's the trouble?'

'Drawbridge stuck open. We're on a trestle. Better go back in and keep your shirt on, mister.'

The lights grew dim, the car turned cold. Roger heard occasional shouts and saw an occasional lantern. At last the ancient locomotive sighed, struggled, and started across the draw, which somehow had been wheedled back into place. A few minutes later it bustled into Boston.

Roger stumbled down the steps, hurried through the station concourse and climbed into a taxi, which finally deposited him before his door. He let himself in quietly, kicked off his rubbers in the vestibule and flung down his hat and coat on the nearest chair. It was Emily's custom to leave a room pleasantly lighted, even when they went out; therefore, it came as no surprise to him to see that the library was not in darkness. But he was puzzled by the murmur of voices. He pushed back the *portières* and walked in.

David and Emily were seated close to the fire, so absorbed in what they were saying to each other that neither was instantly aware of his entrance.

For a moment, Roger had the strange feeling that he was the interloper, that it was David who really belonged there in the library, beside the fire with Emily. He tried unsuccessfully to suppress it as both preposterous and morbid, and went forward, making an effort to speak cordially and naturally. Emily had not come into the hall, to welcome him home with a loving caress, the way she had always done before; instead she sat very still, her white dress dazzling against the crimson of her chair, her lovely face almost expressionless. David, on the contrary, leapt up, holding out his hand and exclaiming, 'Hallo, there! You *have* had a day of it!' before Roger himself could think of anything to say. Yes, it was as if David were the host, as if he were the outsider and as if Emily did not belong wholly to him any more.

When, half an hour later, the front door had closed behind David, Emily rose and came over to Roger, putting her lovely arms around his neck.

'Darling,' she said gently. 'Darling, I'm so sorry you've had such an awful day. I couldn't seem to say anything before David, but now we're alone we can have a good talk. First though, you've got to have a drink and something to eat. Ellie's

89

left everything ready, in the pantry. Please sit down and rest, while I get it for you.'

He was too tired to protest, too tired to say she must not wait on him, or that he wasn't hungry, or that all right, he would get the whisky and sandwiches himself. Emily brought them in, quietly and expertly, and set them down on the table before him. Roger drank slowly, and as the warmth of the whisky filtered through his veins, he began to take slow bites from a sandwich. But all the time he kept thinking, *Emily's treating me as if I were a child who needed her care, not as if I were a man who could take care of her. If we had a son, this is the way she would act towards him. She wouldn't act this way towards David, if he were her husband.*

'After you telephoned, I called up Uncle Homer and told him I was afraid you couldn't make the dinner, that perhaps he'd better ask one of his old friends to fill in,' Emily was saying soothingly. 'But he wouldn't. He said of course you'd make it. Then he called me back at seven, just to assure himself you'd got home. When I told him you hadn't and that I had no idea how to reach you, he said in that case *I'd* have to find someone to fill in—*he* couldn't.' *Yes, and I know just the way he said it. You're trying to spare me as much as you can, Emily, but I know. I know Homer Lathrop told you again just what he thought of me, he intimated you'd made your own bed, in spite of all he could do to prevent you and now you'd have to lie on it. He wouldn't help you out. Couldn't? Of course he could have!* 'Well, I tried to think and think fast. I thought first of Pell. But I remembered you said he didn't own dress clothes, that he hired them when he needed them.'

'I see.' Vaguely and ironically, Roger felt relieved to learn that Pell and not David had been Emily's first choice in her dilemma. He took another drink, and though his glass was nowhere nearly empty, Emily poured a little more whisky and put another lump of ice in it. 'You didn't think of Brian, I suppose?' he asked, biting into his sandwich again.

'*Brian!* That uncouth, clowning Mick! I certainly didn't. You haven't forgotten, have you? That ham actor entrance, that awful red tie, those terrible stories——'

'No—no. Of course you couldn't risk having anything like that happen a second time. I'm afraid we're not going to make much headway with the plan we had—you know, about having

90

our home a centre of good feeling, a place where better understanding could be promoted.'

'Well, we will yet. You'll see. It's just because you're so tired, Roger, that you think we can't—eventually. But, in the meantime——'

'In the meantime you couldn't ask Pell to fill in because he doesn't own dress clothes and you wouldn't ask Brian in because he wouldn't bother to wear them unless he felt like it. And you faced a major crisis because your trustee was short one man for a dinner party on account of your husband's unavoidable absence.'

For the first time since their marriage, he was speaking to her sarcastically and bitterly. But if his tone surprised or hurt her, she gave no indication of it. Instead, she went on speaking in the same soothing way as before.

'In the meantime I thought perhaps David was my best bet. And he got here in no time at all. I don't see how he managed, dressing and everything. He lives on Aspinwall Avenue, way out by Coolidge Corner. But he said he was used to doing things on the double.'

'There's no doubt about that.'

Again he spoke sarcastically and again she disregarded his sarcasm. 'You should have seen Uncle Homer's face when I walked into the club with David,' she said, almost gleefully. 'I hadn't called him back myself—Ellie did that for me—and he understood her to say I was bringing a Mr. Sulloway. Of course he thought it was one of the New Hampshire Sulloways and he was terribly pleased. He took me aside as soon as he could and asked me if I'd gone crazy. He said, "You can't take that fellow with you to the Waltz Evening, Emily. You'd never be asked again if you did." I told him I wouldn't dream of going to the Waltz Evening without you, that I was coming back here to wait for you, as soon as the dinner was over, but that I'd taken him up on his dare.'

'So you knew it was a dare, when he told you to find an extra man?'

'Of course. And did I turn the tables on him? David was the great success of the evening. He was so entertaining that everyone wanted to listen to him and so attractive that no one could help looking at him. Before we came away, several people had asked him to drop in for cocktails and the Amorys had invited

91

him to Sunday dinner. I could see that Uncle Homer was fairly foaming at the mouth with rage.'

'Well, evidently we can drop our philanthropic plans as far as David's concerned. He'll be pretty well launched after tonight.'

'Why, I hadn't thought of it that way! But I guess he will be.'

'You can be damn sure David's thought of it that way. I only hope he's properly grateful to you.'

Roger set down his glass and laid his half-eaten sandwich beside it. 'I seem to be pretty well bushed,' he said. 'Let's go upstairs, shall we?'

The spaciousness of the Joy Street house permitted the use of a hall bedroom as a dressing-room for Roger, and this dressing-room included in its equipment an Empire day bed. As a matter of fact, Roger had never slept there, even when he was ill, and he and Emily had often joked about the alleged advantages of separate apartments for married couples, while lying cosily side by side. Now, for some reason that he could not define, he felt that he wanted to be alone, that solitude would mean even more to him, in his exhausted state, than the nearness of his beloved. But he felt sure this would wound Emily deeply and that was the last thing on earth he wanted to do, especially when she had been so understanding and so kind. He went to the threshold and paused there, hoping that the right words would come.

Emily was already in bed, but she had not turned on her side, with one arm under her head, as she generally did when she was beginning to grow drowsy. She was sitting up, with two pillows behind her, her soft hair hanging in two long braids over her breasts. Above the lace of her nightgown, her skin was luminous. He had never seen her when she looked more lovely; yet at the moment he did not desire her. He wanted only to say good night and leave her. But when she saw him, she smiled; and her smile, like her eyes, was welcoming. She held out her arms.

'Dearest,' she said. 'Dearest——'

He could not deal another blow to her pride, he could not let her know that he did not want her. The conviction of this was so strong that it impelled him to assume an urgency he did not feel. Her instant acquiescence, her passionate response, betrayed the degree of her own yearning and her own need. . . .

Long after she had at last gone to sleep, Roger lay wakeful and wretched beside her, dwelling on this new revelation. He had grown up in the belief that in his marital relations a gentleman was always 'considerate' and he had scrupulously lived up to his code. Now, for the first time, he realized that Emily had wanted ardour rather than tenderness, that she had expected domination rather than reverence. Since this was so, he had failed her in another way from the beginning. . . .

PART THREE

FEBRUARY 1939 TO JANUARY 1940

ROGER AND BRIAN

CHAPTER VI

Cora Donlan, the harried receptionist of Cutter, Mills and Swan, who sat at the switchboard near the elevators, a typewriter stand beside her, had looked up with a start as soon as the formidable visitor began to speak. As she found no suitable opening for interruption, however, she waited for the tirade to end before attempting to say anything in self-defence and then going on to the usual routine question, 'May I help you?'

'You may show me the way to Mr. Field's office, if you can leave the switchboard and the elevators and the typewriter that long.'

'I think Mr. Field and Mr. Salomont are in conference. But I'll be glad to find out,' Cora said. She still spoke patiently and politely and, at the same time, she reached to plug in a jack and ring Roger's cubby-hole. 'Who shall I say is calling, please?'

'You needn't say. I can see Mr. Field's name on the door over there at the right. If I'd only noticed it in the first place, I wouldn't have had to waste all this time.'

Under the circumstances the best Cora could do was to let Mr. Field know someone was on the way. Roger was indeed deep in discussion with David at the moment, though their argument could hardly be characterized as a conference.

'I'm not sure I want to take your advice, Dave,' he was saying. 'This isn't a movie. These are real people and they're in a jam. They need a lawyer and besides, I ... Why, hello, Mrs. Forbes! I'm awfully glad to see you! Won't you sit down? You remember David Salomont, don't you? Excuse me a second, while I catch that call.'

'Never mind the call. It's just to tell you I'm here, which you've already found out for yourself. And of course I remember David Salomont. How's your stepfather, David? Tell him we still have good borsch on Louisburg Square.... What are you and Roger quarrelling about?'

'Oh, that wasn't a quarrel! Roger was just telling me where to get off. Quite right too. I keep forgetting he's a big boy now. Could I take your coat? And thanks for the invitation. I'll call up Dad and see if some night next week would be convenient. Right now I have to get on my horse. Good-bye, Mrs. Forbes. So long, Rog.'

Mrs. Forbes, adjusting the sable wrap which, a quarter of a century earlier, had represented the ultimate in elegance and which she had never seen fit to have remodelled, settled her imposing person in the least uncomfortable chair available and permitted her penetrating gaze to rest upon David as he took his easy departure. Then she turned to Roger, who was still standing, his expression rather tense, beside his desk.

'Is there more to this than meets the eye, Roger?'

'I'm not sure I know just what you mean, Mrs. Forbes.'

'Well, I've had the growing impression for some time now that you and David Salomont weren't hitting it off as well as you did at first. You're not jealous of him by any chance, are you?'

'There's no reason why I should be, is there?'

'Just that he's making a name for himself pretty fast as a lawyer and attracting a good deal of general attention besides. More than you are. Not that I feel there's any reason why you should be jealous of him on that account, as you say. Especially as you've got so much that he'd give his eyeteeth for and won't ever get. There's a balance about these things. But sometimes young fools don't have enough sense to realize that. Incidentally, David made a good move, leaving those weird relations of his who live way out on Aspinwall Avenue and setting himself up in a bachelor apartment on Lime Street. Very attractive he's making it too, so I hear. But of course you've seen it for yourself.'

'No, I haven't been to his apartment. He's asked Emily and me there twice—I believe he's giving a series of small suppers— but we had something on both times. And right now, you know Emily's awfully busy with rehearsals for the Vincent Club Show. She's in the Drill again and she's doing a lot of work on the lyrics besides.'

'Yes, I know. Well, I didn't come here to talk about the Vincent Club or about David Salomont and his various successes. I've got other matters on my mind.'

'I'd feel very much complimented to have you tell me about

them, if you would.'

'Of course I would. I've just said that's what I came here for. Your father-in-law, Roger, is behaving very badly. I want you to take measures to stop him.'

Roger, who had always secretly felt that Sumner Thayer was more sinned against than sinning, and who could not imagine what new dereliction was now being laid at his door, wisely waited for Old Mrs. Forbes to go on.

'When the Gloucester Street house was closed for the summer, after your wedding, this was done exactly as it had been for twenty-five years. I mean the silver was put in the bank and the rugs were sent to storage and the furniture was slip-covered —that sort of thing. And since I didn't care about using the Dublin house this last summer, I was glad enough to have Sumner and Eleanor go there. I said they were welcome to stay as long as they liked. Naturally, I didn't suppose they'd like it there in the winter-time. Of course, Eleanor hasn't been in Dublin much since October. She's been here, there and everywhere with those vapid Southern friends of hers, as you and Emily must know. And whenever she's come to Boston, she's stayed at the Chilton Club—well, you must know that too. It didn't strike me as strange at first, because of her perpetual servant troubles. You know how your mother-in-law harps on servant troubles, Roger.'

Roger murmured a vague agreement.

'Well, as I was saying, it didn't seem to me strange that Eleanor should stay at the Chilton Club when she came to Boston without Sumner, or even that she *did* come without Sumner—until she kept on doing it,' Old Mrs. Forbes continued. 'But she's done it too often. And she's acted more like a fool than usual when she has been here. I'm not going into that—at least not now. But yesterday she told me they'd meant for years to get rid of the Gloucester Street house as soon as Emily was married, and that if they'd only had a good offer for it, they'd have sold it. Well, they haven't had an offer for a sale. But they have had a chance to lease it for five years to some dentists who do extractions and all that sort of thing! And Sumner and Eleanor would take the rental money from the house my husband gave his daughter as a wedding present and live abroad on it! Sumner says he's willing to live with Eleanor if she'll go abroad. He says he'll never live with her in Boston again after the way she's acted—well, as I told you before, that's neither

98

here nor there for the moment. And where do you think they're talking about going? To the shabby, stupid little place on the Riviera, where Letty, Russell's ex-wife, lives with that crazy fiddler! Sumner and Eleanor have actually been in correspondence with Letty and she says she's found them just the place—a villa on a hillside where the terrace is simply overhung with geraniums. *Geraniums!*'

Old Mrs. Forbes paused for breath, and this time Roger knew he must say something as promptly as possible, and still not so quickly that he erred in discernment through haste. Obviously, it was his mother-in-law, rather than his father-in-law, who had really been 'behaving badly' and, until he knew just how badly and in what way, there was not much he could say along those lines. He had probably better concentrate on the subject of real estate, now that the horrible little Gloucester Street house had suddenly become both a symbol of family unity and of family dissension.

'I don't wonder you're upset about all this,' he said earnestly. 'And I can't tell you how pleased and touched I am that you've come to me about it.'

'Well, after all, you're in the family now,' Old Mrs. Forbes replied. 'I don't believe in washing dirty linen in public, if it can be helped. The point is, can it? I mean, are you capable of handling a case of this sort?'

'I'll have to know a little more about it before I can be sure,' Roger said cautiously. 'But so would any lawyer. And I'm afraid there isn't anything that could prevent Mr. and Mrs. Thayer from selling their house, if they wanted to, because it's theirs. But I'm not so sure they can lease it—that is, for use as a dental parlour or any other business purpose. The zoning ordinances may prevent it. In that case, I think quite possibly they could be enjoined from doing what would be so distasteful to you.'

'You do? How long would it take you to find out?'

'Not long. I could let you know by tomorrow at the latest—that is, if something else wasn't suddenly sprung on me that I had to do for the firm.'

The telephone rang and Roger picked up the receiver. 'Hello—why, hello, dear! How's the rehearsal going? Oh, that's too bad! ... Well, of course, if you think you ought to. Yes—yes. Good-bye.' He hung up and turned towards Old Mrs. Forbes. 'Emily says everything's at sixes and sevens with the show.'

'It always is, at this stage,' Old Mrs. Forbes replied, with something like a snort.

'Well, Emily seems to be worried about it. She thinks she ought to go home with Marion, after the rehearsal, and work on the lyrics. She'll have dinner with the Swans.'

'What do you do with yourself, the nights she stays out to dinner?'

'It isn't *nights*, Mrs. Forbes. This is almost the first time.'

'It won't be the last,' Old Mrs. Forbes said conclusively. Then she added, more hastily than was her wont, 'What I mean is, she'll be putting a lot of work into these rehearsals and those lyrics during the next few weeks and I'm glad of it. But you ought to have some independent interests too. Have you ever thought of joining the First Corps Cadets?'

'No—but it might not be such a bad idea.'

He turned towards the viewless window. Old Mrs. Forbes allowed a moment to elapse without further comment. Then she picked up the thread of her previous remarks.

'I intended to have a word with the head of the firm, about interrupting your work for me, before I left here, in any event,' she said conclusively. 'That is, if you felt you could handle the case. And I see that you can. But there was also something else on my mind. I have not finished talking to you about Sumner. He is not satisfied with saying that he will never come back to Boston and live here like a gentleman. He has been making trouble for me with the tax authorities.'

'The tax authorities?'

'Yes. That property of mine in Dublin isn't handled by the Federal Street Trust Company, like most of my belongings. It couldn't be, as I understand it, because it isn't located in Massachusetts, and now there is trouble about the so-called "profits" of my dairy farm, trouble stirred up by Sumner.' Old Mrs. Forbes opened her handsome bag and extracted from it a sheaf of papers which she laid on the corner of Roger's desk. Then she leant forward and shoved them a little nearer to him. Irrelevantly, he noticed that the great signet ring, which Morris Brucker had given her, was now the only one on her right hand, though her left was still laden with diamonds; and the observation revived the dormant curiosity which the gift had aroused when it was made. Conscientiously striving to dismiss this from his mind, he picked up the papers and scrutinized them.

'It doesn't surprise me that these have puzzled and disturbed you, Mrs. Forbes,' he said, speaking quite sincerely. She was by no means the first person of more than average intelligence whom he had seen thus baffled and consequently thus upset; and women particularly, however quick to grasp the *raison d'être* for many of the law's workings, usually seemed to have a blind spot when it came to tax matters, just as they usually saw no reason why they should not smuggle, however meticulous they might be in other matters of honesty. There was, nevertheless, one aspect of the present difficulty which he himself did not find quite clear.

'I think I understand the root of this trouble, Mrs. Forbes,' he said at length. 'And if I do, we ought not to have too much difficulty getting rid of it. But I still don't quite understand why the Federal Street Trust isn't looking after this for you.'

'Neither do I. That's just what I said to myself. But all Mr. Adams, who is obviously in his dotage, could suggest was that I refer the tax matters to Fiske, Ford and Gibbons. But those whited sepulchres declined to have anything to do with my problems, on the ground that they represented the Trust and that there might be a conflict of interests. They didn't say whose interests and it's quite evident they weren't thinking about mine! All they did was to ferret out a tax accountant who heaped more reproaches on me and, on top of everything else, in came that green form!'

Old Mrs. Forbes glared at the offending document lying on top of the other papers, and then pushed them still farther away from her with such force that they fell, scattering, to the floor. The great emerald in the signet ring glittered with the sweep of her hand. Roger, resolutely glancing away from it, retrieved the papers and put them on the other side of the desk, beyond his caller's reach.

'I'm very sorry you've had so many things to bother you,' he said calmly, 'especially as it seems to me that most of them were unnecessary.'

'Unnecessary! Do you mean to tell me these miscreants have been persecuting me merely for the fun of it?'

'No, I don't mean that. But I do mean there's no reason why one person . . .'

Again the telephone rang and Roger picked up the receiver.

'Hello,' he said. 'Yes, Mr. Mills. Yes, sir, of course you may count on me.' He had managed to speak evenly, betraying neither annoyance nor agitation at the inopportune interrup-

101

tion. But, as he turned from the telephone to face his caller once more, his words came with a rush. 'What I was trying to say, Mrs. Forbes, was just this: I'd like very much to have a try at handling your affairs for you myself, if you'd let me. I know you must feel I haven't had much experience. But I'd do the very best I could for you. Not just because you're Emily's grandmother either; but because you're about the grandest person I've ever known and I'd be proud to be of service to you.'

He stopped abruptly and, for a moment, they both sat very still, looking at each other. But, as they did so, Old Mrs. Forbes found nothing in Roger's earnest and direct gaze which would cause her to doubt that every word he spoke was true and he found nothing in her appraising glance except astonished respect. She rose, gathering her sable wrap around her.

'No, don't come with me,' she said emphatically, as he hastened to rise also. 'I prefer to go alone. As I told you, I want to have a few words with Roscoe Cutter before I leave this building and I am not interested in having a third person present at the interview. . . .'

The door had hardly closed behind Old Mrs. Forbes when Roger snatched up the documents she had left on his desk and plunged excitedly into his tax project. He was soon so completely immersed in it that he did not realize the afternoon had slipped away, until the door of his office slowly opened and Brian, having first peered around with an air of great caution, entered on tiptoe, his battered felt hat in his hand. Laying this and his brief case down on the chair earlier occupied by his associate's new client, he salaamed deeply several times.

Roger laughed, throwing down the pencil with which he had been figuring and pushing aside a sheaf of loose-leaf account sheets.

'Cut it out, Briny. What's got into you?'

'As if you didn't know! And realize that everyone else in these here parts must know by now. Why, the grapevine's been so busy it's had to put out new tendrils!'

Roger laughed again. 'Sit down and let's talk about it. This is a pretty big thing, Briny. I'm going to need lots of help and I'm counting on you for some of it. Of course, I've already got in touch with a couple of accountants and called the tax office for copies of all requisite forms, but I think I ought to set up a separate account next. Don't you think I should discuss this at a bank?'

'Of course. And I'd go straight to Ellery Stockbridge. You know he's president of the Third National now and I don't need to tell you he's one of our best clients. But you can't call him tonight, the bank's been closed for hours.'

'Good grief! I had no idea it was that late!'

'Time to call it a day and then some. You and I are closing up the joint this evening. There's something I've wanted to get off my chest for a long while, so I thought——'

'Shoot!'

'Well, I guess there isn't any graceful way for a man to admit he's made a damn fool of himself. But that's what I know I did and I'm sorry as hell. Honest to God though, I didn't set out to mess up your wife's dinner party. When you asked me to your house, I really did think it was for an evening with the boys, like what we'll be having at home tonight. If I hadn't, I wouldn't have come dressed like a bookmaker and I wouldn't have stopped for a couple of quick ones with Tim. I wouldn't have——'

'Say, let's skip it!' Roger found Brian's obvious sincerity moving and his embarrassment contagious.

'Well, I guess you realize I wouldn't go in for clowning on general principles. But what about your wife?'

'Why, Emily——' Roger began. But his tone failed to carry conviction. 'Why don't we just forget the whole thing?'

'You mean you don't want to ask her——'

'It's not exactly that. But I couldn't tonight, anyway. She won't be home until late and then she'll be dead tired. She's been rehearsing all afternoon for the Vincent Show, and she telephoned a while back to say that something didn't quite come off in one of the lyrics. I'll be dining in solitary state when I get home—if I ever do get home with all the work I've still got ahead of me here.'

Roger motioned, half proudly and half desperately, towards the pile of papers which littered his desk. Brian shook his head.

'You can't straighten all that out at a sitting, no matter how hard you try.'

'Well, I've got to keep on trying anyway. And not just to straighten out this tax deal. There's another job Mrs. Forbes wants handled too, and I haven't even made a start on that, because I got side-tracked. Look here—you don't happen to know anything about the zoning set-up in the area around Gloucester Street, do you?'

'Well, I know this much: I know my uncle, Barney Garvin, is secretary to the Zoning Board of Appeal. And I know he can fix things so that any ten blocks beyond the golden streets of heaven would be off limits to the saints. Would that help any?'

'Would it help? How soon . . . I mean, would it be convenient for you to introduce me to your uncle some time, so that I can ask him which side is up?'

'Some time? He's coming to our house tonight. He always sits in on our little poker parties. Why don't you come along and meet him right now, instead of "dining in solitary state"? It's a foul night, but you won't get any wetter going to South Boston than you would going to Joy Street. The whole family'd be tickled to death to have you take pot-luck with us and all your zoning troubles would be fixed, but good, before the first bluff of the game had been called. What do you say?'

The City Point car crossed a bridge which seemed to surmount railroad tracks and then plunged up and down a succession of small hills, its progress mildly suggestive of a ride on a roller-coaster. This plunging motion rendered any scrutiny of the route doubly difficult, and this was already obscured by the early dusk and the big snowflakes. However, as nearly as Roger could make out, they were passing through a business district where small shops and large signs predominated. Eventually, Brian signalled to the conductor and nodded to his guest.

'Car turns off Broadway here,' he said. 'We have to walk a little over a block. I'm sorry it's such a foul night. But you don't mind, do you? It'll be nice and warm after we get there.'

'Of course I don't mind. I'm interested in seeing this section of the city.'

' "Parts unknown", eh?'

'Well, I didn't mean that exactly,' Roger replied in some embarrassment.

'I know you didn't—at least, not offensively. And maybe you'll have a happy surprise, at that.'

The guess was correct. Roger knew that Brian's people were well to do; but he had assumed that some strange attachment must have caused them to cling to the quarters their immediate forbears had occupied as immigrants, for he had never thought of South Boston except in terms of drabness interspersed with squalor. Therefore, he was amazed to see that the houses on the hill they were now mounting were not only sizeable and substantial, but that hardly any of them gave any evidence of a rundown condition or of multiple occupancy. Brian closed his dripping umbrella and ran rapidly up the steps of the largest and handsomest house in sight, proclaiming his presence in a ringing voice at the same moment that his key turned in the latch.

'Hello, everybody! Where are you all keeping yourselves? Come see who I've brought home to supper!'

A radio in some room beyond was blaring a tune so loudly that Roger wondered how Brian could possibly make himself heard above it, especially as the noise it made was only part of a general tumult. Nevertheless, there was an instantaneous response to his greeting.

'Easy now. You don't want to scare our visitor off with all your ructions. He's not used to the like of this. Roger, this small hellion here is Queenie. And right behind her Della and Doreen —my other sisters aren't home. Bearing up to the rear of them is my collegiate brother Ray and my clerical brother Mat, and still farther off, Himself and Herself. And yes—I thought so, Uncle Barney Garvin. Folks, this is my friend, Roger Field.'

The drink, with which Father Mat promptly presented him, was so good that Roger was persuaded, without much trouble, to have a second one. The assembled family was now in the sitting-room, forming an uneven circle; and though the radio was still going, Brian had turned it down to something resembling normal volume, so that casual conversation could proceed in a more or less natural tone, though nobody seemed to feel any compulsion to create small talk. The large square room lent itself readily to companionship; and Roger was so pleasantly aware of the overstuffed sofa's comfort that he hardly noticed the upholstery of pressed plush, the Axminster rug, the chromo of the Sacred Heart, flanked by family portraits, or even the rather gory crucifix hanging above the mantelpiece. Both Brian's father and his Uncle Barney gave such an immediate impression of goodwill and geniality that he found it difficult to associate either one with crooked politics and generally shady practices, in spite of all the tales he had heard to the contrary, and Father Mat's conviviality came as a great and welcome surprise. But it was Mrs. Collins who affected him most profoundly. She sat calmly in a large armchair, her face benign above an ample figure and a nondescript dress, her expression suffused with such genuine loving-kindness that he could not take his eyes off her.

Eventually Mrs. Collins rose, saying she must see to the steak, and signalling Della and Doreen to go with her. Brian, making a sign to his uncle, withdrew to the farther side of the room and engaged him in earnest, but low-voiced conversation, of which Roger thought he could guess the purport. Ray, spreading open a well-thumbed textbook, asked Father Mat if he would mind going on where they had left off; and soon thereafter Roger caught, intermittently, the cadences of vaguely remembered passages from Virgil. Mr. Collins, lifting Queenie on to his lap, shifted his chair a little nearer their guest.

'As Briny told you, two of our daughters aren't here tonight,' he said genially, stroking Queenie's curls as he spoke. 'I'm sorry they wouldn't get to meet you—but then, you'll be coming again, now you've found the way here, and we're lucky enough to have Mat right at the Gate of Heaven Church and Sheila a teacher at St. Brigid's School. Then Terence, that's Katie's husband, will be coming along soon—he won't fail us for poker, even if he does miss out on the steak. A grand boy he is, one of the best. I don't know what I'd do without him in my business. Of course, any father's proud to have a son of his go into the Church or into the law. But when a man's two eldest both leave him in the lurch that way, in a manner of speaking, and his third isn't through with book learning by the time his father needs him ... Why, then it's a great thing to have a son-in-law stepping right into the breach!'

Roger agreed that it must be, and Mr. Collins, having insisted that their drinks needed a little freshening, said that he would like to tell Briny's friend a few things about the contracting business later on in the evening, but that, meanwhile, it was Queenie's turn to talk. Queenie was in the first grade already, would Mr. Field ever believe it now? And she spoke pieces. Maybe she would speak one for him. At this point, Queenie put her finger in her mouth again and, nestling up against her father, retreated behind her curls. While he was still trying to tempt her, with appropriate bribes, to demonstrate her talents as an elocutionist, Della appeared in the doorway and announced that Doreen was just bringing in the steak.

There was an immediate surge to the dining-room, which led out of the room where they had been sitting, and Father Mat asked a quick, cheery blessing, as everyone gathered around the long table which was covered with a white cloth. Mrs. Collins

106

was already ensconced at one end of this table, with two well-heaped, smoking hot vegetable dishes before her. Mr. Collins took his place at the opposite end, and began to carve the steaks, which were spread imposingly over a huge platter. They were nearly three inches thick, broiled to a turn and garnished with crisp onion rings. When he had placed a generous portion on one of the plates piled in front of him, this was passed down the table to Mrs. Collins, who flanked it with mounds of mashed potatoes and string beans and then sent it along again, repeating this process until everyone had been served. Meanwhile, milk, butter, jelly, pickles and hot rolls had been circulated from the sidelines. For a few moments, the requirements of healthy appetites effectually put a stop to the flow of talk and remarks were limited to requests for another roll, more butter and a second helping of beans. But, by the time the vegetable dishes had been refilled and more steak brought in, hunger was sufficiently appeased so that conversation gradually became animated again.

'I ate up my meat and potato a long time ago. I want my dessert,' Queenie managed to break in at last.

'Of course you do, darling. We all do. Mr. Field's been telling us a nice story and we didn't want to interrupt. But Della and Doreen are going to change the plates right now. And guess what's coming next!'

'Ice cream?' inquired Queenie hopefully.

'No. Guess again.'

'Chocolate chiffon pie?'

'Right you are. And Mother's going to cut you a great big piece!'

The two teen-agers cleared the table quietly and quickly. Then the telephone rang again and Doreen hastened to answer it, returning presently with the announcement that it was for Uncle Barney. His absence was prolonged and, during the course of it, Queenie abandoned the last few crumbs of her pie and began to rub her eyes. Then, after some urging, she bestowed moist smacks, supplemented, in several cases, with big hugs, on everyone in the assembled group, though she hesitated for a moment when she came to Roger. Then she wriggled herself into place on Mat's and Briny's clasped hands and put her arms around their necks. They straightened up and marched out of the room, singing: 'Come, little queen, in your flying machine.' At the top of the stairs, Father Mat interrupted the song to call down to Mrs. Collins.

'I'll hear her prayers, Mother. Don't bother to come up.'

'Two years already, she's undressed herself,' Mrs. Collins told Roger proudly. 'But sometimes she skimps a bit on her Hail Marys. You know how it is with a child. Mat'll take care of that all right, though. And I'll have a look at her later on, when the girls and I have done the dishes and you men are having your poker game. . . . Well, Terence! Briny was just saying you'd be along any minute now. Meet his friend, Roger Field, that we're lucky enough to have with us tonight. Would you have a bite of pie and a sip of coffee while you're telling us about Katie and the baby?'

Terence Lenahan acknowledged the introduction in the same hearty way that the others had done and, falling in with his mother-in-law's suggestion, took the chair vacated by Queenie. 'We'll be getting him and Katie home day after tomorrow,' he said in conclusion. 'I was thinking of speaking to Mat about the baptism.'

'He'll be down in a minute, when he's finished hearing Queenie's prayers. . . . Well, Barney! It wasn't any bad news, I hope, that kept you so long at the telephone?'

'No, not what you'd call bad. But I've just heard that it looks now as if the legislature might go along with the Governor on those cuts he wants made in the budget. If it does, there won't be enough cash to go around. Not that I'm really worried. But could be Shaun and Terence won't get all they thought they had coming to them on the new highway contracts and I'd be sorry if——'

'Well, there'll be no bids submitted tonight and no contracts let, either,' Mrs. Collins observed with what was apparently never-failing cheerfulness. 'So why not put the whole matter from your minds and get started on your pocket? . . .'

Roger's expressions of appreciation for her hospitality were cut short by the obvious impatience of the other men to begin their game; in fact, Barney Garvin and Terence Lenahan, who were discussing with Father Mat the Cardinal's visit to Rome, had already strolled out of the dining-room with the priest before Roger left it, accompanied by Mr. Collins and Brian.

'From what Uncle Barney's been saying, I think maybe we made a mistake not to get in on this gold mine, Dad,' Terence said as they gathered round the table in the den. 'Especially if those rumours about a cut in the budget are true, as I'm afraid they may be. Once Saltonstall gets started on this damned econ-

108

omy programme——'

'Even if he does, the less we have to do with gold mines, away off in Nevada or some such place, the better,' Mr. Collins announced decidedly. 'All too often they turn out to be gold *bricks* instead. And I understand they're calling this one Curley's Luck —which hasn't been any too good lately, more's the pity! Besides, you heard what Herself said, bless her heart—there'll be no bids submitted and no contracts let tonight. So we might as well forget about economy and Republicans and all such blights and get on with our game.... You don't know our ways yet, Mr. Field, so you may not have noticed that here's bourbon and Scotch and, praise the saints! a bottle of Bushmill's on the sideboard over there. You'll be helping yourself as the spirit moves you, I hope, the same as the rest of us will.'

As a matter of fact, Roger had already observed the prodigal display of whisky, which was supplemented by a thermos bucket, presumably ice filled, a pitcher of ice water, bottles of soda and ginger ale and tall glasses. As he took the place now indicated as his, Barney Garvin stripped the jokers from a new deck and riffled the cards skilfully, while Brian measured out six stacks of chips.

'Ten dollars each okey with everybody?' he asked. 'Ten-cent ante and fifty-cent limit—table stakes—dealer's choice—everybody antes for draw, only the dealer for stud—and whoever gets caught bluffing loses the pot.'

Uncle Barney passed the cards to Shaun Collins for a cut and then began to deal them swiftly.

An hour later Barney Garvin was heard to grumble, 'I ought to know what's going to happen to me when I sit down to the cards with one of these I-don't-hardly-even-know-the-game fellers. You'd think I'd be gun-shy by this time. But no, Uncle Sucker always comes back, asking the boys please to skin him pretty. That's me all over.'

'Yeah, too bad about you,' gibed Brian. 'They tell me that down at the Athletic Club you sent all the boys home for fresh money last week.'

' 'Tis a slander, indeed,' retorted Uncle Barney. 'I may have won a few dimes. No more. And I am like to lose them three and four times over to this innocent from Joy Street who has come down here to spoil the Egyptians.'

'Incidentally, that's not all he came down for, as I hinted to you before supper,' Brian remarked. 'He's got a zoning problem you might give him some advice on.'

'Advice is cheap enough,' observed Shaun Collins.

'Tell him about it, Rog,' urged Brian. 'Meantime, we'll all stop and have a drink, just to keep you from fleecing us while our attention's distracted.'

'Why, it's like this,' Roger began a bit diffidently. 'My wife's grandmother, Mrs. Forbes, came in this afternoon to ask for my advice. I'd like very much to be helpful to her, if I could. Briny thought you would know whether I could do anything for her. It seems that her daughter, Eleanor—my mother-in-law—and her husband want to lease the house where they've lived ever since their marriage to a firm of dentists and Mrs. Forbes finds this a very distasteful prospect.'

'What's wrong with dental parlours?' asked Father Mat bluntly.

'Why, nothing, really,' conceded Roger. 'But Mrs. Forbes is an old lady of very decided views and she can't bear the thought of having a family possession, such as a house that her late husband gave his daughter for a wedding present, become a commercial establishment of any kind, maybe with a big, tooth-shaped signboard swinging in front of it and a glass case full of dentures beside the doorway.'

'Where is this house now?' asked Barney Garvin, pulling at his pipe and releasing the smoke in a trickling cloud.

'Number sixteen Gloucester Street—near Marlborough.'

Garvin nodded. 'I know the block well. It's a residential area and if you like, I can have the word passed down to the painless pullers that the Commissioner won't give them a permit. That'll knock a hole in the deal all right.'

'I can't think of any way to do the trick more neatly,' Roger agreed heartily. 'And I don't know how to thank you enough, Mr. Garvin. I didn't have any idea——' He had started to say 'I didn't have any idea it could all be handled so simply.' Opportunely, Brian interrupted.

'Now that's as good as settled, let's get on with our game,' he said. 'Here, let me freshen that drink of yours, Uncle Barney. Whose deal is it, anyway? Yours, Ould One? Well, deal it out then and let's see if we can win back some of this greenhorn's ill-gotten gains.'

It was nearly midnight when Roger went quickly up the steps of his house, whistling softly, but jubilantly. He could not help

110

thinking of the night when he had returned from Salem, so completely discouraged that he could not seem to take heart, even when Emily received him with loving-kindness and revealed her passionate yearning for him. He knew that from now on his status with Cutter, Mills and Swan would be vastly improved; the problem about the Gloucester Street house was as good as solved already; and on top of his big day at the office, he had spent an evening in a way so gladdening to him that the glow of its prevailing good-fellowship warmed him still. Last, but by no means least, he had in his pocket almost seventy dollars that had come from his winnings at poker—the first money which had ever come to him easily and pleasantly.

He was still whistling as he turned his key in the latch, but suddenly remembering that it was very late, he suppressed his impulse to call out to Emily. She might very well be asleep by now—in fact, she should be, after her long, hard rehearsal. To his amazement the portières of the library instantly parted and Emily, still in street clothes, came hastily towards him.

'Roger!' she exclaimed. 'Where on earth have you been? What happened? I've been worried to death!'

'Why, I'm terribly sorry, darling,' he said soothingly. 'Didn't Ellie tell you that——' he broke off. His departure from the office had been so precipitate, his invitation from Brian so unexpected, that he had entirely forgotten to telephone and say he would not dine at home.

'Ellie said she hadn't heard a word from you. Deirdre kept your dinner warm for hours and both she and Ellie sat up until I got home. Then I telephoned every place I could think of. And no one else had heard a word from you either. Caroline's been worried to death too.'

'I'm terribly sorry, darling,' he said again. He put his arms around her and kissed her in the usual fond way that marked his homecoming; but though she returned his embrace, something was lacking in it, and he suddenly realized that there was an element of annoyance in her anxiety. As far as he knew, Emily had never been annoyed with him before—at all events, he had never been aware of such a feeling on her part. Distressed that she should have it now, and with reason, he tried, quickly, to explain.

'I had a pretty full day at the office. Your grandmother came in and offered me a wonderful piece of work. I was awfully pleased—pleased and proud and—well, rather touched that she

111

should show so much confidence in me. So, after she left, I plunged right into this new job and I didn't realize how late it was until Brian came in and reminded me. Then, on the spur of the moment, he asked me to go home to supper with him. In the general excitement, I just plain forgot to telephone I wouldn't be home to dinner.... I'm terribly sorry, darling,' he said for the third time. 'I wouldn't have worried you, purposely, for the world, you know that. And I'll try to make my peace with Ellie and Deirdre in the morning. It shouldn't be too hard.'

They had continued to stand, with their arms around each other, in the hall, and now Roger tried to draw Emily closer to him and to kiss her again. To his bewilderment, she stiffened slightly.

'Of course I'm very glad that Grandmamma's given you some important work to do,' she said. 'But I still don't understand why you should have been so excited over an invitation from Brian Collins that you'd forget everything else. I shouldn't think you'd have even wanted to go home to supper with him, after the way he acted here.'

'It wasn't just an invitation. Perhaps I can explain better if I don't have to do it standing here in the hall. I've been hoping for the last five minutes that you'd invite me into the library—at least.'

His tone was now light and loving. But Emily did not respond to this either.

'I think I'd better call up Caroline. Or that you had.'

'I will. Where shall I look for you afterwards? Upstairs, downstairs or in my lady's chamber? I confess to a preference for the latter.'

'All right, I'll meet you there.'

Caroline kept Roger on the telephone for some time, in spite of his efforts to cut her short; she too was feeling injured. When he reached the big bedroom, Emily had taken off her tweed suit and put on a pink cashmere dressing-gown. She had lighted the fire and was stretched out on the chaise-longue near it. There was, of course no room for Roger beside her, but there was an easy chair on the opposite side of the hearth and a well-laden tray stood on a near-by end table. Emily was smoking and had already made herself a nightcap.

'I didn't fix a drink for you, because I didn't know whether you'd want one. But everything's right there.'

'Well, I'll fix myself a light one for the sake of sociability....'

He mixed his drink and sat down, wishing that she would ask him some more questions, so that he would know where to begin. Instead, she went on quietly smoking her cigarette and sipping her drink. He decided that the only thing to do was to plunge into his subject.

'You said you didn't see why I wanted to go home with Brian Collins, after the way he acted here. Pehaps I ought to begin by telling you he's very apologetic about what happened the night of our dinner. That was what he'd been wanting to say to me for so long. He'd stayed overtime on purpose, because he never seemed to get a chance before.'

'I should think he could have managed, if he'd wanted to very much. I should think he'd have apologized to us both.'

'Well, as he said himself, there's no easy way and no graceful way either for a man to admit he's made a damn fool of himself. But he knows that's what he did and he's sorry as hell. When we asked him here, he really thought it was for an evening of poker with the boys, like what they were having at his house tonight. Afterwards, he said he knew you must think he was about as crude as they come, and he's sorry about that too, because he likes you and he wishes you liked him. He ended up by saying he hoped I'd tell you tonight that if there were any way he could show you ... I was afraid I wouldn't have a chance to tell you tonight. I thought you'd be so tired when you got home you wouldn't feel like talking. I'm glad you weren't—glad the rehearsal didn't whip you down, and glad I've had a chance to tell you right away what Briny said.'

'I am tired. But I'm not sleepy now that I'm not worried any more ... Is that why you're so late, because you've been "having an evening of poker with the boys"?'

'Yes. But first we had supper with the family. There were ten of us. Just the same number we had for our dinner. And there wasn't a servant in sight, or any sign of confusion or commotion either. It was a wonderful supper too—great, huge juicy steaks and lots of well-cooked vegetables and rolls and chocolate pie that really melted in your mouth.'

'It doesn't sound like a very imaginative menu.'

'It wasn't. It was just plain good. I don't believe the people who ate it are particularly imaginative either. They're just plain good too.'

'Including the contractors who've been tremendously successful in their line and the great political power?'

'Look here, Emily, you're not trying to pick a quarrel with me, are you? I know that contractors, especially Irish contractors, are all supposed to be crooks; but there must be some who are reasonably honest, just to keep up the law of averages. And Barney Garvin's making it possible for me to do something your grandmother was afraid couldn't be pulled off. It certainly isn't any worse, at least in my book, to grant a favour of that kind than to ask it.'

Setting down his drink Roger rose, stopped to poke the fire somewhat harder than its condition necessitated and then, straightening up, stepped closer to the chaise-longue. He looked down at Emily, who was staring at him incredulously, with an expression he had never seen before.

'Anyway, when I said they were just plain good, I wasn't thinking so much of the successful contractors and the great political power. I was thinking mostly about Mrs. Collins, who's had eight children and kept them all close to her, not just physically, but mentally and spiritually too. That's something no woman we know has done or could do. If either you or I had had a mother like that, we might have amounted to more ourselves. All her grown children are doing something that counts in the world, and the others will too, as soon as they're old enough. What have I done, compared to Father Mat and Brian? And what have *you* done, compared to Sheila with her teaching and Katie with her babies? And still you look down on the Collins', you don't want them for friends, you don't even want me to have them for friends! Well, that's just too bad, because I'm going to be friends with them! I'm going to their house as often as I please and I'm going to have them here too, as often as I please!'

'I've done nursing and you know it! And it isn't my fault I'm not going to have a baby—you know that too! You'd better stop insulting my family—after all they've done for you! You can go and see your precious Collins' whenever you like—I don't care! But I won't go with you and I won't have them here in my house!'

Emily had leapt up and was facing him again, not in half-allayed anxiety and mild annoyance and complete bewilderment as she had downstairs, but in deep resentment and unreasoning mutiny. He seized her arms, gripping them hard, not with the compulsion of passionate love, but with its ugly counterpart of passionate anger. The primitive male instinct to overpower a

114

rebellious woman by sheer physical strength had been roused, without warning, from civilized dormancy. Then, suddenly appalled by the realization of the violence to which he had come so close and the injustice of which he was already guilty, Roger released his angry hold and gently encircled Emily's waist.

'Forgive me, darling,' he said tenderly. 'That is, if you can. Of course you've done things that count—I do know it. You're wonderful. I don't see how I could have said what I did. I don't see how I could have made such a comparison between you and Sheila, or between you and Katie either. I know it's a terrible disappointment to you that you haven't a prospect of a baby yet. But of course you will have a baby—just as many as Katie's had. And you'll be a marvellous mother. Your children will be willing to go through fire and water for you—just as I am, even if I don't show it. Please believe me. Please say you forgive me.'

He bent his head, but she had already buried hers on his shoulder and he could not reach her lips. Then he felt her body trembling against his and heard her sobbing. More and more appalled, he tried to comfort her with caresses and whispered endearments. When she finally raised her tear-stained face and answered him, it was with contrition equal to his own.

'I'm just as much to blame as you are,' she said, between sobs which were beginning to subside, but which still shook her intermittently. 'I've been hateful to you ever since you came in. But I was worried, terribly worried, for hours. And when I found I needn't have worried, after all, somehow I wasn't just relieved; I was piqued too. I don't see why. It was unreasonable. It was—it was *small*. I've been small about Brian too,' she went on. 'I knew all along he felt the way you say he does. But I wanted him to tell me so. I wanted him to humble himself and then I would have been gracious and condescending. And when I found out he'd told you instead, I was jealous. I was jealous because you'd had such a good time without me too. You have no idea how terrible it is to be jealous.'

'Yes, I have, dear. I've been jealous lots of times. I guess everyone is.' Fleetingly, he thought again of the night he had returned from Salem and found David alone with Emily. But he was not jealous of David now; he knew that Emily had never been so wholly his as she was at that moment.

'Really?' She looked up at him again and this time, when she did so, he kissed her mouth. 'Of course I want Brian to come

115

here,' she said, when he gave her a chance to speak again. 'You'll ask Brian here right away, won't you? Brian and all his family.'

Roger laughed, contentedly. 'Well, not all his family, at one fell swoop. I'm afraid that would be too much of a good thing. And I won't ask him right away. It would be a little too pointed if I did, wouldn't it? He'd know that we'd talked this all over. He might even suspect that we'd quarrelled.'

'But we've never quarrelled before! We're never going to again!'

'No, of course not. But Brian's pretty shrewd, you know. I think it would be better to wait a week or so then suggest that I might give a poker party here—something like the one he thought he was coming to the first time.'

'You mean—just men?'

'Yes, just men. After dinner. More or less on the spur of the moment. Some night when you have to work on lyrics again.'

'Then I wouldn't even be here?'

'No. Except that probably you'd get home during the course of the evening and look in on us to say hello. Then, the next time Brian came——'

'Yes. Yes, I can see how it would all work out. Simply and naturally and pleasantly. And I've been making mountains out of molehills all winter. I must be the dumbest girl you ever knew. And the meanest. I should think you'd hate me. I should think you'd want to beat me.'

'You know you're not dumb or mean either. You know I don't hate you. You know I'm crazy about you. But maybe I'd better stop telling you. Maybe I'd just better try to show you.'

CHAPTER VII

Afterwards, Emily said several times that it was almost worth while to quarrel, because, unless you quarrelled, you could not make up, and making up was undoubtedly among the most wonderful things that it was possible to do. Roger did not altogether agree with her. He was amazed and disturbed to find how hard it could be to forget words spoken in anger, either by himself or by his wife, and the memory of them continued to pain him. But since obviously Emily did not have the same sad experience, he wisely did not mention his own.

Besides, the next months were so pleasant and profitable, in almost every way, that he realized he should not tempt fate by asking too much of it. As he had foreseen, his status at the office took a turn for the better after Old Mrs. Forbes had been there to consult him professionally; but he would not have dared to hope for such an immediate improvement as the one which took place.

Old Mrs. Forbes was already in a mellow mood over the news Roger had brought her from Barney Garvin; and it mellowed still further when she learned that her tax difficulties should soon be a thing of the past and that her other financial affairs were already in order. Roger had filed a letter of protest concerning past taxes, in order to gain access to the capable conferees in the office of the Internal Revenue Agent, and had prepared the return currently due on a basis revised for her benefit. He had also opened the bank accounts and established the bookkeeping methods necessary to carry out his control of her funds; deposits were being made and expenses met in an orderly fashion, and, of course, Cutter, Mills and Swan charged a substantial sum for services rendered. On this occasion though their distinguished client paid their bill without a murmur, her cheque was enclosed in a note which stated that she assumed all charges were divided on a percentage basis and that her grand-

117

son would benefit by such a system. It was so obvious that this assumption was based on her wishes, and that therefore her continued favours would be based upon it also, that Mr. Cutter summoned Roger into his handsome corner office, and looked up from the fire which he was industriously poking long enough to state that the time had now obviously come for a second raise, and that Mr. Field might also expect a percentage from the payments received from Mrs. Forbes.

Roger's financial advancement and his progress in self-confidence and initiative at the office were paralleled by an increasing number of outside activities which varied his interests and widened his outlook. Monday poker with Brian and Brian's relatives became a regular though not an inflexible part of his schedule: it was understood that if Emily wished to make other plans for that evening in which, almost automatically, he should be included, he would be available; otherwise he went straight from the office to the Collins' house or Brian came to his. The first postprandial game on Joy Street proved generally enjoyable; and Emily's brief, incidental appearance was obviously regarded as a compliment and not an intrusion from the viewpoint of the guests, while from hers it was an agreeable if novel episode. Thankfully, Roger realized that the strain between her and Brian had slackened of itself and that neither pressure nor artifice was necessary to bring about better mutual understanding. The next time that it was 'his turn to shout', he asked Brian to come home to dinner with him, in the same casual way that Brian asked him to the big house in South Boston. Brian accepted with a spontaneity which suggested genuine pleasure at the invitation; and after that, his presence at the Fields' table on poker nights was taken for granted, both by them and by him. The other men continued to come in later, but the slight remaining diffidence on their part was also on the wane; Roger knew that it would not be long before this was overcome. Meanwhile, Brian had achieved the status of family friend.

Roger had never been privileged to enjoy such a friendship before and, next to the fulfilment of his love for Emily, he found it the most enriching experience of his life. His father, in a fond but ineffectual way, had tried to make his schoolmates welcome in his boyhood home; but this, lacking the presence of a wife and mother, had lacked so many other vital elements as well that most of the youngsters Roger knew preferred to seek diversion elsewhere. After Mr. Field's death, Caroline had discouraged company, at first with the pretext that it was 'unsuitable' for her and Roger to 'entertain' while they were in mourning, and later on the grounds of 'expense' and 'extra work'. Roger had lived at home all through college and law school because it admittedly cost less that way—in cash; Caroline never knew how much it had cost him in kind.

Now, at last, there was no question of unsuitability, of extra work or expense; he could entertain as much as he chose. Though Emily had been sincere in deploring her own lack of capability, she actually had great potential gifts, both as a housekeeper and as a hostess. Not the least part of her largess to her husband had been the creation of a home which—as she herself had said from the beginning—was designed and intended for the pleasure and profit of their friends as well as themselves. She had long spoken, without constraint, of that first dinner party and, as time went on, she did so less and less seriously, characterizing it as 'silly' instead of 'disastrous'. But she had never referred again to the first Waltz Evening, except to tell Roger how pleased and proud she was when Fleency belatedly accepted her husband's suggested compromise. In spite of her silence, however—possibly because of it—she had given a great deal of troubled thought to the incident which had put an abrupt end to her spontaneous reception of David as a habitué of the house.

As she had freely told Roger on his return from Salem, David had dominated the group at the Somerset Club, charming all Homer Lathrop's other guests, besides saving the situation for her. In asking David to go home with her afterwards, she had primarily desired to pick up the gauntlet which her trustee had thrown down; but while also sincerely feeling that she could not have a pleasanter companion to while away the time until Roger's return, she had not thought of David as a stimulating, much less as a disturbing, presence.

This had still not occurred to her when she returned to the library from the pantry, after assuring herself that everything was in readiness for Roger's substantial refreshment when he came home, late and tired, and that the makings of a drink were available for David whenever he chose to have one. Meanwhile, David had turned on the radio to an inviting musical programme. He bowed to her with mock solemnity as she re-entered the room and then, straightening up again, he smiled at her engagingly.

119

'There's no reason why we shouldn't have a dance of our own, is there, just because I wouldn't be acceptable at the Waltz Evening?' he inquired; and, almost before she could answer, 'Of course there isn't!' he had swept her into his arms.

Almost immediately she was aware that he was far and away the best waltzer with whom she had ever danced; presently, of a vague wish that the music would go on and on; then of the magnetic attraction of their united motion and physical proximity. Rather startled, she murmured something inconsequential and unconvincing about not being able to keep up with such an accomplished partner. David laughed lightly.

'Nonsense! Of course you can. Didn't you ever dance before? I mean really? Well then, it's high time you learned—it'll do wonders for you. Don't stiffen so—just relax and float along. It's a marvellous feeling.'

'Yes, I—I know. Just the same, I think we'd better stop.'

'You mean you're not enjoying this?'

'Of course I'm enjoying it. But——'

She tried, ineffectually, to disengage herself. David laughed again and drew her closer to him, in a way that was both compelling and intoxicating. After that, she ceased to think of release. In fact, she did not try to think at all. As the music rose to a crescendo, David bent his head and, pressing his face against hers, kissed her on the mouth.

Instantly she wrenched herself free and confronted him, trembling and incoherent with rage. He walked over to the radio, switched it off and then, opening her favourite cloisonné box, helped himself to a cigarette and lighted it. When she paused, breathless, in her tirade, he spoke with the utmost calm.

'I'm sorry you feel that I insulted you. I certainly didn't mean to. I felt as if a kiss were a suitable climax to our dance, that's all.'

'You know we shouldn't have danced in the first place.'

'Wouldn't you have danced if you'd gone to the Waltz Evening?'

'Yes, of course. But not—not like that.'

'I said I didn't believe you'd ever really danced before. I told you I thought it would do wonders for you to learn. Well, it has—already.'

'You've made me so ashamed that I don't see how I'm ever going to look my husband in the face. If you call that doing wonders for me, I—I'm sorry I ever let you into this house.'

'Emily, are you sorry we've had such good times, sitting in front of the fire together while we had tea? Are you sorry you went with my stepfather and me to your grandmother's house when he took her the signet ring? Are you sorry I suggested going out on the town the night of that dreadful dinner? Are you sorry I came to your rescue tonight? If you can say yes to all that, looking me straight in the eye, I'll leave here this minute and I'll never come back.'

Without answering, Emily sank down in one of the big chairs flanking the hearthstone and put her hands to her face. David seated himself opposite her and quietly awaited her answer.

'No,' she said at last, without looking up, 'I'm not sorry for any of that. I shouldn't have told you I regretted ever letting you into this house. I did exaggerate. I've—I've enjoyed everything you've mentioned. But that doesn't mean I'm not ashamed of what's just happened.'

'Didn't it occur to you that something of the sort might happen sooner or later—as a result of the rest?'

'Of course not. I thought we were just friends. I thought you were *Roger's* friend. I thought you were——'

'A gentleman? Emily, if you say that, it'll be the last straw.'

'But I *did*. I thought——'

'Didn't you ever think of me as a man? Didn't you ever think of yourself as a woman?' David asked. He spoke slowly and still very calmly; but somehow he made every word sound ominous. 'All right, let me tell you something: from now on you'll know that two people like you and me don't ever stay "just friends". You'll recognize my kind of man when you see one. You'll know he's a potential lover. Eventually, you'll want him for an actual lover. What's more, you already know—at last—that you're a woman and not just a lady.'

It was at this moment that Roger had parted the portières and come into the library, to find David and Emily so absorbed in what they were saying to each other that they did not even hear his approach.

During the ensuing months, Emily had never seen David alone again. If Roger thought it was strange that his fellow junior no longer dropped in at tea-time, he did not say so. In fact, he mentioned David very little and he tried, conscientiously, to overcome his instinctive antagonism, telling himself that it was both unworthy and baseless; but he did not succeed

121

in completely rooting it out. The office association between the two was pleasant enough, except for an occasional slight clash, and, not infrequently, they formed part of the same downtown luncheon group; but Roger found plausible pretexts for declining invitations to the handsome new apartment on Lime Street and he did not suggest that David should join the weekly poker parties. He did mention these to Pell; but he accepted, without insistence, Pell's simple and straightforward statement that he could not afford to play poker. Early in the spring Roger joined the First Corps Cadets and shortly thereafter, asked Pell why he did not do the same. This time the suggestion was accepted, and frequently they walked together from Joy Street to the armoury where the drills were held and home again afterwards. Roger's admiration for Pell's character and ability increased all the time; but he did not try to force the status of hail-fellow-well-met upon the young Italian, since this was obviously unwelcome; it was Brian who had become his intimate and, with every new day, this friendship meant more to him than it had the day before.

Emily did not resent any of Roger's new interests; she herself was increasingly preoccupied with Priscilla, who was at Joy Street more and more, and with her housekeeping, which seemed to demand a great deal of her time. Dolly had now been permanently added to the domestic staff, but larger and larger numbers of guests were coming to the house. These added responsibilities were obviously enjoyable rather than burdensome to Emily; and Roger's own sense of well-being was disturbed by only two aspects of the general situation. The first was the attitude of Emily's parents. They were both displeased when Old Mrs. Forbes turned over the management of her financial affairs to him, completely shutting Fiske, Ford out of the picture, as far as she was concerned, and they betrayed this; when the further news leaked out that Roger had been instrumental in blocking the lease of the 'horrible little Gloucester Street house', their displeasure flamed into anger.

They did not reveal these feelings simultaneously, during the course of a family conference, as they would have done in the past; the estrangement between them, though it did not have the status of an official separation, was sufficiently established so that they almost never appeared in each other's company; and though they both went to the house on Louisburg Square and—less often—to the one on Joy Street, they did not do so together.

Roger had regarded Old Mrs. Forbes' remarks to him on the subject of her daughter and her son-in-law as a professional confidence, and had not spoken of it, even to Emily, until she herself brought up the matter.

'Grandmamma says she's told you Father and Mother aren't getting on so well,' she remarked, as casually as she could, on one of the increasingly rare evenings when they were alone.

'Yes. I'm very sorry.'

'So am I. Especially that they should choose just this time to blow up. After all, they've gone along a good many years without worrying about incompatibility—or anything worse. Mother just went her way and Father went his—or rather, Mother went her way and Father sat at home and moped. I don't blame him; he's always had a cheerless sort of life. But, after letting Mother have her head so long, I think he might have done it one more year—until Priscilla really got under way. It won't help her any if there's a family scandal right now.'

Roger was conscious of the slight irritation he always felt when the subject of Priscilla's début was treated as one of paramount importance. But he had never voiced this irritation.

'Is there really a question of scandal?' he asked, also speaking as casually as he could. 'Don't tell me, of course, if you'd rather not.'

'Not any more than there has been in a long while. To put it bluntly, Mother likes men. Probably you wouldn't think so, to look at her—she's so completely the classic Bostonian type, even more so than Aunt Elizabeth. You'd think it would be just the other way. Because, after all, Mother did marry young and she's always moved in mixed society, while Liz is an old maid and spends a lot of time way off in a lonely farmhouse when she isn't teaching at a girl's college. As a matter of fact, I don't believe Mother's ever gone off the deep end. I hope you won't misunderstand me when I say I don't believe it's so much a matter of principle with her as that she simply hasn't got the kind of courage it takes to do that. Now I can see that Grandmamma might have had. But Mother does love to skim over thin ice,' Emily continued. 'So Father finally said he wouldn't put up with it any longer! He's self-conscious even about going to his club because he thinks people are gossiping. And he hasn't much of anything else to do, now that he's resigned from Homer Lathrop's brokerage firm. Not that he does much when he goes to the club. If he played cards it would be different. But he promised Grandpapa he never would again after his college gambling debts were paid. And he's kept his promise all these years. It must have been awfully hard for him. I think he deserves a lot of credit.'

'So do I,' said Roger heartily, thinking with gratitude of his pleasant poker games. It soon became evident that Emily had been thinking about them too.

'Do you know, I wouldn't be surprised if your poker games didn't have something to do with Father's feeling about you? We've agreed that jealousy can be a terrible thing. If he were playing poker himself, with that crowd that does it regularly at the Algonquin ... Of course, poker wasn't his game and the Algonquin isn't his club. But you must see what I mean.'

'I do. And I'm sorry about that too. But don't you think he'd have got more out of life if he'd been more adaptable?'

'Of course I do. I think Father's had an awfully empty, futile life. As far as that goes, Mother has too. So she's kept aimlessly pursuing something she hasn't found. Now Grandmamma's different. She's had everything.'

'And made the most of everything she did have. But we seem to have strayed from the main subject. You began by telling me that your father and mother weren't getting on so well—which of course I knew already. Did you have anything special in mind that we might do about it?'

'Well, I thought perhaps as you'd blocked his lease business, you might think of something else that would bring them in money. Now that Father's resigned his position with Uncle Homer, their joint income is pretty limited, especially since Grandmamma has stopped supplementing it. Grandpa left almost everything to her—except for my trust fund—you know that too. Apparently he adored her to the day of his death. Mother and all his other children got mere pittances from his will. And Father didn't have much more—outside his salary, I mean.'

'Would you like me to try and see what I could do about the Gloucester Street house? Shall I try to sell it?'

'Do you think you could?'

'I could try. Fletcher's been saying his wife wants to live in town for the winter, now that the children are school age, and perhaps if your father and mother would let it go at a bargain. ... Maybe you'd better sound them out, since I'm in their bad graces. Meanwhile, I should think your grandmother could be persuaded to let them go on staying in Dublin—that is, to let your father go on staying there. Your mother spends most of her time visiting, anyway.'

'Well, Grandmamma might, at that. Especially as she doesn't want to stay there herself. She wants to take Priscilla to Europe. Priscilla doesn't want to go, but Uncle Sherman and Aunt Sue have actually agreed to it. They still won't do anything for her themselves, but they've begun to see that somebody must.'

There it was again, that annoying subject of Priscilla's début. Once more Roger suppressed the impulse to express his irritation.

'About selling the house. I think maybe you've got something there,' Emily said thoughtfully. 'I'll sound Father and Mother out, as you suggest. And I'll ask Grandmamma about Dublin. Incidentally, you wouldn't mind having Priscilla come and spend the rest of the spring with us, would you?'

'Of course not. I told you last fall, when you first spoke of it as a possibility, that I'd be glad to have her. I like Priscilla very much. But I don't especially like——'

He wished that it did not seem advisable, quite so often, to leave statements unfinished even when he had begun them at all. He knew he must not say, 'But I don't especially like the way you're all trying to railroad her into doing something she doesn't want to do. Suppose she doesn't "make" the Junior League and the Vincent Club? Lots of wonderful people don't even know they exist and don't care if they do know. Suppose she doesn't get asked to all the right parties or have a whirl at the ones she does go to? She may turn out to be a one-man girl, the way I was a one-girl man. It does happen. And there hasn't been time for the one man to come along yet. She isn't ready for one. Suppose she is gun-shy? She'll get over it, if you'll give her a chance. Just a year or two might make a difference, if she could develop naturally. I was shy myself, I know she must really suffer. Why don't you let her alone?'

He should not say all this and he did not, as was so often the case. But afterwards, as was less often the case, he was glad of it. For, as it turned out, Priscilla proved to be his second source of disturbance that spring, and he would have been the last to recommend that she be allowed to go her own way. He was thankful that no one could lay her wilfulness to his door.

Since Priscilla had not attended a major private school, it was

125

impossible for her to obtain the official status of a débutant upon her graduation from one of these. It was therefore decided, through general family conference, that it would be well for her to come up from the Cape early in the spring, settle down at the house on Joy Street and gradually drift into the current of the proper preliminaries to a formal entry into society. In this way, she would—or should—be well established when everyone began to go away for the summer, at which time Old Mrs. Forbes would take her to Europe, inviting some girl whom she had found particularly congenial, to accompany them. They would leave Boston early in June and return in September; with this schedule Priscilla would have gone to several important luncheons at the Chilton Club and one or two outstanding house dances before they sailed; and they would still reach London in time for the last Court. They would be back early enough for her to attend the Usher's dinners on the North Shore, dances at the Essex County Club and the Myopia Hunt Club and the correlative week-end parties.

For fear of mutiny, the details of this schedule were revealed to Priscilla only by degrees; but to everyone's amazed relief, she made no objection to any of the activities proposed. Without argument—indeed with every appearance of amenity—she arrived at Joy Street on the appointed day; unpacked her belongings in a manner indicative of expecting prolonged occupancy of the small spare room with the spool furniture; and, apparently quite on her own initiative, remarked that she supposed she ought to go shopping, because she did not have enough clothes to last 'until she got to Paris'. She did not resist advice and she did not stipulate that she should go on her shopping expeditions unaccompanied; but it was soon obvious that she needed surprisingly little guidance. The wardrobe she selected contained exactly the right proportion of extremely well-tailored tweeds and serges, superlatively smart silks, prints and linens and a collection of evening dresses which varied in hue and design, but which were uniformly gauzy, girlish and bewitching.

Neither Old Mrs. Forbes nor Emily had ventured to hope that Priscilla would make much of an impression at the Empire Dance or the Freshman Jubilee, and were therefore agreeably surprised to find that she was able more than to hold her own on both of these occasions. They had taken it for granted that she would do better at the pseudo-rustic barn dances which were featured among the spring festivities, the synthetic Hofbrau on Stanhope Street and the four-course picnic suppers on Buzzard's Bay. They had likewise felt almost certain that she would ride in the Memorial Day Horse Show and, with this in mind, had decided somewhat hesitantly to include Elliot Berkeley among the guests at the first dinner given in Priscilla's honour, which, because of the greater prestige which would inevitably be attached to it under these circumstances, was scheduled to be held at Old Mrs. Forbes' house instead of Emily's. It was when Emily and her grandmother submitted this dinner list to Priscilla for inspection that she asked her first disturbing question.

'Aren't you going to ask David Salomont to the party?' she inquired with genuine surprise.

'Why, no. We hadn't thought of doing so. You see, he's older than the crowd you're going with and——'

'He isn't any older than Elliot Berkeley, is he? I thought he was younger.'

'Well, he is, a little. But we made an exception, in the case of Elliot Berkeley, because we thought you might find him especially congenial, on account of his interest in horses. We asked Caroline so that there'd be an older girl too.'

'I don't see why you're so worried about people being congenial. David's a very good mixer. I know the Stockbridges like him and the Amorys. They've told me so.'

'Then we'll ask David and the Stockbridges and the Amorys to a small party at Joy Street if you like. But how did the subject of David Salomont happen to arise between you and the Stockbridges? Or between you and the Amorys?'

'Joan Amory and her beau had the next table to David and me at the Ritz last Saturday. We went there to a late lunch after I finished my shopping. He went shopping with me too. We went back to David's apartment for a drink afterwards. And all three girls have called me up to tell me how attractive they thought he was.'

Old Mrs. Forbes and Emily exchanged glances, and there was nothing fleeting about the looks they gave each other. Then Emily spoke with an obvious effort at restraint.

'But, Priscilla, you never told us you were shopping or lunching with David Salomont. And you know you're not supposed to drink at all until after graduation.'

'You never asked me who helped me choose my clothes or

who took me out to lunch. I'd have told you if you had. And you acted as if you weren't much interested in David Salomont any more. Every time I've started to talk about him you've changed the subject. I didn't understand why, because, after all, he was your friend and Roger's before he was mine. His stepfather's a friend of Grandmamma's and I met David here at her house for the first time.'

All this was so unanswerable that neither Old Mrs. Forbes nor Emily attempted an immediate reply.

'Did Faith and Olivia tell their mother that they went to David's apartment with you?' Emily asked finally.

'I don't know. I suppose they did if she expected them home at a certain minute and she asked them why they were late. And I don't suppose they said anything if she didn't. I don't see why they should.'

'Priscilla, you've simply got to be more careful. The next thing you know, you'll overhear something, while you're under the dryer after your hair's been set, or in a powder room or in a——'

'Of course I'll overhear something. I can't help doing it all the time.'

'I mean you'll overhear that you're running all over town with David Salomont, that you're even letting him choose your clothes and going to his apartment without a chaperon for drinking parties. And the next thing you know, you'll find yourself left out of the parties you'd especially like to go, because David isn't the sort of man——'

'Isn't *what* sort of man? He's well educated, isn't he, even if he did go to Columbia instead of Harvard? He knows how to dress, doesn't he? He's been all over the world, he knows people everywhere—people who've *done* things. He's good looking, he's amusing, he's charming, he's——'

'Priscilla, I am sure that David Salomont would be very much complimented to know that you have such a high opinion of him. But it really isn't necessary for you to rise to his defence quite so vehemently. Neither Emily nor I would dream of denying that everything you've said is true.'

Old Mrs. Forbes had now recovered from her surprise and gathered her forces.

'All Emily means,' she said, 'is that there are a lot of very stodgy stupid people in Boston who don't know how to appreciate a young man like David Salomont, for the very reason that

128

he *is* so much better educated and more widely travelled and more sophisticated than their own sons and the callow youths who went to college with them and who represent about all there is in the way of available material as beaux for their daughters. The Stockbridges and the Amorys may be exceptions to the general rule—I hope they arc. Anyway, we'll soon find out. But, taken by and large, the parents of the girls you're meeting now and that you'll be thrown with next winter wouldn't welcome David Salomont because he's *different*. They'd recognize this without recognizing the reason that he's different is that he's superior and they'd resent it—perhaps unconsciously, but they would, just the same. Thinking as highly of David Salomont as you do, I'm sure you wouldn't want to do anything that would jeopardize his career—especially when he's made such a brilliant beginning, when there's no reason why he shouldn't rise to great heights in his profession.'

'No, of course I wouldn't——'

'If you listen to me, you won't stop seeing David Salomont, but you'll see him quietly—at his house and at Emily's. As often as you please. You'll ask him to small parties, in which you'll include such people as the Stockbridges and the Amorys that you know like him too. But you won't insist on including him in groups where there might be the least chance of antagonism to him, and you won't so much as hint that anyone outside your own family should ask him to a party. Let the suggestions come from the other side—they'll have a great deal more weight that way. Does what I've said make sense?'

'Yes, sort of.'

It was now obvious that Old Mrs. Forbes had really begun to strike home, and she decided that it would be unwise to press her advantage further for the moment.

Nothing more was said about David Salomont that afternoon; and Priscilla made no comment when her grandmother told her that she had been able to improve their reservations by taking an earlier sailing for Europe than had originally been intended. They were going on the *Normandie* instead of the *Ile de France*, which was one of those things which should be 'even more exciting'. The small dinner, which included David as well as the Stockbridges and the Amorys, was a great success and so was the larger one at which none of these persons was present; therefore, no occasion for unfavourable comparison arose between the two. Both the Stockbridges and the Amorys had already invited David to their houses, before Priscilla appeared on the scene, so there was nothing forced about the fact that they should do so again, and Priscilla now felt free to invite him as often as she liked—without running the risk of appearing to attempt monopoly—to both Louisburg Square and Joy Street.

David, it appeared, felt equally free to avail himself of these invitations; and it was thus that, quite innocently, Priscilla proved a source of disturbance to Roger. For, though she was the ostensible attraction, he was convinced that she had furnished a convenient pretext for the resumption of David's visits to Emily. What was even more to the point, Emily was convinced of the same thing—so thoroughly convinced that she broached the subject to David one evening when Priscilla had gone out with someone else and he strolled in, clad in immaculate Shantung, with the idea of asking her whether she would care to drop in at Zero Hereford Street for a pre-dinner drink.

'Almost everyone I've talked to lately seems to be making vacation plans,' she said. 'What about yours?'

'Well, of course, I have to spend two weeks at Camp Smith, and that won't leave me much time to do anything else, if I can't fix up something with the Artful Dodger. But I hope I can.'

'I don't seem to know about Camp Smith or why you have to go there.'

'Camp Smith, my dear girl, is in Peekskill, New York, and I have to go there for so-called duty in the field, because I am a reserve officer, holding a commission as second lieutenant in the National Guard. While I was in Columbia, I joined the officer candidates' school of New York's Twenty-seventh Division.'

'You did! That's all very impressive. Proud to know you Lieutenant Salomont.... And if you can drive a bargain with the Artful Dodger, what else would you do this summer besides "duty in the field"?'

'I think I'll probably go to Venezuela. In addition to the pleasures of the voyage on the *Santa Paulo* or the *Santa Rosa*, I can look forward to others in Caracas. Some of my father's relatives, that we used to visit regularly when he was alive, have a rather nice place there. Mother's always kept in touch with the family and my stepfather gets on well with them too. Mother and Dad thought they'd like to go to South America for a change and they've suggested that I should go with them. These relatives of ours have a *quinta* in the country too—I wouldn't know how many acres. But I do know there are three girls in the family. I haven't seen them in the flesh for a long while, but they sent us pictures of the wedding party when their brother was married and they were all bridesmaids. I must say they were quite easy to look at. That picture rather influenced my decision about a vacation.'

'No doubt you'd make a very favourable impression on them too,' Emily said, delighted that she had been provided with such an advantageous approach to the subject she wished to discuss. 'You certainly have on Priscilla.'

David smiled, with a slight deprecatory shrug.

'It's nice to know I have the unqualified approval of some member of the family,' he remarked.

'I don't see why you say that. I understand from Priscilla that you've visited on the Cape several times this past winter, so I gather that Uncle Sherman and Aunt Sue must have approved of you too. And I'm sure Grandmamma's been just as nice as she could be to you.'

'I have the impression that Mr. and Mrs. Sherman Forbes act on the principle of live and let live and apply it even to the very young,' David replied. 'And of course I benefit because Old Mrs. Forbes is grateful to my stepfather on account of Feodor.'

'Feodor?' exclaimed Emily, diverted in spite of herself. 'Feodor who?'

'Romanoff. But of course grand dukes didn't use their surnames. Surely you know that. And I believe your grandmother always called him Freddie anyway.'

'I haven't the least idea what you're driving at.'

'Surely that doesn't worry you?'

Emily flushed and bit her lip. 'We were talking about Priscilla,' she said. She spoke rather severely, but she was, in fact, dying to hear more about the Grand Duke, whose existence had been definitely disclosed to her for the first time.

'Excuse me. I thought it was you who was talking about Priscilla. I don't particularly wish to discuss her. But I strive to please. What more did you want to say?'

'Only that she seems to have what's commonly called a crush on you and that I hope you won't take it very seriously. Of course she's a great deal too young to know her own mind.'

'I thought you'd already found out I never take things of that sort very seriously. And I might add it isn't only girls in their teens who sometimes don't know their own minds—though

131

sometimes they do. But occasionally girls in their twenties don't either.'

Emily flushed again and turned away. There was no use trying to spar with David. He was a great deal better at it than she was.

'Incidentally, my mother and stepfather are planning to give a party in honour of Old Mrs. Forbes and her young charges the night before they sail,' David went on. 'It might be good. You and Roger better come over to New York for it too. You could take in a few shows at the same time.'

'It's very kind of you to suggest it, but I don't believe Roger can leave the office. He's got an awful lot of important work on his hands.'

'Yes, things have certainly changed since your grandmother took over that situation.... Well, if Roger can't get away, why don't you come over to New York without him?'

'Because I'd rather stay at home than go anywhere he can't go with me.'

'If you came to that conclusion on the basis of one kiss, that must have made quite an impression on you.'

'I don't care to discuss the episode in question with you, David.'

'Well, I didn't want to discuss the question of Priscilla. But, as I said, I strive to please. You might strive to please, too, once in a while, Emily. You'd be ever so much more lovable if you did. All the same, I'd like very much to kiss you again, in spite of the fact that you're not especially lovable—you're very attractive none the less. Some day I shall. Meanwhile, if you make any further objections to my perfectly innocent attentions to Priscilla, I shall draw the inevitable conclusion. You're not the only person who can draw conclusions.'

'You're not ever going to have a chance to kiss me again.'

'Would you like to bet on that?'

'Yes. I'll bet on it. Whatever you like.'

'All right. I'll take you up. But not right now. All our most interesting conversations seem subject to interruption. If I'm not mistaken, the luck of the Irish is about to intrude upon our delightful solitude *à deux*. Isn't that his special signal?'

David was quite right. Brian was jiggling the old brass knocker which Emily had attached to the new door that had been cut through the brick wall at the side of the transformed back yard, so that visitors could enter there, instead of through the old rear door leading into the alley, where trash cans were perforce placed. It was Monday and, as usual on poker nights, Brian had come straight to Joy Street from the office. Emily hastened to let him in and greeted him with even greater cordiality than was her habit.

'Hello, Emily! I thought I'd find you here,' he said, 'that's why I didn't bother to go through the house. Hello, David! Gosh, you always manage to get through earlier than any of the rest of us, don't you? Is it good luck or good management?'

'Both in about equal proportions. And apparently Roger is still the one to shut up shop, in spite of the favourable turn of fortune's wheel.'

Brian had nodded, almost casually, to Emily as he came in, without shaking hands. Now, without paying much apparent attention to David, he draped his rumpled coat over the nearest chair and sank back on it, throwing his hat on the ground and wiping a moist brow.

'Whatever he's doing I hope he isn't late for poker. Can you pinch-hit for him until he gets here, if he is, Dave?'

'Thanks for the compliment. But I've got a dinner date. In fact, I ought to be on my way right now. I've kept thinking Priscilla would be along any minute and I wanted to have a word with her about that *bon voyage* party—I'm to call my mother about it at midnight. Well, I'll catch up with Pris somehow and somewhere before then.... Sure you can't get over to New York for the great event yourself, Emily?'

'Yes, I'm very sure.'

'Sorry. Well, so long.'

He brought his empty glass back to the table and set it down on the tray. Emily said good-bye without getting up; and, with a passing compliment on the growth of her tulips since he had last observed them, David strolled towards the new door in the side of the brick wall, and went out, latching the door carefully.

Brian and Emily were still strolling up and down the diminutive walk, deep in conversation about flowers, with which it appeared Brian's mother had always had great success, when Roger came in, half an hour later. Emily ran to meet him with a glad cry of welcome and Brian stood by, grinning, while the young couple embraced. Afterwards they all three sat down while Emily mixed fresh drinks and then both men fell in heartily with Emily's suggestion that they should have a picnic supper.

133

The rest of the poker players and also Priscilla and Stanley Lyman arrived more or less simultaneously, before Roger and Brian and Emily finished supper. Uncle Barney and Father Mat had both eaten, they said; but Shaun Collins and Terence Lenahan confessed that they had been kept late at the office and that they could do with a bite along with their drinks; as for Priscilla and Stanley, they were frankly ravenous. Presently, everyone was hobnobbing with everyone else as if they had known each other all their lives. Eventually, Priscilla and Stanley said they must leave to get ready for a dance in Concord and the poker players repaired to the library. But Emily sat for a long time in her little garden, looking at the stars, wondering if she dared to ask her grandmother about the Grand Duke Feodor, and why David thought she was not lovable, and what she should do to prevent him from making love to her, and why he should imagine for one moment that she should be jealous of Priscilla. But it was so quiet and pleasant in the garden that, although she pondered these things, she did not worry over them. She felt happy and at peace. . . .

She was still sitting there when Roger came to tell her that the poker players were gone. He also said that there had been no chance to tell her about it when he came in, with so many people around, but he had another piece of good news for her— he had pulled off the sale of the Gloucester Street house. The Fletchers had actually made him a very advantageous offer, on their own initiative; he had not been obliged to press them at all.

'What's more,' he went on, 'when I telephoned the good news to your mother, she said that she and your father had agreed to go together to Commencement since it's his twenty-fifth reunion. Anyway she feels that she should take a stand for Governor Saltonstall, and of course she couldn't do it—that is, not as a reunioner—if she and your father made their separation official. She's talked it over with him and he sees her point. He agrees that they ought to be seen at Commencement together, and if they do that, they might as well see Priscilla through too. In fact, I wouldn't be surprised if, eventually, they wouldn't be almost sorry they sold the Gloucester Street house, especially as your father's practically decided he may as well resume his connection with Homer Lathrop's office. But, of course, there's always the Chilton Club and the Somerset Club.'

'So it's beginning to look like the best of all possible worlds to

Father and Mother again and they're even ready to hold out a helping hand to their fellow creatures?'

'Well, things certainly do look better than they did a while ago. But I wouldn't go quite as far as to say that. After all, everyone can't be as happy as we are.'

There was an undertone of amusement in his voice, as there had been throughout the conversation. But he also spoke as if he too were happy and at peace, which was not strange, because he also felt that way. It had never even crossed his mind to be troubled or jealous when he came home and found Emily and Brian alone in the garden together.

CHAPTER VIII

Before the month of June was out, the sale of the Gloucester Street house had been consummated to the satisfaction of all concerned, and the Class of '14 had celebrated its twenty-fifth reunion in a manner befitting the best traditions of Harvard College. Perfect weather had prevailed throughout Commencement Week, Harvard won the baseball game against Yale, and the paraders, led by the Governor who was also a gentleman, presented a striking sight in their fanciful blue blazers and variegated headgear. Eleanor Thayer's slight misgivings about the congeniality of the reunioners with whom she and her husband might be quartered in the Yard proved to be groundless; they were Philadelphians of unimpeachable background. With such a generally satisfactory set-up, it was not strange that she could find the way towards complete reconciliation with her husband smoothed.

Final courts at Buckingham Palace were later than usual that year, because of the visit which the King and Queen made to the United States. However, Old Mrs. Forbes, Priscilla and Olivia Stockbridge, accompanied by the faithful maid, Doris, and Clark, the equally faithful chauffeur, had departed for Europe by the end of the month and soon thereafter, Brian, Pell and David went off successively on their vacations. Their absence, inevitably, meant more work for Roger and both he and Emily began to take his lateness as a matter of course, and to accept the fact that he would usually be too tired to go anywhere in the evening, after an abnormally long day at the office, even if they could put sufficient dependence on his departure from there at a certain hour to permit the making of definite plans. However, they continued to enjoy their garden and, on week-ends, they usually went either to Manchester-by-the-Sea or to Dublin, where Old Mrs. Forbes had instructed Roger to 'keep an eye on how things were going'. Less frequently they visited Sue and

Sherman Forbes on the Cape, finding an unexpectedly warm welcome whenever they did so; and, stealing one extra day, they went for the Fourth of July to Elizabeth Forbes' old brick farmhouse, in Vermont, where she was already contentedly installed for the summer.

During the week-end, lengthened to include the holiday, Emily found herself taking almost as much pleasure in the hours she spent with Elizabeth in the house and garden as she did in the hours when she and Roger went swimming and riding together. Roger was just recovering from another attack of bronchitis, which seemed even more severe than its predecessors, probably because it was so unseasonable. He really felt more like stretching out in a hammock, with a pile of books and a pitcher of orangeade beside him than like making any physical exertion. The realization of this robbed Emily of her own zest for exercise; of course she could go swimming and riding alone, and once or twice she did. But she did not stay out very long. She was soon back on Hollyhock Hill, as she had christened her aunt's place, weeding contentedly around the moss roses, which were still at their prime, or discussing with Elizabeth the possibility of further improvements and embellishments for the house.

While they talked one day the two were sitting in Elizabeth's bedroom alone.

'You know, Liz, it is wonderful here for Roger,' Emily said. 'I can't help worrying about this recurrent bronchitis of his.'

'He's been examined, of course?'

'Yes, of course. And Dr. Blaine says there's no cause for alarm—whatever that may mean. I *am* alarmed though. I suppose it's silly of me, but I'd have been happier if Roger hadn't gone out in the summer-house today, even if there isn't a particle of wind and it is July!'

For a time neither of them spoke. Emily continued to think of Roger and Elizabeth, of the satisfaction to be had from making her home a haven for them both. Presently Emily went out to join Roger in the summer-house.

When she told him that she and Elizabeth had been talking of possible improvements to the house, he answered, lazily, that he thought the place was almost perfect as it was, but that if she and Elizabeth were bent on gilding refined gold and painting the lily, he supposed there was nothing he could do to stop them; as far as he was concerned, he hoped they would let him

137

lie still and enjoy the view in peace. Falling in with his mood, Emily sat down on the ground beside the reclining chair in which he was stretched out and, clasping her hands around her knees, gazed across the intervening hills and the valley where the Connecticut River wove its peaceful way between fresh fields, towards the White Mountains beyond. A slight mist was rising from the meadows, which veiled them without hiding them; but above it, there was almost perfect clarity; and when the sun set behind the wooded foothills at the west, everything seemed covered with a delicate sheen of glory.

Yes, it was perfect as it was—perfect to sit there, in the gathering darkness, with her hand against Roger's knees and his hand on her hair. All her perplexities, all her worries, were relegated to another sphere when they were together like this. She no longer felt worried about his illness. She forgot that she had wondered about the Grand Duke's ring, that she had been concerned about Pietro's accident and piqued by Simonetta's elusiveness; she had even forgotten that Priscilla had become a problem and that a passage-at-arms with David always ended in her defeat. As Roger said, it was unimportant whether Elizabeth made any changes on the place. In fact, it seemed rather a shame that she should toil all summer, instead of sitting quietly in the garden like this. Only of course Elizabeth had no one to sit in the garden with her—at least, no one who counted. That made all the difference. She had said to Emily once, 'I love this place so much that I would give up teaching and stay here all the time, if only——' Then she had flushed and she had not finished her sentence. But Emily knew she meant, 'If only I had someone to live here with me. Some man whom I loved and who loved me.' Suddenly, Emily felt very sorry for Elizabeth, who had never known the fulfilment of love and who had never sat in the dusk with her head against her husband's knees and his hand on her hair. But presently she ceased to feel sorry, because such complete contentment filled her being that there was no room for anything else.

They left determined to return in September, but as it turned out, they could not. Roger and Pell, as members of the First Corps Cadets, were sent to Camp Edwards the first two weeks in July; and in view of David's absence, which had not only covered his duty in the field at Camp Smith, but had been prolonged to cover his desired trip to Venezuela, work at the office inevitably piled up. Then late in August, the news from

France, became suddenly disquieting and Roger felt impelled to cable Old Mrs. Forbes, urging that she and her charges should return to the United States immediately.

A week later Europe was at war, and world conditions, though not yet chaotic, were admittedly menacing. David and Brian had already made plans of long standing for the Labour Day week-end and Roger had a preliminary hearing in an equity case coming up Tuesday morning—the most important entrusted to him so far. Besides, he did not feel justified in leaving Pell to grapple alone with any problems which might unexpectedly arise, even if he had been in the mood for Hollyhock Hill just then. He urged Emily to go there without him, knowing how disappointed both she and Elizabeth would be by her failure to do so. But though the disappointment was real enough, Emily was not in the mood for Hollyhock Hill either. The memory of the radiant evening which she and Roger had spent in the summer-house together had become much more vital to her than her eagerness for material improvements; though she was still interested in seeing these, she wanted to do so with him. Besides, if she had gone to Vermont, she would have missed the home-coming of her grandmother and Priscilla; she wanted to hear the account of all their exciting adventures, without any delay.

They had arrived safely in New York, were both well, both in high spirits and both inclined to regard their precipitate departure from the scene of impending conflict in the light of a lark. In like measure, Old Mrs. Forbes was insistent that no change should be made in their programme for the autumn and winter, except, if anything, to crowd it more full of festivities than she had originally planned. She did not actually say, '*Après nous, le déluge*', but it was implicit in all her actions and her attitude was by no means an isolated one. Both the débutantes and their elders realized that this year might well be the last when the supply of suitable escorts from Harvard remained undiminished and were determined to make the most of the opportunities furnished by this provident university while they still survived. Priscilla was immediately caught up in a whirl.

In the wake of her own ball at the Somerset, Priscilla went to countless other hotel balls, to country club balls and hunt balls; to dances at the Chilton Club and at the Duxbury Yacht Club; to cocktail parties, supper parties and theatre parties; to football games and hockey games. She poured at innumerable teas; she

ushered at morning musicales. As if Boston and its smarter sub-
urbs did not offer sufficient diversion, she was rushed off to an
Assembly in Philadelphia, to the Bachelors Cotillion in Balti-
more and to the coming-out party of Hal Roosevelt's daughter,
Eleanor, at the White House. Having promptly become a provisional member of the Junior League, she began her volunteer
work at the Perkins Institute for the Blind and the Canton
School for Crippled Children, and also attended the requisite
course of lectures at Zero Marlborough Street where the League
had its headquarters. It was after she had gone to several of
these that she betrayed a marked lack of appreciation.

'If all those girls sitting on those hard, straight-backed chairs
in that pinky ballroom are really the cream of Boston society,'
she remarked caustically to Emily, 'I shudder to think what the
skim milk is like.'

'Priscilla, it's very ill-bred to talk this way about your friends.
Very—very ungrateful.'

'They're not my friends. I never said I wanted them for my
friends and I'm sure they don't want me for theirs.'

'If Grandmamma heard you talking like this, she'd just about
die.'

'Oh, no, she wouldn't! It's exactly the sort of thing she says
herself. Only she doesn't say it about the provisional Junior
Leaguers of this year. She doesn't want anything to "go
wrong". But give her time! A little later, when she isn't hampered, she'll say things that will make your hair curl.'

Except for occasional captious comments of this character, it
was not until after the League's Christmas performance at the
Peabody Playhouse, in which she took a leading part, that Priscilla showed any further signs of surfeit. Then, unexpectedly, as
she did so many things, she voiced sudden discontent.

'I've been to all the luncheons and done all the ushering I can
stand. I want to do something different for a few days at least.
If I don't, I'll go crazy.'

'Just what do you mean by different?' inquired Emily, laying
down her pen and trying to speak patiently.

'I've never been to Hollyhock Hill,' Priscilla said. 'That ought
to be different.'

'Yes, it is ... Well, I don't know Elizabeth's plans, but I can
ask. When would you want to go?'

'Next Thursday.'

'You seem to have this pretty well thought out already. Do you

140

want to be alone, like Greta Garbo, or do you want a big boisterous house party?'

'I don't want either one. I want you and Roger, of course. And Olivia.'

'No men, except Roger?'

'Naturally. Don't *hurry* me so, Emily! I heard Roger talking to Brian about Hollyhock Hill the other night, and Brian said that he'd never been to a place like that, that he'd give anything to see it. I think he meant what he said. I think he'd probably like Hollyhock Hill. And Olivia isn't interested in anyone special just now. She's had a row with her high-particular, as she calls him. And she isn't snobbish. She'd be polite to Brian.'

'Damn white of her, as Brian would put it himself. Yes, I've heard him say he'd like to go to Hollyhock Hill too and I'd be glad to ask him. I think Elizabeth would be glad to have him. You knew he'd just been elected to the City Council, didn't you?'

'Yes, I heard Roger talking about it and saying it was just the first rung of the political ladder—that he was sure Brian would get to the Senate some day, which is what he wants.'

'Well, I wouldn't go so far as that. Our senators are pretty firmly entrenched and, after all, one of them's my uncle, so naturally I wouldn't want to see him defeated by an Irishman—not that I dislike Brian.... Would I be hurrying you—or prying into your affairs or doing anything I shouldn't—if I ask whether you're interested in anyone special just now and what man you had in mind for yourself?'

'I want to ask David.'

Emily pressed her lips together, and, picking up her pen, placed it in an upright position, ran her thumb and forefinger down its length and, turning it over, repeated this process several times. She had not seen David alone since the spring evening when he had told her he was not sorry he had kissed her once and that he intended to do so again, in spite of the fact that he did not find her particularly lovable, adding that he gathered she was jealous of Priscilla.

'Why David?' she asked noncommittally.

'Well, he and Brian are great friends, aren't they? Besides, I've seen hardly anything of him lately. And I've missed him a lot. If he went off in the country like that, with us, we could be together all day and every evening.'

'Somehow, I don't believe David would care for Hollyhock

141

Hill,' she said cautiously. 'I don't even know whether he can skate.'

'Of course he can skate. I've been skating with him. He's a wonderful skater. He skates just the way he dances.'

'I thought you said you hadn't seen anything of David lately,' Emily remarked.

'I said, hardly anything. Of course I see him once in a while. After all, he's one of my best friends.'

'I didn't know you considered David one of your best friends.'

'Yes, you did too. You like to pretend you don't, that's all. I can't see why. It isn't as if you were a girl and wanted him yourself.'

This time Emily did not lay down her pen; she threw it down.

'It certainly isn't,' she said almost sharply. 'All right, I'll telephone Elizabeth and if she can manage a house party over the New Year's week-end, I'll speak to the others.... Was there anything else you wanted to talk to me about just now? If there isn't, I'd really like to finish balancing my cheque-book, so I can pay this month's bills. I'm late getting to them as it is.'

'I don't see why you bother to balance it. You know you have plenty of money in the bank. And it wouldn't matter, even if you were overdrawn. The cashiers are very considerate, when they're told to be. I happen to know. I'm overdrawn more than a thousand myself right now. I just bought myself a very snappy ermine jacket. I was sick and tired of that old squirrel number. It looked like something left over from your time.'

Emily did not reply; she did not trust herself to do so. Assiduously, she bent over her accounts.

Later, when Emily telephoned, Elizabeth was delighted. She had rather wanted to invite Mark Merriweather, who taught biology at Dartmouth and who had recently lectured at Bryn Mawr, to spend the New Year's week-end at Hollyhock Hill; she had hesitated because—well, just because she had. Since the others were coming, she would get in touch with him right away. Of course they would not make too much work—Jenny was with her as usual and Una Randell would come in whenever they needed her for dishwashing and cleaning. There was any amount of snow, the tobogganing would be wonderful. And she would have the pond cleared off. She had not been skating, because it was not much fun, all alone. But she was sure the ice was inches thick. . . .

Olivia, Brian and David all expressed themselves as equally delighted when the invitation was extended to them, and Roger, if anything, seemed even more pleased.

The sleighs which Elizabeth had sent to meet them at the station swung immediately into the back road where the snowploughs had not penetrated and, for several miles, while the bells jingled and the horses jogged easily along, the members of Priscilla's party—as they had all agreed to call it—gave themselves up to the quiet enjoyment of an experience which was new to more than half of them. Then the lights on Hollyhock Hill came into view, shining warmly through the cold glitter of the night. There were big fires in all the fireplaces, the house was as warm as toast and gaily decorated with Christmas greens, and Elizabeth had on a red dress; there was colour in her cheeks to match it too, colour that neither Roger nor Emily had ever seen there before; and Mark Merriweather, her biology professor, who did not seem too professorial or too elderly either, was helping everyone with bags, and saying how about hot buttered rum or would somebody rather have plain toddy and seeming and acting like the most genial of hosts. And next there was one of Jenny's fine suppers, a big ironstone tureen full of corn chowder and chicken pie and hot rolls and a huge baked Indian pudding. . . .

By the time they had finished coffee, Emily was so sleepy that she wondered whether she could keep awake long enough to get out of her clothes before she tumbled into the candle-flame bed. Roger was equally drowsy and they were soon fast asleep, with their arms around each other for extra warmth and comfort. It was not until they waked the next morning, with the sun streaming into their room, that Emily, cuddling closer to her husband, smilingly reminded him that they were supposed to be the chaperons of the occasion, and that they had not even made a pretence of finding what the others were up to before they tumbled off to bed themselves.

'Why, Liz is the chaperon, isn't she?' Roger inquired unconcernedly. It was certainly very pleasant in this bright, warm room and this big, soft bed and he saw no reason why he should give anyone except Emily even a passing thought.

'Go on! She has a beau of her own now! And am I glad, after all these years! We're the old married couple, lending respectability to this gay gathering, darling.'

Fragrant aromas were soon stealing pleasantly through the house, and Roger and Emily did full justice to their share of the excellent breakfast when, belatedly, they joined the others round the dining-room table and good-naturedly responded to the jokes made at their expense—though some of these jokes were rather broad, in Emily's opinion, considering the presence of Priscilla and Olivia. She was astonished to learn that everyone else had gone skating the night before in the moonlight and had stayed up for hours, entranced by David's execution of fancy figures; also that intermittent tobogganing had already been going on that morning too. She hastened to get bundled up and go outdoors herself; and from then, until the sun went down behind the foothills in a blaze of rose, radiantly reflected on the distant snow-covered mountains, she did not come into the house at all, except for lunch. Then she was amazed to find that she was already tired and sleepy again.

'We're all hoping you'll join us tonight,' David said. 'We're going to have a small bonfire, so you wouldn't be cold. And I can take down a bench. You could sit on that and rest if you found you couldn't keep up with us.'

'You don't need to talk as if I were a thousand years old. Of course I'll come skating, if everyone else is going. I didn't know everyone was going last night.'

'I did open the door a crack and tell you so,' Brian interposed. 'But you must have been sound asleep already. Myself, I just stumble around on skates. Why don't you and Roger and I go down to the pond for just a little while and then come back to the house and get our well-earned rest, leaving the others who don't work as hard as we do to their childish pastimes?'

She looked at him gratefully; there was really something very pleasant about Brian, after you got to know him. But his kindly suggestion did not serve to counterbalance David's taunt. Determined to show him that she could stand up under long hours and violent exercise as well as anyone, she went early to the pond, and was already gliding quietly over it, hand in hand with Roger, when Priscilla and David came down the slope which led to it. Brian made his way clumsily over to Roger and Emily and nodded towards the pair on the hill.

'Olivia's given me up,' he said good-naturedly. 'But those two are certainly making a go of it, aren't they?'

'Looks that way,' agreed Roger. 'Here, you and Emily have a

144

try. I'll go and take on Olivia. Talk about making a go of it! Liz and her prof don't seem to know that there's anyone else on the ice.'

Emily accepted Brian's hands in place of Roger's without comment. Her eyes were still on Priscilla and David, who had now reached the pond. Briefly, David knelt to help Priscilla change her stadium boots for her shoe-skates and put on his own; then they were off together, cutting figure eights, playing leapfrog, separating and meeting, waltzing, locked close together. It was a beautiful exhibition. Mechanically, Emily gave Brian a few helpful directions and showed proper patience when he revealed no skill at following them; but as soon as he suggested that they should go and sit down by the fire, she readily agreed. He piled more logs on it, and they bent over it together, enjoying its cheerful glow. Then, as Emily glanced up, she caught his arm.

'Oh, Brian, look!'

'Gosh almighty! What would those be? Not really northern lights, that you read about?'

'Of course. You don't just read about them, you know. They exist. But they're rare around here. I haven't seen them many times myself. And never as bright as this. Look! They're mounting higher and higher all the time! And they're not all white any longer. They're getting more and more brilliant every moment!'

It was true. The manner in which these multicoloured rays slanted towards each other gave them the effect of striving to meet and make a dome; and gradually this lustrous mass took shining and complete form overhead. Equally rapt, equally awed, Brian and Emily sat gazing at it, both unaware that, in the excitement of the moment, she had let her hand slide down his arm, and that their fingers were now tightly interlocked. They were still thus absorbed when David swung gracefully up to them, alone.

'Quite a sight, isn't it?' he said agreeably. 'Well! You two have been in such a daze that you haven't noticed our number is now reduced. Olivia actually doesn't like northern lights; she's heard they're an omen of some sort. Anyhow, Miss Forbes and Roger have taken Olivia up to the house and she's going to bed. The others said they'd be back in a few minutes and that they'd bring a thermos of hot chocolate with them—sounds good to me. Meanwhile, the prof's taken advantage of his lady-love's

145

absence to make up to Priscilla. If you really don't want to skate, Briny, you won't mind if I lure Emily away from you, will you?'

'Not if luring's what she wants. I'm going to go right on sitting here. What I'm looking at beats any skating I'll ever do.'

Emily was inclined to feel much the same way. But as Brian made no effort to detain her and David was smiling engagingly, she told herself it would be pointed to decline and permitted David to raise her to her feet. As they glided away, she understood almost instantly what Priscilla had meant by saying that he skated in the same way that he danced; the ease and grace of his movements made them seem not only natural but inevitable. Emily felt a surge of pride in the consciousness that her own performance was worthy of his, even before he voiced his approval of it.

'You're really an excellent skater. I had no idea.'

'Have you made up your mind I don't do anything especially well?'

'On the contrary. You do a great many things exceptionally well. You know it and so do I. I never said you didn't. All I said was, that you'd never really danced, until I made you, and that you weren't especially lovable, but that you might easily become so, under the right influence.'

'I'm afraid you and I haven't the same ideas about what constitutes a good influence.'

'Very possibly not. But couldn't we discuss that some other time? It really seems too bad to bicker just now. It's a night in a million. Come on, make a bargain with me!'

'What kind of a bargain?'

'Just that if you don't denounce me all the time, I won't do anything to deserve it. We'll simply skate—and look at that great dome of light.'

His tone held no suggestion of sarcasm now and none of sensuality either; it was merely pleasant and persuasive. Emily found it amazingly easy to listen to. They circled the pond a few times, passing Priscilla and Merriweather, who were circling it in the opposite direction, and nodding gaily each time they did so. Then, by mutual, unspoken impulse, they began the execution of simple figures which gradually became more elaborate. As they finally paused, both breathless, David crowned his compliments with a question.

'You wouldn't like a race to wind up with, would you?'

'A race! What kind of a race?'

'The ice is solid on the brook a long way up beyond the dam and it's clear of snow to the end of the pasture. Priscilla and I raced on it last night.'

'Who beat?'

'I did.'

'Well, I'm not going to let you beat me!'

She was off with almost unbelievable speed, so fast indeed that her head start gave her considerable advantage. Emily skimmed over the ice, still keeping her lead, and she did not stop when she heard David begin shouting to her. She could not hear his words, only his voice, and she did not feel that words mattered. The only thing that mattered was that she was winning the race, that she could skate faster than David, that she was doing something Priscilla could not do. . . .

Then suddenly she was conscious that she had hurled herself against something hard and unyielding, something that hurt almost unbelievably, something against which she could not prevail. After one terrible moment of pain, the shock of it stunned her. Again she was conscious of David's voice, but not of his words, as she went down hard on the ice, twisting one foot underneath her.

He had tried to warn her of the solid fence, forming the boundary line between her aunt's land and the Randells', and he had been too late.

Almost instantly, everyone was crowding around her, questioning her solicitously and trying to lift her up. David, who had been close behind her, of course reached her first; however, Brian, for a man who was clumsy on skates, got there surprisingly soon and so did Priscilla and Merriweather; Roger and Elizabeth, who had just come down the hill with the hot chocolate, were delayed while they put on their shoe-skates again.

'Here, take a small swig of this,' Brian said helpfully, extracting a silver flask from his pocket and unscrewing the top. 'You've been telling all these people you're a convert to Irish whisky. Just show them now.'

Obediently, she tried to swallow, gagged and then tried again, as he continued to hold the flask against her trembling mouth. When the whisky had done its good work, she looked up at the anxious faces encircling her and tried to smile.

'I—I think I'm all right now,' she said. 'I'll just get on my feet and then——'

'Indeed and she'll do nothing of the sort, will she, Roger? That must have been a bad tumble you took, and you've a sprained ankle, if nothing worse. You couldn't skate now to save your soul, and you'd be crazy to try to walk. Roger and I will just make a chair for you, the way he's often seen me do for Queenie, and we'll have you back at the house in no time.'

'You two carry her part way and then let Merriweather and me take over,' David interposed.

But Brian brushed aside this suggestion. He had assumed control of the situation with such ease and ability that no one except David questioned his right to do so. The skaters started back towards the pond with Brian and Roger, carrying Emily, bringing up the rear, and the others casting backward glances to make sure everything was going all right. Brian laughed and joked as they went along; but though he was apparently still in good spirits, the accident had depressed everyone else and by common consent, the skating party was over. When the pond was reached, the shoe-skates were hurriedly changed for boots and the ascent of the hill began. Roger was very tired by this time and Emily knew it; the realization added to her distress. But she also knew that it would humiliate him to acknowledge publicly that he did not have Brian's powers of endurance and she kept turning her head towards him, whispering that she was sorry she had made so much trouble, while Brian, in a louder voice, kept saying, well now, they were almost there. They were both rewarded by the triumphant look on Roger's face when Emily was finally lowered on to the candle-flame bed.

'There! And didn't I say all the time we could do it?' Brian inquired with a broad grin. 'Now, if Miss Forbes has got some Epsom salts in the house, I bet it would do that foot of yours a lot of good to soak it in a strong, hot solution.... I don't suppose there's much chance of getting a doctor this late at night, is there, Miss Forbes?'

'Oh, country doctors are used to being called at all hours of day and night, but it is pretty late and I do have the Epsom salts. I think, between us, Roger and I could make Emily pretty comfortable for the night, if the rest of you will get out of the way and let us see what we can do for her. Then we'll send for Dr. Ives the first thing in the morning.'

An exchange of good nights was accompanied by many expressions of sympathy and assurances that, of course, Emily would soon be right as rain again. Then one by one, the unrelated guests departed, leaving Elizabeth in charge, with Roger to help her. Priscilla found that Olivia had already fallen asleep and that she was rather resentful at being waked; she reminded Priscilla of what she had said about northern lights bringing bad luck and Priscilla retorted, rather snappishly, that no one but a nincompoop would imagine that northern lights had anything to do with bumping into a fence—as far as that went, no one but a nincompoop would do that either. The exchange of comments in the 'sleigh' room was not any more complimentary. Once out of Emily's presence, Brian's apparent good humour evaporated and, in brief, ugly terms, he upbraided David as a damn fool and then some; David was obliged to remind him, in tones which were none the less angry because they were low and controlled, that the walls between the rooms were extremely thin and that doubtless Roger and Emily, and Miss Forbes too if she were still in there with them, would overhear every word that was being said. Only Mark Merriweather, in the peaceful isolation of the library, was wrapped in contentment, as he lay in his foldaway bed, which he had unfolded and made up himself; he sipped a nightcap and read a detective story which he put down from time to time, in order that his thoughts might wander more freely on the pleasant and promising nature of his courtship.

In spite of Mark Merriweather's geniality, breakfast was far from being a successful meal; and, as the doctor arrived before it was over, everyone felt impelled to await his report before beginning the day's sport. Nothing but a bad sprain, he announced cheerfully, when he came downstairs, to the rather grumpy group assembled around the library fire. He had bandaged Mrs. Field's ankle now, but the Epsom salts had been a good idea. Of course Mrs. Field was feeling the effects of her fall in other ways than merely because of the pain in her ankle; she had had quite a shock and he had given her a mild sedative. The quieter she kept, the better off she would be. A few days' rest in bed were essential; but these would fix her up, he was sure.

When the overworked, conscientious little doctor had left, Elizabeth, speaking with more sprightliness than she felt, said, 'What about snowshoeing?' Rather half-heartedly, it was agreed that snowshoeing would be a good plan. So Olivia and

Brian, followed by Priscilla and David, went tramping off across the pasture in the direction of the foothills. Elizabeth said she must stay at home to be near Emily and see to her household, in case anything were needed, and Merriweather wanted to finish the detective story he had begun the night before. When the others returned Elizabeth was a little vague on the subject of Emily's progress and Merriweather equally vague as to the outcome of the mystery; but both were in very good spirits, and the long walk through the snow seemed to have had a beneficent effect on the frayed tempers of the others. However, they had had all the exercise they wanted; they were going to spend the afternoon playing bridge.

'Why not skate again and postpone the bridge?' Elizabeth asked. 'It's a beautiful day again, but the barometer's falling. Tomorrow may not be so pleasant.'

Nobody wanted to skate, so the bridge table was brought out and the game went on and on. Everyone had eaten rather too heartily and eventually everyone felt stuffy in the warm room which, by this time, was hazy with cigarette smoke. There were no real outbursts of ill-humour, but it was evident that tempers were on the point of fraying again, so that when Elizabeth said there was to be a baked bean supper, followed by dancing at the village hall that night, and that perhaps some of her guests would like to go, the card players agreed with alacrity that it would be a good idea. But once more their hostess excused herself from going with them; Emily had slept a good deal during the day, but now she was restless; the sprained ankle needed to be soaked and rebandaged and Roger had no experience in such matters. Besides, Roger seemed very tired himself.

'And as I said, he had no business trying to carry Emily all that distance,' David reminded her. 'He wouldn't have done it, either, if you hadn't practically dared him to, Briny.'

'You're a great one to talk about dares. If you hadn't dared her to race with you, no one would have had to carry Emily. Not that I wasn't glad to do it.'

'I have a feeling those two aren't getting on so well together,' Elizabeth confided to Merriweather, when the foursome had departed for the dance. 'Or the two girls either. I'm terribly sorry. I thought they all seemed so congenial at first.'

'Well, anyway, Roger and Emily are congenial. Obviously, they're a very devoted couple. And you and I are pretty congenial too—aren't we, Beth?' He had never called her that before. No one had ever called her that before. She looked at him, colouring with surprise and pleasure. The name, as he said it, was more musical than she had ever thought her name, or any other, could be. While she was pondering on this, he said something that surprised and pleased her still more.

She told Emily about it the next day, after the soaking and the bandaging was over. The sheets had been changed too and Emily, who had been sponged off with tepid water and Old English Lavender and clad in a fresh nightgown, was lying back among her pillows, looking and feeling very much better than she had the day before—so much better, in fact, that if Elizabeth had not told her this exciting news, she might have found the hours dragging, for Brian, who had got up at an unearthly hour and gone off by himself to Mass at the Junction, had now persuaded Roger to come downstairs and play poker.

'Oh, Liz, I'm terribly glad! I can tell, just by looking at you, how happy you are! And I think Mark's just as nice as he can be! When are you planning to be married? Will you let me be your matron of honour? Are you going to give up teaching and live here all the time, the way you've wanted to?'

'How can I answer so many questions all at once? Nothing's decided yet—after all, it was only yesterday.... I'd love to have you for my matron of honour. Though, of course, at my age, it'll be a very quiet wedding.'

'What do you mean at your age! Honestly, Liz, you don't look a day over twenty-five at this moment.'

'Well, I am a day over twenty-five—a good many days. It must be the happiness you were talking about that makes me look younger. Because I *am* very happy. And I think we'll be married in June, as soon as college closes. About living here— well, I'm not sure. You know how I feel about Hollyhock Hill. I love the mountains and the river and the valley and the pasture and the brook and the foothills. I love the little white church with its lovely small spire in the village and the quiet old houses clustering around that and the village hall and the public library and the general store. I love the sort of people who live in those houses. They're sincere and intelligent and kindly. They do more thinking and more reading too, along with their hard physical labour, than almost anyone at Bryn Mawr. And yet they always have time to be neighbourly with each other. They're not neighbourly with me, but I think they would be if I lived here all the time, if they didn't still put me in the class with "summer people". I wish I could stay here all my life. I—I hope when my time comes, I can die here—in my own room, with the firelight flickering and the sunlight streaming across my bed. I want to be buried in the little cemetery on the hill, with white birches screening my grave. I want——'

She stopped, her voice trembling. But she had spoken after the manner of one in whom certain wellsprings, long sealed, had at last been released, and Emily knew that the reason Elizabeth could do this was because of Mark; apparently when a woman found that the man she loved also loved her, it transfigured her life in every way, it made of her a new being. Emily did not try to answer Elizabeth; for a moment, she could not. And then, after that moment, Elizabeth went on, speaking calmly and collectedly again.

'Well, to answer your question, of course I'd like to live here all the time and Mark thinks he would too. But he wouldn't be content to live on my money. We'd have to think up a way he could earn some—writing, perhaps, or teaching locally. And I'm not blind to the fact that Hollyhock Hill is terribly quiet— terribly remote. Perhaps, after a while, a normal, active man wouldn't be satisfied with such an uneventful, unstimulating life. On a day like this, for instance, you almost feel as if you weren't in a real world any longer.'

She rose and went over to the window. The dancers had reported that it was 'spitting snow' when they came in late the night before; now the snow was falling steadily, though very quietly. There was not a breath of wind and, as the flakes fell, they clung to the branches of the trees, transforming them into fairylike boughs, and mantled the ground with a covering smooth as white satin.

After a little, when Elizabeth left—to 'see to the housekeeping' as she put it, smilingly disregarding her niece's correction, 'to see Mark, you mean'—Emily drifted off to sleep. Once or twice she half waked, but the feeling of drowsiness, mingling, as it did, with the release from pain, was delicious; she did not try to combat it. When she finally roused to greater consciousness, she saw Roger sitting beside the bed and realized that the reason she saw him dimly was not only because she was still sleepy, but because the room was in semi-darkness. He leant over and kissed her.

'You slept straight through lunch, darling,' he said. 'Liz and I both came and looked at you several times, but you were

152

having such a wonderful sleep that we hated to disturb you—we knew you needed rest more than anything else. I'll see about getting you something to eat in just a minute. But first, I think I ought to tell you that I'm afraid I must start back to Boston. If I don't leave tonight, I might not be there by Tuesday morning. The storm's getting worse by the minute. Listen to that wind!'

Looking beyond Roger towards the window, Emily could see that the branches of the trees, which had been so beautiful in the quietude of their dark covering earlier in the day, were now waving about, dark and naked again.

'The barometer's still falling and the radio says that a blizzard's on the way,' Roger continued. 'I can't risk getting stuck here. That equity case of mine is the one that's coming up January second. You know how important that is to me personally, as well as to the firm.'

'Yes, I do. Well, I suppose it can't be helped. And I suppose I've got to lie here, like a good girl, until this miserable ankle's really well.'

'Of course you have. And you won't be lonely. I'm the only one who can't afford to take a chance. Mark's vacation isn't up until next week and neither Briny nor Dave has anything especially urgent on the calendar. Besides, Stanley Lyman's there to run errands, you know. It isn't like the old days.' They looked at each other, smiling. They could afford to smile now at the recollection of the days when Roger had been the errand boy. 'Briny's going to drive me to the Junction, right after an early supper,' he continued. 'And I'm not worried about you because I'm leaving you in such good hands. Even if the doctor can't get here tomorrow, Liz will look after you all right. And your ankle's ever so much better already, isn't it?'

'So much better that I'm sure I could walk on it, if I had to.'

'But you don't have to and you'd better not try. Promise!'

'All right. I promise.'

'Good! Now I'll go down and look into the food situation and then I'll come back and throw some things into my suitcase.'

He reappeared, five minutes later, carrying a well-laden tray. 'I've got to get busy on my packing right off,' he said. 'Brian thinks we'd better not stop for supper, that we might as well snatch something at the Junction.'

153

He talked disjointedly while he was throwing things into his suitcase and then bent over to kiss her fondly. David called from the hall below.

'Briny's shouting to you from outside. He can't seem to make you hear. But he's ready and raring to go.'

Roger snatched one more kiss, picked up his suitcase and hurried out of the room and down the stairs. The wind was blowing harder now, the panes in the old windows were rattling and there was a whistling sound in the chimney. Elizabeth said she would look in at bedtime and bring some hot Ovaltine and sandwiches. In the meanwhile, there were books within reach, and she noticed that Emily had brought some knitting; she would put that within reach too.

Emily thought the knitting was a good idea, and her thoughts as she knitted were, for the most part, agreeable. She was very pleased about Elizabeth and Mark. Emily counted up and realized that Liz was not forty yet, that she might even have one or two children. Emily had a momentary pang at the thought of her own continued childlessness, but it did not last. Of course she was going to have children eventually. It was just as well, saddled as she had been with Priscilla, that there was not a baby in the house too. . . .

She was glad that Priscilla was really launched now, that the girl had 'made' the Junior League and the Vincent Club and done all the other things for which Emily had been obliged to assume responsibility, because of Sue's shiftlessness. Well, she was not going to be responsible for Priscilla any longer; the girl could go her own wilful way. Not that it was doing her much good, at least as far as David was concerned. . . .

When Elizabeth came back, with the Ovaltine, and wished her Happy New Year, Emily was amazed to learn that it was so late. Elizabeth was delighted to find that she was feeling so much better, that she was not minding the storm. It was really very bad now, the worst one Elizabeth could remember. Brian had telephoned from the Junction; he and Roger had made it all right, but they had had hard work getting there, and he had decided that he would not try to come back to Hollyhock Hill that night.

'I'm afraid he won't have a very comfortable night. And I'm sorry he missed seeing the New Year in with the rest of us—we've been making popcorn and toasting marshmallows in front of the fire. Just the same, I think he was right to stay where he was.'

'So do I. And I don't believe Brian minds a little discomfort. Good night, Liz. I *know* your New Year's going to be happy.'

'Good night, dear. Don't hesitate to call if you need something. If you can't make me hear you, or the girls, I'm sure David would, and he could come and get me. Remember, he's right in the next room.'

'Yes, I remember.'

But she had not remembered until that minute. In the midst of all her pleasant meditation, she had not once thought of David, except in connection with Priscilla's futile pursuit of him and of her own easy victory over him—a victory which had really been worth the price of a bad fall and a painful ankle. For the first time, she had seen him when he was not self-assured and self-satisfied, but humble, contrite, alarmed. Even his wish to help Brian and Roger carry her had been set aside. All this had been extremely gratifying to her.

Now that her wish to bring him to such a pass had been fulfilled, however, and that Elizabeth had innocently reminded her of his nearness, she began to think of him in other ways, of his skating, which, as Priscilla had said, was so much like his dancing. Of his charm—of his magnetism—of his virility—of his kiss. . . .

She lay in the dark, thinking of all this, her heart thumping in her breast. Now there was no doubt at all in her mind that her thoughts were sinful. She knew they were. Because suddenly she realized that she wanted to have David kiss her again, that she wanted to have him make love to her. She thought she knew what his lovemaking would be like—vehement, possibly even violent. But the thought of such violence did not frighten her; it fascinated her. And this fascination had no kinship with her feeling for Roger. She did not even think of Roger in connection with her wickedness. Her shame was for her own sinful desire. . . .

She sat up in bed again, reaching in the dark for her dressing-gown. She did not want to turn on the light, for fear it would shine through the cracks in the old panelling of the door which connected her room with David's. If he saw a light, he might call to her and ask if anything was the matter and then, even if she said there was not. . . . No, she would not turn on the light.

She would grope her way to Elizabeth's room in the dark. She would try to walk in spite of her promise to Roger. It was better to break such a promise than to risk staying where she was, a moment longer, alone with her sinful thoughts. . . .

The snow was beating against the house, and suddenly it swirled down through the fireplace and across the room, in a series of small, glacial gusts. At the same moment, the door into David's room blew open. Emily now had only one thought: to reach the door and close it quickly. If David were already sleeping soundly, he would not know it had blown open. But if he woke and realized what had happened, he might think she had opened it. He might not think of the wind. He might believe that she had opened it as a sign. There was no telling what he might think—or what he might pretend he had thought. Or rather, it was all too easy to tell.

It did not occur to her that he would hear the door blow open at the same moment she did, that he would hasten to close it too, that he would hope to keep her from being wakened by its banging. But with a conviction as compelling as hers—that the door must be closed immediately—he had leapt out of bed and rushed towards it.

They reached it at the same moment, meeting on its threshold.

PART FOUR

AUGUST 1940 TO MARCH 1943

ROGER AND PELL

CHAPTER IX

Despite the disrespectful nickname of Artful Dodger, bestowed upon him by his juniors, Cleophas Mills was a man who always referred to himself as a worker, with the unmistakable implication that he alone bore the burden and heat of the day in the firm of Cutter, Mills and Swan. He deplored Mr. Cutter's preoccupation with rowing and Elliot Berkeley's enthusiasm about horses. He resented the fact that Brian had roused Roger's interest in baseball and that David went skating with Priscilla Forbes. Pell escaped his censure only because, with characteristice reserve, Pell never disclosed what sports, if any, attracted him.

Mr. Mills sat thinking irritably of all this one very warm day in August, when Mr. Cutter was disporting himself at Bar Harbour and Mr. Swan, disheartened by the impossibility of visiting England, had retreated to the Congressional Library to do research for a paper which he expected to deliver the following winter. Several matters had already come up since their departure, for which Mr. Mills had been obliged to accept the responsibility of decision, not to mention putting in considerable time; and though in theory all this was his delight, in practice it irked him greatly, Miss Riley, his secretary, had inconsiderately chosen the same time to fall ill; and Miss Smythe, Mr. Cutter's secretary, who was deputizing for her did not understand his ways or cater to his tastes, she could not even read his handwriting. He felt injured as well as irritated, and he had just decided that there was no use in killing himself, if no one else was going to do any work at all, when David Salomont unceremoniously entered his office.

'I'd like to have a few words with you, if you don't mind,' David said, drawing up a chair which he had not been invited to take.

'David, I'm in no condition for further conversations tonight,' said Mr. Mills. 'I'm feeling very far from well and I'm also very much upset. I'm starting for home immediately and I shall go straight to bed. I'm not at all sure that I'll be able to come to the office at all in the morning. But, if I am, possibly around eleven-thirty——'

'Just as you say, Mr. Mills. But I got a letter from the Adjutant-General of the Army in the afternoon mail and I thought——'

'The Adjutant-General of the Army!' repeated Mr. Mills angrily. 'Why on earth should the Adjutant-General of the Army be writing to you?'

'Well, I believe that the Judge Advocate-General requires the services of a few young lawyers who've had reserve officer training. You know I trained at the Seventh Regiment Armoury while I was at Columbia, and apparently my record's been examined and found satisfactory, both then and since. This is the second letter I've had from the Adjutant-General. The first one merely said that consideration was being given to ordering me to active duty in the Army of the United States, with my consent, for the period of one year, and requested that I reply, by endorsement thereon, advising as to my availability for subject duty. If further requested that I indicate the earliest practicable date of availability. I didn't think it was necessary to mention the first letter, because there was nothing definite about it. But of course I answered immediately that I would be available any time. I'm not sure just what my duties will be, but no doubt that'll be very quickly explained as soon as I get to Washington.'

'As soon as you get to Washington!' Mr. Mills shouted, the echo much angrier this time. 'May I ask what made you think you were free to start off for Washington at the drop of a hat, just because an interfering old busybody like an Adjutant-General writes you a couple of letters? They're probably nothing but forms, anyway. No doubt the clerk who mailed them out with several thousand others expected you'd just drop them in the waste-basket.'

'They don't sound that way to me. I brought the second one along, so that you could see for yourself what's in it.'

David extended the envelope and Mr. Mills snatched it from his hand.

'You'll have to say you can't go, David,' Mr. Mills said authoritatively when he had read through the letter. 'If Elliot Berkeley weren't deserting us at this crucial time, of course I'd be glad to release you. But he's just told me he's leaving on Saturday.'

'I'm sorry, Mr. Mills, but I don't seem to feel the same way about this that you do,' David said courteously, 'I've already said that I will go. I did that after I got the first letter. What's more, I think I ought to get to Washington as soon as I can. I think I'm needed there.'

'You're needed right here. We can't lend our juniors out to every pompous government official who suddenly decides to enlarge his department.'

'I'm sorry, Mr. Mills,' David said again, still speaking very courteously. 'I don't like to leave without your approval.'

'It isn't a question of my approval. It's a question of my consent and I won't give it.'

'Then I'm afraid I'll have to go without it.'

'If you do that, you'll leave for good.'

'Do you really mean that, Mr. Mills?'

For a moment Mr. Mills hesitated. He was aware that he had gone too far; David Salomont was not only a very brilliant and promising lawyer, he was a singularly personable, gifted and versatile young man; and these attributes of his were great assets to the firm. If his connection with it was severed, this might well represent a great loss, not only now, but in the future, for he was bound to make a success of almost anything he undertook. But, having taken a stand, Mr. Mills could not, with dignity, retreat from it.

'Yes, I really mean that,' he said tersely.

'Very well, sir. I'll try to leave everything in good order. Shall I discuss unfinished business with Mr. Fletcher?'

'You'd better sleep on this, David.'

'I would, ordinarily. But this doesn't look to me like an ordinary situation. And it isn't as if I didn't know the rest of the boys would take care of things all right. They're a fine bunch. Good night, sir.'

'Good night,' muttered Mr. Mills.

Without waiting to sign the letters he had dictated that morning, or to put his cluttered desk into even a semblance of order, Mr. Mills picked up the brief case which he always carried from force of habit, whether it contained anything of importance or not, and hurried out of his office on the very heels of his insubordinate junior. He was still very angry, and he was also in a state of amazement not untinged by humiliation. Within an hour, two persons whose activities he was supposed to control had eluded him, and one of them had successfully defied him. Nothing like this had ever happened to him before; and when Roscoe Cutter had left him in charge of the office, the senior partner had certainly not foreseen that such an emergency would arise, or that he, Cleophas Mills, would not be able to cope with any that did. He knew that Cutter, who probably could have done no better himself, would blame his partner for the turn things had taken, and he dreaded the long-distance call which he knew he must make without delay. But he was determined to escape first; in his disturbed state, he visualized the entire staff as barging in upon him and forcing him to face unpleasant facts of one sort or another. He rushed down the corridor without glancing into the juniors' offices, and rang the elevator bell, having omitted his usual brief good night to Cora Donlon, who had been carefully protecting him from calls all day and who still sat patiently at the switchboard. Once in a taxi, he began to breathe more freely, for there he was free from intrusion; but its crawling progress through the congested evening traffic added to his sense of irritation. After reaching his suite at the Puritan, he took a stiff drink, which helped a little, though not as much as he thought it should; and the dinner he ordered from room service and swallowed in solitary state was tepid and tasteless. He knew that once he had finished it, he could no longer put off the evil moment of telephoning Roscoe Cutter.

A week from the following Monday, the working day began with a strangely altered set-up in the firm of Cutter, Mills and Swan. Brian was engulfed in minute books and stock records, and he was doing this intensive study in the pleasant office recently vacated by Elliot Berkeley. The severity of his labours was relieved not only by the comfort in which he worked, but by the agreeable consciousness that, as soon as the preparation of new partnership papers had been completed and new signatures affixed, he would be a junior partner in an important law firm—before he was thirty. He dwelt on all this with pardonable pride, both in his private thoughts and in his companionable talks with Pell and Roger, which he usually began by saying, with a broad grin, 'Now any time I can do something for you juniors, just tell your Uncle Briny. He hasn't forgotten that he was young and struggling once himself.'

161

'All right,' Roger retorted one day. 'The poor young strugglers, yourself among them, have said over and over again that it would help them to bear their lot with better grace if the big shots would only say it was a matter of regret that they didn't have much to offer their juniors, in the way of creature comforts, but that their plans for the future included improvement along these lines. We've gone on, hoping against hope, but those improvements have never materialized. Of course, Pell has moved up to your cubbyhole now and I've moved to his—with Dave gone, I was able to take two intermediary steps forward, instead of one, thank the Lord. But the big shots don't deserve any credit for that.' He paused briefly, dwelling on the change brought by David's departure, with a degree of satisfaction that was not caused only by the fact that he himself now had a better place to work in; he was also doing this work without being needled in one way or another; and though neither of them had put the feeling into words, he was aware that, for some unknown reason, Brian shared his satisfaction to a certain degree. Only Pell had been genuinely sorry to have their brilliant and engaging associate leave them. 'What I'm getting at is this,' Roger continued. 'Couldn't you suggest to the Artful Dodger that a few partitions might come down? After all, he keeps telling us that he hasn't got a prayer of finding another junior this fall, that we've got to put our shoulders to the wheel, et cetera, et cetera. So why not have the four cubbyholes made over into small offices, neat but not gaudy? Pell could actually get two windows that way; and though I wouldn't have but one, I'd like to see poor Stanley get a few extra feet too. I've got just as good a memory as you have, Uncle Briny.'

'I think you've got something there, my boy—not just about the matter of money, but about the matter of partitions. I'll take it up with the Artful Dodger the first thing in the morning— around eleven-thirty. Of course I'll check with Miss Riley first, to make sure nothing unexpected has come up,' Brian remarked, grinning more broadly than ever. 'And if he tells me he doesn't see how he'll ever get the work done, what with the scarcity of materials and labour, not to mention the exorbitant price of everything, I'll ask him did he never hear about the firm of Collins and Lenahan and what is the use of that close connection if you never get the good of it, begorra?'

Brian was as good as his word and his word accomplished wonders. There was no use in doing a patchy job, he said, now that they were started on it. Mr. Mills winced and groaned as the work progressed, but his actual protests were feeble. If he had been driven to it, he would have been obliged to admit that the charges made by Collins and Lenahan were reasonable and the improvements on the premises very great. In an unbelievably short time, Pell and Roger were settled in more commodious and attractive quarters than any juniors hitherto associated with Cutter, Mills and Swan; and thanks to Roger's reference to memories, Stanley Lyman's comfort and convenience had not been overlooked in the course of the improvements. He was most touchingly grateful, especially when he learned that Roger was responsible for the betterment of his lot; and he was quite content to run the firm's legal errands, without looking for anything more important to come his way. As for Pell and Roger, the now adjacent position of their offices almost automatically lent itself to a furtherance of their already congenial relations and the community of their interests. Besides, they, no less than Brian, both had cause for satisfaction in these days and this served to promote harmonious feeling, as well as to stimulate earnest endeavour. Their offices were now side by side, for Pell had been moved into Brian's cubicle, and Roger into Pell's; so that they kept dropping in on each other to discuss their respective cases and, almost automatically, they went out to lunch together. Sometimes Brian went with them, but more often he snatched a sandwich while he studied his minute books.

Meanwhile, David had not only taken leave of the firm, but had also been engaged with various other leave-takings.

When his interview with Mr. Mills was over, he returned to his cubicle, closed the door and settled down to several hours of hard work. It was nearly nine o'clock before he finally locked the drawers of his desk, having arranged the few remaining papers on top of it in neatly clipped piles, labelled with care for easy reference in the morning. The other offices were long since deserted, the gloom of the long corridor unrelieved except for a glimmer from the reception hall beyond. But, as he stepped out into this, he saw that Cora Donlon was still seated beside her quiet and unwinking switchboard, her normally busy hands lying loosely clasped in her lap, the precise parting in her well-waved hair seemingly preternaturally white against its darkness because of her bent head.

'For heaven's sake, Cora!' David exclaimed. 'What are you

doing here at this hour?'

She raised her head and looked at him with swimming eyes. It was obvious, from the redness of her swollen face, that she had been crying for a long while.

'It isn't true, is it?' she asked brokenly.

'Isn't what true?' David inquired. With characteristic quickness, he had now guessed why Cora was still at the switchboard and why she was upset; and, like most men, he was antagonized and not moved to sympathy by the sight of tears. But, having recovered from his first astonishment, he spoke calmly and rather coolly.

'That you're going away,' Cora sobbed. 'Please don't be angry with me, Mr. Salomont. I simply couldn't bear the thought of——'

'I'm not angry, but I'm slightly annoyed and rather puzzled. I always thought you were a very sensible girl, not at all the type who would cry over a silly rumour or wait around for hours to spring questions on a tired, hungry man.'

'But it isn't a rumour. You've as good as said yourself it was true. And I didn't mean to annoy you, Mr. Salomont, really I didn't. I just couldn't make up my mind to go home until you told me. But I will now. I know you must be tired and hungry. It was very thoughtless of me to delay you.'

She rose, reaching for her hat and her handbag, which lay on the small table beside her, and walked towards the elevator, without pausing to apply fresh make-up. David stepped in front of her.

'See here,' he said, 'you're not going out looking like that, are you? I've got a much better plan. Why don't you come home with me instead? That is, after you've fixed your face. Because you're mistaken in supposing the elevator man won't notice. If you go away from here looking like Niobe, when there's no one else left in the building but you and me, he'll imagine the worst, even if we carefully space our separate departures half an hour apart. And I'm sure neither of us wants to stay here that much longer. Come on, let's see if you can put on make-up in the same record time that you can put through calls.'

Cora hesitated. Her mother had cautioned her that she should never, under any circumstances, go except as one of a group to a bachelor's establishment. However, her hesitation was only momentary. David had several times taken her out to dinner at pleasant and inconspicuous restaurants where the food was excellent, and had been to her apartment, where she had done her best to make ready-mixed drinks and canned products attractive and appetizing. But he had never before invited her to go home with him; and the grapevine, which Miss Smythe so carefully nurtured, had brought her numerous alluring accounts of the *décor*, the service and the cuisine at 40 Lime Street. These accounts had not only piqued her curiosity, they had aroused her envy of the fortunate beings who were encouraged to share these delights with David Salomont whenever they chose. Among these privileged persons—also according to rumour—was Miss Priscilla Forbes; and this young lady had returned to the Cape, as soon as the social season was over, with the flat announcement that she was through with Boston for good and all. Cora could not understand how any girl in her senses could be so indifferent to her opportunities. Heartened by the engaging smile, which had displaced the abnormally blank expression with which David had first regarded her, she swiftly applied powder and lipstick, smoothed her still-tidy hair, and assured herself that she had tilted her hat at its most becoming angle. She was just drawing on her spotless white fabric gloves when the elevator, which David had summoned, appeared to receive them.

'It was awfully good of you to stay this evening and help me out, Miss Donlon,' David said as they stepped inside. 'I don't know how I could possibly have managed, if you hadn't, with all that stuff which was suddenly dumped on my desk.' Then, as the doors of the elevator opened to the ground floor, he nodded, first to the operator and next to her. 'So long, Tom. Don't let them treat you as if you were a lawyer and make you work until all hours. . . . Good night, Miss Donlon. Thanks again.'

Cora understood that she was to turn in the opposite direction from the one David took, and though she did this with no apparent vacillation, her progress towards the side door, where she knew he would rejoin her, was not an altogether happy one. She knew that if he had been escorting Miss Priscilla Forbes, he would have done so not merely openly, but proudly; and the very fact that his technique with her was different indicated some cause for uneasiness, as well as some cause for resentment. She had practically decided to tell him that she had changed her mind and was going straight home after all when she was aware of his hand lightly placed under her elbow and of his easy guidance towards the exit.

'We're in luck; there's a taxi right now,' he said, hailing it;

and, once they were inside, he added, 'Too bad the parking problem's so bad. If it weren't, I'd go to and from the office in my roadster—I can't seem to acquire the Boston passion for walking, just for the sake of walking.... Well, all that'll be different in Washington—like lots of other things. No doubt I'll have a parking place allotted to me.... But I'll tell you what: we'll take a spin around Jamaica Pond later on, if you like. A pleasant breeze always seems to spring up there in the evening, for some reason. You haven't seen my new roadster, have you?'...

By the following afternoon, everybody at Cutter, Mills and Swan had learned, through legitimate channels, that David Salomont was leaving the firm and, one by one, different members of the staff had come to his cubicle, in the wake of Cyrus Fletcher, to express their regret. These visits, while gratifying—especially in the case of Mr. Fletcher—constituted a series of interruptions which seriously interfered with David's purpose of putting everything in the best possible order, in the least possible time. In this light, he rather resented them; as far as he was concerned, his association with Cutter, Mills and Swan was already relegated to the realm of past experiences. Nevertheless, he did not fail to notice that, whereas Pell paid him a long and almost ceremonial visit, Brian merely stuck his head in the door with the terse remark, 'Hear you're off to Washington to take charge of things there. Hope they appreciate you,' and, up to five o'clock, Roger had not been near him. David found himself involuntarily dwelling on this omission, and wondering whether it had any special significance, when Roger, looking even more wilted and dishevelled than he usually did at the end of a warm day, appeared on the threshold.

'I've been trying to get in here all the afternoon,' he said apologetically. 'But I've been going around in circles. That Jerry Donovan case is certainly something! You know the background of it, I suppose?'

'I don't believe I do,' David answered, in a tone which, civil as this was, unmistakably indicated that he had neither the time nor the inclination to hear it now.

'Well, I won't go into it,' Roger responded. He had not failed to catch the implication; but, as a matter of fact, he had not wanted to tell David about the Jerry Donovan case. He talked to Pell about that and Pell was always a ready listener; he had no need of any other. Besides, he was very tired; he had only wanted to explain what he feared might have appeared like a discourtesy. 'Of course I felt like telling you how much you'd be missed,' he went on, determined not to take umbrage at David's attitude. 'I know you've been told that so many times already today that you must be tired of hearing it. Just the same, I wanted to say it too.'

'Well, thanks a lot,' David said. Roger Field really was a well meaning kind of guy; it was a pity that his good intentions did not prevent him from being a blunderer and a bore.

'Also,' Roger persisted, 'I wanted to ask you if you wouldn't come up to the house some evening before you left, I know you've got a lot ahead of you, but I thought perhaps we could have some kind of a little farewell party that you'd enjoy. If you would——'

'It's nice of you to think of it, but I do have a lot to clean up here. I expect to work late every evening this week. I told that bastard, Mills, I'd try to leave everything in good order and I meant it. You know yourself what it's like to break off in the middle of a job. It usually means you have to start all over again, at the beginning. And it's also usually impossible to tell just when you'll finish it.'

'Of course, if you feel that way——'

'I'm sorry, but I do. However, if you'd let me, I'd just like to drop in on you some evening after I *have* finished. Then I wouldn't be under any strain. I could stretch out in a big chair beside the fountain in that pretty little garden Emily's made and imagine I was one of my ancestors back in Granada—well, anyway, I'd feel just as important and know I was in just as pleasant a place. And we could have a good long talk and a couple of nightcaps and still get in a decent night's rest.'

'All right. Since that's what you'd prefer.... It doesn't seem like showing you any special courtesy and we'd like to; but it *is* pleasant in the garden these summer evenings. I'll tell Emily to expect you. We're nearly always home—it seems more sensible than to go tearing around looking for a better place. There just isn't any. Good night, Dave. And best of luck.'

'Good night. Thanks again.'

Roger went out, leaving the door open, as he had found it. Nobody kept doors closed these days; it was much too warm. Just the same, open doors led to distractions and David wanted none of these; he wanted to concentrate. As he picked up the brief again, he could hear Roger's footsteps in the corridor, Roger's good night to Cora at the switchboard, Roger's greeting to the operator as the elevator door slid open; and these sounds were unwelcome out of all proportion to their apparent importance. The footsteps were slow, almost dragging; they suggested extreme weariness. Of course the warm weather and the lack of a proper vacation could be partly responsible for that. In addition to his fortnight at Camp Edwards, which certainly could not be classed as a holiday, Roger had been offered only one week's absence from the office, which he and Emily had spent at Old Mrs. Forbes' place in Dublin; and doubtless various problems regarding the model dairy had been laid before him there. Even so, he should not be as tired as he seemed. David himself was not in the least tired, and he had not been given a proper vacation either, because of the extra time he had taken off the summer before in Venezuela. If Roger were weary now, when the office was fully staffed, he would certainly be continually exhausted after the almost simultaneous departure of Elliott Berkeley and David Salomont. David could visualize Roger as he would look if he were continually exhausted, and it was not a cheering picture. . . .

Weary or not, of course Roger would have to stop and say good night to Cora. Courtesy was part of his code; he would be polite on his deathbed. David, who could, when he chose, be charming to a degree which Roger never could hope to achieve, could also be brusque when it suited his purpose, or completely neglectful of all amenities when he was not in the mood to observe them. He had been brusque with Cora the previous evening, before he decided that it would be better if he were kind. Roger would not have acted as he did, either to begin with or later on. He would have been moved by Cora's tears and he would have tried, immediately, to comfort her. However, he would not have forgotten for one moment that he was married to Emily. But then, Cora would not have cried if she had found out that Roger was going away; the news would have left her entirely indifferent. So, after all, there was no sense in wasting time on reflecting how Roger would have acted under the conditions which confronted David.

A little smile played around David's mouth as he recalled these. He had told Cora the truth when he said she was helping him to pass a pleasant evening; once she had stopped crying, she had been just the sort of companion he required then—not only undemanding, but touchingly grateful for whatever attention he chose to show her; he had been faintly amused by such humble appreciation. The degree of admiration which his establishment had evoked, and the terms in which she had expressed this, were pleasantly amusing too; he had not realized that such naïveté still existed, in a grown girl. It was rather refreshing. So was the way in which she responded to his suggestion that they should go for a drive around Jamaica Pond before he took her home. Obviously it did not occur to her that the drive might take them farther afield, or that it might serve any ulterior purpose. For a girl who had been on her own since a tender age, there was still something surprisingly virginal about Cora, something surprisingly sweet. . . .

All this was delightful to recall. But, just as Roger's courteous good night to Cora had revived these agreeable recollections, so the sliding doors of the elevator revived the mental picture of the operator's expression when David had thanked Cora for staying late to help him at the office and said he would be seeing her in the morning. He would not put it past an elevator operator to develop a sixth sense about such sayings, which he must have heard voiced not infrequently. It might be just as well to give the man a farewell present when he, David, left for good. Not enough to look like bribery or concern about blackmail, of course; but just enough to make sure that Cora would not be annoyed by any insinuating remarks or surly demands after he had gone. Though, as far as that went, he thought it was quite possible that Cora might soon be leaving too, that he really could find a place for her in Washington. . . .

Hang it all, he did not seem to be making much progress with that brief. Instead, the train of thought which Roger had evoked went on and on. David found himself following those slow footsteps across the Common. It would not occur to Roger to take a taxi home, no matter how tired he was; like most Bostonians, he would walk as a matter of course. Pell would walk with him and they would talk about the Jerry Donovan case; he and Pell were seeing more and more of each other these days. And when he reached home, he would find the house—darkened to keep it cool—shorn of its rugs and draperies, with its ornaments put away and its furniture slip-covered in colourless linen, because all this was also in conformity with established Boston custom. But at least he would not go on over the crest of Beacon Hill, like Pell, and end up in a small suffocating tenement. . . .

Apparently Pell had nothing to live on but his inadequate salary, or he would have left that dingy district long before. No influential relative had ever demanded that he should be put on a percentage basis and, of course, that skinflint, Mills, would never have done it of his own accord; and apparently Pell was supporting not only himself, but the shrewish, middle-aged woman and the beautiful girl with whom he lived and who had figured in the suit which got him his position. Of course the beautiful girl was his mistress—if she had been his wife or his sister or his cousin, he would not have been so silent, not to say secretive, about her. As far as that went, there were plenty of places where he would not have felt it incumbent on him to be silent, much less secretive, about an illicit relationship. But Boston was not among them. . . .

Doubtless Pell did not begrudge what it cost him to keep his mistress, in spite of his meagre means. David had seen her, once or twice, and he was more than ready to admit that a mistress with a face and figure like hers would compensate for a good deal—though not, as far as he was concerned, for living in a tenement. But then, he would have found some way of making enough money to get out of the tenement, which, for some strange reason, Pell had not.

But his errant thoughts had now taken him past the point to which Roger's slow progress would finally have brought him. He would not have gone on with Pell to the tenement on the farther side of Joy Street, no matter how deep they might have been in conference when they reached the crest of the Hill, for the simple reason that Pell would not have invited him to do so; and though Roger very probably would have asked Pell to step in for a drink, the chances were that Pell would have gone straight on home to his beautiful mistress. So after Roger had washed up, in the ground-floor lavatory under the front stairs, he would have continued on to the garden which Emily had made out of the back yard and he would have found her there.

David's thoughts had skirted the subject of Emily for some time, but now they were definitely focused on it. He did not consider her colourless, as he did her husband. He had been attracted to her from the first; and the consciousness that she had also been immediately attracted to him struck him as a feather in his cap, considering both her conservative upbringing and her newly wedded state. Her unfeigned indignation at the first advances he had made to her, and her refusal to compromise with her conscience by seeing him afterwards as if nothing had happened, also impressed him favourably; conquests which were too easy had very little significance, and the compliance which seemed rather touching in a girl like Cora, would have seemed merely cheap to him, in a girl like Emily. Even after their every chance meeting resulted in a passage-at-arms, he found this stimulating rather than annoying; in spite of the fact that he could always carry off the honours in an argument, he could not do this so easily as to make it tame; and he recognized the mutual antagonism which became stronger and stronger with the passage of time, as a vital element in mutual attraction.

When he had told Emily that some day he would really make love to her and that she would be glad to have him, he had meant it; and over and over again afterwards he had dwelt on the vision of her first instinctive recoil, of her gradual acquiescence and of her ultimate rapturous response. Yet, when fortuitous circumstance had fairly flung her into his arms, he had not seized upon the chance to make the vision a reality.

When he and Emily had met, on New Year's Eve, at the threshold of the door which connected their rooms, the actions themselves had been simple enough and seemingly spontaneous. He had immediately put his arm around her and he had also instantly realized that, if he had not, she would have fallen; she was already reaching towards the jamb for further support. Then he remembered her sprained ankle and knew that it must be hurting her horribly.

'Hold on to that jamb for a moment and let me get both my arms underneath you,' he said. 'Then put your arms around my neck and I'll have you back in bed before you can say Jack Robinson.'

'The door——' she began.

'Don't you worry about the door. With this gale, I'm surprised it wasn't blown right off its hinges. But I'll take care of that as soon as I get you fixed up. Now then ... Who says I can't make a chair, without anyone to help me too. And I can make a pretty good job of carrying you by myself. I'm glad of a chance to prove it to you!'

She had obediently encircled his neck, as soon as she was aware of his two supporting arms, but he could feel the trembling, first of her fingers, and then of her whole body. The room was bitterly cold; probably she was half frozen, in her lacy nightgown and her silk robe. This conviction was strengthened

171

when he realized that her teeth were chattering too. She was not the sort of girl to be frightened by a storm—or by a man. But somehow he resented the quivering of her body; strangely, it robbed this of allure. When he laid her down on her bed, so easily as to indicate that it had cost him no effort to carry her, he would not even have kissed her if it had not seemed abrupt to leave her without some sort of a casual caress. But the kiss was only a light one on her brow.

'If I remember rightly, you were told to stay in that bed for three or four days and give that ankle of yours a chance to get well,' he said, looking down at her in much the same way that he might have looked at a child of whom he was fond, but whom he found rather troublesome. 'I hereby charge you not to get up again until that nice little village doctor gives you permission. If you hear any sounds that frighten you, ring that cowbell Liz left with you. It ought to wake the dead; certainly it would wake her. But I promise you the door won't blow open again. It's banging isn't going to be one of the things that might disturb you.'

Though David was by nature an analyst, he was still balked, nearly eight months after the occurrence of this episode, in his attempts to resolve the reasons for his behaviour. Emily's trembling could not in itself have been responsible for this, though it was undoubtedly a contributing factor; and akin to it was the crippled condition which was also vaguely distasteful to him. As a perfectionist, even more than as a sensualist, he instinctively felt that bodily beauty should be unblemished to insure enjoyment of it against disillusionment. The conquest he had visualized had been one of a proud and glowing woman, not a shivering, broken one.

There was perhaps another explanation for his withdrawal. He had never yet experienced a sense of guilt after the satisfaction of any appetite and it did not seem likely that he would now begin to do so; but there was a disturbing, though slight, possibility of this. He might successfully dismiss the thought of Roger most of the time, but he could not do so all of the time, and Roger, whom he might designate as colourless, he still could not designate as negligible. He had long since guessed, of course, that Roger did not like him, and why; but the dislike had not prevented the plodding, tired man from coming in to tell David that he would be missed, from offering him farewell hospitality

172

and from wishing him Godspeed. There was something so essentially fine about Roger Field that it illumined his otherwise unprovocative person and all the humdrum tasks he performed; it also illumined his attitude towards his wife and his relationship with her. If David beclouded this attitude, or undermined this relationship, the consciousness that he had done so might be persistently disturbing.

Even if there had been no question of Roger, there remained the question of Emily herself. There was no doubt whatsoever that if she were unfaithful to her husband—and that was the way she would put it—however great her transitory rapture, her permanent sense of guilt would be much greater. And if the act of adultery were repeated, the consciousness of grave culpability would not only soon be almost unbearable, as far as she was concerned; it would also communicate itself to David, in such a way as to destroy all pagan delight in possessing her.

Little by little, he had come to at least one definite realization: if he and Emily had allowed themselves to be engulfed in mutual passion, they would almost inevitably have succumbed to it again and yet again. Their attraction for each other was too strong to find easy or swift appeasement; indeed, it was quite possible that it might grow stronger and stronger with every secret meeting, for a long time. Conceivably, under the right tutelage, Emily might become a *grande amoureuse*—indeed, the more he reflected on it, the more clearly David could see her potentialities in this role, which he believed her grandmother had played with both daring and magnificence. But she could never be a light-of-love; though she might be sinful, she could not be casual. Perhaps some submerged instinct had warned him of this and kept him from kindling flames which he could not extinguish....

Yet, as he sat thinking of all these things, that warm August evening after Roger had left him, he suddenly knew that it would be very hard to say good-bye to Emily. As long as they were in the same city, where it was possible to seek her out at any time, it had not been too hard to resist the temptation of doing so. Besides, for a period, he had been inclined to regard the abortive quality of their meeting on New Year's Eve as more or less significant; whatever the reasons, and however sound, that he had not taken her that night, the fact remained that she had not proved irresistible to him on an occasion when everything had conspired to make it easy for him to do so. Therefore

173

he had argued, more or less successfully, that she must have began to lose her attraction for him, and of course that was all to the good; any emotional involvement would have been very awkward. But now the image which rose before him in the gathering twilight was unexpectedly lovely. It was the portrait of a lady that he saw, highly bred, delicately nurtured, intelligent, sensitive and refined; but it was also the revelation of a woman ready for love and ripe for motherhood, whose capacities for great emotional experience had never yet been fully tested and whose barrenness was a reproach and a waste.

'Good God!' David exclaimed, unaware that he was speaking aloud until after he had done so. 'Am I falling in love with that girl? Really in love? Have I fallen in love with her already? Is *that* the reason I couldn't ...'

It was unbelievable and yet, apparently, it was true. The feeling which now swept through him bore no resemblance to any which had previously caused him to embark on a passionate adventure. If anything, it was stronger; but it was also compounded of elements which had hitherto been altogether alien to him in connection with passion: tenderness, respect, admiration, sympathy, understanding, a longing to protect as well as to possess, an awareness that integrity must be the cornerstone of any enduring relationship, a consciousness that physical communion was incomplete unless it were beautified with spiritual communion.

How long he sat alone in the darkness, grappling with his new-found knowledge and his overwhelming emotion, he never knew. But when he finally left the deserted office and went home to his empty house, it was with the conviction that before he left the city he must see Emily and tell her what was in his heart. He could not leave her believing he did not care. He would not leave her without telling her of the strange revelation that had come to him of a new heaven and a new earth.

CHAPTER X

He found her, as he had hoped he might, in the little garden and, as he had not dared to hope, alone. Although he did not make an informal entrance, the way Brian would have done, through the side gate, Ellie, who answered his ring at the front door, admitted him and led him straight through the house, without announcing him. He had been there so often in the past that she took his welcome for granted. He had impressed Ellie very favourably from the beginning.

Emily who was stretched out in a long chair, did not rise or even turn when the door from the basement opened, and it was obvious that she had at first assumed the intruder upon her solitude was only Ellie, bent on some trivial errand. Then, as the sound of his footsteps betrayed the newcomer as a man, she looked up and swung her feet to the ground.

'Why, David!' she said in a startled voice. Then, quickly regaining her composure, she added conventionally, 'How are you? Won't you sit down? What can I offer you?'

'I'm very well, and I'd like very much to sit down,' he said, drawing up a chair and suiting his action to his words. 'But I don't care for a drink just now, thanks. Perhaps a little later.... Didn't Roger tell you that he very kindly offered to give a party for me, and that I said I knew I'd have to work late at the office every night, so I'd rather just drop in, like this?'

'Yes, he did. But I don't think he expected you quite so soon—or else he forgot to tell you that this is his regular drill night.'

'I see.... Yes, he did forget to tell me. Or rather, I suppose he thought I knew which night he drilled. I should have, he's been doing it so long now. But I didn't.'

As if she felt that nothing further needed to be said on the subject, or indeed on any other, for the moment, she relapsed into silence. David felt that she had provided him with an opening, which, while not ideal, at least made it possible for him to approach, without too great abruptness, the subjects he wanted to discuss.

'I didn't deliberately choose an evening when I knew I'd find you alone, Emily, but I have hoped there would be one, some time before I went away, because I wanted to have a talk with you, and it isn't the kind of talk to have in the presence of a third person. *Any* third person.'

'You mean what's generally called a heart-to-heart talk?'

'Exactly. In a very literal sense.'

'Do you think there's any reason why you and I should have such a talk?'

'Yes, I do. I thought so before, and the way you ask that question makes me a good deal surer of it. I don't want to leave Boston feeling there's any misunderstanding between us.'

'What makes you think there is?'

'I don't *think* there is. I *know* there is. I'm surer of it every minute.'

Again Emily did not answer.

'I told you once, Emily, that some time I was going to make love to you again, really make love to you, and that you'd like it.'

'I'm sorry, but if you start talking that way to me, David, I'll have to go into the house. I can't stay here and listen to you.'

'This is important to all of us. Please, Emily! I'm not going to try to make love to you. I'm not going to say anything that will make you feel you're disloyal to your husband while you're listening. I just want to explain certain things to you. Won't you even give me a chance to explain? I won't take any longer than I have to.'

She had already risen when she said that she could not stay and listen to him. Now something in his tone, more than in his actual words, impelled her to sit down again.

'It's like this,' he said, seizing upon her hesitation. 'I did mean what I said when I told you that some day I'd make love to you. I did think perhaps that I could get away with it, once anyway, perhaps often. I won't go into all the reasons why I thought so—probably you can make a pretty fair guess, when it comes to that. I don't think it's necessary for me to explain what I meant by "love-making", either. That's beyond the point anyway. The point is, I was mistaken in what I said. I found I couldn't.'

176

'You mean you found you didn't want to.'

She was speaking scornfully now and, once more, she made a slight movement, as if she were about to leave him. Again the swiftness and sincerity with which he spoke deterred her.

'I want you to get this absolutely straight, Emily. I didn't want to the night of the storm. You're right, that far. I didn't want to take advantage of a series of circumstances like your accident and Roger's departure and a banging door to stage the setting for a glorious adventure. It wouldn't have *been* a glorious adventure under those conditions. Can't you see that?'

She turned her head away and, for the first time, he leaned forward and reached for her hand. She did not draw it away, but there was no responsive pressure as he took it in his.

'Can't you?' he persisted. 'Don't say yes, if you can't; but don't say no, either, if you don't mean it.'

He had to wait for his answer, but when it came, it was the answer he wanted. 'Yes,' she said at last, 'yes, I see that. I didn't before, but I do now.'

'And don't you feel better, since you do understand?'

Again she hesitated, but it was obvious that the hesitation was occasioned because she was turning the question over in her mind and not because she was trying to evade the issue. Then she looked up at him. 'Yes,' he said, with a note in her voice that was very like surprise, 'yes, I do feel better. I suppose—well, I suppose my pride was hurt when you left me the way you did. You'd told me you wanted me, and I believed you; and then when I realized you didn't—that you didn't want to *enough* to take advantage of a situation like that one, I couldn't help thinking. . . .'

'After that night on Hollyhock Hill,' David continued, 'I began trying to think things through. I myself didn't understand very well, at first, why I'd instinctively acted the way I had and I wanted to find out. I also wanted to find out what—well, what the *whole* score was. I think I've done it, but it's been a long, slow process. And a hard one. Because I didn't stop loving you, Emily. I began.'

She looked up at him with the same startled expression that had marked her greeting and drew a quick breath. But she did not try to free her hand.

'It wasn't love before,' he went on with convincing earnestness. 'It was strong mutual attraction at first and then—we're going to be absolutely honest with each other, aren't we?—it was something much more powerful and passionate than that. Something that's a normal and vital part of love between a man and a woman. But only a part. By itself, it isn't really love.'

'No, I suppose not,' Emily said in a low voice.

'Don't misunderstand me now, either. When I really began to love you, that vital part of my feeling didn't disappear. Nothing's happened to weaken it. But it took its natural place among all the other elements that make up love. And when it did that I realized we mustn't let our strong mutual attraction get out of hand. I realized how you'd feel—afterwards. How *I'd* feel afterwards, if I knew you were weighted down by a sense of guilt on account of me. I couldn't bring shame and suffering to you, Emily. And you would have been ashamed, you would have suffered.'

'Yes,' Emily said, almost in a whisper.

'So I—take back what I told you before. I'm not going to make love to you, but I can't go away without saying that I love you. I think I have a right to tell you that. If things had been different, if they ever could be different.... But they aren't. They can't be. Probably it's better that they shouldn't be. Roger's a great guy. You knew that when you married him. You still know it. He's your kind. He's worth ten of me.... And that's all I wanted to tell you before I went away. Good-bye, Emily.'

He raised the hand he had been holding to his lips and then he released it quickly and walked rapidly towards the garden gate. As he was lifting the latch, he turned, and Emily knew that if she had held out her arms to him, he would have come back, that he would not have been able to help it. But instead of holding out her arms, she bowed her head. She wanted to be sure he would not see the yearning in her face. She did not think he could, in the dim light, but she had to be certain. She heard him say, 'Good-bye, Emily,' again and this time she thought he added, 'Good-bye, darling.' But she was not sure, and if he did, he was already half outside the gate. Then he was gone.

The next day Roger told David how sorry he was that he had forgotten to mention the weekly drill; it was very stupid of him, he said. But he had thought of something else—it was stupid of him not to have suggested that in the beginning too: they could have a Sunday party at the Joy Street house. Surely David would not have to work all day Sunday?'

'No,' David answered readily. 'But I'm going down to the Cape for the week-end. I'd planned to before I knew I was leaving for Washington, and I can't very well change the arrangements now.'

'Of course I wouldn't ask you to. But you're not sure yet exactly when you're going to Washington, are you? Perhaps there'd be another week-end before——'

'No, I'm not sure yet just when I'm going. But I have to get packed up sometime. And, as a matter of fact, I'm more or less expected down on the Cape every week-end. Not that there's anything arbitrary about it. But it's become sort of a habit.'

Roger did not stress the feasibility of a Sunday party any further and David did not again refer to week-ends on the Cape. As a matter of fact, while it was true that these had become more or less of a habit with him, it was also true that there was nothing 'arbitrary' about them and he did not take them very seriously. Priscilla's family had made him very welcome from the first time that he went to their wide-spreading, grey-shingled house, and he had found this a pleasant place to visit as well as a convenient centre for both summer and winter sports.

But David did go, as planned, to the Cape on the Sunday following his conversation with Roger. He was late in starting, however, and barely had time to reach his destination, by the most direct route, for dinner. After dinner, when Priscilla suggested that they should walk along the dunes, he agreed readily enough; but they did not walk very fast or very far. Presently he said that he had always heard that the climate of the Cape was extremely relaxing, and he had decided that this might be true, especially in early August after a hearty dinner. He would rather lie down on the sand and talk than to walk any farther.

'I think you ought to tell me more about your plans,' Priscilla said in her direct fashion.

'Very well, I will. Not that there's much more to say. I wrote your father a note about them and I talked to the whole family about them all through dinner. Which, incidentally, gave everybody but me a chance for second helpings.'

'You don't need second helpings, leading the sedentary life you do. Now, if you would only get out and walk or ride——'

'Priscilla, if you start lecturing me, I won't tell you anything about my plans.'

179

'All right, I won't then. I do want to hear about Washington

She listened without interruption, to everything he said, bu she made no stray comments on her own initiative along th way; and finally she was silent for so long that he said jokingly 'A penny for your thoughts, Pris.'

'They're worth more than that.'

'A nickel then.'

He reached in his pocket, brought out a handful of loose change and, selecting a coin, tossed it smilingly into her lap. She picked it up and turned it over several times, still without speak- ing.

'Look here, no cheating. That nickel had a string attached to it.'

'All right, you asked for it. I was wondering whether I couldn't go too.'

'Go too! Go where?'

'To Washington, of course.'

'My dear child, whatever would you do in Washington?'

'I could do just the same things I did in Boston, couldn't I, if I had to? They must be just about the same in one place as in another.'

'Probably. However, I didn't realize you had any special yen for going to Washington.'

'I didn't have before. But I have now.'

'Why?'

'Because you're going to be there, of course. What makes you ask such a silly question?'

'I didn't think you were such a silly girl. I thought you were quite sensible, for your age.'

'You're talking now as if I were about ten years old. That's not the way you talked to Emily about me. You told her I was old enough to know my own mind.'

'Excuse me. If Emily reported that conversation to you, she must have done so inaccurately—quite unintentionally, of course. What I said was, that the fact a girl was only in her teens didn't *necessarily* mean she didn't know her own mind— that some girls knew their minds younger than others.'

'Well, I'm one of those that makes up her mind young.'

She spoke calmly, but conclusively. Involuntarily, David sighed.

'Where would you live in Washington?' he inquired, feeling, even as he did so, that the question was inadequate, that doubtless Priscilla had this all figured out by now. He was quite right.

'You seem to forget that I have an uncle in Washington. Isn't it just as logical that I should live with an uncle in Washington as with a cousin in Boston?'

'No. Emily has a very nice house, with plenty of room for you. Your Uncle Russell's lived at a hotel since his wife left him.'

'Yes, and Grandmamma thinks that's a very poor arrangement. She's said so over and over again. If I went to live with Uncle Russell, he'd get another house. I could be his hostess.'

'My dear child, I don't like to discourage you, but I'm afraid you're a victim of "vaulting ambition which o'erleaps itself and falls on the other". From all I've heard, it's quite a job to be a successful senatorial hostess.'

'Maybe. But I think I could manage. And if I couldn't, Grandmamma could come down and help me out. There's nothing she'd like better. She adores Washington.'

This was undeniably true. David, who had begun by being mildly annoyed, was fast becoming appalled. Priscilla had this thing far too well mapped out.

'What makes you think your uncle would like to have you live with him?' he asked, again conscious of inadequacy.

'Well, Emily really didn't want me to live with her. She put up with it because she thought it was part of a proper pattern. So would Uncle Russell, if he thought so. Grandmamma could convince him that it was.'

This was also undeniably true. David could visualize Russell Forbes, who was no match for his mother when it came to determination, as already domiciled in a handsome house near the embassies on upper Massachusetts Avenue, entertaining lavishly and launching a debutante niece on the Washington scene, with the help of an efficient social secretary. It was as good as half done already.

'You don't seem to like the idea,' Priscilla remarked, in the same calm, conclusive way she had spoken before. 'I've got another one. But I'm not sure that you'll like that any better.'

'Let's hear it anyway. I might.'

'Then let me repeat that you mustn't say, later on, that you didn't ask for all this. The other idea is that you and I could get married.'

'Why, you pert little baggage!' he exclaimed, abruptly attempting to veil his consternation, which was becoming very real, in something like levity. 'The idea of making advances to me like that!'

'They're not improper advances. You can't say I asked you to have an affair with me. I wouldn't be at all interested in an affair. I think they're rather messy, almost always. But I'd like very much to marry you. It isn't a new idea. I've had it quite a while already. But I'd have probably waited a little longer for you to get the same one, if you hadn't been going away. You would have in course of time and any girl would rather have a man propose to her than to do the proposing herself.'

'Priscilla, I don't want to hurt your feelings, but you're mistaken. I think you're a perfectly grand kid and I'm very fond of you, but I'm not in love with you. There's not the slightest chance that I ever will be.'

'I don't see why you're so sure.'

'There are quite a number of reasons. I don't think it's necessary to go into them. But even if there weren't, I wouldn't ask you to marry me now.'

'Why not?'

He hesitated, then he went on slowly, 'There's a war on and unless I miss my guess, it won't be very long before the United States is in it. There hasn't been any doubt in my mind what was going to happen, not since Hitler sent his troops into the Rhineland, and neither France nor England did anything to stop him, because they were so damn jealous of each other and so afraid of each other. The sooner *I* can get in a war against that archcriminal, the better I'll be pleased. That's why I went to an officers' candidate school in New York. That's why I'm jumping at this job in Washington. It may make just the difference between being in at the kill and doing some of the killing—or maybe getting killed myself—and getting stuck at some camp in the Middle West as an orderly in a military hospital.'

'You'll never be an orderly in a military hospital, David.'

'You're damn right, I never will be. Because I've taken good care not to get caught by waiting for the draft that's bound to come. But Brian Collins may find himself emptying bedpans. Serve him right too, with all his talk about England's war. He's never heard of Hitler's war, apparently.'

'Yes, he has, David. I can't stand it not to have you fair, when I lo—care for you so much. But it doesn't touch him as closely as it does you.'

182

'I'll say it doesn't. He's one of a large family and they're all well and prosperous and safe. I'm one of a large family, too, even though I'm an only child. I have a number of aunts and uncles and cousins. My stepfather and my mother, and other relatives in this country, have done everything in their power to get those miserable people into the United States. My relatives are pretty powerful—they haven't lacked money, they haven't lacked influential connections. In a few cases they've been successful.' David broke off, abruptly. 'I'm sure I don't know why I told you this. I'm sorry.'

'I'm not sorry. I'm very glad. Because people only talk that way to people they like a lot and trust a lot.'

'I do trust you a lot, I do like you a lot, Priscilla. I told you before that I'm very fond of you and I meant it. But I'm not in love with you. You wouldn't want me to marry you if I weren't in love with you, would you?'

'You might fall in love with me afterwards.'

'I just tried to explain to you, without using any more brutal language than is absolutely necessary, that there may not be any "afterwards". I mentioned in passing that I might be one of those who got killed. You don't want to run the risk of being left a widow, do you? A very young widow, with a Jewish name and maybe a half-Jewish baby, and no one to try and make up to you for the discrimination we all know about.'

'Of course I don't want to be left a widow, because I love you and I want to live with you all my life.' A few minutes earlier, Priscilla had still shrunk, with typical New England reserve, from using the word 'love'. But she was making rapid progress and she now brought it out boldly. 'Just the same, I'd rather be your widow than not marry you at all. And if I had a baby, I could fight for him, even if I had to do it alone. I wouldn't let him suffer from discrimination. Maybe it would be a good thing if a girl from an old Boston family put up a fight like that. Perhaps it would make at least a few people see how un-American it is to discriminate, how it puts us almost in the same class as the Nazis.'

'Well, supposing I wasn't killed. Suppose that instead I came home blind? Or without any arms and legs? Or not a whole man in—well, in some other way, if you know what I mean?'

'Of course I know what you mean. You're talking to me again as if I were about ten years old. We could show our love differently. And if you were blind I could read to you, couldn't I,

183

and take care of you? It wouldn't be so hard; you could have a seeing-eye dog to help me. And I suppose you've heard of such things as crutches and artificial limbs. Anyway I have. You imagine. *We* could manage.'

She looked up at him, her whole being awake with love. In spite of himself, David was deeply moved. He found himself unable to resist the impulse to cup her mobile little face with his hands and, tilting back her head, look into her eyes. There were no tears in them, no despair and no sadness—only complete trust, deep devotion and unflinching courage.

'Priscilla, I'm—well, I'm terribly touched that you should care like this,' he said at last. 'I didn't dream that you did. If I had——' It was too late now to tell her that, if he had, he would not have helped her choose her clothes and invited her to luncheon at the Ritz; he would not have gone to a house party on Hollyhock Hill and spent week-end after week-end at her parents' house on the Cape. In a certain sense, he had felt sorry for her; she had been so obviously unprepared, when he first met her, to swim in the social stream into which she had suddenly been flung. Almost instinctively, he had wanted to keep her from sinking, and he had taken a secret pride in the knowledge that it was he, whom most of the 'best' people declined to receive, that had prepared her not only to survive, but to hold her own in their midst. Besides, he had found her plucky, amusing and original. It was true that she was ignorant. But he knew she was not mistaken in believing that, given a fair chance, she would be quick to learn. Meanwhile, she had the natural endowments of good sense and mother wit. He had genuinely enjoyed his association with her, and he had not been blind to the fact that she had been attracted and that she had become attached to him. But it had not occurred to him that she had really fallen in love with him, and that she would be ready and eager to go to any legitimate lengths to prove her love.

Only one trump card remained in his possession and, at last, unwillingly, he decided to play it. Still holding her face in his hands and looking into her fond and fearless eyes, he spoke with unwonted gentleness.

'Priscilla, I've told you several reasons why I wouldn't and couldn't marry you and I've tried hard to make you see that they're all good. There's one more I haven't mentioned. I don't want to mention it now. But you almost force me to. When I asked you if you'd want me to marry you without being in love

184

with you, your answer was that I might fall in love with you afterwards and you weren't frightened when I told you there might not be any afterwards. But let's assume that there might be. I couldn't possibly fulfil your hopes of falling in love with you then, either. Because I'm in love with someone else.'

She shook her head furiously, freeing her face from his hands.

'Of course you expect me to pretend I haven't the slightest idea who it is. If you won't have an affair with her, what are you waiting for? A dead man's shoes?'

The ugly question came as a shock, the greater in that it revealed a kernel of secret truth. David's vehement denial lacked weight because it lacked complete candour.

Priscilla did not ask him any more questions. She continued to look at him fixedly for a few moments and then she made an uncompromising and final statement.

'If that's the way things are, I think you'd better leave here. You can say you've been suddenly called back to Boston. Or you needn't say anything at all. You can just go. No one will care. You can be damn sure I shan't.'

She turned quickly and ran off. He did not try to stop her and he did not see her alone again. As soon as he had put all his pending cases in competent hands, and left everything else for which he was responsible in perfect order, he took his departure.

Later he wrote to Cora from Washington, saying he was sorry, but that he had not been able to find a situation for her after all. He had not realized that the scene would already be so overcrowded with stenographers. He was enjoying his new work and he wished her the best of luck.

He did not write to either Emily or Priscilla at all.

CHAPTER XI

The evenings were already beginning to be cool and it was now the exception rather than the rule that Emily waited in the garden for Roger's return on drill nights. On the other hand, she seldom went to bed before he came home; he generally found her in the library, reading or knitting beside the open fire. Therefore, he was surprised to find that the library, though, as usual, pleasantly lighted against his return, was empty. He turned out the lights and went upstairs, only to find their bedroom and his dressing-room vacant also. He had talked with her over the telephone late that afternoon, to say that he would not be home to dinner, and she had said nothing about going out; he had almost decided that the unexpected arrival of some guest had taken her to the third floor, when Emily opened, from within, the door leading into one of the unfurnished rear rooms behind their own quarters and came towards him.

'Hello, there!' he said, going forward to give her the fond kiss which was still his habitual form of greeting. 'What are you doing? Pursuing mysterious sounds which might mean there are robbers in the house?'

'No. I was merely pursuing a train of thought.'

'Yes? Is it a secret one? Or are you going to share it with me?'

'Of course I'm going to share it with you. I've been looking over those back rooms and wondering how you'd feel about having me fix up one of them as—well, as a sort of boudoir. After all, you have your dressing-room and I haven't anything that quite corresponds to it. I've taken it into my head that I'd rather enjoy doing so. Not that it's important.'

For a moment he did not answer. When he had first looked at the house from the outside, he had visualized it as having double drawing-rooms on the ground floor and an immense second-storey library, like Old Mrs. Forbes' house on Louisburg

Square. Emily's decision that one drawing-room was enough for their needs, both present and future, and that the library should be located directly behind this had resulted in the impression that she was saving the rear rooms on the second storey for nursery purposes. Later this impression had been confirmed in loving and intimate words. But it was a long time since the subject had been brought up and now, in Emily's suggestion of a boudoir, Roger caught the implication that she thought they were never going to need a nursery. He tried to suppress his own pang of disappointment and to make up for his hesitancy by heartiness.

'Why, of course! I think the idea of a boudoir's quite amusing. Traditionally, the *décor's* rather voluptuous, isn't it? Cupids and divans and all that sort of thing? I don't believe there are many boudoirs on Beacon Hill.'

'No, I don't either. And I hadn't visualized that sort. Just something rather chintzy and cosy and feminine. Perhaps I should have said an upstairs sitting-room.'

'Well, after all, "what's in a name?" I know you'll make it very attractive, whatever you call it, and I do think you should have a room that's essentially yours and not ours, just as I have. I don't see why neither of us thought of it before. But since, at the moment, there isn't any furniture, chintzy or otherwise, in this future sitting-room of yours, let's use our bedroom, shall we? I've turned out all the lights downstairs and there's something I want to talk to you about.'

'You haven't had bad news, have you?' she asked quickly, as he put his arm around her and guided her towards an easy chair.

'Well, I don't suppose it could be called good. We were told at drill tonight that the National Guard's to be inducted into the Army.'

'Does that mean war—war for the United States?'

'Not necessarily. That is, I don't think so. But it certainly means the international situation is getting worse instead of better. With the exception of married men, the members of the First Corps Cadets are instructed to report for medical examinations on their next drill night. Married men may withdraw from the Corps if they want to before the others go to Camp Edwards for intensive training, prior to being shipped off somewhere else.'

'And that's what you wanted to talk to me about?'

'Yes, darling. I want to know how you feel about having me withdraw.'

'How do *you* feel?'

'I'd feel terribly ashamed to do it. It isn't as if you were dependent on what I earn for support. You've got plenty to live on. And it isn't as if—well, as if we had a family. I think when there are children——'

Suddenly he saw those empty rooms at the rear as Emily had seen them, suddenly he realized her need for making them less vacant, even if she did so in a seemingly frivolous or futile fashion. Children gave a purpose to marriage which no unfruitful union possessed; they might even justify a man's desire to remain at home as long as possible, though his country was preparing for war. But without children. . . .

'Of course you know I'm going to tell you to go. You're right in saying it might be different if you had to support me or if we had a family. But since you don't, since we haven't——'

There was a break in her voice. He put his arms around her, comforting her, telling her, as he had told her so many times before, that it was too soon to give up hope—and knowing, as he did so, that his words carried no conviction, because he had given up hope himself.

The army doctor, who was making one chest examination after another, laid down his stethoscope and scribbled a few lines on the card, labelled FIELD, ROGER, that lay before him.

'You say you've been subject to bronchitis, Sergeant?'

'Well, I've had it several times—a number of times.'

'You've been seriously ill with it?'

'I wouldn't have said "seriously". But then of course, I'm not a physican. I wouldn't know whether that was the right word. I can ask my own doctor.'

'It won't be necessary. I'm sorry to tell you that when I examined you the *râles* were quite pronounced.'

'The *râles*?'

'Yes. Abnormal sounds accompanying the normal respiratory murmur.'

'But those aren't serious, either, are they?'

'They can become so at any moment. You quite obviously have chronic bronchiectasis. There's also a slight heart murmur in addition to this respiratory murmur. I shan't be able to pass you.'

188

'You mean—I can't go to Camp Edwards with the others?'

'I'm sorry,' the doctor said again. But he was already glancing towards the next man. There were a great many young men to examine and it was already very late. He had put in a hard day, as had all the other specialists.

Roger had put in a hard day too. He had been working intensively on the Jerry Donovan case, in which he had his new bill of complaint almost ready to file. He knew he would put in still harder days, while he continued to work on it. No one would suggest that he was not well enough to do that. And he would not be able to talk the case over with Pell any longer. Because Pell would be at Camp Edwards. He had been examined before Roger and had been passed without question.

As it turned out, Pell came up to Boston several times during the weeks that he was at Camp Edwards, and dropped into the office to see Roger, but he never stayed long, partly because he realized that Roger was hard pressed for time, and partly because he himself did not have much time to spare. He seemed to be in good health and in good spirits and his uniform set off his natural good looks to great advantage. From Camp Edwards, his outfit was ordered to Camp Hulen and it was some months before he returned to Boston on brief leave.

In the meanwhile, Brian, like every other man of his age, had of course registered for the draft, but he had viewed the requirement almost airily; it was ten to one, he told Roger, that his number would never come up and that, if it did, this would only mean he would have a few weeks of pleasant outdoor life, such as David had previously enjoyed at Camp Smith and Roger and Pell at Camp Edwards. He had always pretended to be somewhat sniffily superior to their duty in the field; while he was admittedly too young to be old, he was also too old to be young, and boy scouting was for boys. He was a man now, doing a man's work, which, as far as he was concerned, was legal work; though it might have been medical work or clerical work or any other kind of adult male work, if he had made a different choice of a profession; and then, of course, there were politics on the side. . . .

As a matter of fact, Brian had been preoccupied with politics since early fall when he had been nominated in the primaries. His registration for the draft had not affected his campaign and he had won, hands down, against a burly tavern-keeper. In

189

January, he took his seat in the General Court and, from then on, his presence in the office was necessarily subject to the interruptions caused by his attendance at the legislative sessions of the House. The senior partners and Cyrus Fletcher could not effectively object to this course of action on Brian's part, partly because, in spite of his many absences, he continued to handle, with brilliance and dispatch, the corporate cases which had been entrusted to him and partly because there was no one available to take his place, or even to supplement his intermittent labours. Other established lawyers had their hands full too, because, one by one, their own juniors were leaving them, either to enter government departments in Washington or officers' training schools; and the new crop of legal talent was swallowed up in much the same way. They should be thankful, Mr. Cutter told Mr. Mills irritably, whenever the latter complained about Brian's breezy ways, that they could be sure of anyone who was efficient and who was not crazy to be off here, there or anywhere.

Sometimes, when Mr. Mills' grumbles became growls, Mr. Cutter added they had also better admit that Roger Field was turning out to be a good deal more capable than they had originally had any reason to expect. He had brought in the Sears account as well as the Forbes account, and neither of those was small potatoes; he was looking after any number of minor cases successfully, without asking for help or advice from anyone; and he was not doing at all badly with some major ones—for instance, the Jerry Donovan case, which was now ready for hearing. Besides, no one could say that Field was not a worker; he did not even go out to lunch any more, unless he were entertaining a client, now that de Lucca's absence had automatically put a stop to those long sessions the two used to have at Durgin-Park. He ordered milk and sandwiches sent in from Schrafft's and had a snack whenever he saw the chance; this saved him a whole hour at noon. And it was generally he who shut up shop at night. Evidently his wife—and his servants —did not care what time dinner was served.

This was quite true. Emily's attitude throughout this trying period was sympathetic, understanding and helpful; and, to a remarkable degree, she had the co-operation of her household staff. She had laid the situation before Deirdre, the morning after Roger had come home with every vestige of colour gone from his face, and had told his wife, in a tone which he managed to keep steady only by making his statement brief, that he had not passed his physical examination and that this meant his rejection by the Army. And Deirdre, after stooping over to stroke her cat, Kilkenny, and then wiping her eyes with the corner of her apron, had said sure, it would be hard on the lad to see his friend Mr. de Lucca go off without him and all and all, especially now that his friend, Mr. Collins, was that busy he couldn't play much poker any more. 'And are these same doctors going to say just how many hours in the day and just how many days in the week a man who can't stand up under training at a camp can stand up under work at an office?' she asked.

'No, Deirdre, I'm afraid they aren't. I wish they were. But wishing won't make it come true. So all you and I can do is to make him comfortable and keep him contented.'

'We can make him comfortable by giving him a hot, tasty dinner and getting him into a nice soft bed, with a pretty young wife to keep him company,' Deirdre said decisively. 'As for the girls, if either of them lets a yip out of her about extra work or late hours, it's the back of my hand she'll be getting.'

There was nothing else Emily felt she should say to Deirdre at the moment; in fact, having made her point about Roger's dinners, Emily was impatient to be on her way to Louisburg Square. She had seen less than usual of her grandmother lately, and she had missed the *tête-à-tête* luncheons with the old lady, which had come to mean as much to her, in a different way, as the luncheons with Pell at Durgin-Park had come to mean to Roger. Early the previous spring, Old Mrs. Forbes had given up her place at Manchester-by-the-Sea to English refugees and now kept welcoming more and more English children to Dublin, where she herself had spent the major part of the summer, leaving Eleanor in charge of them during the course of her own occasional excursions to town.

'Apparently, a good many changes have been taking place at Cutter, Mills while I've been in New Hampshire,' she said briskly. 'Roger wrote me that Elliot Berkeley had decided to hunt around Middleburg instead of around Hamilton for the present. Of course Roger didn't put it just that way, but that's what it amounts to. I knew Elliot would find some excuse for fading out of the local scene after Priscilla turned him down. I don't think it ever occurred to him that she wouldn't jump at the chance of marrying him. He's regarded himself as the Greatest Catch in New England Waters for so long, and been so encouraged in this belief, that it isn't strange he should sulk in his stables for a while. But he'll get over it.'

'It never occurred to me that he *had* proposed to Priscilla.'

'I've always thought you were a reasonably intelligent girl, Emily, considering the limitations of your upbringing. But the number of things that don't occur to you is appalling. It doesn't take psychic powers to see that Priscilla is the sort of girl who gets a good many proposals. She's no siren, but she has the bounce of a rubber ball and men like that. She's turned down Stanley Lyman and Elliot Berkeley and several others I know of, which means there must be at least as many others I don't know of. But that's neither here nor there, as far as Cutter, Mills is concerned. I dare say that bold-faced young Irishman, who has plenty of bounce himself, will do very well in Elliot's place. He probably won't devote any more time to politics than Elliot did to horses. . . . Well we're still not catching up very fast with the news. Roger also wrote me that David Salomont has preceded Brian Collins to Washington, in a somewhat different capacity from that to which the latter aspires.'

'Yes, but I don't believe Roger's written you the latest news, because he only heard it himself last night. He was turned down when he took his physical examination at the armoury.'

'Turned down! Why on earth should he have been turned down, I'd like to know?'

'Well, the army doctor said Roger had chronic bronchiectasis, whatever that may mean. He wouldn't pass him. So now Pellegrino de Lucca, who was passed without the slightest question, is starting straight off for Camp Edwards and Roger is left holding the bag at Cutter, Mills.'

'Without anyone to help him except that Lyman boy?'

'Mr. Mills says it isn't possible to get anyone to help him.'

'Cleophas Mills always has some sort of an excuse for not doing anything he doesn't want to do. He thinks he can get away with giving one young man the work of four and pocketing the equivalent of the extra salaries. I'll have a talk with him myself and I warrant that when I get through with him he'll see things in a different light. Don't you worry about Roger. . . . I suppose you are worrying about Roger?'

'Of course I'm worrying about Roger. He hasn't had a real vacation since we went to Europe—just those weeks at camp for duty in the field, which didn't do any good, as things have turned out, and those short visits in Dublin, when he spent hours every day going over farm figures.'

'Why don't you and he go to Hollyhock Hill for a little while? Elizabeth and Mark will be leaving there pretty soon, and you and Roger could have it to yourselves. Heaven knows that must be restful, from all I've heard. As you know, I've never seen the place myself and never want to. But you and Roger have always liked it there.'

'Yes, we used to, very much. But it had changed somehow, the last time we went there. I don't think it's especially suited for house parties.'

'I wasn't suggesting you should have a house party. I was suggesting——'

'I know. But I think of it now in connection with a house party, because there was one the last time we were there.'

Emily rose and walked over to the bay window. Then she stood for some minutes looking down on the little park, where a few leaves had already turned from green to gold and a few more had already fallen on the grass. Her grandmother made no attempt to call her back to the fireside. Old Mrs. Forbes did not pretend to have psychic powers herself; but she had felt certain for a long time that a sprained ankle, a bad storm and the inevitable disintegration of a house party's initial hilarity were not alone responsible for Emily's unenthusiastic and uncommunicative attitude regarding the holiday outing which had begun so auspiciously. Not that she seemed in any way to begrudge Elizabeth her happiness. On the contrary, Emily had insisted that there should be no references to an 'autumnal' romance and that the wedding should not be shorn of any of the splendour which would have automatically surrounded a younger bride. Thanks to Emily, Elizabeth had presented an unforgettable picture of old-time elegance and dignity; and the ceremony, which had taken place by candlelight in Old Mrs. Forbes' drawing-room, transformed for the occasion into a chapel, had been one of equal beauty and distinction. Emily herself had been second only to the bride as the centre of attraction, not only in her role of matron of honour during the service, but as the motivating spirit throughout the reception which followed; her grandmother had watched her with admiration untinged by envy, feeling, for the first time, that her own power and personality would not be buried with her, but would survive in her favourite grandchild. Furthermore, it was Emily who brought her grandmother the great news that Elizabeth was already 'expecting', before Elizabeth could summon courage to do so herself. ('A case of nine months and ten minutes if I ever heard of one,' Old Mrs. Forbes had said succinctly; but she had been highly pleased, just the same.) And it was Emily who had made all the arrangements for Elizabeth's confinement, which, it had been agreed, after a family counsel, should take place in Boston; because when all was said and done, Elizabeth was not in her *very* first youth, and if there should be complications, which of course no one foresaw, there was no hospital on earth to compare with the Boston Lying-In and no doctors who could hold a candle to the obstetricians who staffed it.

While Emily stood looking out on the little park and the falling leaves, Old Mrs. Forbes sat thinking of all this and told herself again that there was certainly something about that house party which had never been explained to her. Emily's attitude towards Hollyhock Hill was entirely at variance with her general attitude towards Elizabeth and Mark; and Old Mrs. Forbes, who was not without a normal share of curiosity, would have given a good deal to solve the mystery. However, she sat, twisting her signet ring around on her finger and asking no questions, and finally Emily turned away from the window and came back to the fireplace.

'Besides, I couldn't persuade Roger to take a vacation right now,' she said, quite as if there had been no break in the conversation. 'He knows he's needed at the office and that's all there is to it.'

'Well, if that's the way he feels about it,' agreed Old Mrs. Forbes. It was seldom she said anything which she knew to be so inadequate. 'But don't worry about Roger any more than you can help,' she went on. 'He'll be safe at home anyway, and what's more, you can be thankful you won't have anyone else to worry about, if we do get into this war. You haven't a brother, or even a cousin, of draft age. No one you care about will be in danger——'

She stopped suddenly. Emily had turned swiftly and gone back to the window again. But not before her grandmother had caught a glimpse of her face. . . .

The signet ring slipped from Old Mrs. Forbes' finger and fell to the floor. Emily heard the slight, sharp sound that it made as it struck the hearthstone. She turned once more and saw it lying there and also saw her grandmother stooping over, trying to retrieve it, and failing because of her lameness. Emily crossed

he room and picked it up and when she returned it to her
randmother, the old lady replaced it carefully on her finger
nd sank back in her chair. Then she raised both her hands and
rew the girl down beside her.

'There,' she said, 'there, my dear. Tell me all about it. You'll
eel better afterwards. And you needn't be afraid that I won't
nderstand.'

CHAPTER XII

Old Mrs. Forbes had just returned from the annual meeting of the Proprietors of Louisburg Square. She sank back on her thronelike chair and unburdened herself to Roger and Emily who had been entertaining for her. The Selectees from Camp Devens now came to Old Mrs. Forbes' house three evenings a week.

'So I said, "Well, of course, we can't have any squirrels in Louisburg Square." And everyone agreed. But if it hadn't been for me that committee would still be talking about squirrels. And afterwards, no one was in the mood to discuss anything serious. The question of whether we should support the Beacon Hill Association and other civic groups didn't even come up. Now if the meeting had only been here, I could have spoken to Mr. Dorr beforehand and reminded him how important it was we should talk about that. It was sidetracked last year too. And as it was, I couldn't catch his eye, I couldn't make him hear me. He's failing very fast. We certainly should have a new chairman. But of course nothing was done about that, either.'

'It's a shame, Grandma. I don't wonder you're upset. You're right—it would be better if the meetings could be here. We'll have to see about arranging it that way next year.... Yes, Pearson?'

The aged butler had opened the folding doors so quietly that Old Mrs. Forbes had not heard him, though no one would have ventured to suggest that perhaps she herself might be getting deaf. Pearson acknowledged Roger's question with a bow, but his answer was addressed to the chatelaine he had served so faithfully for nearly fifty years.

'If you please, madam, Mrs. Field is wanted on the telephone.'

'What did you say, Pearson? Mrs. Field?'

'Yes, madam.'

196

'Did you ask who was calling?'

'Yes, madam. It was Mr. Merriweather. It seems he was speaking from the hospital and——'

Emily leapt up and rushed across the library to the instrument which was conveniently placed on the big desk, though no bell rang there. She picked up the receiver and spoke breathlessly.

'Yes, Mark. Yes, this is Emily.... Oh, Mark, how *wonderful*! Yes, she's right here.'

Old Mrs. Forbes took the telephone with hands that trembled a little, and, for once, she listened more than she spoke. After a few moments, she replaced the receiver and handed the instrument back to Emily. Then she looked around her—at the book-lined walls, at the long, richly draped windows, at the great Persian rug on the floor and at the portrait of herself, when she was young and beautiful, hanging above the mantel.

'They're going to name him after your grandfather, Emily,' she said slowly. 'Another Archibald Forbes in this house. Well, he'll have a goodly heritage.' She paused and looked around her again and Emily knew that she was seeing not only her immediate surroundings; in her mind's eye, she was visualizing everything in the house from the hand-blown bottles, filled with mellow rum, in the attic, to the great bins of vintage wines in the cellar. Finally she reached for her cane, and waving away Roger's helping hand, she made her way over to the window and stood looking out of it with observant pride. 'It's a good thing we Proprietors haven't given those scalawags down at the State House a chance to spoil this Square,' she said, in a tone of great satisfaction. 'If we had, we wouldn't have been able to keep it the way it is for the children who are coming along. The next time we have a meeting, I'm going to vote for those sandboxes. And I'm sorry I said what I did about the squirrels. A little boy would have liked to watch squirrels in the Square when he stood like this, looking out of the window!'

Ten days later Elizabeth was discharged from Richardson House with little Archie and for the next month Old Mrs. Forbes was in the seventh heaven of delight with Elizabeth installed in the third storey front bedroom; and Elizabeth's decision to take Archie home to Hanover, when he was less than six weeks old, raised her dark suspicions. In spite of her daughter's assurance that she was quite equal to taking up the reins of housekeeping again, and that she did not think it was

197

fair to deprive Mark of the pleasure he took in his son—whom he had been able to see, so far, only at week-ends—Old Mrs. Forbes said all she could to prevent it, stressing the severity of the New Hampshire climate at that season, and hinting darkly that Elizabeth would lose her milk if she undertook so much; then what would happen, with summer coming on? If the poor child were to be moved at all, he should go to her own farm at Dublin, where she could guarantee the products of the model dairy. But it would be much better for him to remain right where he was for several months more. Had Elizabeth forgotten that there should be a christening? Of course everyone was saying that the number of parties should be cut down, because of the European war. But a christening was not really a party; no matter how many guests you invited or how much champagne you served, it was still a religious ceremony.

Elizabeth agreed to the christening, stipulating only that it should take place somewhat sooner than her mother thought advisable, and invited her Uncle Russell and Homer Lathrop to act as godfathers and Emily as godmother. The function, which followed the baptism and which was naturally held at Old Mrs. Forbes' house, indubitably bore a certain resemblance to a party. But no one seemed to enjoy it the less on that account and, as she said, it had a certain pious trend, since it served to bring the family together as nothing else would have done. In this respect, she was undoubtedly right; all four of Mrs. Forbes' living children were actually under her roof simultaneously, for the first time since Elizabeth's wedding, and there was no apparent friction; though Russell's attitude was characteristically pompous, though Sherman persisted in using colloquial speech, though Eleanor remained detached and superior, none of this resulted in irritation, as it often had in the past. Somehow Elizabeth's radiant happiness redeemed and transfigured it all.

When the last guest had departed, Old Mrs. Forbes persuaded Elizabeth to go and rest and she herself withdrew to her own ponderously furnished bedroom, summoning Emily to go with her—not, she insisted, that she was in the least tired, but the best feature of a par—that is, of any special occasion, was the fun of talking it over afterwards.

'Priscilla told me she was going to Warrenton for the Gold Cup. Did she tell you?' she asked when she was settled on her *chaise longue.*

'No. I didn't have much chance for a talk with Priscilla. She was surrounded all the time.'

'Yes, she certainly doesn't seem like the same girl she did three years ago, at your wedding. Do you remember how she retreated into a corner and stayed there until David Salomont lured her out of it?'

'I remember.... Perhaps if she's going to Warrenton that means she's softening a little towards Elliot Berkeley. He's probably responsible for the invitation.'

'I haven't the slightest doubt of that. But Priscilla doesn't look to me as if she's softening towards anybody. On the contrary, there's a hard line around her mouth when she isn't laughing and I don't like it.'

'Maybe she's just growing up.'

'Maybe.... I was glad that Brian Collins came. *He's* good-natured, heaven knows. In fact, there's something rather likeable about him.'

'Yes, there is, once you get to know him.'

'I overheard part of his conversation with your Uncle Russell. He seemed very well informed on national and international affairs.'

'He makes it a point to be. He has his eye on Uncle Russell's seat in the Senate.'

'He has? Well, Russell had better look out. A smart, up-and-coming youngster like Brian Collins might really give him some trouble. Russell's still priding himself that he was against the League of Nations.'

'Brian would have been against it too, if he'd been old enough to know anything about it. He's talking about "England's war" right now.'

'He won't much longer, now that things have come to such a pass that the United States has had to send Marines to guard the American Embassy in London. You can't drop a hundred thousand bombs there, as the Germans just did, without hitting some Americans in the process; and Americans don't take kindly to being hit by German bombs. But we'll let Brian Collins find that out for himself.... Incidentally, I sent invitations to both David Salomont and Pellegrino de Lucca. You might tell Roger. Naturally, I knew they couldn't come. But I thought perhaps it would please him to have me do it. And David sent Archie a beautiful present—a complete *couvert* of *repoussé* silver; the cup is gold lined and gold bordered and the knife and fork and spoon are all gold trimmed. It must be very valuable and very old. David wrote me a nice letter too. I thought perhaps you'd like to see it. I put it over there on my desk.'

A number of letters were rather carelessly piled on one side of the big blotter; the envelope with the letterhead of the War Department lay by itself in the middle of this. Emily glanced at her grandmother, whose expression was completely blank. Then she picked up David's letter and read it through slowly.

Dear Mrs. Forbes,

I can't tell you how much I appreciate the kind and thoughtful invitation to little Archie's christening. Already, in the short time since I've been in Washington, I've come to feel I'm living in another world, one of indecision and confusion. Your letter, so indicative of your deep feeling for the established order of things, so emphatic in the determination it reveals that this order shall not be changed in its essentials, or undermined by war and rumours of war, took me back, even if all too briefly, to the world you live in—one that is still stately and gracious and composed.

Having said this, I must now say, most regretfully, that I can't come. It's virtually impossible to get leave. And, even if by some near miracle I *could* get it, I wouldn't feel that I should. The office of the Judge Advocate General—here commonly called the JAGO—which, as you know, I left Boston to enter, is the best military assignment for a lawyer—now. But though, technically, we're not in the war yet, in my opinion it is only a matter of time before we will be, and the sooner the better, again in my opinion. We know on which side we belong and the die is cast. I don't see how we can stay out of the shooting and we're not ready for it. (One pays a great penalty for not being militaristic in a militaristic world!) So I don't want to slacken my efforts towards helping to *get* ready, even for a single day; and, as soon as we *are* ready, I want to be out of Washington and on my way 'Over There'. My chances for that will be a lot better if I can prove my usefulness here first. I know you'll understand.

Of course I'm writing you confidentially, so I may as well go a step further and say I believe you understand, that there are other reasons which have nothing to do with the war why I think it is better for me not to come back to Boston, and, more specifically, to a family gathering in your house, right now. I've said certain good-byes and, once that's been done, it's better not to unsay them, unless and until all the circumstances connected with such farewells have changed, including the feelings of the person's involved. I'm one of those persons and my feelings haven't changed; there's still a certain tightness inside of me that hasn't had time to loosen. And, as far as I know, there's been no change in circumstances. Enough said.

I never knew Washington well before and, in some ways, it's to me a bewildering city—overgrown, overcrowded, top heavy with government bureaux, essentially unorganized and therefore becoming daily more disorganized, just when organization is most needed. I've got delightful living quarters, which is a great piece of good fortune, because there's a terrible housing shortage. The lovely thatched cottage of my dreams is a tiny house in Alexandria, which like all the others near it, is really perfect of its kind, both inside and out; and, as I have my father's old servant, Ramón, who was with me in Boston, here to look after me, I'm extremely comfortable and come home to a good dinner every night that I'm not invited out to one, which, I'm glad to say, is pretty frequently.

Well, I've rambled on long enough. Again, let me say how sorry I am—in one way!—that I can't be at the christening and how glad I am—in another!—that I'm just where I am. Under separate cover, I'm sending a small gift that I hope will please your honoree's parents, even if he himself doesn't appreciate it at present. It's another specimen of that Russian handicraft for which I know you have a certain penchant. Let's hope your excellent taste will be inherited!

My best—in the usual sense—to everyone in the family, of course. To you my sincere and devoted homage.

DAVID SALOMONT

'I thought you might be interested in it,' Old Mrs. Forbes remarked, as Emily replaced the letter in its envelope without comment, and laid it carefully back on the middle of the blotter. 'I was.'

'I was too, of course. It—it was very kind of you to ask me to come to your room, so I'd have a chance to read it.'

'I asked you to my room to talk over the par—the christening.' Old Mrs. Forbes said sharply. 'And some other things. . . . Elizabeth persists in going to Hanover next week. But she says

201

that, as soon as college closes, she's going to Hollyhock Hill. She also says that she hopes you and Roger will make her a nice, long visit. I think you ought to do it. For her sake. And also for Roger's. He wants to go there too.'

'Did he tell you so?'

'Of course he told me so. You don't think I'm making this up as I go along, do you? He told me so yesterday when he came here to go over my personal chequebook with me, as he does regularly four times a year now. You know about that.'

'Yes, I know about that, but I didn't know how many other things you talked about on the side.'

'We talk about a good many. Roger's a good listener when I get started on something that really interests me. And he isn't a bad talker, either, when he gets started on something that really interests him. I may as well admit to you, Emily, that Roger is turning out to be more of a person than I expected, when I first discussed him with you. Not that I think, even now, that he'll set the world on fire. But, as you very reasonably remarked, on the occasion to which I am referring, you weren't concerned with a fiery world—then.'

Emily made no reply. She could not think of one that was especially apt and Old Mrs. Forbes did not seem to expect any. Instead, she reverted to the subject previously under consideration.

'If Roger wants to go to Hollyhock Hill, Emily, I think you owe it to him. Just as much as you owe it to him to stay in town all summer, when he can't get away. You're very conscientious about that.'

'I try to be conscientious about everything, Grandmamma.'

'I know you do. If I didn't, I wouldn't make such a point of this. Roscoe Cutter has got to give Roger a vacation this summer. He realizes it. He kept poking the fire all the time I was talking to him, but he finally admitted it.'

'I didn't know you'd talked to Mr. Cutter about a vacation for Roger.'

'There are lots of things I do that you don't know about, Emily. And lots of things I've done!' Old Mrs. Forbes smiled suddenly, and Emily saw how beautiful her grandmother's face still could be, momentarily, when she smiled. But Emily also noticed that there was no beauty left in the hands, which had once been so shapely and white. These were the hands of an old woman, and while Emily sat looking at them, watching as her grandmother twisted the signet ring around on her misshapen fourth finger, the girl suddenly shivered a little. When people grew old, this meant that it would soon be time for them to die; and it came as a shock to Emily to realize that perhaps the day was not far distant when she could not go to her grandmother's room like this.

'I won't ask you to tell me about all the things you've done,' she said, trying to speak lightly, 'that is, I won't ask you about all the naughty things you've done in the past, if you'll promise not to do too many things behind my back in the present. And since you've bull-dozed Mr. Cutter into giving Roger a vacation at last, and wrung an admission from Roger that he wants to go to Hollyhock Hill, I'll go there with him. I agree with you that it's very silly of me to stay away from there for ever just because——'

'I didn't say anything about your being silly. I think you're fairly sensible, on the whole. But incidentally, there's something else I've been meaning to tell you—something that seems rather strange, but that happens fairly frequently: when there hasn't been a baby in a family for a long while and one finally arrives, it often has a little cousin almost before you can say Jack Robinson. You mark my words, we'll be having another christening before long.'

Mr. Cutter did not go back on his word. He had promised Old Mrs. Forbes that he would give Roger Field a vacation and he knew he had to do so. But he had not said exactly *when* this vacation would be granted, and in June he observed with satisfaction that Roger, while attending faithfully to office routine, was also working so intensively on the Jerry Donovan case that any interruption would really have been unfair to him. July and August, as well as June, were consumed in this manner; and it was not until just before Labour Day that the chaos had been resolved to such order that Roger felt the general situation could do without his legal supervision for a few weeks. When he so advised Mr. Cutter, the senior partner could find no sound reason for disagreement.

Roger was really glad it turned out like that, he told Emily; didn't she remember they had hoped, two years before, that they might get to Hollyhock Hill for Labour Day? Then they had been disappointed. Well, now they would make up for it. He had visualized them as recapturing that sense of peace and detachment which had pervaded them both in the early summer, when they first went to Hollyhock Hill together; but the peace of the world had been rent asunder, and there could be no complete peace for anyone again, until this was restored to those who had suffered from the loss of it. Neither could there be detachment, for the same reason.

To all appearances the old brick house facing the quiet valley and the eternal hills beyond was as remote from tumult as ever; but a subtle change had come over its atmosphere, which betrayed its tiny part in a tangled pattern. Mark and Elizabeth, instead of being wholly absorbed in each other and their baby, read the newspapers avidly, listened to the radio intently and discussed their duty with troubled faces. Whether they actually heard these conversations or not, Roger and Emily were conscious of them, and very often they were drawn into such discussions and asked to give their opinions. They did not sit out in the sunshine or before the open fire, for long hours at a time, while they conversed; they talked while they worked. Both the young male Randalls were already at camp and Una was helping her father with his chores. Mark and Roger did the stable work with the awkwardness of inexperience and also with the resultant fatigue. Elizabeth and Emily, who were both accustomed to gardening, insisted that they could do this alone and usually won their point. Afterwards, when they sat down briefly to rest, Mark told Emily and Elizabeth what he had said to Roger while they were feeding the horses, and Elizabeth told Mark and Roger what she had said to Emily while they were weeding the garden; and though these conversations went on and on, they all boiled down in the end to the same thing: Mark did not want Elizabeth to go back to teaching and she thought she ought to do so, because it was the only contribution she could make to the defence programme....

So far, Emily had not been troubled because she was not making more of a contribution to the defence programme, but now she began to give this matter conscientious thought; and she was very definitely troubled about Roger. He woke up in the morning, saying he felt fine, but by noon he was slowing down and long before evening he had given up all pretence and gone to sit, with an unopened book in his hands, in the summer-house, or to lie, with half-closed eyes, in the hammock on the terrace. When Emily went to sit beside him he did not put out his hand to take hers, or to stroke her hair. He looked up every now and then and spoke anxiously of conditions at the office.

'I hope that building encroachment case of Pell's doesn't get reached for trial before I get back. I know more about it than Briny does, because he and I didn't talk things over, the way Pell and I did. It's fairly well down on the list, but unless a case is in the first half-dozen, you never know. . . . I wish that trustee of Mrs. Sims' would resign of his own accord, instead of making me show him up. There's no doubt at all that he's incompetent and I'm very much afraid that he's dishonest; but I hate to think of all the dirty linen he'll make me wash in public, if he doesn't quietly fade out of the picture.'

Sometimes, even before Roger spoke of these problems of his own accord, they obtruded themselves upon him. Presumably, his whereabouts were unknown to his clients; but sometimes these were so insistent that Stanley Lyman, who had been told to 'use his best judgment' about revealing the fact that Roger was at Hollyhock Hill, felt that he should do so. Then Jenny Griffin would appear in the kitchen door and shout loudly in the harsh voice which was so at variance with her great kindness.

'Boston calling, Mr. Field. It's very urgent.'

Roger would force himself to get up and try to hurry towards the house, and then a long conversation would ensue, rendered doubly difficulty because the connection was so bad. Such calls would be laborious, and afterwards Roger would feel he should write one or more letters, confirming the telephone conversation; then these letters had to be taken to the Junction, so they would catch the night mail. When that had been done, all Roger wanted was to tumble into bed.

Once or twice the clients did not telephone. They arrived, unannounced by car, bringing their families with them. Then the quiet of Hollyhock Hill was completely dissipated. The clients' children chased each other around the garden, trampling the zinnias and the asters or jumped in the hay, scattering it over the barn floor as they shouted to each other. The clients' wives asked endless questions about Elizabeth's antiques, and wondered if they could not be taken somewhere to purchase similar ones, while their husbands were 'talking law'. The clients themselves propounded questions which could not be solved without reference to office files and various legal authorities, and Roger would often have to go back with them to Boston for a day or two.

'I don't see why people can't let you alone. They didn't bother you this way two years ago,' Emily said at last, indignantly.

'No, dear. Two years ago I hadn't taken over the Forbes and Sears accounts, or organized that minority stockholders' meeting in the Jerry Donovan case. Almost nobody knew there was a lawyer named Roger Field. Now quite a number of people know it.'

'Then the more successful you are, the more of this sort of thing we've got to expect?'

'I'm afraid so. But you wanted me to be a success, didn't you, Emily?'

Of course she wanted him to be a success. Of course she wanted people to feel that Roger Field was the most promising young lawyer Cutter, Mills had ever taken into the firm, one of the most promising young lawyers in Boston. She also wanted people to stop talking about David Salomont's brilliance and the great loss his departure had been to the firm, and to talk instead about Roger Field's soundness and reliability and the great asset he had become to the firm.

Resolutely, she tried not to think about David. She was glad there was so little time to go swimming, because the pond reminded her of him; she did not see it as warm and blue, under the September sun; she saw it as cold and glittering, under the northern lights. She was glad there was so little time to go riding, because the horses reminded her of David; she did not see them ambling quietly along under the saddle; she saw them trotting briskly to the sound of sleigh bells. Most of all, she was thankful that the nights were so clear and still; if there had been another storm, if a door had blown open again....

Roger realized nothing of this inner conflict; he realized only that Emily's loving-kindness had deepened into solicitude, that she supported and comforted him and ministered to his every need.

'You're not having any fun at all, darling. It's a rotten shame.'

'I didn't come here to have fun. I came here so that you could have a rest. And you're not getting it. That's much more serious.'

'I'm getting some. But I do seem to feel tired all the time. And I keep thinking about poor Stanley struggling along alone at the office.'

'Stop thinking about him. And the next time someone tries to get you on the telephone, let me answer. I'll say I don't know where to find you. It won't hurt my conscience at all. It won't hurt my conscience to turn away a client from the door, either.'

'I can't let you do that, Emily. Anyway, perhaps there won't be any more telephone calls, perhaps there won't be any more inopportune visitors.'

But he knew, even while he was talking, that there would be. And finally, the morning mail brought in this letter:

DEAR ROG,

Well, I might have known that the draft would catch up with me sooner or later. Last Thursday I got one of those Cordial Greetings from the President, which, being interpreted, means that, within a fortnight, I must be on my way to Camp Devens, where I will be tossed into a uniform, inoculated, and otherwise pushed around as I begin the gruelling process of thirteen weeks' basic training. It also means that you'll have to start back to Boston as soon as you get this letter. I hate like hell to say this, but I don't need to tell you there just isn't anyone else to take over.

At this point, I'm so sore, I don't know whether I'm sorrier for myself or for you.

My best to Emily, Elizabeth, Mark and the heir of the Radcliffes.

Yours,
BRINY.

Brian had already departed for Camp Devens when Roger returned to the office, and the confusion in which he had left his desk was a striking contrast to the perfect order that David had achieved. For the next few days, Roger was fully occupied with the attempt to cope with this chaos. Even after the papers had been sorted, the scrawled notations which, in many instances, were all Brian had left in the way of records, were incomplete and illegible. His secretary, Rose McCarty, did her level best to help him and so, to give him his due, did Cyrus Fletcher. But even, with their help, Roger had a difficult time until, after some weeks, he had a surprising letter from Brian in which he wrote:

Well, and have you heard the great news or may I be the

first to congratulate myself in your presence? The Army, in that infinite wisdom which I mentioned before, has now ruled that all of us draftees—only of course it is stressed that we shall be called selectees—who are twenty-eight years and over shall be released to the E. R. C. (which, being interpreted, means the Enlisted Reserve Corps) and sent home. Evidently a great fear has arisen that the infirmaries will be filled with men confined to their beds by the maladies peculiar to old age and babbling with senile dementia, or that we will trip over our long white beards while we are drilling.

Be that as it may, I bless God, His angels and His saints, that I was twenty-eight on Michaelmas, so even if I got under the wire by the skin of my teeth, still I did it, and if that isn't the luck of the Irish for you, then begorra, I'd like to know what is?

However, there's one catch to this, as there is to most things that look like luck at first glance: I am still subject to immediate recall as an infantry corporal of the United States Army. (Did I tell you before that, because of my superior education, cultural background, immense wealth, varied accomplishments, and winning personality, I have been promoted to that proud rank?) Therefore, though you may expect to see me—and you may bet your bottom dollar it will be in civvies—at the office next Monday, I cannot assure you that you will have the pleasure of my company long; for my first act, before turning my attention to any little odds and ends of work will be to apply for a Commission in the Navy. The rule is that an enlisted man shall be released to accept a commission from any other branch of the armed services. But there is also a lot of flap in such cases, the Army saying we'll release him when he gets his commission and the Navy saying we'll give him a commission the moment he's released.

Well, we shall see what we shall see. Meanwhile, as I said before, I'll turn up Monday morning and do my best, before either the Army or the Navy gets me, to clear away that mess I left you to tackle alone.

Brian was as good as his word; for the next six weeks he toiled early and late, reaching the office as early as Roger did and never leaving it, except in connection with his legal work, until late at night. Even on Sundays he went to early Mass, and was at his desk before eight o'clock. Roger, to whom church-going had always been a social habit rather than a religious obligation, entirely abandoned it now, and the two managed to surmount the enormous 'backlog' during the long uninterrupted hours when the office was empty except for themselves, and no telephone calls got through. But finally the Sunday came when they went home to find their families gathered around their radios with horror-stricken faces and to stare, almost unbelievingly, at the headlines in the extras, which announced the destruction of Pearl Harbour.

Brian's commission reached him by the first mail the following morning, and he rushed down the corridor, throwing on his overcoat and jamming on his hat as he went and calling out to Roger that he was on his way to 150 Causeway Street to be sworn in and get his orders. When he returned to the office about noon, having gone straight from the Naval Procurement Office to Littlefield's to order his uniforms, he found that the second mail contained the call to serve as an army corporal. He carried the notice into Roger's office, grinning broadly.

'A miss is as good as a mile,' he said, 'but I'll also say, at the risk of having you tell me I'm mixing my metaphors, that it was a pretty close shave—too close for comfort, if you ask me. But my orders are to "report" for indoctrination at Northwestern, not to "proceed" there, so I've got a little leeway. For this next week at least we'll go right on with the work as we have been doing, my boy.'

'Except that we won't talk any more about "England's War",' Roger could not refrain from observing.

'Thanks for the "we". Come on now, let's get going. We've no time to lose,' Brian answered, more soberly than was his wont.

The day after Brian left for his indoctrination school at Northwestern, Roger went to see Tim Tupperty at the Joy Street Station, in response to a notice asking for volunteers who would act as air raid wardens. Tim received him courteously, but not enthusiastically; indeed, he gave Roger the impression of having matters on his mind which seemed to him of greater importance than the question at hand. However, after shuffling several papers about and studying the charts which had been sketched on these, he said that Mr. Field might be responsible for Joy Street between Beacon and Mount Vernon; of course he would have to take a training course and participate in practice raids. Roger thanked him, as if the policeman had done him a great favour; and thereafter he visited all the houses in the indicated area, gave instructions about blackouts and saw that these were carried through. His next efforts were along the line of preparation for bomb extinction, a duty that was complicated by the fact that some experts recommended a solid stream of water for this purpose and others a fine spray; the compromise of advising the use of one method one week, and the other the next, did not seem wholly logical, either to Roger or to the persons he was striving to instruct. But the places assigned to the sand-pails, as probable danger-points, were stationary, and the insignia he wore—a white helmet and a white arm band—also remained unchanged, though the latter was somewhat delayed as to issue. He tried hard to feel, when he put this on, that it had some meaning and might be of some service.

Because he was not wholly successful in this effort, he responded as soon as he had made the necessary arrangements with his alternate warden, to Governor Saltonstall's appeal for volunteer workers at the Boston Information Centre, to which, like everyone else, he was soon referring as the B.I.C. Even before Pearl Harbour, there had been some daytime activity at this centre; now the airplane plotters were operating there on a twenty-four hour basis; and since the graveyard shift between midnight to six A.M. was the hardest to supply, Roger chose to serve on this one.

Simple accommodations were provided at the centre for operators who wished to sleep there before or after they went on duty and, as time went on, more and more of them took advantage of these. A little restaurant was opened, and frequently workers who came on duty in the morning breakfasted with those who had been on duty throughout the night. All types were represented—rich people, poor people, elderly men, young women, prominent executives, janitors. Junior Leaguers, stenographers, shopgirls.

Roger, breakfasting by himself, because he was too tired to talk with anyone, looked towards the ships going in and out of the harbour, and reflected, with surprise, on the others' phenomenal capacity for work and, with discouragement, on his own inadequacy. For, in spite of conscientious application to his duties as an air-raid warden and his operations on the graveyard shift, Roger could not escape the feeling, as time went on, that everyone else was contributing more to the war effort than he was. Brian had graduated from the indoctrination school for naval officers at Northwestern University and was now assigned to the naval station in New Orleans. David was still in Washington, but he had written Old Mrs. Forbes that he might not be much longer. Pell had gone from Camp Hulen, in Texas, to the Mare Island Navy Yard at Vallejo, California, where the First Corps Cadets were stationed as part of the defence of San Francisco Bay immediately after Pearl Harbour; afterwards, he had been sent to Camp Hahn, at Riverside, to undergo desert training in the Mojave. He still wrote infrequently and briefly, but it was obvious that he was preparing intensively for combat duty; Roger envied him far more than Brian in New Orleans and David in Washington.

His feeling of failure was intensified, not only because of what his former associates at Cutter, Mills were doing, but because almost every girl and woman of his acquaintance seemed to be doing so much more than he was, in one way or another, for the common cause. Dolly was the first in his household to go. She tried to be very fair; she gave a month's notice, instead of the requisite week, and she helped both Ellie and Deirdre with their housecleaning, so that everything would be spick-and-span, from attic to cellar, when she took her departure. But Ellie and Deirdre both realized that Dolly felt the time was not far distant when Deirdre should manage alone, thereby releasing Ellie to something more essential to the war effort than polishing all the silver every week and serving her employers' meals in courses.

Emily had already resumed her work as Nurse's Aide at the Massachusetts General; and she was helping her grandmother to supervise the sock-knitting bees which were now regularly held in Old Mrs. Forbes' drawing-room, where hand-turned machines had been installed. She was also giving blood to the Red Cross, with the feeling that this was another small service performed on Roger's behalf as well, for his failure to prove acceptable as a blood donor had been among his many disappointments. It was better, Emily decided, to let the domestic situation ride for the present; if and when Ellie showed signs of restiveness, there would be time enough to take the next indicated step.

So Dolly departed alone to take up her work at the Hood Rubber Company and, at the end of her first week there, reappeared at Joy Street with the announcement that she was in a car pool which included Miss Marion Swan! Elizabeth had gone back to her teaching, in spite of Mark's protests; Eleanor Thayer was spending practically all her time, most enthusiastically, at the newly organized Officers' Club, and reported, with admiration, that Caroline Field was one of her ablest assistants. Roger did not take the activities of his mother-in-law and his sister too seriously. Without wishing to disparage the patriotism of the ladies responsible for the entertainment of these gentlemen, Roger could not believe that they found it much of a hardship. Indeed, he noticed a certain smug satisfaction in the face of his sister which he had not seen there before, and something in his mother-in-law's expression recalled her look at the time when her husband had found her behaviour unbecoming to a Boston matron. Roger had been relieved to think that there was no need for further anxiety on that score; now his doubts were raised again. But it was Priscilla who gave the family its first devastating surprise.

She appeared at her grandmother's house late one afternoon when the elderly ladies who had assembled there for the knitting bee were just beginning to disperse. She accepted a cup of tea, and sat quietly to one side until the last guest had gone and only Old Mrs. Forbes and Emily were left in the drawing-room with her. Then she threw her bombshell.

'I'm going overseas,' she announced.

'What do you mean, you're going overseas?' her grandmother and her cousin asked simultaneously.

'I happened to be in New York, and I told a taxi driver that I wanted to go overseas as a WAC and he said, "You do?" All right, and he drove me to a large building on Madison Avenue and told me to go up the stairs and sign my name. I did it and when I came down he said, "Kid, you're in the Army now." And he was right. Afterwards, I got a letter, telling me to go to 10 Commonwealth Avenue here in Boston for a physical examination and now I have another letter, telling me to report for duty. I'm being sent to Camp Oglethorpe for basic training. But of course that's just a preliminary to going overseas.'

'The whole thing sounds absolutely crazy to me, the way you tell it,' Emily said, rather heatedly. 'Why do you want to go overseas, anyway?'

'What did you think I wanted to do all through the war? Pick cranberries? Or pour tea for British officers every afternoon?'

'You didn't visit the Bruckers, by any chance, while you were

212

in New York, did you, Priscilla?' Old Mrs. Forbes asked, inconsequentially.

'Yes, I did. I've visited them several times. Is there any reason why I shouldn't?'

'Not the slightest.... Shall we be seeing you again, Priscilla, before you leave for Camp Oglethorpe?'

'No, I'm going home tonight. I just thought I'd come in and say good-bye.'

'I'm very glad that you did, my dear. Good-bye and the best of luck.'

Old Mrs. Forbes sat for so long, with her eyes closed and without speaking, after Priscilla had gone, that Emily finally decided she must have gone to sleep and tiptoed out of the room. Her grandmother did not move until the front door had quietly closed. Then she reached for her cane and, leaning heavily upon it, walked up the stairs to her bedroom and crossed over to her desk. Picking up the envelope, with the letterhead of the War Department, which lay on the middle of the blotter, she drew out the single sheet of paper which it contained and read this slowly through for the second time.

DEAR MRS. FORBES.

This is just to tell you that my hopes have been fulfilled. I have been put on the requisition and the Adjutant General has cut my orders for overseas duty.

When I see all the poor fellows who are frozen here for the duration, to fight the Battle of the Potomac, I realize how lucky I am. I'll write to you again when and as I can. I'll never forget your very great kindness to me while I was in Boston, and you've given me the feeling that you'd like me to keep in touch with you. So, as you see, I'm acting on it.

Yours, most sincerely and gratefully,

DAVID SALOMONT.

Old Mrs. Forbes replaced the letter in its envelope. She had meant to show it to Emily after the knitting bee was over. But in the course of Priscilla's startling visit she had changed her mind. Now she suddenly felt very tired. She rang for Doris and, when the maid appeared, she said she did not want any dinner. She would have just a cup of soup, after she was settled in bed....

However, Emily did not lack for exciting news. When she reached home, she found that Roger had returned from the office earlier than usual, to tell her that Pell was in Boston. Roger had received a telephone call from him, saying he wanted to see Roger at once—privately. He was coming to the house that evening at eight-thirty. He said the matter was very urgent.

CHAPTER XIII

When Pell arrived Roger and Emily were in the upstairs sitting-room, listening to the war news on the radio. Emily had carried out her plan of creating something 'personal, chintzy and cosy' before the war had made all such improvements and embellishments seem like luxuries and extravagances; and both she and Roger were glad that she had been able to do so. He enjoyed the room almost as much as she did; it had become their preferred centre, at the end of a hard day, because it had more intimacy than the library and more space for music, reading and relaxation generally than their bedroom, which they had gradually drifted into the habit of calling 'Emily's bedroom'. Not that Roger had ceased to share it with her, as a usual thing, but he was no longer self-conscious about sleeping on the day bed in his dressing-room, if he came in very late or unusually tired. Emily, who was usually very tired herself, had a hard day at the Massachusetts General, even when she did not also give blood or superintend knitting, took it as a matter of course that sometimes he would do so.

Roger's response to Pell's appeal had been unhesitating and cordial. Moreover, as Pell had been specific in asking that their conference be private, Roger and Emily agreed that, unless Pell definitely asked for her, she would not go downstairs.

Ellie, who was still doing the dinner dishes and who had been told to expect him, answered his ring, ushered him into the library and announced his presence. He was standing at the window, and as he turned, Roger was immediately aware of the change in him. His skin, naturally dark, was burnt to a deep copper colour; his heavy black hair was clipped so close that the last vestige of its wave was gone. Even his lips seemed to have lost their fullness; his expression, instead of being one of winning grace, was one of determination. He was as handsome as ever, and his uniform set off his trim figure to great advantage.

But the troubadour was gone; this was a knight in armour.

'Hello there, Pell! Am I ever glad to see you!' Roger exclaimed. 'What can I offer you? Scotch? Bourbon? Bushmill's?'

'Thanks, not a thing. I just wanted to talk to you——'

'You know if there's anything in the world I can do.... Shan't we sit down? You'll smoke anyway, won't you? And let me know if you change your mind about a drink.'

'I don't suppose you remember the first time we ever saw each other,' Pell began hesitantly.

'Of course I do. It was right in front of this house. You were leading a group of carollers—you and a very beautiful girl.'

'Yes, that's right. But afterwards you didn't identify me, when we met at the office and worked together.'

'No, I didn't. And Emily didn't identify you either, when you came to our wedding, though she'd seen you that same Christmas Eve—I believe she told you so when you came here to dinner and that you explained to her you'd sung outside her house. It was only after she repeated to me what you'd said that I was able to identify you.'

'I did tell her I'd sung outside her house, so that she wouldn't keep on being puzzled over where she'd seen me. But I didn't answer her questions about the beautiful girl who was with me.'

'No, she said you didn't. And later on, when she accidentally met this girl——'

'Yes. That is what I wanted to explain to you. It's rather a long story. I hope it won't bore you.'

'Of course it won't bore me. I'm very much interested.'

Roger settled back more deeply in his chair, puffing companionably on his pipe. Pell leant forward.

'The story goes back to my grandfather, Antonio Pacetti. He and his bride, Bianca, with some cousins by the name of Barrata, were the first of our family to emigrate. They left Naples and settled in New Bedford during the latter part of 1890. The Barratas moved away before I came along, and I never knew Bianca, either; she lived only a short time. But she had three children, two daughters and a son—Carmela, Adelina and Nazareno. Adelina was my mother. She married a man named Felipe de Lucca. And they were both killed in an accident when I was a baby. My Aunt Carmela brought me up. She wasn't married when my parents were killed, but later she did marry.

216

Her husband, Edmondo de Lucca, died in the 'flu epidemic of 1918.'

'The two husbands were related, I suppose?'

'No, not at all. It was just a coincidence that their surnames were the same.' For the first time, Pell smiled faintly. 'It's a funny thing, but when foreigners have the same name, Americans take it for granted they must be related. But you wouldn't expect a Neapolitan to leap to the conclusion, if he met two men named Field, that they must be brothers or at least cousins.'

'You're right, I wouldn't.... So your aunt, Carmela de Lucca, was widowed in 1918. You'd lived with her after she was married?'

'Yes—there wasn't anyone else to take care of me, because, as I told you, my grandmother was dead already. So Aunt Carmela brought me with her when she came to Boston. Edmondo de Lucca was a Bostonian.' Again Pell smiled faintly. 'At least that's what he called himself. Of course most of the Bostonians you know wouldn't call him one.'

As Pell went on talking, Roger realized how circumscribed his environment had been when he was a boy, how greatly he had been conditioned by it in the past; and a feeling of thankfulness that it was no longer so circumscribed and so conditioned, because of his friendship with Brian and Pell, permeated his being.

'It's strange that the Boston Brahmins don't think in terms of the Christmas carollers,' Pell continued. 'I've been one of those, you know—one of the outsiders getting a glimpse of the beauty of those old houses, instead of one of the Proprietors who lives there. And even those glimpses mean a lot to the outsiders.'

'Emily's always understood that. She spoke of it the night she first saw you—the night she and I got engaged.'

'She did? Well, I should have known she might, I'm glad you told me.... Anyway, I seem to be running on and on about something that's always interested me and puzzled me, instead of sticking to the point. I got sidetracked when I said my uncle by marriage, Edmondo de Lucca, considered himself a Bostonian. In one way, the Italians and Irish are very much alike; they're clannish, they keep together, they do everything they can for each other, unless they're actually enemies, and they lay a lot of stress even on distant realtionships. Perhaps you didn't fully realize this. They have their own churches and their own newspapers, their own clubs and their own cafés, and unless they really rise in the world, they cling to their own language, quite stubbornly. I know Italians who've been in this country for years and who hardly speak a word of English.'

'I did realize this in a general way, but it's never happened to affect me very closely, so I've never given it much thought, any more than I had the other things you talked about.'

'That's what I imagined and that's why I've stressed the point, because it may help you to understand my Aunt Carmela better. Until she was married, she and I had lived with my grandfather and my uncle, Nazareno, who's still alive and who's still single. Is this getting too complicated for you?'

'No, it's perfectly clear to me. Two sisters, Carmela and Adelina Pacetti, married Edmondo and Felipe de Lucca, who weren't related at all. Adelina and Felipe were killed in an accident, leaving an infant son, Pellegrino, and his Aunt Carmela did her best to mother this orphan, both before and after her marriage. That's all straight so far, isn't it?'

'Yes, absolutely. Then, after Aunt Carmela's husband died, she had a baby of her own—Simonetta.'

Pell stopped for a moment, almost as if he were lingering over the name. But he did not seem to expect any comment and Roger wisely refrained from making one.

'It had been pretty bad, that winter of the 'flu. I was seven. But my recollection of it is quite vivid. My aunt had very little money. My grandfather sent her some for my care and clothing, but it wasn't enough even for that, much less for all our needs. He had disapproved of her marriage, so she says, and had never shown her the same affection that he had towards my mother and my Uncle Nazareno, whom she hates, and who evidently hates her. Uncle Nazareno's an agnostic, like Antonio Pacetti, and Aunt Carmela's very religious—almost fanatically so. She thinks my uncle influenced their father against her. At all events, the winter of 1918 and 1919 was a very bitter one. We were cold all of the time and hungry most of the time, except when the neighbours took pity on us—which, bless them, they tried their best to do. But my aunt didn't want to accept charity. She withdrew more and more from her friends, she grew silent and morose in her sorrow and her need. But she never failed in kindness to me. And finally, spring came. And, with the spring, the beautiful baby.'

Again Pell paused, smiling reminiscently.

'Of course we couldn't let the baby go cold and hungry,' he said, looking across at Roger with a new light in his eyes. 'So that was when I became a wage-earner.'

'When you were *seven*?'

'Yes. Lots of kids go to work when they're seven—not kids like the ones you knew, of course, but plenty of them that I knew. I found all sorts of odd jobs to do, during my vacation and outside of school hours. And I didn't feel the same way about our Italian friends that my aunt did. I went to them when she had to have more money than I could earn. You see, Aunt Carmela's never been the same since her husband died. She felt she'd been singled out for poverty and sorrow. She still feels that way. And she began by being bitter against her father and her brother and she's ended by being bitter against everyone except Simonetta and me. Of course no one could feel bitter against Simonetta.'

'You've always loved Simonetta, haven't you?'

Roger thought it was all right for him to speak now and to say what seemed natural. Nevertheless, he was relieved when he found he had not been too precipitate in following his impulse.

'Yes. Yes, I've loved her from the day she was born,' Pell answered, his words coming in a rush. 'I'm glad you didn't think a boy seven years old was too young to love anybody, the way you thought he was too young to get a job. After all, the Catholic Church recognizes seven as the age of reason. And by and large, the Church is pretty wise.'

He paused, and then went on slowly, 'I couldn't wait to get home from school or from work to see Simonetta in her cradle. I did everything for her—fed her, bathed her, dressed her, whenever I could—not just because I wanted to help my aunt, but because I was never so happy as when I was taking care of the baby. I always thought of her as my little sister, dearer to me than anyone else in the world.'

'And that was perfectly natural.'

'Yes, and I suppose it was also perfectly natural that eventually I should stop thinking of her as my sister. I suppose it was inevitable that, when I grew up, I should fall in love with her—deeply, passionately in love.'

'I suppose so, too. And I don't see——'

'We're own cousins. We're within the forbidden bonds of consanguinity. Unless we defy canon law, there's nothing we can do.'

219

Pell made this statement with the finality of complete hopelessness. In the face of it, Roger was inevitably halted. His sympathy was strongly stirred, but he knew he must search for the right words in which to express it. When he finally spoke, it was with great restraint and gentleness.

'Are you sure? I don't know much about canon law, of course. But I'm almost sure I've heard of cases where there were dispensations.'

'There have been. We've tried to get one. We've been refused.'

'You say "we". I take it that means Simonetta wants——'

'Yes. She's desperately in love with me too.'

'Can't you appeal to a higher clerical authority?'

'We *have* appealed to a higher clerical authority. And we got the same answer. The very fact that we were brought up together, that lots of people have always thought we really were brother and sister—that's against us, you see. And Aunt Carmela is against us. She sides with the Church. It's a dreadful thing to say, when she's always been so kind to me, as far as everything else is concerned, but it almost seems as if she didn't want us to be happy, because she hasn't been happy herself. I've told you she's been growing more and more morose, more and more bitter, for years. She won't let anyone inside her flat if she can help it—well, Emily found that out, I'm sorry to say. I haven't lived there myself since—well, since Simonetta and I realized that I shouldn't, any longer. We knew that if we kept on living in the same flat, that some night . . . So I've lived with Mrs. Danielli and Pietro on the floor above. No one's questioned the arrangement—that is, I haven't *heard* anyone question it and I'm sure Simonetta hasn't either, or she'd have told me. I said I needed more space for my paper and things and Mrs. Danielli needed the money she could get from a lodger and altogether—well, I don't think it sounded too illogical.'

He paused, looking to Roger for agreement. Roger nodded, not trusting himself to speak at once. Obviously, an illicit love affair had never occurred to either Pell or Simonetta as a substitute for marriage and somehow this was infinitely moving to him.

'No, I don't think it does,' he said finally. 'And I think if you go on applying to other authorities, sooner or later you'll find one with more understanding.'

'We might, if we had time to go on trying. But I'm leaving

Boston next week. I haven't any idea when I'll be back. Perhaps never.'

'And you wouldn't consider—marrying out of the Church?'

'No. We'd never be happy if we did. Of course we're not happy now. But at least we don't feel guilty as well as—unful-filled.'

'So you're accepting the decision as final? You're leaving without trying to do anything more?'

'What more can I do?'

'I don't suppose you can do anything more, since you feel this way.'

Silence fell on the room and it was Pell who finally broke it.

'Well, you see that. So I hope and believe you see why I've come to you now and why I couldn't before. Since I couldn't explain about Simonetta, I couldn't bring her here and I couldn't ask you and Emily to come and see us, even if Aunt Carmela had been willing. But now that I'm going away, now that I've found you understand, I want you and Emily to watch over Simonetta for me.'

'Pell, I don't know how I can ever tell you——'

'You didn't need to. You've told me everything already that I need to know. But there's something else I want to tell you. A little while ago, my grandfather died.'

Roused to fresh alertness, Roger looked attentively at Pell.

'It wasn't in the least a source of sorrow to me. After all, I hadn't seen him in years, and I thought he'd treated my aunt very shabbily—not to mention the way he'd treated me. Evidently, he'd become well-to-do in his old age, perhaps because he did so much penny pinching when he was younger. Anyway, this legacy's big enough to assure Simonetta's comfort if—well, if anything should happen to me. You'll be here, you could take the necessary steps to be sure that she got what she needed.'

'What steps do you want me to take?'

'I want you to be the executor of my will. I want to leave everything to Simonetta outright, except what I want handed over to her right away. I'll give you a power of attorney to take care of that part. The capital isn't tied up, like in your Boston trust funds. I want Simonetta to have "advantages", the kind girls you grew up with take for granted. She hasn't even had any more schooling than the law requires, because her mother persisted in keeping her at home—it was just part of the general

221

picture of withdrawal I've told you about. Of course I've taught her what I could, in odd moments, and she's very intelligent—very eager to learn. Besides, she's got natural musical talent—you knew that, because you've heard her sing. Aunt Carmela did let her do that because the singing was connected with church. But I want her to have lessons from good teachers—music lessons, English lessons, all sorts of lessons. You'd know how to arrange for that.'

'Emily would. Emily would do that better than I could. Not that I wouldn't be glad to try.'

'All right, have Emily do it then. Perhaps you'll talk to her about all this after I've left tonight, and then, later on, the four of us can discuss it together.... But there's a hitch. That's another thing I'm coming to. Aunt Carmela wasn't pleased about my legacy. She thinks *she* should have had a substantial legacy, so that she could handle it according to *her* views. After all, Simonetta's her child and she's Antonio Pacetti's daughter. I'm only Simonetta's cousin and Pacetti's grandson. There's some reason on her side.'

'When you put it that way, of course I can see that there is.'

'So she was upset on that score. And when she found out that, besides the sum he'd left me, Antonio Pacetti had left a very flourishing restaurant and, apparently, quite a little money, as well, to his son, Nazareno—her brother and my uncle—she saw red. She said the money should have been evenly divided between herself and Nazareno, with perhaps token legacies to Simonetta and me. Then just today, another lawyer, named Fopiano, turned up here and persuaded her to contest it. I suppose he's filed an appearance for her already.'

'Fopiano? Is he from New Bedford too?'

'Yes, he is, and I don't like what I've been able to find out about him. I made inquiries at the Bar Association.'

'And how about this contest, from your point of view? Would you get more or less if your aunt can knock out the will?'

'Probably more. But I don't want money that way. And I'd be very grateful if you'd represent me and agree to any kind of compromise that will keep the peace and still take care of Simonetta. I think that ought to be possible. But I'm afraid Aunt Carmela, with Fopiano telling her what to do and trying to muscle in for a big fee, will make it pretty tough for you.'

'Maybe it won't be too hard if your uncle will play ball with me.'

'I rather think he will. He has no use for my aunt, as I've told you. I haven't seen much of him, but I doubt if you'll have any real trouble there, especially after you've persuaded him that I feel the way I do about the restaurant.'

'I'll go to see Autori right away. I don't believe he'll raise any objections if I say I'd like to talk to your uncle. . . . May I see the will?'

'Yes, I brought a copy of it to show you. I bet my grandfather just asked Autori, casually, one day, when they were talking about something else, how many witnesses you need to have, and, after finding that out, went home, and wrote this up, happy in the conviction that he'd saved at least twenty-five dollars.'

Pell took an unsealed, commercial-sized envelope from his pocket and handed it to Roger, who drew from this a single typed sheet and read:

NEW BEDFORD, MASSACHUSETTS
July 17, 1937.

I know I am going to die.

I give my grandson, Pellegrino de Lucca, who lives in Boston and who has worked hard and done well, fifteen thousand dollars.

I give Carmela de Lucca two thousand dollars.

I give my beloved son, Nazareno, everything else and I want him to run my restaurant and carry on the business after I am gone.

/s/ Antonio Pacetti.

WITNESSES:
Guilio Fulginnetti
Paul Lavaroni
Francis J. Desmond

Roger smiled and sighed.

'He left out a lot of stuff they put in the form books, but it looks to me as if it would hold water.'

'Then can you carry on from there?'

'I'll do the best I can.'

'All right. I don't need to know anything more. Now I can put what little spare time I have into trying again for that dispensation. I'll try to see the Cardinal. If I could marry Simonetta this week. . . .' He broke off and looked away. 'Any-

223

how,' he went on after a moment. 'I'd be very happy—Simonetta and I would both be very happy—if, after you've told Emily about all this, you and she would spend an evening with us—as our guests. I'm sorry we can't ask you to the flat. But you understand now how that is. And I know of a quiet old restaurant where we'd be undisturbed. I think you'd find it pleasant. Perhaps when I bring the papers in for you to sign, you'd tell me whether Emily would accept our invitation.'

It was very late when Pell finally said good night; but Roger found that Emily was still waiting for him in the chintz sitting-room, as he expected, when he went upstairs.

'It's a long story,' he said. 'Sad and baffling and—beautiful. Pell told me to tell you everything he said to me; we both felt that, if I did, perhaps you could help us lighten the sorrow and solve the mystery and keep the beauty. That isn't the way he said it, but it's what he meant. Are you too tired to listen now? The time element's very important, so if you're not——'

'Of course I'm not. I sat up on purpose. I didn't know you'd be able to tell me everything, but I hoped you'd have permission to tell me something.'

They sat down side by side and hand in hand on a big comfortable sofa and for the next half-hour Roger talked almost without pausing, and Emily listened almost without interruption.

'What would you think of going to bed? It's nearly two o'clock,' Roger asked at last when he reached the end of Pell's story.

'I'm willing to go to bed, but there's still one more question I want to ask.'

'Then let's have it.'

'I'm quoting verbatim now. When Pell said he'd like to have Simonetta and her mother live in a better place, after the lease on their flat was up, you told him you had an idea. What was it?'

'There's a little old house, wedged in among the tenements, on the farther side of Joy Street. It's the only one of its kind in that locality, so I think you must have noticed it. It's not unlike the Paul Revere house, but it's smaller. And it's really got quite a good deal of charm. Well, the former owner of that house died recently, and I understand her heirs aren't interested in keeping it. I've admired the house so much, myself, that I've been meaning to ask whether you'd care to buy it, as an investment. I

224

think it might be a pretty good one. Then, after Pell said what he did tonight. . . .'

'You will find out about it, right away, won't you? Because it would be perfect if. . . .'

Roger agreed that he thought so, too, and they went to bed. There was no question as to where he would sleep that night. He and Emily still had a great deal to say to each other about Pell and Simonetta.

Pell telephoned again the next morning and suggested a late lunch at Durgin-Park. He had already drafted a will, he said. It was almost as simple as his grandfather's and he wanted Roger to approve it; when that was done, they would get Stanley and Rose and Cora to witness it, and that would be the end of the matter. He assumed that Roger had the power of attorney ready for him to sign.

Roger was able to give him the assurance he desired, and they ate their lunch with a mutually satisfactory feeling of picking up again where they had left off two years before, as their favourite waitress automatically brought Roger his chowder, and Pell, after studying the pastel-coloured slips, decided on mushrooms and kidneys.

'You mentioned some cousins named Barrata, who emigrated at the same time as your grandparents. Have you any idea where they are now?' Roger asked when they had been served.

'They might be in Lynn. I believe that's where they went first after they left New Bedford. But I'm not sure. And they could have moved half a dozen times since then.'

'You never met them at all?'

Pell pondered for a moment. 'Why, yes, in a way I "met" them,' he said. 'I went to visit them once or twice, with Aunt Carmela, when I was very small. And I think they came to my Uncle Edmondo's funeral. Now that you speak of them, I believe they did—Italians go in for funerals in a big way, just as they do for weddings. But I had my hands so full, pretty soon afterwards, trying to take care of Simonetta, that I never thought of them again. I've certainly never seen them *since* the funeral. I don't think Aunt Carmela has, either. I'm almost sure I'd have known of it, if she had.'

'Do you remember how many of them there were?'

'Not exactly. As I say, it's all very vague in my mind. I think there were a couple of women, about my grandfather's age, or maybe a little younger, and an older man. One of the women was married, so of course her name wasn't Barrata any more. I haven't the dimmest idea what it was.'

'You see,' Roger pursued, 'if we could get in touch with these cousins, perhaps we could find out what caused the trouble between Carmela and her father and that may have an important bearing on the case. I talked over everything you told me with Emily, the way you said I might; and Emily felt that differences of religious opinion wouldn't be strong enough to alienate a daughter from her father. Anyway, there's just a chance that Emily's got something, and that the long-lost cousins could throw some light on the subject. Isn't there a way that Simonetta could ask her mother about them, without rousing antagonism or suspicion?'

'Perhaps. I can speak to Simonetta about it anyway and let you know what she says.'

'And of course, if Autori raises no objection, I'm going to call on your Uncle Nazareno as soon as possible. I'll see if he has anything to offer about the Barratas. He might, one way or another. Meanwhile, here's something else. If you really want Simonetta and her mother to move into better quarters. . . .'

It was obvious that Pell felt no interest in his cousins, and that he did not regard them as probable sources of important information. On the other hand, his enthusiasm about the little house was immediate and unbounded. Roger had already verified the reports that the present owners would 'consider an offer' for it and were willing that it should be inspected. Before he saw Pell again, he secured the keys for him. But when Pell came rushing back to say that he and Simonetta had been through the house, that they were both enchanted with it and that they wanted Roger to get it for them before anyone else could snap it up, he felt obliged to urge a little patience.

'Easy there. I haven't had time to look up the title yet.'

'Well, we'll pray for luck. Here are the keys back. You and Emily can go to see the house before tomorrow night, can't you? Because Simonetta and I thought that would be a good time for our little party. We'd like you to meet us at the Old Venice Restaurant on Hanover Street, around seven-thirty, if that would be convenient.'

'Quite convenient and very pleasant. Thank you. We'll be there.

Pell and Simonetta were waiting for them when they reached the restaurant, which was otherwise almost empty, and came forward to welcome them. In spite of the fact that the meeting with Simonetta had been so long deferred, there was no constraint about it. Pell now gave the impression, not only of being entirely at ease in almost any situation which might arise, but of being capable to control and even command it. His presence gave Simonetta a degree of self-confidence which she might otherwise have lacked and her slight remaining shyness became her; somehow it added to the quiet charm of her manner. She was dressed simply, but very effectively, in soft white, and Emily guessed that Pell had insisted on a new outfit for this occasion and had not only supplied the wherewithal for it, but had taken a hand in its choice.

'Roger and I went to see your house last night, Simonetta,' Emily said when the drinks had been ordered and the major-domo had taken his departure.

'*My* house! Is it really——'

'Well, it's going to be, of course. But I thought perhaps we could plan improvements and decorations for it together. Then I could get started on those as soon as the wartime building restrictions permit and still I'd be sure that everything I was doing was the way you'd want it later on. For instance, I like its interior arrangement, but——'

'Hasn't Roger said anything to you about clearing the title, Emily?' Pell asked whimsically. 'Because, if he hasn't, I'm going to raise all sorts of objections. You should have heard him stall when I tried to talk to him.... Well, here's Mr. Maturo with the vermouth, both plain and reinforced. Let's drink to a clear title!'

Pell sounded so happy that Roger and Emily both wondered whether he could have had good news from the Cardinal, whether it were possible that he and Simonetta were to be married that week, after all.

'Thanks to you, things look a lot better to me than they did when I came to your house the other night,' he said, looking at Roger. 'So I'm not going to gripe because they don't look better yet. I'll get all I can out of this week; if it isn't all I want, still it's a good deal. And when I'm on my way, I'll know I'm leaving everything in good hands. The very best.'

The meal progressed happily and the major-domo, who had removed the shrimps *cacciatore* and brought in *scallopine* and

227

green salad, had now retreated again. Emily and Simonetta were still engrossed in a discussion of improvements for the little house, as enthusiastically as if it were already in the possession of one or the other. Roger leaned forward and questioned Pell in an undertone.

'Did you have any luck with the Cardinal?'

'No. His secretary received me very courteously, but said he would have to await the return of His Eminence to lay the matter before him. Perhaps you didn't know. . . . There's quite a dividing line between the Irish Catholics and the Italian Catholics in Boston. Of course there shouldn't be, any more than there should be that narrow viewpoint as to what constitutes a "real" Bostonian, which we discussed the other night. But I can't help feeling that, if I'd been an Irishman or if the Cardinal had been an Italian—— Anyway, I can see there's no chance of our getting a dispensation this week.'

'I'm terribly sorry, Pell. If there were only something I could do to help. . . . Perhaps there is. Not that I've any direct contacts with the hierarchy, but I've got indirect ones that might do some good. Are you willing I should try?'

'*Willing!* But don't worry if you're not successful. You're doing plenty as it is. You've *done* plenty. . . . Anything else on your mind?'

'Yes, one other thing. I want to know whether you succeeded in getting any information about those cousins of yours. Somehow I'd feel I had a clue as to why your grandfather left his money the way he did if I knew a little more about them.'

'I'm sorry, but I haven't found out a thing. I did speak to Simonetta about them and she managed to ask her mother, without having the question seem too pointed. Just the same, Aunt Carmela shut up like a clam, exactly as I thought she would.'

'Then I guess your Uncle Nazareno's my best bet.'

'I guess he is. Sorry I haven't time to run down and pump him myself. But you can see what's keeping me here.'

He looked lovingly at Simonetta and, as if conscious that his eyes were upon her, she turned away from Emily and looked at him. The gaze had the quality of a caress; and Emily, who was watching them, thought of that embrace in the street on Christmas Eve and thought, too, for a moment, that they might exchange one now, with almost the same spontaneity and lack of self-consciousness. Then she realized, with sadness, that prob-

228

ably they did not feel free to embrace each other like that any more, since they had come to realize both the intensity of their love and the laws which prevented its fulfilment. Probably they would kiss each other good-bye, and that would be all. And perhaps they would never see each other again. . . .

Two nights later, Pell and Simonetta came for a garden supper with Roger and Emily, and again Pell seemed in good spirits. They did not talk so much about the little house this time; Pell apparently regarded that question as settled, along with all questions pertaining to his insurance and will, to the allotment of his pay and his legacy, and to Roger's acceptance of his case. Instead, they talked about Simonetta's future education, which he now wished to discuss in greater detail than had been possible on the occasion of his first visit. He wanted Emily's advice about finding a new music teacher—a first-class one—and he wanted Simonetta to have a new piano, the best available under present conditions; the new teacher should be able to give advice about that.

'How would you like to go to the New England Conservatory of Music, instead of taking private lessons at home, Simonetta?' Emily asked. 'Of course you'd have your new piano at home, you'd practise there. But you'd meet interesting people, you'd have the benefit of teamwork, you'd get the stimulus of competition.'

Simonetta turned towards Pell and he answered for her. 'I think that's a grand idea, Emily,' he said heartily. 'But then you're full of grand ideas—you and Roger both.'

'Perhaps Mother will not permit me to go to the Conservatory,' suggested Simonetta, for the first time speaking with hesitation and obvious anxiety.

'I'm afraid she won't like it. But she can't stop you, Simonetta. You're twenty-three years old. You're free to do whatever seems best to you and Pell. You mustn't let your mother interfere with your life any longer.'

Roger spoke kindly, but firmly; and when Pell said, 'That's right,' Roger felt emboldened to say more.

'I think your studies at the Conservatory will use up most of your time and strength. But if they don't, you ought to take courses somewhere else—perhaps at Simmons, perhaps at one of the good Catholic colleges. We'll see what can be arranged. But I think Emily's right—I think the Conservatory should come first, because you and Pell both love music so much. When he comes home, when you and he are married, just think what it will mean to him if you can fill the house with melody.'

'You said, "*when*" we are married,' Simonetta began falteringly. 'But——'

'Yes, I did say "when". I didn't say "*if*". I feel sure you and he are going to be married some day. I'm certain that when he comes home the way will be cleared for your marriage. I don't know how yet, but somehow. Please believe me, Simonetta. I think Pell half believes me already. If I can make you believe me, he will too.'

'I do believe him, Simonetta,' Pell said in a low voice. 'Not just halfway, either. That is, I don't see how it's going to be possible, any more than he does. But I think he's going to find out. I—well, I'm practically sure of it. If I weren't, I couldn't have been so happy this week. I wasn't, when I first came home. I was in despair. But I'm not any longer. And you mustn't despair, either. You must be hopeful too.'

He put his arm around her. 'Tomorrow, you and I will go and choose your engagement ring,' he said. 'Even if I can't have you for my wife before I leave, I can have you for my betrothed. We'll plight our troth to each other, in the presence of witnesses —Roger and Emily—just as our people used to do in olden times. It will be a solemn betrothal service. After that, no one should come between us—not even your mother. Your first thought and your first obligation will be to me.'

After the simple ceremony held in their house the following afternoon, Roger and Emily did not see Pell again. This would be his last evening at home, he said, and he and Simonetta would spend it by themselves. He wrung Roger's hand and told him again how grateful he was to him and how much he trusted him. And he kissed Emily and said he knew Simonetta would be safe in her keeping. Then he was gone, taking his betrothed with him.

Late the next evening, when Roger and Emily were in the chintz sitting-room, they were suddenly conscious of an unfamiliar sound and realized that someone was knocking at the garden gate. There had been a heavy storm in the afternoon, and there were still intermittent flashes of lightning and distant rumbles of thunder; it had been too wet for them to eat supper in the garden or, indeed, to stay there at all. Now they were startled that anyone should come to the gate in such weather and at such an hour. Then they heard a cry above the knocking and it was a cry of desperation.

'Someone must be in terrible trouble,' Roger exclaimed, jumping up. 'Stay where you are, Emily, until I find out.'

'No, I'm coming too.'

He did not hear her because he was already hurrying through the hall and down the stairs, snapping on lights as he went. She hastened after him, catching up with him as he reached the garden gate. He unlatched it and threw it open to reveal Simonetta standing on the threshold. She had thrown a shawl around her shoulders and tied a scarf under her chin, to protect herself from the rain; but the effect was one of reversion to old familiar custom. She was weeping bitterly, and she threw herself into Emily's arms, abandoning herself to her grief.

'He has gone,' she sobbed. 'He has gone and I know he is not coming back. I shall never be his wife, for he will be killed. And my mother has turned against me, calling me dreadful names and cursing me. She has driven me away from her. I was ashamed to tell our neighbours. I had to come here. There was nowhere else that I could go.'

CHAPTER XIV

Daylight was already fading and a chill was creeping into the crispness of the autumnal air as Emily and Roger left the tangle of traffic in Quincy behind them and headed south. They were nearly halfway to New Bedford before either of them made more than a few desultory remarks. Both had a succession of hard days behind them and were thankful for brief respite; both wanted to improve that rare opportunity for undisturbed reflection. It was very seldom, lately, that they had been motoring together. Only the fact that this was primarily a professional trip, and that their mission stood a better chance of success if it were undertaken after normal business hours, when there were fewer interruptions and less sense of pressure, would have justified the present consumption of petrol. They were on their way to see Nazareno Pacetti, who had cordially invited them to dinner.

As Roger had foreseen, Fopiano had immediately begun a formal challenge of the will by filing an appearance for Carmela; and he had also contested it more specifically on the grounds that it was improperly executed and witnessed and that Antonio had been unduly influenced by his son at the time it was made. Furthermore, Fopiano was trying to persuade the probate court that these issues should be heard by a jury; and Roger and Autori, Nazareno's lawyer, were both fearful that, if his motion for this purpose were allowed, Fopiano might be able to present a fairly plausible case, founded on the close association of Antonio and his son in the restaurant business, and on Nazareno's increasing amount of authority there.

Roger had hoped that the interview with Pacetti might take place promptly after Pell's departure. But he had of course been obliged to wait on Autori; and, when the way was clear, as far as his move was concerned, the firm of Cutter, Mills and Swan had received another body blow: Cyrus Fletcher, who had visualized more clearly than any of the senior partners the difficulties under which Roger and Stanley were labouring, and who had done his best to lighten and share these labours, was suddenly stricken with cerebral haemorrhage. He died without regaining full consciousness. Roger had been closer to him than anyone else in the firm, both through the nature of their professional association, and through the friendly relations which had developed between Sumner Thayer and Cyrus Fletcher after the sale of the Gloucester Street house. Therefore Roger was the logical person to take over the work which poor Fletcher had so abruptly left unfinished; and he had not only felt it incumbent on him to attend the funeral, but to help arrange for this, and to offer every possible service to the widow.

Roger had been thinking of these things when at last he broke the silence.

'We've got to do something down at the office. Everyone is run ragged and still we're not getting anywhere. There's no one to do the leg work and the clients aren't getting any kind of service. We're sending the girls on some errands, but they can't go into court—or at least they shouldn't. And they're all tired out too. Of course they're trying to do something for the war effort. Rose is putting in odd hours at the Travellers Aid in the South Station—so many servicemen are going through there now that the regular force can't handle them. And Cora's at the USO, off and on. We try to make allowances for them. But that doesn't help us to get rid of the leg work. It was bad enough before Fletcher died. Now it's a great deal worse. He wasn't much to look at or talk with, but he really pulled his weight.'

'Have you ever thought of a woman?'

'What do you mean, have I ever thought of a woman? Oh—you're talking about a female lawyer! Not if I could help it. As far as I know, almost none of the big firms in Boston has one on its staff.'

'But they do in other places, don't they?'

'Maybe. I should think they might be all right for tax and title work. But I never saw one yet who made a good appearance in court.'

'You're a hidebound old Bostonian, that's what you are! I won't make any more suggestions.'

'Go right ahead. You might come up with something yet. . . .
By the way, I'm sorry I couldn't accept Homer Lathrop's invitation to serve on his committee for the Bay State Club. I hope

I convinced him I'd really like to. But you know what time I've been getting home lately. And with air-raid practice and plotting, I honestly don't see how I can do anything more.'

'I don't either and I'm sure Uncle Homer understands. He was just trying to pay you a compliment.'

'Well, I guess we have to let compliments go for the present.... Gosh, look at that little lake! Isn't it pretty and wouldn't it seem good to get out on it for a while? Just you and I, in any old kind of a boat; but that sort of thing will have to go for the present too.'

It would indeed have seemed good to get out on the water in 'any old kind of a boat'. But Emily knew, as well as Roger, that there would be no chance for 'that sort of thing' at present and probably not for a long while; and this was not only because of Roger's preoccupations, but also because of her own. The time which she and Deirdre had foreseen, when Ellie would feel she should follow Dolly to a factory, had come that fall. True, they had not lost Ellie altogether; she continued to live with them and did what housework she could after factory hours and on Saturday afternoons and Sundays when she would otherwise have been free. But Deirdre now sent up breakfast on the dumb waiter, and Emily was dressed and downstairs, ready to receive it when it reached the butler's pantry, and to take it into the dining-room; for Ellie had already left for the factory, even though breakfast was now much earlier than it used to be. There were no more pleasant leisurely bedside meals before Roger went to the office. Emily served the breakfast herself, washed the breakfast dishes and did the chamber work and as much dusting as she could before she went to the hospital; then, on her return, she saw to the marketing, the mending and other incidental tasks. Together, she and Ellie devoted Saturday afternoons to vacuum cleaning; and Ellie laid fires, brought up wood and washed windows, a few at a time, after her later return from the factory on other weekdays.

Though she was adjusting herself to more and more physical labour and giving less and less attention to superfluous amenities, Emily worried because the house was already so cold and because she knew it would be much colder when winter really set in. The allotment of oil for heating purposes was entirely inadequate to keep the large, high-ceilinged structure at an even temperature of moderate warmth. The open fireplaces helped and she had been able to get some wood from the Dublin farm;

but actually, Deirdre's kitchen, with its big stove, which they were fortunately still able to feed with coal, was the most comfortable room in the house. Emily did not blame Deirdre for clinging to it. As a matter of fact, she did not mind the cold too much herself, especially now that she was so active. But she worried about it on Roger's account. Every time he had an attack of bronchitis, it was more severe than the one before; and finally, the family doctor had taken her aside and talked to her privately about her husband's condition.

'I don't like to see Mr. Field so overtired all the time. And I wish there were some way of getting him out of this Boston climate in the worst winter months. In fact, as his physician, I'd say it was imperative. Isn't there any way you could persuade him to take more time off every week, Mrs. Field? And go to Florida or the Gulf Coast during January and February?'

Now, as she sat watching the sparkling waters of the little lake, while Roger slowed down the car so that they might at least have a good look at it as they went by, she wished that she and Roger could have gone boating once in a while; if they could have got out more frequently in a car, as they were doing today, or stolen a weekend now and then at Hollyhock Hill, neither of them would have been so tired all the time. And Roger had told her, over and over again, how much he would like to see the Gulf Coast. She finally decided to broach the subject.

'Well, couldn't we?' she asked.

'Couldn't we what?'

'Get out in a boat?'

'Just when?'

'Well, whenever you like.'

'Whenever I *like*!'

'Well, whenever you could manage to. Because, honestly Roger, I don't believe you can go on indefinitely without taking some time off. I don't think you ought to.'

'I don't imagine Pell and Brian and David are getting much time off, do you?'

'No, but——'

'Let's skip it, Emily, if you don't mind.'

Well, she had hurt him, as she had feared she might. She would not try to say anything more about getting away.

It was growing dark as they entered New Bedford and found a side street dominated by a red neon sign on which the name

235

PACETTI'S appeared in large scroll letters. Having carefully parked and prudently locked their car, they went in to find that the place was pervaded with good cheer; it was redolent with the mingled odours of herbs, spices, liquor and tobacco; and it was crowded with customers whose genial talk and hearty laughter resounded through it. Almost at once, a short, stocky man, with wiry, iron-grey hair and noticeably fine teeth, who was neatly dressed in a dark, double-breasted suit, hurried forward to meet them and introduced himself as Nazareno Pacetti.

He shook hands with every evidence of good feeling, and ushered them ceremoniously into a small private dining-room, where a table covered by a white cloth and adorned with a stiff little bouquet of paper flowers was set for three. At the moment, only a basket of bread and a carafe of water flanked the flowers; but the prodigal display of cutlery and the variety of goblets revealed the lavish proportions of the impending feast.

'Sit down, sit down,' Pacetti said jovially, drawing out the chairs. 'We shall eat first and talk business afterwards, shan't we? That way, we'll be better fortified to face any unpleasant subject which may arise—not that I anticipate disagreement. I hope you like Italian cooking. We can't do as well for you as we'd like, hampered the way we are with rationing. But we'll do our best. And you'll come back, I hope, after the war's over and find out more about our specialities.'

The Fields found Mr. Pacetti a likeable host. He gave an impression of enormous energy and great goodwill; and he was obviously bent on being friendly and on showing his friendliness in the way which was most instinctive, by plying his guests with food and drink. When the strong black coffee and the sweet golden Strega were brought in, Roger was finally obliged to take the initiative by plunging into the subject he had come to discuss.

'Mr. Pacetti,' he began, leaning forward with one arm on the table, 'may I ask how much you can tell me, of your own knowledge, about the execution of your father's will?'

'Not much, I'm sorry to say. In some ways, my dad and I were very close. In others, he kept his distance. He brought me into the restaurant when I was just a kid—first to wash dishes and then to wait on table, outside of school hours. Afterwards, he kept me in the kitchen and sent me to the markets; I learned to cook and to buy foodstuffs. He took me with him when he went to get supplies and ideas. All in all, we visited a good many famous restaurants, both in this country and abroad and, incidentally, we met a good many famous persons.' Nazareno smiled and, in his turn, leaned forward. 'My dad was more interested in having me learn the business than he was in seeing I had a good time,' he said. 'I managed to do both and to pick up a fair education along the way. But I never wanted to be anything except a restaurateur. I always wanted to carry on here.'

'And you always expected to? Your father expected to have you?'

'Of course. Dad kept telling me, from the time I began to wash dishes, that some day I'd be running the business. On the other hand, he didn't want to make me his partner. He wanted to be the boss, see?'

'Yes, I see,' Roger said thoughtfully.

'He was always bound to have his own way and keep his own counsel. That was how it was with the will.'

'Yes?' Roger said again. But this time the word formed a question.

'I don't even know when he made it,' Pacetti went on earnestly. 'Probably while I'd gone out on some errand. Anyway, one day he showed me an envelope and said, "This is my will. I'm leaving the restaurant to you, just as I always planned. I know I can trust you to see that our patrons get good food and sound wines and that they're treated like friends. I'm putting this in our office safe and, when I'm gone, take it out and give it to Mr. Autori. He'll do the necessary and then this place will be yours."'

'So you're sure there was nothing sudden about his decision? And you're equally certain you didn't influence him in any way as to the terms of the will?'

'Of course I'm certain. I told you that before,' Nazareno repeated, speaking, for the first time, with a touch of annoyance. 'And, after dad died, I did just what he said. I never knew what was in the will until Autori told me. But I've spent my whole life working for the restaurant and my dad always meant me to have it. Carmela is a wicked woman. Supposing she does spend half her life on her knees and fast until she's faint? What does that prove? If she weren't wicked, she wouldn't try to stop me from getting what's lawfully mine.'

His tone had become more and more indignant as he went on. Roger tried to speak soothingly.

'I don't blame you for feeling the way you do. And there's no doubt that Mrs. de Lucca is a very strange woman. You knew, of course, that she'd turned against Pell, after treating him like her own child for years and years. But perhaps you didn't know she'd turned against her own child too. She drove Simonetta out of her house the night after Pell went away.'

'She did? What happened to the poor girl?'

'Fortunately, she came to us. And I think she's quite happy now—as happy as she can be with Pell in a combat zone. Those two are very much in love.'

'And of course Carmela would do everything she could to block that, that mean old woman. Why didn't they get married? Own cousins can get married in Massachusetts. Plenty of them do. It's legal, all right.'

'I know that and so do they. But they're very sincere, themselves, in feeling they must be married in the Church. They hope, in time, they can get a dispensation in spite of Mrs. de Lucca. Meanwhile, Pell's overseas and Simonetta's studying at the New England Conservatory of Music. She has a great deal of talent and she's progressing beautifully. She comes to us two or three times a week, she's living at Franklin Square House. For the first time in her life, she's meeting lots of nice girls her own age, with interests similar to hers. It's been a revelation to her.... Pell doesn't know yet that her mother was so cruel to her. We thought that should be kept from him as long as possible, because of course this isn't any time for him to have additional worries. It had been agreed that he'd write to her in our care anyway, because—well, because we wanted to be sure the letters weren't intercepted.'

'What did I say in the first place about Carmela?'

'I know. And I said I understood your viewpoint. But we mustn't keep harping on that. We must try to find out why your father felt the way he obviously did about her. He didn't realize she'd try to prevent you from getting your rights; he didn't know she'd turn against her foster son and her own daughter. Can you think of anything beside the fact that she was the first to make the break, and that she became a fanatic, that she could have turned your father against your sister?'

'Not right off the bat. If I do later on, I'll let you know.'

'Good. Now here's another question. What can you tell me about your cousins?'

'My cousins? What cousins?'

'Pell told me you had some cousins, named Barrata, who came to the United States at the same time as your parents, but that they didn't stay in New Bedford.'

'Well, that's so. They moved away before I was born. Carmela might remember them. She's older than I am. For that matter, so was my other sister, Adelina—Pell's mother. I was the youngest in the family.'

'I think Mrs. de Lucca does remember them. But she won't talk about them. You say you and your father went to her husband's funeral? Didn't you see these cousins of yours there? Didn't your father speak to them?'

'He didn't speak to anybody. He was disgusted because the funeral was so showy. He came straight home from the church. He didn't even go to the cemetery. He didn't go to Carmela's flat. I didn't know that any of the people in the church were our cousins. My dad never told me so.'

'Well, wouldn't that show there was *something* strange? I mean in connection with the cousins?' It was Emily who put the question.

'Well, supposing there was, Mrs. Field?' Nazareno said tolerantly. 'What then?'

'As my wife just said, she'd been interested in those cousins of yours from the beginning,' Roger said, answering for her. 'This happens to be the first case I've ever fully discussed with her— of course the relations between a lawyer and his client are usually confidential. But Pell wanted Emily to know everything there was to know, on account of Simonetta. And I agree that we should try to track the Barratas down—especially in the light of what you've told me about the funeral. Obviously your father, who'd taken the trouble to go all the way from New Bedford to Boston, would have gone to the cemetery and the house, unless something happened to disturb him very much— to make him very angry. My guess is that something was connected with those cousins.'

'And so? My dad's dead. He can't tell us what it was. Carmela's raging, she won't tell us what it was. We don't know where the Barratas are and it would be like hunting for a needle in a haystack——'

'Well, you wouldn't have any objection if Roger *tried* to find them, would you, Mr. Pacetti?'

'Of course not, if he's got nothing better to do. But it seems to me we've got enough else to worry over. What about this

239

trumped-up charge of Fopiano's that the will wasn't properly witnessed? What's he shooting at?'

'Well, as I've told you right along, I think the will's okay legally. But it was obviously homemade. If it had been drawn up in a law office, it would have recited, above the witnesses' signatures, that your father told them it was his will, and also, that he and they all signed it in the presence of each other. I'll have to go and see these three men and, if possible, get their sworn statements that this was done.'

Emily took another sip of her Strega and then set the small glass aside. 'You brought a copy of that will with you, didn't you, Roger?' she asked. 'Could I have another look at it?'

'Sure, Mrs. Sherlock Homes,' he agreed, and Nazareno laughed.

Roger drew the document from his brief case and handed it to her. She was still studying it intently when, after a few moments, he said, 'Well, I guess that's about all for now, isn't it? Unless there's something else on your mind. I'm afraid Emily and I ought to be getting back to Boston. You've given us a wonderful dinner and a very pleasant evening. As far as I'm concerned, I'd be only too glad to come back.'

He glanced towards Emily, awaiting her corroboration of his move towards departure. She looked up from the will, which she had continued to hold, but she did not return it to him, or rise.

'Just a minute,' she said almost pleadingly, 'I want you to look at this with me for a moment, Mr. Pacetti, if you wouldn't mind, and tell me if you don't see something strange about it.'

'Mrs. Field, I've told you and your husband, half a dozen times now, that I know there's nothing the matter with that will.'

'I know you have. And I know there isn't anything the *matter* with it. That's not what I said. I said there was something *strange* about it. I said so to Roger when I first noticed that your father spoke of his "*beloved*" son and of his "*grandson who'd worked hard and done well*", but he didn't speak of Carmela as his beloved daughter.'

'He couldn't, without being a terrible old hypocrite. He didn't love her any more than I do.'

'Yes, but she was his daughter, wasn't she?'

'Of course she was his daughter.'

'Then why didn't he *say* so? Why does he speak of his beloved "*son*" and his "*grandson*" who's worked hard and done well and only say, "I give Carmela de Lucca two thousand dollars"? I know you always thought she was his daughter, I know he brought her up like one. But I believe she knew she *wasn't*! I believe that, when he came to die, he wouldn't pretend any longer!'

The courtroom in New Bedford really bore a striking resemblance to the one in Salem, where he had tried his first case, Roger told himself. It was no imagination—or fever—that made him think so. He seated himself at one of the counsel tables, unstrapped his brief case, spread out his papers and opened his loose-leaf notebook. It was the sort of trifling preparation for trial which any lawyer made almost mechanically in a courtroom; but every move cost him an effort, and the mental exertion essential to concentrated thought was harder still.

For nearly a week now he had felt under the weather and during the last two days he had been coughing a little and running a low fever; then his head had begun to ache. Emily had begged him to go to bed and send for a doctor. He had declined, at first rather nonchalantly, and then with increasing annoyance.

'You know just as well as I do what that would mean—a postponement of the trial. And I don't propose to have this trial postponed. I've been to court any number of times when I've felt sicker than I do now and won my case even if I did have a headache. You haven't worried like this before.'

'Yes, I have. I always worry when you begin to cough. I wish you'd let me go to New Bedford with you. I hate to have you go alone.'

'Darling, you ought to know by this time that a man doesn't want *anyone* to take care of him while he's about his work; the time he likes to be coddled is after he gets home. And it gives most men the willies to have members of the family looking on, with bated breath, while they're doing their stuff. It does me, anyway.'

'Then at least go down to New Bedford the evening before the trial and get a good night's rest.'

'A good night's rest! In a hard hotel bed without enough blankets! and going over and over the darned evidence in my mind, the way I used to do when I first tried cases.'

'Said he, tugging at his long white beard. All right, have it your own way. I'll stay here and keep the home fires burning—as brightly as possible under present fuel restrictions. And of course I'll be on pins and needles until I know you've come out. But I might even have some rather exciting news of my own for you when you get back.'

Ordinarily, his curiosity would have been piqued by such a statement. But this time his attention was hardly arrested; all his interest, all his thoughts, were focused on the impending trial.

He had taken some aspirin, he had drunk some coffee, and still he did not feel any better. Here he was in the courtroom, with the trial about to begin, and he was coughing so hard that he had been obliged to stop, while he was arranging his papers, and steady himself by holding on to the counsel table. Behind him, the crowd of spectators was rapidly increasing in size. Some of these people looked eager and some bored; some chattered unceasingly, some sat in solid silence and some edged away from their fellows and buried themselves in their morning papers. All this was dully familiar. But gradually Roger realized that there was a difference. This crowd was excited. They were all waiting to find out what the papers he had drawn from his brief case would disclose, and how he would handle these disclosures. As the friendly janitor who had directed him to the courtroom had said, when he entered the building, word had got around that this was going to be good.

Autori came into the enclosure with Nazareno, and shook hands with Roger; then Nazareno retired to a public bench and Autori stayed at Roger's table. Fopiano appeared with Carmela, and Roger eyed them both with attentive interest. Fopiano was a small, brisk man, with more nose than either brow or chin. Carmela's face still had remnants of beauty; but her mouth was hard and there was a malignant glitter in her eyes.

Everything followed the familiar pattern: the lawyers shook hands formally, the court officer and stenographer appeared, the assistant registrar took his seat at the clerk's table, and all rose as the judge came in and the crier spoke his piece. The judge, pink of cheek and white of hair, gathered his black robe about him and seated himself in his high-backed chair. Then he greeted the assistant registrar, court officer and counsel, and glanced quickly at the papers the assistant registrar handed up to him.

'We are today hearing the motion of Pellegrino de Lucca to strike from the petition for probate the name of Carmela de

Lucca as an heir of the deceased Antonio Pacetti,' he announced. 'This motion also asks that the Court strike her appearance in opposition to the will of the deceased.' He turned the top paper over and read the notation which appeared on the back. 'You may proceed, Mr. Field,' he concluded quietly.

Roger rose, trying hard to stifle a cough. 'I shall not make any formal opening, unless your Honour so desires,' he said. 'May the witnesses be sworn?'

The assistant registrar directed all witnesses to rise, whereupon Carmela, Nazareno and an elderly unidentified man, who was with the latter, stood up and were sworn.

'Who is that character?' Fopiano inquired of Roger, in a stage whisper, jerking his thumb in the direction of the stranger.

'You will find out in due time,' Roger responded. Then he turned towards Carmela. 'Mrs. de Lucca, will you please take the stand?' he said, with formal politeness.

Fopiano rose. 'And make her your witness?' he asked in astonishment.

'Yes. A hostile witness. Why not?' rejoined Roger. 'Of course I have no reason to fear that she will not be truthful.'

Carmela, guided by directions from Fopiano, stepped on to the stand and clutched its railing.

'Your name?' Roger inquired, again addressing the witness and watching her as he asked the question.

'Maria Carmela de Lucca.'

'That is your married name, isn't it?'

'Yes,' Carmela answered.

'And before you were married your name was Maria Carmela Pacetti?'

'Yes.'

'And Antonio Pacetti left you two thousand dollars in his will?'

'Yes,' she replied a third time, the single word charged with indignation.

'He came to this country in December, 1890?'

'I think so.'

'And with him was his bride, Bianca?'

'Yes.'

'And also his cousins, Luisa, Beatrice and Ernesto Barrata?'

'So I am told.'

'By your family?'

'Yes.'

243

Fopiano apparently felt the time had come for self-assertion. 'My brother is beginning to ask questions which can be answered only through hearsay,' he objected.

'I presume these preliminary questions are based on general reputation in the family, as the witness has testified,' the judge answered. 'Technically, she is the adverse party. You may continue, Mr. Field.'

'In the next generation, you were the eldest?' Roger asked, much encouraged.

'Yes.'

'And next to you in age was Adelina Pacetti, the daughter of Bianca and Antonio Pacetti and the mother of Pellegrino de Lucca?'

'Yes.'

'And next to her in age was Nazareno, the son of Bianca and Antonio Pacetti?'

'Yes.'

'Bianca Pacetti died when you were a small child, did she not?'

'Yes.'

'So you hardly remember, I suppose?'

'No.'

'But Antonio Pacetti did his best for these three motherless children, and they were all very fond of him, I am sure?'

'Yes! yes! yes!' This time the response was almost eager.

'And he was very fond of you all?'

'*Si! si!*'

'You and Adelina and Nazareno had many good times together when you were children, no doubt?'

Her answer was voluble and affirmative.

'You had Christmas parties?'

'Yes, a party every Christmas.'

Glancing at the outline he had prepared, Roger went on slowly, 'Am I correct in believing that your birthday was May 23rd, 1891?'

'I was born May 23rd, but I do not remember the year.'

'A lady's privilege,' interjected Fopiano.

'Well,' said Roger, drawing a paper from his brief case, 'I show you this paper and I ask if to you it appears to certify correctly the facts of your birth?'

Carmela looked at the paper. She hesitated and turned her

glittering eyes towards Fopiano, who rose. The room was very still.

'If that is a certified copy of a record, it does not need her testimony to qualify it,' he said scornfully.

'Now, Mrs. de Lucca, suppose we get back to those Christmas parties. They were all at Mr. Pacetti's house?'

'Most of them.'

'Some were at the Barratas'?'

'Yes.'

'They had moved to Lynn?'

Again Carmela glanced towards the unidentified witness, whose gaze was steadily fixed on the portrait behind the judge's bench. Carmela's glittering eyes next fixed themselves on Fopiano, as if seeking a signal. 'Yes,' she said belatedly.

'And you were fond of them too?' inquired Roger, who had closely observed all this.

'Yes.'

'Did you call them Aunt Luisa and Aunt Beatrice and Uncle Ernesto or Cousin Luisa and Cousin Beatrice and Cousin Ernesto?'

'Aunt and uncle.'

'And what did they call you?'

'They called me Carmela, of course.'

Almost everyone in the crowd tittered and a number shifted about. Roger felt that he had lost ground and tried to retrieve it.

'As you grew older, you spent more time with them, didn't you?'

'Yes. My mother had died and my father was very busy with his restaurant. He didn't know much about taking care of children anyway.'

'Then Adelina and Nazareno went with you, I suppose, to stay with the Barratas in Lynn?'

'No, there were neighbours in New Bedford who took care of them. These neighbours would have taken care of me, too, but I liked to go visiting.'

'Your Aunt Luisa had married, hadn't she?'

Once again, Carmela glanced nervously at the elderly man seated beside Nazareno. But she did not hesitate so long this time.

'Yes. One time she got married.'

'But her husband wasn't at the Barratas' when you visited

there, was he?'

Carmela, looking more and more troubled, answered vaguely that her aunt's husband was 'away'.

'As a matter of fact,' insisted Roger, 'they were divorced. I offer this certified copy of a decree of divorce between Leopoldo Mafalda and Luisa Barrata Mafalda.'

'Just a minute!' howled Fopiano. 'May I see the certificate?'

'Of course.'

Roger handed it over and Fopiano glanced at it. 'I object,' he said tersely.

'How can you—after calling for it and looking at it?'

'That was merely to see it while you were offering it. It is immaterial, in any case.'

'I will take it *de bene*,' the judge said, intervening. 'If Mr. Field does not connect it with pertinent evidence at the close of the testimony, Mr. Fopiano, I will entertain your motion to strike it from the record.'

'And Mr. Field's questions about it?' urged Fopiano.

'Those may go out, too, in that event. Now, let us get on with the case.'

Roger, again encouraged, read into the record the title of the decree, reciting a divorce between Luisa Barrata Mafalda and Leopoldo Mafalda, on grounds of desertion, in 1891.

'Now,' he continued, 'suppose we return to Mr. Pacetti. You were, of course, greatly grieved by his death, Mrs. de Lucca?'

The witness nodded and began to sniffle.

'And went to his funeral?'

'Yes, of course.' The sniffle had now become a sob, and Carmela's words were increasingly muffled. But their drift was still completely clear.

'And then you heard about his will?'

She nodded again and sobbed more convulsively. Roger waited for her to collect herself. 'So you consulted Mr. Fopiano? And, as a matter of fact, it was he who explained Mr. Pacetti's will to you, wasn't it?'

'Yes,' Carmela responded, beginning to sob again.

Fopiano rose. 'If it please your Honour, the witness has been visibly affected. May we have a recess?'

Roger closed his loose-leaf notebook, replaced some of his papers in his brief case and walked from the bar enclosure to the public bench where Nazareno and the unidentified witness were awaiting him.

246

'You're doing fine, Mr. Field,' Nazareno said in a hearty undertone.

'Well, I don't believe things are going too badly, but we're not out of the woods yet. Mr. Barrata, I may need to call on you fairly soon now. Don't be surprised if I do. On the other hand, I may not have to call on you at all, as I told you before. It depends on how much I can get Mrs. de Lucca to admit herself. Of course she's talking to Fopiano about you right now. But I want to tell you again how grateful I am for your willingness to help. It may make all the difference.'

'I was glad enough to do it, after I understood how things were. That first time you came to Lynn I didn't. Of course my wife didn't, either.'

He spoke with apologetic and convincing sincerity. There had indeed been a great change in his attitude since that first call at his house in Lynn. As Roger, after exchanging a few more desultory remarks with the cousins, went off in search of a water cooler, where he washed down ten more grains of aspirin, he found himself thinking of that discouraging episode, instead of dwelling, as he knew he should have, on the next moves in the trial. It was getting harder and harder to concentrate. He must have had more fever than he realized when he started out that morning. . . .

Well, he must not review the rest of that episode now. It was time to return to the courtroom. Carmela was already back on the witness stand, where a chair had now been provided for her, at Fopiano's request, on the grounds of fatigue. Her black-gloved hands were folded in her lap, her glittering eyes were less restless and her expression more secretive. Roger resumed his place at the counsel table and continued his examination.

'Tell me, Mrs. de Lucca,' he said, 'have you discussed your testimony with Mr. Fopiano?'

Instantly Fopiano was on his feet again. 'Of course she has!' he blurted out.

'Your Honour, if Mr. Fopiano is going to testify himself, I should like to have him sworn and submitted to cross-examination.'

'I am surprised that anyone from an office with the standing of Cutter, Mills and Swan should ask such a question of a help-less widow!' shouted Fopiano.

'Gentlemen, gentlemen!' admonished the judge wearily. 'The question was proper, even if hackneyed. You will please not intervene in the testimony, Mr. Fopiano. You will please keep to the point, Mr. Field.'

'You did discuss your testimony with Mr. Fopiano?' Roger inquired, turning back to Carmela.

'Yes.'

'Did you tell him about your recent trip here?'

'What trip?'

'Didn't you come here to get your birth certificate, for the purpose of introducing it at the trial,' Roger said.

'Yes, I did.'

'And when you came to New Bedford, you went to the city clerk's office? And what did you ask for, in the clerk's office?'

'I asked for my birth certificate.'

'What did you say?'

'I said I wanted it.'

'Mrs. de Lucca—didn't you ask the clerk if he had a record, showing the birth of a baby born May 23rd, 1891, to *Luisa and Leopoldo Mafalda*?'

With a smothered exclamation, Carmela half rose and then sank back again, grasping the arms of her chair. But almost instantly, she sprang to her feet, vehemently shouting in Italian. When no one answered her, she cried out in English, 'How did you know that?'

There was a tense pause, unbroken by any sound in the courtroom.

'And the clerk told you he had no such record?' Roger pursued.

'*Si.*'

'So then you asked him if he had a record, dated the same day, of a baby named Carmela born to *Antonio and Bianca Pacetti*? Be very careful. Remember that you are under the oath.'

There was another long pause. But finally, she spat out the single word, '*Si!*'

'And that is the certificate you had ready to introduce here?'

'*Si!*'

'But you didn't know then, and you don't know now, what your name really is, do you?'

This time she burst into genuine tears and her reply came with tragic intensity.

'No. I have never known my real name. I have never known who was really my father.'

A sudden murmur arose in the courtroom, swelling gradually in sound. A sheriff rapped for order and failed to get it. The judge spoke in a voice of authority.

'The courtroom will be quiet. Proceed, Mr. Field.'

'May it please the Court,' Roger said slowly and distinctly. 'I offer this certificate, showing the birth of a child, Adelina, to Antonio and Bianca Pacetti, in New Bedford on September 29th, 1891. I also offer the marriage certificate of the said Antonio and Bianca Pacetti, dated in Naples, November 30th, 1890. I submit that these certificates are both relevant and material, as is all the evidence concerning the Barrata family. It would have been impossible for Bianca Pacetti to give birth to a child in May and to another in September. Therefore, if Antonio had been the father of a child born in May, it must have had a different mother and there is no evidence that this occurred. I therefore further submit that Carmela was the daughter of Luisa Barrata Mafalda and that, as the said Carmela was born less than six months after her mother's arrival in the United States, her father is unknown to us. Your Honour may infer from this that Antonio Pacetti registered the said Carmela as his child, in order to shield her mother, Luisa Barrata Mafalda, from disgrace, and that the father of the child was also unknown to him, as it was to Leopoldo Mafalda, who instantly left his wife upon the discovery of her pregnancy by another man. All this evidence is therefore admissible on the issue before us, namely: will your Honour allow the motion of Pellegrino de Lucca to strike the name of Carmela de Lucca from the list of Antonio Pacetti's heirs, *since she is not his daughter*?'

Roger guided the car mechanically, stopping and starting almost instinctively as the traffic lights changed. Against the grey clouds, at the top of every rise, he seemed to see the black-clad figure of Carmela, as she had appeared on the stand, at first confident, then frightened, and finally violent and vindictive. But with the dark vision came the compelling knowledge that she had not been able to prevail against him. He had trapped her even without recourse to other witnesses; neither Nazareno nor Barrata had needed to testify; they had been superfluous and ineffective, after all. But it had been a tough day; Pell would understand that, not only as a friend and as a man, but as a lawyer. Pell would feel that his trust had been justified—

again not only as a friend and as a man, but as a lawyer. He would write immediately to Pell, explaining everything, both about the present situation, as far as Simonetta was concerned, and about the trial step by step. It was tremendously important that he should do this. Or was it? Did it matter? Did anything really matter except that his head was bursting and his heart pounding, that he had never felt so ill in his life, or dreamed that it was possible to be so ill and still be on a highroad, driving a car?

Roger's errant thoughts, as always, returned to Emily. Without her initiative he would not have been able to piece the pattern of the case together, and he must try to make up for his unfairness in excluding her from his triumph by relating every detail of the trial to her when he reached home. But, in the course of doing this, he would also be justified in mentioning the important move he had made on his own initiative, when it dawned on him that Carmela might have gone to the city clerk's office to make sure that she had not been recorded as the daughter of Leopoldo and Luisa Mafalda and thereby automatically disqualified as a next of kin. The question which he had accordingly put to her, based on pure guesswork, had startled her into telling the truth. Emily would applaud this as an inspiration on his part. They would go to the chintz sitting-room together and he would forestall her eager questions by telling her everything there was to tell. Also, he must not forget to ask her what she had meant when she told him she might have some news for him too. He should have shown immediate interest when she said that. He must have hurt *her* feelings. And he would not have hurt Emily's feelings for anything in the world. He would make her understand that. Or would he? Could he?

He hoped he could, because there were so many things he wanted to tell Emily before he went to sleep. Several times that day he had thought how much this trial resembled his first one—in the physical aspects of the courtroom and the spectators, in his abnormal degree of nervousness beforehand, in his feeling that a successful outcome was imperative and must be won at any cost. But this time he would have Emily all to himself; he would not find an interloper on his hearth. Briefly, and with a sensation bordering almost on amusement, he recalled his jealousy and rage over David's unexpected presence on that long-ago night. How could he have been so crazy as to imagine, for one moment, that David was a menace to the happiness and harmony of his marriage? Why, David had hardly left the house when Emily urgently welcomed her husband to her arms, revealing a capacity for passion hitherto not only undisclosed, but unimagined! And she had scarcely seen David since then, except when circumstances which she neither directed nor controlled had brought him into her company. He had disappeared from their lives and Roger did not even know where he was at present. Someone at the office had said he had gone to England and Roger had felt no curiosity to learn anything more. It would be rather nice to hear from good old Briny once in a while, to know he was safe and getting along all right in the South Pacific—Roger had a vague impression that Briny was somewhere in the South Pacific now. But there was no hurry about hearing—any time would do. Of course he would be hearing from Pell and he was glad of that, because of the reasons for it. But there was no hurry about that, either. There was no hurry about anything, except to get home and talk to Emily.

He never knew how he reached Joy Street. He had no recollection, later on, of drawing up to the curb in front of his house and mounting the steps and unlocking the door. He had a dim impression that he called to Emily and that she answered him, but everything was very hazy, for all at once vertigo overcame him completely. When she reached his side, he was lying unconscious on the floor.

After that, there were moments of awareness. He knew that he was in his big soft bed and that Emily was standing near it. He heard the doctor saying, 'There's no cause for uneasiness, Mrs. Field. Pneumonia isn't what it used to be, you know. Why, we'll have his temperature down with penicillin, inside of twenty-four hours.' Roger was meant to overhear that, he knew. But he was not so sure he was meant to overhear what the doctor said when he came the next time. 'Well, of course, occasionally there *is* a case. . . . I think perhaps I'd better arrange for oxygen.'

Roger did not care what they had arranged for, because, in the meanwhile, Emily had told him her news and he was supremely happy. She had not wanted to say anything until she was sure, and she had been disappointed so many times. . . . But she had been examined by a famous obstetrician in the morning that Roger went to New Bedford and he had told her there would be a September baby.

Soon after that, Emily read him a letter that had come in from Roscoe Cutter, congratulating him on his signal success in New Bedford. He was not to hurry back to the office before he was really able, though they would all be glad to see him there for both personal and professional reasons. As a matter of fact, Mr. Cutter and Mr. Mills wished to discuss with Roger the possibility that he might now be interested in a partnership. This communication, gratifying as it was, seemed unimportant compared to Emily's great news. For the first time, in more than six years, Roger did not seem to have the office work on his mind. He did not worry about anything. He did not feel there was anything to worry about.

Emily always stayed in his room. She did not ever seem to get tired or anything and she understood, better than the nurses, what he wanted and needed. But then, she had always been understanding—understanding and loyal and loving. She had made him very happy. There it was again, that consciousness of joy. The doctor looked graver and graver, whenever Roger noticed his presence; Roger did not see why. There was nothing to be grave about. He had won his case. He was going to be a member of the firm. Simonetta and Pell were going to be married. And after all these years, he and Emily were going to have a baby. Only Emily was in the room with him now. Well, he did not need anyone else. Just Emily, so that they could share his victory.

PART FIVE

MARCH 1943 TO NOVEMBER 1946

EMILY

CHAPTER XV

For the first few weeks after Roger died, Emily was mainly conscious of numbness; then she was aware only of overwhelming fatigue and incomparable apathy, tinged with sorrow.

She did not argue when Old Mrs. Forbes, who was undoubtedly in league with the obstetrician, said that Emily would be much better off in that famous third-storey bedroom on Louisburg Square. Deirdre needed a vacation; she had appeared to accept Roger's death bravely, but, as a matter of fact, she had been completely crushed by it. When she had pulled herself together, Emily could take her to Hollyhock Hill, if she choose, for the warm summer months. But for the present . . .

So the shutters were closed and the shades were drawn in the Joy Street house. The silver was put in the bank, the rugs in storage and the furniture was slip-covered with clean, colourless linen.

Old Mrs. Forbes talked briskly all through their *tête-à-tête* luncheon, when Emily first arrived at Louisburg Square, but Emily could not think of much to say, and afterwards she could not think of much to do. For the next month nearly all her days seemed equally aimless and equally empty. She had a number of callers, some of them very old friends, and she saw them because she could not excuse herself on grounds of ill-health or pre-occupation; but she would have been just as contented to remain alone.

One day, Sister Mary Theresa came and, after a little desultory conversation, she hesitated. 'You used to come and see us quite often, Mrs. Field. We know you've been busy these last years, that you haven't had much time for visiting. But we've missed you very much. We hope now you're so near . . . The chapel is always open.'

'Thank you,' Emily said again. But she had no desire to go to St. Margaret's Convent or anywhere else, and no intention of

254

doing so. She thought Sister Mary Theresa understood this.

Quite often Simonetta came to see Emily. Simonetta did not try to talk to her about anything; she sat and played the piano and sometimes she sang. She played and sang more and more beautifully all the time, and she seemed to grow more and more beautiful herself, all the time too. Emily realized that she ought to ask Simonetta what she had heard from Pell, and kept telling herself that the next time Simonetta came she would do so. But Simonetta did not seem to expect questions and she did not offer any information on her own initiative. Emily sat still and listened to the music and that was all that happened.

Eventually her physician told her that she should be getting outdoors more and taking more exercise, so every pleasant day she walked up the Hill and sat for a little while in her garden and then walked back to Louisburg Square. She had not told anyone about the habit she had formed of going there, so she had no reason to expect that she would be disturbed; and she was slightly startled when, one evening, someone knocked at the gate. She went and opened it and, to her surprise, saw her father standing there.

'I hope I didn't frighten you,' he said. 'I went to your grandmother's house and she told me you were here. She said she thought you might be glad to see me, so I walked on up.'

'Of course I'm glad to see you, Papa. Won't you come in and sit down?'

He accepted a chair and laid his hat and gloves on the table beside it. Then he looked around him with approval.

'I'd forgotten how pleasant you'd made this,' he said. 'It's rather a long while since I've been here.'

'It *is* a long while. Of course you've been in Dublin so much of the time—— Would you like a drink, Papa? I haven't been in the house since I left it, but I have my keys in my purse and I'm sure there's still something in the wine cupboard. Deirdre comes in to clean, so I told her to keep the small refrigerator going. I think I could get some ice cubes fairly quickly.'

'Thank you, Emily. A drink would be very refreshing.'

She was gone for some minutes and, when she reappeared at the back door, she was carrying a well-laden tray. He hurried to take it from her.

They sat for some time over their drinks and they did not talk much; they had never been particularly close to each other, and there did not seem to be much to say. But the silence was com-

255

panionable. When it began to grow dark, and Emily said she must go back to Louisburg Square, or her grandmother would worry about her, her father carried the tray back to the kitchen, and insisted on drying the glasses she washed and putting the bottles away. As they went out into the street together, he cleared his throat.

'I've enjoyed this very much, Emily. I'd like to do it again.'

'Then I hope you will.'

After that, they sat together almost every pleasant afternoon, until she went to Hollyhock Hill. And little by little, they found they had more to say to each other, more than they ever had before.

'Do you hear anything from Priscilla these days, Emily?' he asked one afternoon.

'She doesn't write to me, but she does write, once in a while, to Grandmamma. And Grandmamma passes on the news to me, if I'll listen. It hasn't been particularly thrilling, so far. The last I knew, Priscilla had been ordered to Camp Kilmer for overseas training and was doing K.P. duty there.'

'And you don't know whether she's gone overseas yet?'

'Grandmamma hasn't spoken about her lately, but she may well have. That's what she was determined to do.'

Another day he asked her if she ever heard what had become of the young men who had been with Roger at Cutter, Mills. It seemed all right, now, to mention Roger's name, and Sumner had long suppressed the curiosity of an idle man to know what more active men were doing.

'I believe David is still in England and Brian in the South Pacific. They both wrote to me when they heard about Roger, of course; but they didn't say much—naturally they couldn't on account of the censorship and they just sent brief notes of condolence anyway. I got the same kind of a note from Pell, as far as news was concerned, but it was longer, because it was filled with expressions of deep gratitude and strong affection. Roger and Brian were good friends, but he and Pell were really devoted to each other. I know Roger's death is a great personal loss to Pell. It would be easy enough to find out more about him from Simonetta if you're really interested.'

'Well, I am interested, Emily, but naturally I wouldn't want to seem prying.'

'You wouldn't. I think she'd be glad to have me ask.'

The next afternoon she was late in reaching the garden, and

when she got there she told her father her tardiness had been caused by the fact that she had been talking to Simonetta.

'I'm awfully glad you asked after Pell, Papa. It seems Simonetta's been worried about him, and that she didn't like to tell me so, especially as I hadn't asked, because I'd been in trouble myself. Pell was wounded in the North African campaign—not seriously, but badly enough to be hospitalized for several weeks. Now he's been transferred from the anti-aircraft outfit he was with to the A.M.G., much to his disgust—and of course greatly to Simonetta's relief. She believes he won't be in Africa much longer—in fact, she's not at all sure he hasn't already left there. Incidentally, he's a captain now and I think he's already had some kind of a citation. She's so proud of him she doesn't know what to do.'

'Did you go ahead with your plans to buy the little house for her?'

'Yes, one of the last things Roger did at the office was to clear the title and get the deed for me. I haven't been in the house again, since Roger and I went there together, but it's mine. That means, of course, that it'll be Simonetta and Pell's, whenever they're ready for it.'

'I should think you and she would like to go down there some day and look it over. As a matter of fact, I'd enjoy walking down there with you myself.'

'All right. The next time Simonetta comes to Louisburg Square I'll speak to her about it.'

Emily really did not feel much interest in the little old house. But Simonetta's response to her suggestion was so eager that Emily was sorry she had not made it sooner, and she decided to discuss with her father at the first opportunity the propriety of making a start on the remodelling of the house.

But, as it turned out, both information and help came from an entirely unexpected quarter. Emily and her father were still talking about what it was right to do and what it was possible to do when they were aware that someone was jiggling the old brass knocker in a way that suggested a special signal. Emily leapt up, crying out in amazement and unbelief.

'That's the way Brian always knocked, when he came to play poker. He and Roger called it his password. Why, it can't be——'

But it was Brian, leaner, browner and seemingly taller, stood on the threshold, grinning broadly. Emily threw her arms

257

around his neck and hugged him hard, still uttering little cries of unbelief which, nevertheless, were tinged with joy. Her father, watching her and listening to her, did not fail to observe that these were the first signs of any emotion she had betrayed since Roger's death.

'Briny, Briny, are you real? Are you *all right*? Wherever did you drop from?'

'I'm as right as rain and as real as the sun. And I didn't drop from anywhere. I alighted, with my usual unimpeachable dignity, from a plane. In the normal course of events, I wouldn't have got home for six or eight months more, when I'd have been entitled to a tour of stateside duty. But the medicos took on about an infection I got as if I'd cut open my head instead of my foot and the brains were leaking right out of it. I tried to tell them it was the other end of me that counted, but they wouldn't listen. I don't know what's going to happen to me next. I may get shipped back to the South Pacific or I may be sent to the B Docks in Norfolk. Anyway I'm spending a little time in Boston, much of it, I hope, in your company. Incidentally, I've got a whole pocketful of petrol coupons. What about a nice long drive out into the beautiful spring countryside?'

'You mean now?'

'Well, tomorrow would be just as good if there's something else you'd rather do now.'

'No, I wasn't doing anything special. When you came, Papa and I were talking about Simonetta's house and wondering how we should go about getting materials and labour for its restoration.'

'Simonetta's house? Go back to the beginning on that one, will you?'

Briefly, Emily explained. While she was talking he had begun to show signs of impatience, and the immediacy of his response disclosed the difficulty he had had in restraining himself.

'Why in hell didn't you ask my old man to help you out?' he inquired.

'Your—why, I never thought!'

'For a reasonably intelligent girl, the number of thoughts you don't have is really staggering. I take it your telephone is still connected?' he said as he disappeared into the house.

'My luck's holding,' he announced cheerily when he came back, 'I got my old man and Simonetta both on the telephone, the first try. He's going to stop at Franklin Square House and bring her over here. Then we'll all go together and look over the premises—probably Terence will come along too. Mark you, I haven't any black marketing in mind. But, as Mr. Thayer told you, anything can be done, within the law, to get a home ready for a returning veteran is all to the good in the way of keeping up army morale. I imagine Simonetta drops a line to Pell once in a while—not just microfilms or voice letters, either. She'll tell him what we're doing and he'll get a great kick out of it. . . . When we've looked over Simonetta's house, why not come back to my house for supper?'

'It's awfully kind of you, Briny, but I haven't been anywhere yet and——'

'I haven't asked you to go "anywhere". I've asked you to come to South Boston. We'll have no more talk about it. . . .'

Shaun Collins and Terence Lenahan were both very sanguine about what could be done to the little house. Simonetta listened to them enthralled while they talked about two-by-fours, sheet-rock and semi-gloss. When they finally closed the door of the little house behind them, Shaun suggested that she should ride over to South Boston with him and Terence, since Brian's car was only a roadster; and without making something of a scene on the street, Emily could not object, then and there. However, when she and Brian were actually on Broadway, she tried to argue.

'You were really pretty high-handed, Briny. I was delighted to have you come to the garden. I'd be delighted to have you come again. But, as I tried to explain to you, I'm not going anywhere just now. As far as that goes, you ought not to need an explanation.'

'You mean because you're going to have a baby and are beginning to show it?'

'Of course.'

'Well, that's not a very convincing argument to the eldest of eight children.'

'You know there's another reason. It's less than three months since Roger died.'

'Yes, I know that too. All the same, you ought to be in a state of expectancy pretty soon.'

'I'd be more inclined to believe you were right if I hadn't been such a failure thus far.'

'A failure? How?'

'Well, I failed in everything I meant to do on Joy Street, didn't I? I didn't help Roger as I wanted to.'

'Why, Emily, you made him completely happy! Do you call that failing! No wife could have been more loyal and devoted than you were! And you were an inspiration and a help to him in his work besides! Suppose your house wasn't the sort of centre you'd planned—don't get the idea for one moment it wasn't the sort that meant most to him, in every way. *It meant a lot to me, too! It meant a lot to Pell!* You haven't thought of it in terms of those poker parties that *did* bring about good fellowship among alien groups. You haven't thought about it in terms of medieval betrothal service, that had all the solemnity of a marriage and transfigured two persons' lives. Why don't you? Why can't you?'

'I—I don't know, Briny.'

'Well, won't you try? If you will, I think you'll stop seeing the Joy Street house as a failure.'

'Yes, I'll try.'

'That's all I want to know, right now. If I know you're trying, it'll help me try too.' He paused a moment, and then went on slowly, 'You know that I went around for more than two years talking about "England's War", don't you? That I didn't apply for a commission in the Navy until I was faced with the probability that I'd be recalled as an infantry corporal in the United States Army? How do you think I've felt about that, ever since Pearl Harbour? How do you think I feel about never getting combat duty—I've tried and tried for it. David tried and got it—at least he's going to have it. Pell didn't even have to try for it. He got it without trying, he's won the Silver Star already. A lot of citations I'll get for fooling around on the B Docks. And it serves me right too!'

'Briny, I had no idea you felt like this!'

'How did you expect me to feel? As far as that goes, how do you think I felt when Roger died? He was a war casualty all right—doing the work of three men besides himself, only one of them good enough to lick his boots, at that! I'd have done more for the war effort, as it's turned out, if I'd stayed in the office, too, than I've done in that stinking South Pacific port. Roger might be alive if I had!'

'Briny, you mustn't talk like this. You're not being fair to yourself.'

'All right, don't let me hear you talk the way you have been doing, either, then. As a matter of fact, we can't either of us talk this way or any way much longer right now—we will some other time though. Meanwhile, I've got to take you to the house before the hungry hordes eat up all the scrod. There aren't any big platters weighted down with steak in our dining-room any more, worse luck. But scrod's pretty good eating at that, the way my mother fixes it. You'll see.'

Several hours later, when he took her back to Louisburg Square, she confessed to him that she was glad he had made her go out, that she had really enjoyed the evening with his big cheerful family. The general atmosphere was still contagiously hearty and Mary Collins was still the personification of loving-kindness. Inevitably, Emily responded to this and, as she did so, she became suddenly conscious of release from the constrictions of the past months. When she went to bed that night, it was not to lie wretched and wakeful for hours, but to fall almost instantly into quiet and refreshing slumber.

In the course of the next week, Brian persuaded her, without too much difficulty, to go off with him on several all-day trips in his car, and he sat in the Joy Street garden with her and her father and dined with her and old Mrs. Forbes on Louisburg Square. When his leave was almost up, he suggested that perhaps she would let him drive her and Deirdre to Hollyhock Hill.

'If you're sure——'

'Of course I'm sure. Look, philanthropy isn't one of my strong points. If I wanted to be night-clubbing instead of driving you around, you can be damn sure that's what I'd be doing.'

Mark and Elizabeth and Archie were not coming to Hollyhock Hill until after college closed; but Una Randell, despite her heavy schedule of chores, had been over to air and clean the house and stock it with enough foodstuffs so that the early arrivals would have the wherewithal for their first supper and their first breakfast. Brian spent the night, but Emily seemed so wholesomely sleepy, after they finished their evening meal, that he did not try to have another serious talk with her; and he had to be up and away at dawn the next morning. However, he left a little note behind him, which Deirdre brought up on Emily's breakfast tray. It had no heading and no closing and contained only two lines:

261

Remember you're not numb any more or apathetic, either. You're just waiting. And you've got lots ahead of you to wait for.

As one tranquil day succeeded another, Emily began to understand more and more clearly what Brian had meant, and to believe, more and more wholeheartedly, that he was right. With the quickening of the child in her womb came a general quickening throughout her whole being, and she began to marvel that she had been so long insensible to those great forces which destroy only to rebuild. Roger would live again in his child and hers and her task now was of preparation for this resurrection.

Although it was so quiet at Hollyhock Hill, Emily was conscious of no tedium, even before the arrival of Mark and Elizabeth and their baby. She occupied herself with minor household tasks and she had begun really to enjoy books again. Without having much aptitude for music, she found that she enjoyed playing on the old square piano; and when Simonetta came up for the week-end, as she did two or three times, Emily sat for hours listening to her. Simonetta brought Pell's letters with her and read them aloud, in part, to Emily. They were growing closer and closer together in every way, all the time and, because of this, Simonetta told Emily many things of her own accord. She spoke of the progress being made on their little house, and of the special courses she was about to take, now that the Conservatory was closed for the summer. She had found some available at Boston University and had decided on a six weeks' session in English and history. Finally, she spoke to Emily about her mother.

'She's gone back to Lynn. Uncle Ernesto and his wife were willing she should come—they said it was time to let bygones be bygones and of course, in a way, their house seems like home to her. I don't know whether she'll stay there permanently or not; if she doesn't, she'll have a little apartment of her own near by. She isn't violent and vindictive any more. Just crushed and hopeless, because she feels life has dealt her one more blow; or she would be, if her Church wasn't such a comfort to her. I'm glad it is.'

'I'm glad too.'

Momentarily, Emily wished that she might have found some comfort in a church, after Roger died, when she herself had felt

262

crushed and hopeless. She thought of Sister Mary Theresa's visit and resolved that she would call at the convent when she went back to town. But as far as she was able to visualize the situation, the only real comfort she had derived had come from Brian. He had made her see that even though life did deal out blows, it also dealt out blessings, and that the better you stood up to hard knocks, the less unendurable they seemed. He had also made her see that she was waiting for something that was worth while.

When the Merriweathers and Jenny arrived from Hanover, Hollyhock Hill became less quiet, but pleasantly so. Archie was a precocious, noisy little boy, unusually knowing and active for his age. In so far as possible, he was encouraged to confine his activities to the rear gallery, which was well railed, and which had only one gate that was always carefully latched. Emily enjoyed sitting on the gallery, watching over Archie while he played there. Meanwhile, she did a little desultory reading and knitting and glanced, every now and then, down over the terraced hill to the brook and to the pond which had been formed where this was dammed. There was no pain in the memories connected with that any longer. She saw it now as it really was, warm and blue under the summer sun, not cold and glittering under the northern lights. She did not visualize it in connection with David—that is, not often.

Then one day when she was sitting on the gallery, quietly and contentedly, thinking of all that the future still held for her, as Brian had begged her to do, she heard a little click, a sound so slight that she would not have been conscious of it, had it not been alien to all the other sounds which Archie normally made. Next she realized that, with fantastic swiftness, he had fumbled at the latch and undone it and that he was pelting down the terrace towards the little pond....

She caught up with him just as he slid over the brink. She slid in after him, drawing him back to safety. Then, unexpectedly sliding a little farther on the slippery mud beneath the surface, she suddenly stepped off into deeper water. She tried to regain her footing, failed and sank but it was only a matter of moments before she had regained the surface and had struggled to the shore....

The same kindly, overworked little man who had taken care of her when she sprained her ankle came to see her; he agreed that any slight sensation of chilliness which she might have had was not likely to amount to anything. But he looked more sober when she told him how she had slipped and struggled for a footing which she could not find.

'You're how far along, Mrs. Field?'

'A little over six months.'

'Well.... Of course I'm very sorry you're not where your own physician can see you. Not that I think there's any cause for alarm—— But perhaps we ought to send you back to Boston in an ambulance. We'll see how you are in the morning. Meanwhile, I'm going to give you a sedative. I want you to get a good night's sleep.'

They did not send her back to Boston in an ambulance and she did not get a good night's sleep. Shortly before midnight, she was seized with violent pain; and in the dark hour just before dawn, she was delivered of a premature baby. It was a little girl, and it breathed for a few minutes before the doctor laid it sorrowfully down, knowing there was nothing more he could do for it. And there was a great deal he must do for its mother, if she were not to die too.

Emily was very ill for a long time. Her recovery was retarded by her belief that, since she had lost her baby, she did not have much to live for after all. Brian, who had been assigned to the B Docks in Norfolk, tried several times to convince her that she was wrong, but he did not make much headway. He had been mistaken before, she reminded him; why should she think he was right now? He realized that she was still very weak and completely disheartened and he did not try to argue with her. But one day she realized, of her own accord, that she was waiting again, and that her expectancy was not only hopeful, but glad.

She was waiting for David to come home.

CHAPTER XVI

In the meanwhile, a great many other things had happened. The most important of these, of course, was that the war had ended and that, with the cessation of hostilities, a new era had begun for Emily, as it had for everyone else. Her viewpoint, like many women's, however, was personal rather than general; she was more affected by the changes which came into her own life and those of the persons whom she actually knew, than by those wrought in the lives of persons in distant lands. Simonetta was radiant with joy in those days, and Emily caught the reflection of it.

For Pell had indeed proved himself a modern knight in armour. His military achievements had been both glamorous and meteoric; and Emily had shared with Simonetta the mingled excitement and pride with which his beloved had followed his progress. And now his return as Colonel to the United States, and his marriage to Simonetta were only a matter of months. The little old house on Joy Street, completely renovated, was already prepared for them to move into; even the grand piano which dominated the living-room had been installed. Simonetta and Pell were to be married at St. Leonard's, and Emily and Brian were to stand up with them. There would be two wedding breakfasts, one at Old Venice, for the special delectation of Italian friends and connections, and another at Old Mrs. Forbes' house, in order that everyone connected with Cutter, Mills might be entertained in a manner which would seem more suitable to conservative Bostonians. Pell and Simonetta had decided not to take a wedding journey; they preferred to go straight to their little house and Pell was going back to work at the office immediately.

Brian was able to get to Boston from Norfolk reasonably often in these days, and the question of his return to the office had already been raised too; but he had been noncommittal. He made no secret of the fact that, if he were free, in time to enter the campaign, he intended to run against Russell Forbes for the United States Senate. If he won, he would be going to Washington in January of '47; he did not propose to commit himself to anything which would keep him in Boston beyond that date. This decision might easily have caused a coolness between him and Old Mrs. Forbes, had Brian not breezily made it evident that he preferred to see Emily in his mother's house than on Louisburg Square, and had not Emily made equally evident the pleasure she took in going to South Boston. Her grandmother wisely decided that it was better not to make overmuch of an issue which would only serve to separate her from her favourite granddaughter. She had managed to persuade Emily to stay on at her house, first because the girl was really not well enough to return to her own, and next because, for the first time, Old Mrs. Forbes had pleaded loneliness and the handicap of her growing incapacity.

Emily, for her part, felt no special urge to return to Joy Street and she was honestly glad to feel that she was being of some service to her grandmother. She worked in her garden again now, and she and her father continued to meet there, when it was warm enough, and to enjoy each other's companionship during the late afternoons. When Brian was home on leave, he frequently joined them there. Emily kept the wine cupboard well stocked, and went in and out of the kitchen and pantry as occasion demanded; but she had not once been upstairs. Deirdre aired and cleaned the premises and reported that everything about them was unchanged. Emily was quite willing to take her word for it.

However, since Old Mrs. Forbes seemed to feel so strongly that someone should supervise every nook and corner of the house at Louisburg Square, Emily did this meticulously; and one day she asked Brian if he would care to go to the attic with her; she thought he might find it interesting. He did not quite see what an attic might possibly provide that would be intriguing; but he was entirely amenable to going there with Emily, if that was what she wanted him to do. So they climbed the last steep flight of stairs together and, when they reached the door at the top, she handed him a large key. As she did so, he noticed for the first time that she had two small glasses in her hand.

'What are those for?'

'Have a little patience, you'll see.'

He unlocked the door and opened it. Directly in front of him stood rows of great hand-blown bottles filled with rum, and the neck of each was encircled by a chain, to which a tag was attached. He bent over and inspected the nearest one.

' "This rum was taken in this container around the Horn—1830, 1838, 1845",' he read. 'Why, Christ in the mountains! It's more than a hundred years old!'

'Certainly it is. Look at some of those other labels. The old theory was that the prolonged rolling and pitching of sailing vessels improved the quality—in addition to ageing, of course. Now you know what the two glasses are for. We'll draw up a couple of those tavern chairs, over in the corner, and have a drink of Great Grandfather's super-special brand.'

After Brian had placed the chairs where Emily had designated, and filled the glasses from one of the bottles labelled GOOD HOPE, he leant back, alternately sipping and sighing with satisfaction.

'Why didn't you ever bring me here before?' he inquired at length. 'I'd say, without a moment's hesitation, that this is the most interesting place in the house. I'd say it had everything needed for a *tête-à-tête*, too—seclusion, comfort, atmosphere and the means of unlimited refreshment.'

'I didn't intend to have the amount of refreshment unlimited, Briny.'

He set down his glass, suddenly grave. 'That's not worrying you, is it, Emily?'

'Isn't what worrying me?'

'That I might drink too much?'

'No-o-o. I've always supposed you were a little on the thirsty side, as the saying goes. But that's really none of my affair, is it?'

'It might be. So I'd really like to set your mind at rest on that score. I used to drink too much, now and again. But I've never once done it since that historic dinner-party—which is a good reason why you might set it down as a blessing in disguise. I've never wanted to run the risk of being as much ashamed of myself again as I was after that night. I'm pretty serious about this, Emily. You can count on it.'

'I think you deserve all kinds of credit, Briny, for making up your mind to do something that must have been awfully hard for you and then sticking to it the way you have. I think——'

'I'm not trying to take any credit for it. I don't want any. I just want you to tell me you're not afraid I'll ever disgrace you.'

'Briny, I just said it really wasn't any of my affair.'

'And I just said that it might be. Now I'll say that I hope more than anything in the world it will be.'

She had continued to toy with her glass while they talked. Now she set it down on the floor beside her, as he had done with his.

'I'm not sure I know just what you mean, Briny', she said quietly.

'You aren't? Why, you must be! You must know I've been in love with you for years! You must know that I've waited and waited for the time to come when I thought it was decent to ask you to marry me.'

'But I didn't! It never occurred to me that you were in love with me. When Roger died and—and the baby, I thought you were *sorry* for me.'

'I was. I was damn sorry for you. I knew what you were going through. No one could help being sorry for you who knew that.'

'Well, and then you tried to help me realize there was still something ahead of me. Something worth waiting for.'

'Yes. Gradually I tried to get it into your head that you couldn't live all the rest of your life with a memory. You're too young! You're too lovely! You're too—too feminine! You're bound to fall in love again. You were made to have children, you'd be a wonderful mother. You can't thwart nature, the way you were trying to. You ought to be married right now. My God, you're going to marry me, no matter what I have to do to make you! You'll be so glad, afterwards, that you won't care!'

He leapt up, and, pulling her to her feet, threw his arms around her and, taking her in a vice-like hold, kissed her as she had never been kissed before. It was completely useless for her to struggle for freedom; since she could not escape the embrace, she had no choice but to accept it. When Brian finally released his grip to the extent of holding her at arm's length, he looked down at her with savage joy.

'Now kiss back, darling, and then we'll really get some place,' he said, drawing her towards him again.

'No, we won't. Let me go, Brian.'

'And what'll make me, I'd like to know? Not you, my dear. I tell you, all you need is——'

'I *will* make you. I won't marry you. I *can't*. I'm in love with someone else.'

'You're not! You're just saying that——'

'I've told you the truth, Brian. If you don't let me go now, I'll never speak to you again as long as I live. I'll never see you again. You'd better believe me. Because I mean it.'

'You say you're in love with someone else. How long has this been going on?'

'In a way, it's been going on for years.'

'You mean, before Roger died?'

'Don't look at me that way, Brian. It wasn't—I didn't ... I almost told you about it that day you kept saying I hadn't been a failure, that no woman could be more loyal and devoted to her husband than I was to Roger. I was loyal, I was devoted. I put all my heart and soul into the effort, because I was trying to make up to him for—for what I didn't feel for him, for what I couldn't give him.'

'Then he never knew?'

'No. At least, I think he was vaguely jealous, for just a little while, when we were first married, but——'

'When you were *first married*! Then he had made love to you? It didn't matter to him that you were married, the way it did to me?'

'Please let me finish, Brian. He had—he'd attempted a little light love-making. Nothing like—well, nothing like what you did just now,' she added, her colour deepening still further. 'I don't think I was the only woman he kissed casually and talked to that way. I think it was more or less natural for him to do so. I'm sure he was very attractive to women generally, and I suppose that type——'

'Yes. I know all about that type. In fact, we had one in our office.' He broke off suddenly. 'You don't mean to tell me——' he began. Then he interrupted himself again. 'Go on,' he said curtly, after a moment's pause.

'Perhaps you don't know as much as you think you do about that type, Brian,' Emily said calmly. 'Because when this man I'm talking about really had a chance to make all kinds of love to me, when I'm afraid I mightn't have tried to stop him, he didn't do it. He had just as much to do with saving my marriage as I had myself. But before he went away, he did tell me that he loved me. He did say that if things had been different ... He thought he had a right to say that much. I'm not sure

269

whether he did or not, but I know he thought so. I know he wouldn't have done it unless he had.'

'And you didn't hear from him again before Roger died?'

'Never directly. Not once. And when people told me how lucky I was not to have anyone I cared about in danger, I felt like such an awful hypocrite. Because of course I was half sick with worry, because of course I read the casualty lists every day and lay awake every night, wondering . . .'

'But you've heard from him since?'

'Yes, just intermittently. And at first very impersonally. He didn't write love letters—at least not exactly.'

'He didn't ask you outright to marry him?'

'Brian, I don't think you have a right to ask for so many details. The letters have been wonderful. They've made me very happy. They've given me something to live for again.'

'And now you've heard that this man's coming home?'

'Yes. I had a letter this morning. He said he wasn't sure yet when he could get here, but some time this week. He said he'd let me know. He said—oh, Briny, he said he had something very important to tell me, something that couldn't wait any longer!'

Her voice, which at first had been so quiet, then troubled and then calm again, suddenly rang out with gladness. She looked up at Brian with shining eyes.

'I meant to tell you about this today anyhow,' she said. 'I was all ready when—when you interrupted me. And I thought after I'd told you, we would have a second drink—just a little one. A—a sort of toast. I didn't dream, you see, that you felt the way you did—the way you do. I'm terribly sorry, Brian. I think a lot of you. But I'm not in love with you. I couldn't be. You understand that now, don't you?'

'Yes, I understand that now.'

'So, of course, you don't want to drink the toast? Of course you'd rather go downstairs.'

'But of course I want to drink it! Of course I wouldn't dream of going downstairs until I had.'

He picked up the two glasses, lifted one of the old hand-blown bottles with the GOOD HOPE label and poured out the fragrant old rum. Then he put the bottle back in its place and, after handing Emily her glass, raised his own.

'I can't toast you personally,' he said, 'because then you couldn't drink with me and of course that's what I want you to do. So let's drink instead to your married happiness—with a husband who loves you better than anyone else in the world!'

The interlude in the attic left Emily more shaken than she would have cared to admit. After Brian left, she went to her room and, much to her own indignation, burst into a sudden and uncontrollable weeping. When the storm had spent itself, she was so exhausted that, despite her scorn for daytime rests, she flung herself down on the chaise-longue, and it was only after a prolonged period that she told herself, resolutely, she had acted like a Victorian female long enough; if she were not careful, the next thing she knew she would be swooning. She dragged herself up, washed her face and applied a conservative amount of make-up, tidied her hair and, taking David's letter in her hand, went to her grandmother's room.

Old Mrs. Forbes was herself so engrossed in a letter that she did not immediately look up. When she tardily realized that her granddaughter was standing in front of her, obviously waiting to speak with her, she gave a slight start.

'Why, Emily, I didn't know you were there! Don't frighten a poor feeble old lady by creeping up on her like that.'

'May I sit down and hear the latest news?' Emily asked.

'By all means. I'd have sent for you in a few minutes to talk it over with you—at least I'd have sent to find out whether Brian Collins was still here, or whether you'd gone streaking off to South Boston with him.'

'The way you say "South Boston" makes it sound like "South Pole", Grandmamma. Brian left more than an hour ago, and I haven't the slightest intention of streaking off to South Boston or anywhere else this evening.' Then she added quickly, 'Go on and give me your great news. I suppose Elizabeth is going to have another baby.'

'Yes, but that's only one of the important items in her letter. Mark's been offered a professorship at Harvard. He's resigning at Dartmouth, effective at the end of the college year, and they're leaving Hanover as soon afterwards as they conveniently can.'

'Well, good for Mark! I should think he and Elizabeth would both enjoy Cambridge very much.'

'They'd prefer to live in Boston. And of course I'd prefer to have them. I want Archie where I can keep my eye on him. He's a handful all right. Some day this house will be his. I've been meaning to tell you, for some time, that I'd decided to leave i to Archie, on account of his name. After all, you have your own house, and your father and mother persisted in selling theirs, so they don't deserve any special consideration. It's quite obvious Sherman and Sue don't ever intend to leave the Cape and that Russell won't ever have any children. Therefore, as long as this is going to belong to Archie some day, I think it would be very fitting to have him grow up here.'

'You mean you'd have Elizabeth and Mark come here, Grand-mamma? I did just think about my house. But if you would really *rather* have them here I'll decide what to do about my house later. You'll write to Elizabeth tonight, won't you, and ask her? Meanwhile, I have something I wanted to tell you about too. I had a letter from David Salomont this morning.'

'That's not unusual, is it? I was under the impression you'd been hearing from him right along, for some time.'

'I have—not regularly, but fairly frequently until lately. Now he's written to say he's coming home. He might arrive in Boston almost any time this week. And he's got something "very important" to tell me. I'll show you the letter, if you like.'

Her grandmother looked up at her searchingly. Emily's tone had suddenly changed, just as it had when she was talking with Brian, a couple of hours earlier; where there had previously been a forced quiet about it, it now rang with released joy. The expression in Old Mrs. Forbes' face changed too; it ceased to be one of defensive determination and became one of singular sympathy and understanding. It was a long while since Emily had seen that illusive look of beauty which had somehow survived the years.

'No,' Old Mrs. Forbes said with unwonted gentleness. 'No, I don't want to see the letter. If it's the kind you're leading me to believe, no one except you ought to see it. But I'm very glad you've got it—at last. I don't think you'll have so much trouble making decisions from now on. And I'll be very glad to see David Salomont himself, when he gets here.'

The telegram announcing his impending arrival came the following morning. Emily had not dared look for it so soon, in view of the previous noncommittal statement that he would arrive 'some day that week'. She had lain awake, the greater part of the previous night, trying to map out a tentative plan of action. It was all very well to say that the house on Louisburg

Square was large enough to accommodate both herself and the Merriweather family; but Emily knew that such an arrangement would have intangible as well as tangible disadvantages. The household would and should revolve primarily around Archie and the new baby, and secondly around Mark and the requirements of his important position; Emily would represent an alien element in this scheme of things.... Well, she supposed that the Merriweathers would not be moving in until September and that would give her plenty of time for readjustment. Her grandmother had not told her when the new baby was due and she had forgotten to inquire. It might very well be earlier than September and in that case ... She would find out right away. But perhaps it would be better for her to make up her mind, without any more dillydallying, to move back into her own house, temporarily.

It would have been helpful if David had been a little more definite in his letter. It had not said whether he was now about to be separated from the Service, or whether he was merely coming home on leave; in the latter case, he would have only about thirty days. But a great deal could be done in thirty days. A great deal could happen—a great many wonderful things....

She finally fell asleep thinking of these things and then, in the morning, came the telegram. She went downstairs to tell her grandmother that he would be there that afternoon, and Old Mrs. Forbes was delighted. In fact, she seemed to be in a generally mellow mood. She had written Elizabeth directly after her conversation with Emily the day before and Elizabeth, who had received the letter in the morning mail, had immediately telephoned her mother, saying that she and Mark were both very grateful for the invitation and that they were happy to accept it.

'Did she tell you when she expected the new baby?'

'Yes, early in August. So they'll come down here right after college closes. That won't seem like any time at all.'

'No, it's really very soon,' Emily said aloud. Mentally, she added, 'I'll tell Deirdre tomorrow that we're moving back to Joy Street. I'll call up the bank and the storage company. I'll have Pierce's send in some supplies.'

'Have you told that young Irishman David's coming back?' Old Mrs. Forbes inquired.

'Yes. That is, I didn't mention David by name, but I said——'

'You let him know you had other interests. I knew you'd been through some kind of a scene. No doubt he knew to whom you were referring, even if you didn't mention David by name. Well, perhaps Brian will find it convenient to stay a little more steadily in Norfolk than he's been doing lately, after he finds that David's back.'

'Perhaps he will. Just the same, I'm sure he'll want to stand up with Pell, as they put it. They've been writing each other about it for quite a while now—ever since Pell knew approximately when he'd be getting home.'

'And it still looks as if that would be midsummer?'

'Yes. August at the latest. Possibly earlier. And Brian hopes to be separated from the Navy before that, so he's going to campaign for the Senate. His nomination papers are already signed and filed.'

Old Mrs. Forbes snorted slightly. 'I don't believe it will do him much good. He'll find it pretty hard to dislodge a Forbes from the Senate. There's always been one there, ever since I can remember.'

Emily thought that her grandmother, who had seemed so radiant when she herself came into the room a little earlier, already acted rather tired; so she said there were lots of things she needed to do, and went back upstairs. As a matter of fact, she had nothing to do except to wait for David; but she noticed that Old Mrs. Forbes tired more and more easily these days, and she wondered how well her grandmother would stand the strain of having a noisy child and a crying baby and a busy man in the house. She filled in the remainder of the morning with trivial tasks; and immediately after luncheon she did over her hair and manicured her nails and changed her dress. She chose a green one which was especially becoming, and which she felt sure David would like. He had once told her that she looked like the personification of spring, when he had found her in her little garden, wearing a green dress, and the one she put on now was not unlike the one she had worn that spring afternoon so long before. (Was it really six years? Yes, it must be—six or even seven. Well, he would have forgotten by this time. Men did not remember little things like that; it was only women who treasured them.) Now she unlocked her jewel box and studied its contents with care. But, after a moment, she closed it and sat turning it over in her hands. Then for the second time that day, she went to her grandmother's room.

Old Mrs. Forbes was seated in front of her dressing-table and Doris was putting the finishing touches on her hair. Her jewel box stood open, as it usually did at such a time, and she was lifting out one of its velvet trays and peering down into its depths with the unfeigned pleasure that she had always taken in doing so. She looked up at Emily with one of her rare, splendid smiles.

'Well, my dear—this must be mental telepathy. I was just on the point of sending Doris for you. I've been thinking, since last night—as you're not going to have this house, you should have other things correspondingly valuable. I told you, before you were married, that I wasn't sure diamonds would ever suit you —diamonds or brocade. Now I'm beginning to change my mind, at least about the diamonds. You're developing. I might change my mind about the brocade, too. Anyway, the jewel box is already open, as you can see. Tell me if there's anything you'd like to wear.'

'I guess it *was* mental telepathy, Grandmamma. I came down on purpose to ask you if you'd lend me something. I couldn't seem to find anything in my own jewel box that I wanted to put on.'

'No wonder. You've never had any jewellery important enough for the present occasion. I won't *lend* you anything. But I'll *give* you whatever you fancy. Don't look at me like that—I'm not Mephistopheles, tempting Marguerite, you know. Just your poor feeble old grandmother, who's very fond of you and very pleased to see you so happy.'

Emily bent over the box, afraid to trust herself to speak. At last she picked up a necklace formed of a slender, platinum chain, from which graduated diamonds were suspended, a large one in the middle, a small one embedded in the clasp. Then she looked questioningly at Old Mrs. Forbes.

'An excellent selection,' her grandmother said briskly. 'But of course you need the proper ornaments to go with it. These eardrops were given to me at about the same time. I think they'd do very well. And for a brooch and bracelets——'

'Oh, Grandmamma, I don't need a brooch and bracelets, too!'

'Of course you need a brooch and bracelets too. Don't tell me what you need. There! You look very nice, Emily. Run along now! I've told Pearson to show David Salomont up immediately when he arrives. I suppose you'll go to the library and bury yourself in a book—or at least pretend to. I don't imagine you'll have very long to wait.'

It was astonishing how dull reading material could be. Emily tried the daily paper, several weeklies, a biography and a murder mystery, without finding anything that arrested her attention. Then she changed the position of several vases and slightly rearranged the flowers these contained. It was so warm that there was really no excuse for a fire, but she finally lighted one and fed it, slender stick by slender stick, to keep it alive without having it burn too brightly. The period of waiting had begun to seem both endless and unendurable, when Pearson at last opened the folding doors.

'Major Salomont, Mrs. Field.'

She hastened forward, both hands outstretched in welcome, calling his name in a glad voice. She had expected that he would take her in his arms as soon as the doors closed behind the butler. Instead, David clasped her outstretched hands in his, firmly rather than caressingly, and regarded her with smiling approval without drawing her closer to him.

'Emily, how lovely you look! I never saw you when you were half so beautiful!'

'You look wonderful to me, David. But of course you would, anyhow.'

'And of course you would, anyhow. But you really *are* a great deal more beautiful than when I left. It's certainly worth crossing the Atlantic to look at you. Incidentally, those diamonds add just the finishing touch to your costume. I don't think you were wearing those before.'

'No. Grandmamma gave them to me today. In honour of your homecoming. She's very eager to see you herself.'

'No more than I am to see her. I'm one of her most devoted admirers. But we're going to have a talk by ourselves first, aren't we? You haven't asked me to sit down yet, you know.'

'Oh! I'm terribly sorry! Of course. . . . I like this sofa, don't you? . . . Now start at the beginning and tell me everything.'

She spoke with great cordiality, but with some confusion. All the time they had been standing, facing each other with clasped hands but at arm's length, she had been waiting, from one moment to the next, for him to fold her in a fond embrace, to tell her how much he loved her and to invite the response which would have been so immediate. She felt both bewildered and frustrated, and she was not sure she had been able to conceal this, when she so belatedly invited David to be seated, after he himself had suggested it. Her feeling of bewilderment increased as he settled himself at one end of the sofa, with the obvious expectation that she would ensconce herself at the other.

'That's rather a large order, isn't it?' he inquired, picking up the thread of the conversation. 'You know a good deal already, from my letters.'

She smiled, determined now that she had recovered from the first shock of his unexpected behaviour, to show no more confusion and, above all, to betray no surprise or disappointment. Of course there was some explanation, which would soon be forthcoming; he must have something on his mind so important that, until he had unburdened himself, he could not be in the mood for lovemaking. She looked at him confidently, waiting for him to go on.

'Of course you realized it was a great blow to me when I found I wasn't going into Normandy over the beaches,' he began. 'But, as it turned out, I can't be thankful enough I went in with Patton instead. When we actually got into Germany, when we began to lay waste to it, forging farther and farther ahead all the time we were destroying—well, that was when I began to know I was doing what I'd been waiting for, what I'd been living for—years and years and years! The only thing I regret is that we couldn't do more damage and more killing, because there wasn't time.'

He spoke with the atavistic joy of a ruthless conqueror, gloating over the annihilation of a hated foe. Emily murmured something indicative of understanding; however, she sensed that almost any comment, at this stage of his outburst, would seem like an interruption.

'But when we got to Wiesbaden, there was a sort of letdown. There wasn't any point in going farther right then. We'd done such a thorough job, we damn well had to stop for a while. We were damn glad to get into decent quarters and relax. We were damn glad to see some women again.'

Involuntarily, Emily drew a deep breath. So all this had been leading up to a confession—a confession such as almost any man, if he were thoroughly honest, was obliged to make sooner or later to the woman he really loved, to the woman he wanted for his wife. Roger had been the shining exception to the sordid rule. But she had always known that there must have been other women in David's life, and that though he would have been

277

selective, in normal times, because he was naturally fastidious, the time of which he was now talking had been anything but normal. She could forgive whatever he had done, in those first weeks of letdown at Wiesbaden.

'I'm sure you must have been. But you don't have to tell me about that, honestly you don't.'

'Yes I do. That's what I came here for.'

'Why of course it isn't! You've come here because——'

She must not be the one to say it first. Until he had done so, she could not say, 'You've come here because you love me and I love you, because there's no impediment any more to our love, because we're free to express it in every way.' She waited for him to say this and instead, he said something else.

'I've come here to tell you that I saw Priscilla in Wiesbaden.'

For a moment Emily found that, strangely enough, she could not seem to answer. When she did so, she hoped and believed that her voice sounded not only natural but casual.

'Well, I'm very glad. I'm sure you must have found her good company. Priscilla's quite amusing, when she's in the mood.'

'Emily, I know you're not consciously making this harder for me. But what I've been trying to tell you—in fact, what I came here on purpose to tell you—is that I fell in love with Priscilla.'

This time Emily did not attempt any answer. She sat staring at David, in dumb and horrible unbelief, and she did not resist when he leant forward and took her hand. She was vaguely aware that the gesture was meant to be kindly, almost compassionate, but it failed in its purpose. It seemed to have no meaning whatsoever.

'All this is so hard to say that I know I'll do it very badly,' David went on. 'But I've got to begin by asking you to believe that I never lied to you. When I told you I loved you, it was true—so overwhelmingly true that I felt I had to tell you, even though you were married to someone else. You do believe me, don't you, Emily?'

She still could not speak, she still could not make any immediate sign. But after a moment or two, though her lips were still pressed tightly together, she inclined her head, and he took it for a sign of assent.

'I went overseas, still loving you. I still loved you when Roger died. I thought I ought to wait a year at least before I told you so again. And then I heard that you'd lost your baby, that you were very ill. It didn't seem the right time to subject you to any more emotional strain. There are times when a human being can stand just so much. . . . You know that, don't you?'

'Yes,' Emily murmured, at last finding it possible to frame the single word.

'By then we were preparing for the invasion, preparing very intensively. And I thought I'd wait a little longer. Until my declaration of love could be coupled with a sort of paean of victory. I told you I'd say all this very badly, I know I am. But you do understand, don't you?'

'Yes,' Emily said again.

'After that there wasn't any time to write letters. Not the kind I wanted to write, not the kind that would have been worthy of you. But I still meant to do it, I still loved you. My God, I don't know why I keep saying I still loved you as if it were in the past. I love you *now*. As much as I ever did, in one way. But not the way I did before. Not the way I did when I first saw Priscilla again, in Paris.'

'In *Paris*?'

'Yes, I'd seen her there, before I saw her in Wiesbaden. She was at St. Germain-en-Laye for eight months, doing switchboard. Well, you must know all about that too.'

'I know a little. Obviously I don't know everything.'

'Of course I'd seen a good deal of Priscilla before I left Boston, I used to go down to the Cape almost every Sunday and stay at her house. And the last time I went down there, she asked me if I wouldn't marry her.'

'*She* asked *you* if you wouldn't marry her!'

'Yes. Of course I wouldn't tell you this if she hadn't said I might. But after all, there's nothing especially astonishing about that. Any number of girls take the initiative in such matters, these days.'

'Not—not girls like——'

'No, not girls like you. But girls like Priscilla. And by that, I mean what you'd call "nice girls", Emily. Don't make any mistake about that.'

He was speaking in a different way now, more assertively and confidently. 'I laughed her off,' he went on. 'It wasn't a very kind thing to do, because she was already in love with me then —very much in love. But I thought perhaps it would be the best way to handle things.'

He paused, but he did not seem to expect Emily to say anything, and, after a brief interlude, he went on.

'Well, I don't need to tell you that by the time we'd seen each other once or twice in Wiesbaden, Priscilla didn't need to propose to me again. I proposed to her. It was she who reminded me about you. And I wouldn't be telling you the whole truth if I didn't admit that, by then, I needed such a reminder. I'd have married Priscilla right then and there if I could have cut enough red tape to do it and she'd have had me.'

'But how could she remind you about me? You don't mean to say you'd told her——'

'I'd never mentioned you by name. But the same day that she proposed to me I'd said I was in love with someone else, someone I couldn't ask to marry me because she wasn't free. Of course Priscilla guessed whom I meant. She couldn't very well help it. And when I proposed to her in Weisbaden, she asked me point-blank if you didn't have the right of way.'

'And what did you tell her?'

'I told her that you did. How could I say anything else? Even though I'd never asked you, in so many words, to marry me, that was because of a combination and a succession of circumstances. I'd *wanted* to marry you for a long time, and it was implicit in what I'd said to you. It wasn't your fault, either, that I didn't want to any longer. You hadn't done anything to change my feelings. It was just one of those things that happens once in a while, especially in wartime. When two people have been through a war together—well, somehow there's a bond between them that's different from other bonds. It's stronger. It has more meaning, it's bound to be more lasting. What happened as far as you and I are concerned won't happen again. From now on, if you release me, Priscilla'll be the only woman in my life.'

CHAPTER XVII

As Emily knocked once more at her grandmother's door, it was with the sensation that she was completing a cycle. Only a little more than twenty-four hours earlier she had come to this room, her heart overflowing with joy, to say she had heard that David was on his way home. Then she had come there again, still more joyously, to ask for jewels with which to adorn herself in welcome. Now she was coming to say that he had gone out of her life for ever.

Even before she saw her grandmother she realized, from the way she was told to enter, that Old Mrs. Forbes had been waiting to receive David and his affianced in a fitting manner. Emily opened the door, to be greeted by the sight of the old lady, sitting in one of her throne-like chairs, arrayed in her most elegant brocade and literally ablaze with diamonds.

'Where is David?' she asked abruptly.

'He's gone.'

'*Gone!* Gone where?'

'Down on the Cape. He offered to come here with me before he went, but I thought it would be better if he didn't. I thought it would be better if you and I were alone when I told you.'

'When you told me *what*?'

'What he's just told me—that he didn't come here to propose to me, that he's already proposed to Priscilla.'

Old Mrs. Forbes' lips moved slightly, but no sound came from them. Emily drew up a low, square stool, which stood in front of the fireplace, and sat down close to her grandmother.

'You mustn't blame either of them,' she said. 'We've got to be fair. I don't believe, any more, that Priscilla went after him because she was trying to get him away from me. I think she went after him because she loved him so much that she was determined to get him at any cost. I don't think any cost seemed to her too high. I—I understand how she felt. Because I've felt

281

the same way. Only I couldn't go after him. I could only wait for him to come to me. I don't mean just because conditions were different in the two cases, either. I mean because I haven't got it in me to do what she did. I'm not her kind.'

'No, you're not,' Old Mrs. Forbes said fiercely. 'And if you ask me——'

'Please let me finish, Grandmamma. I'm sincere in saying I don't blame Priscilla. I think her kind's very resolute—very brave—very—very splendid. I think David's kind is too. I want you to know I don't blame him, either. I want you to know that I believe he told me the truth when he said he loved me, that he loved me very much then and for a long time afterwards. But he changed ... I tell you I don't blame him for changing. How many men are there in the world who love the same woman all their lives?'

'There are some. And, unfortunately, there are a great many women who are never really in love with but one man. I'm afraid you're one of them. That's why I don't want you to give in to this so easily. I want you to fight back, to tell David you won't release him. He'll probably live to thank you for it. If he could change as far as you're concerned, he could change as far as Priscilla's concerned. And she's young, she'll get over it. She has any number of other suitors—one of them would do for her just as well as David. But no one else will ever do for you.'

'Again you're partly right and partly wrong, Grandmamma. I know I won't get over loving David, but I don't believe Priscilla will, either. And I don't believe David will change again. He said something to me that was very moving—very convincing. He said that when two people have been through a war together, there's a bond between them that has more meaning than other bonds. He said it was so much stronger that it was bound to be more lasting.'

For the first time, Old Mrs. Forbes looked away from Emily and again, though her lips moved, no sound came from them.

'So I'm not going to fight for him,' Emily said quietly. 'And nothing you or anyone else can say will make me change my mind about that. I've released him already. I know I'll love him as long as I live. But I don't want him for my husband any more.'

Her words rang with finality. She rose, setting the stool back in its customary place.

'David is only home on leave,' she announced. 'He's going

back to Germany. He wants to go back there. He's had a chance to serve on Major Wallis' staff at the Nuremberg trial. That means more to him, both as a lawyer and as a Jew, than anything else that could possibly happen to him—to have a part in bringing those arch-criminals, who've tortured his race and tried to exterminate it, to justice. Priscilla's about to come home too—he expects her before his leave is up. He wants to take her with him to Germany as his wife. That's why he's gone right on down to the Cape to tell Aunt Sue and Uncle Sherman they've got to get ready for a wedding. And you'd better make up your mind that you're going down on the Cape, too, at last, whether you want to or not. Because I'll never forgive you if you don't go with me to that wedding.'

The next morning Emily told her grandmother that she had decided to move back into her own house, that she was going there at noon to check on its general condition. If no major repairs were indicated—and Deirdre had never reported the visible need of any—there was no reason why she could not get in almost immediately. The warm spring weather was a great asset; once sunshine had been let into the house again, any lingering dampness would quickly disappear. And of course all bedding would be thoroughly aired. Inside of a week she should be reinstalled, without the slightest danger of overtaxing her strength or taking cold.

Old Mrs. Forbes did not attempt dissuasion. In fact, she was preternaturally silent in the days which followed David's brief visit. Several times Emily thought her grandmother seemed to be on the point of bursting into expostulation. But nothing came of it. Emily was back in her own house within the time limit she had set for herself; but though she had been correct in her expectation that no major repairs would be required, countless small renovations seemed desirable and she and Deirdre were both busy from morning till night. When her father dropped in on her, later afternoons, he found her healthily tired and only too glad to sit back and rest as long as he remained with her. Over and over again, he expressed his pleasure in finding her where she was.

'It's good to have you back here, Emily. I've always enjoyed the garden, of course. But I enjoy it much more now that the house is open too. It never seemed natural to me to see it closed.'

'Well you know what I said when you told me you regretted

the sale of the Gloucester Street house—it seemed the best thing at the time. When I closed this house, that seemed the best thing. Now it seems best to have it open again.'

She knew that he wanted to ask her certain questions and that he refrained, partly through natural reserve and partly because he did not want to run the risk of hurting her feelings. She appreciated his consideration, but she took advantage of it. However, when Brian burst in upon her, unceremoniously, one morning while she was dusting books, she quickly discovered that he had no similar inhibitions and that he not only meant to ask questions but to get answers.

'I had a wedding invitation this morning that came like a bolt from the blue: "Mr. and Mrs. Sherman Endicott Forbes request the honour of your presence at the marriage of their daughter, Priscilla Anne, to Major David Salomont." What's the meaning of this, Emily? I'll bet anything you didn't know it that day you lured me up to your grandmother's attic and induced me to guzzle down your great-grandfather's rum.'

'No, I didn't. . . . Have you been back to Cutter, Mills yet, Briny? Do they know you're already separated from the Navy?'

'I haven't been back there and they don't know it yet. I've got other things to do and other things on my mind. When you told me you wouldn't marry me because you were in love with someone else, you were talking about David Salomont. Yes or no?'

'Briny, I've told you before that you ask too many questions and that some of them are pretty presumptuous. I think it would be a wonderful idea if you'd give me a chance to dust these books while you go down to the office and say you're ready to start work again.'

'That's what you think. Do you want to know what I think? I think David Salomont is a——'

'Don't say it, Brian. Don't you dare say it.'

'All right. Then give me a good reason why I shouldn't.'

Either she would have to tell him, in substance, what she had told her grandmother, or she would have to let him go on misjudging and despising David. She laid down the first edition she was still holding and spoke very gravely.

'I'm sorry you won't take my word for it that there is a good reason. If you ask me to take your word for something, I do it. But, since you insist . . .'

He did not try to interrupt her simple and straightforward recital, and he did not speak immediately when she finished.

But he looked at her with unconcealed admiration and eventually he voiced this:

'You'd have made a good lawyer yourself, Emily. I never heard a case better presented.'

'I had a good case to present.'

'You've almost convinced me of it—not quite, but almost. Well, I won't bother you any more right now. Go back to your dusting. I'll take your advice and get on down to the office.'

A few days later, Emily asked Old Mrs. Forbes if she would like to have the Bruckers invited to stay at the Joy Street house during the wedding festivities since Elizabeth and her family would already be at the house on Louisburg Square by then, as they had purposely hastened their departure from Hanover.

'It's kind of you, Emily—kind and thoughtful. I think the Bruckers would appreciate such an invitation. I'd appreciate it for them.... I've never told you how I happened to know Morris Brucker in the first place, have I?'

'No,' Emily replied, resisting the temptation to add, 'You know very well you never did.'

'Well, I might just as well tell you now, if you'll sit down with me long enough.'

'There's no reason why I can't stay with you today as long as you like, Grandmamma.'

'I'm delighted to hear it.... All right then, going back to some rather ancient history, Morris Brucker's father, Hugo Brucker, was one of the greatest connoisseurs of his time. One of his galleries was in Budapest, and as soon as his son Morris was old enough, Hugo Brucker established him there. That was where I met them.'

'Yes, I remember, the first time David came to call, I telephoned you to find out whether his stepfather could come and see you, and you told me you were quite sure you knew him already. You mentioned Budapest then.'

'So I did.... Well, I used to go to the Brucker Galleries in Budapest fairly often. Your grandfather was minister to Austria-Hungary then and, unlike most people, we preferred Budapest to Vienna. Well, eventually, as you know, your grandfather was promoted. He was very helpful in the Harrison and McKinley campaigns and he was suitably rewarded by being sent first to Rome and then to St. Petersburg, as ambassador. I'd lost sight of Morris Brucker, for a time, while I was in Rome, but when I got to St. Petersburg, I found he'd been promoted too. He was manager of the Brucker Galleries there and he was gradually taking over his father's responsibilities.'

'You saw a good deal of Morris Brucker in St. Petersburg, didn't you, Grandmamma? Another thing I remember is that, when Morris Brucker came over to see you, he said that, when you were first in St. Petersburg, you used to go a great deal to his shop. He spoke of it as a shop, not a gallery.'

'That was just part of the joke. It was a magnificent gallery.'

'Well, anyway, he said that at first you were a good customer of his, that you made a great many selections from his stock, but that after a while you didn't buy anything more, because you had so many presents from grand dukes.'

'And of course that was just part of the joke too.'

'Was it really, Grandmamma?'

'Why should you think it wasn't, I'd like to know?'

Emily hesitated, but only for a moment. 'Partly because of the ring Mr. Brucker brought you. Partly because of something very indefinite David let drop about a grand duke named Feodor. And partly because—well, because I've felt for a long while there must have been a David in your life. I mean, someone you cared for in the same way I've cared for him.'

'There's someone like David in a good many women's lives, Emily.'

'There couldn't be. Because there aren't enough like him to go around. But the Grand Duke Feodor was something like him, wasn't he?'

Without answering, Old Mrs. Forbes began to twist her emerald ring around. Emily put her hand over it.

'If he was, it—it would help to have you tell me so, Grandmamma. Because you've been so magnificent all these years. And if it's been because you lost so much, instead of because you had so much ... If I thought there was some chance that I...'

She did not need to finish. Old Mrs. Forbes freed her fingers and began to stroke her granddaughter's hair.

'Yes,' she said. 'There's a great resemblance between David Salomont and the man I used to know, who was a grand duke and whose name was Feodor. That's enough for me to tell you now. Perhaps I'll tell you more some other time.'

As it turned out, Emily did not have to wait very long to

learn more.

The Bruckers accepted, with alacrity, her invitation to stay with her; and the evening of their arrival Morris Brucker himself, quite unconsciously, picked up the thread of Old Mrs. Forbes' narrative.

'It's good to see this tea service in use again,' he said. 'I always suspected, when it was reported "missing" from the Romanoff treasure, that it had been previously given to your grandmother. There wasn't much she couldn't have had, in those days, without so much as lifting her little finger. There will never be another American ambassadress to equal her, Mrs. Field, in Russia or anywhere else.'

He paused, as if for effect, and glanced towards his wife, who had so far sat silent, sipping her tea. Emily had glanced at her a good many times since she had come into the library. The resemblance between her and David was very marked, in many ways; she had the same fine features, the same air of assurance, and she wore her clothes with the same ease and elegance. Emily would have liked to know whether the mental characteristics of mother and son were as nearly the same. Absorbed as she was in what Mr. Brucker was saying, she longed to talk at length with her other guest too. But Mrs. Brucker continued to sip her tea in silence and her husband went on: 'I wish there was something I could do to show my appreciation for all that your grandmother has done for me.'

'I think you've already done what meant most to Grandmamma. Do you remember that ring you brought her, when you came to see her soon after my marriage? She's worn it ever since.'

Morris Brucker set down his silver-gilt cup. 'Yes,' he said quietly. 'Yes, I thought she might like to have it. It belonged to the Grand Duke Feodor. Your grandmother was always a great belle, from the time I first knew her, but I do not think it was until she met Feodor that any of the homage she received meant much to her. Unfortunately, he was one of the Romanoffs, who met such a terrible death during the worst "terror" periods, in the summer of '18. When the White Forces advanced westwards through the Urals, his desecrated body was one of those found in a deserted quarry.'

Everything connected with the wedding went off beautifully. It took place, on a perfect summer afternoon, in the garden of the big weather-beaten house surmounting the cliffs and the dunes; even Old Mrs. Forbes admitted that, once Priscilla had roused her parents from their lethargy, Sherman and Sue had spared no pains to do themselves and their elder daughter proud. Their younger daughter, Charlotte, was as dainty a bridesmaid as could have been found anywhere, and their two sons, Stillman and Donald, did not betray how unaccustomed they were to white flannels. As for Priscilla, she was really a charming bride. When she raised her head to receive David's kiss, after the ceremony was over, the look in her eyes had a dazzling quality. Old Mrs. Forbes turned away, to hide the tears in her own. But there were no tears in Emily's. Whenever her grandmother, who had been watching her closely, glanced in her direction, she seemed to be the central figure in a convivial group, which usually included Brian Collins. A new green-and-gold brocade was extremely becoming to her, and so was the big green picture hat, trimmed with golden roses, which she wore with it. And she had made a wise choice, in selecting her topazes as the finishing touch for her costume, instead of the diamonds. For the first time, Old Mrs. Forbes, who had always freely admitted Emily's good looks, coupled them with an adjective she had never used before. 'The girl's striking,' she said to herself. 'She stands out in a crowd. She never used to. She can say all she wants to about Priscilla's courage, I'd still say Emily's more than a match for her when it comes to that, and in a good many other ways too. What she's done today hasn't been easy. I ought to know.'

The day had not been easy for Old Mrs. Forbes, either. She was proud of Emily, but she was sick at heart on her account too. Moreover, the old lady had made a great effort, physically, not only in coming to the Cape for the wedding, but in seeing that the bridal party was suitably entertained beforehand. Well, thank God, there were to be no more parties at her house for the present; and now that everything had gone so well with the wedding, now that she was sure Sue and Sherman had insisted on having the Bruckers stand in line with them and that there was plenty of imported champagne for everybody, she wanted to go home. She was not interested in watching the bridal couple start off, in a shower of rice and confetti; she could not begrudge Priscilla her happiness, after seeing that look in her eyes; but she still felt it was Emily who should have been going to Germany with David. She still wondered why he did not seem to know what he had done to Emily, she could not forget that Emily was going to love him as long as she lived. . . .

Old Mrs. Forbes extricated herself with difficulty, from a very boring conversation with Roscoe Cutter, and managed to withdraw a little from the crowd, but presently Emily, who was watchful, came strolling across the lawn, escorted by Brian Collins. The gold roses on her hat, the gold threads in her brocade dress, glittered in the sunlight. She leaned over and put her arms around her grandmother.

'Brian has to get back to town,' she said. 'Something to do with this wicked campaign of his against poor Uncle Russell. Why don't you go with him? It's been a long day for you. I'll explain to Aunt Sue and Uncle Sherman that you were tired, and that you didn't like to break in on the line to say good-bye. I'll come along later with Clark and explain to him too. You can just slip quietly out of the side entrance. Brian's got his car there already.'

If anyone had told Old Mrs. Forbes beforehand that she would welcome the opportunity to drive away with Brian Collins, she would have denied this indignantly; but now she accepted Emily's suggestion with alacrity. 'Why, that's very kind of him,' she said. 'And I think it's an excellent idea. But you'll come in and see me for a minute before you go home yourself, won't you?'

'Of course, if you want me to. But I'll stay till the end here, you may depend on that. I'll be prepared to tell you about cutting the cake, and what Priscilla's going-away dress is like, and everything.'

Old Mrs. Forbes was not asleep when Emily tiptoed into her room, some hours later, and she immediately signified that such was the case. But she was not interested in the cake or the dress. She cut short Emily's description of them.

'Did David say anything special? Did he get a chance to speak to you alone?'

'Of course he didn't say anything special. Of course he didn't have a chance to speak to me alone. What are you thinking of, Grandmamma? A bridegroom on his wedding day!'

'I'm thinking that I hope you'll never be sorry.'

'Sorry for what?'

'Sorry that David was never your lover.'

'I suppose I'll have moments of being sorry. But only moments. And I'll know they won't last. I'll know I never could

289

have been really happy if I'd betrayed Roger's faith in me. David knew it, too, from the beginning. He told me so himself —the same day he told me that he loved me.'

'Well, you're right. And he was right. You and I don't belong to the breed that can take adultery in its stride, or call it fancy names. I found that out a long, long time ago.'

Her voice trailed away into silence and she seemed to be growing drowsy at last. The light in the room was dim, but Emily could see that she was fumbling with her ring. She spoke again, almost fretfully.

'I can't get this off. I want to take it off.'

'Why, Grandmamma?'

'Because I want you to have it. I want to give it to you tonight. I want you to wear it always—for my sake. Help me take it off, Emily. I don't want it found on my hand after I'm dead.'

'But, Grandmamma, you're not going to die!'

'I know I'm not going to die just yet. But I'm eighty years old, Emily. I can't expect to live much longer. I might die in my sleep, some night. I hope I do. And if I did, you wouldn't have any right to take this ring off and keep it, unless you knew it was yours. Besides, as I said, I don't want it found on my hand after I'm dead, the way it was found on Feodor Romanoff's hand when his corpse was taken from the quarry.'

Obviously, she had forgotten that she had never finished telling Emily the story she had begun a few weeks earlier. She went on speaking as if she had done so.

'Just before the state funeral at Ekaterinburg, some of the minor ornaments on the bodies were—retrieved. I don't know how they happened to be overlooked when—when the massacre took place. But they were. And I've always been thankful that this ring came into Morris Brucker's possession. I wish you'd tell him so, for me, if you have a good chance.'

'I will, Grandmamma. I'll be very glad to.'

'Morris Brucker knew I gave it to Feodor. He had it made for me to give the man I really—the man I really——' Again her voice trailed off into silence.

'I didn't have as much strength of character as you do, Emily,' she said at last. 'But I was a great ambassadress just the same. Everyone thought so. Most of all your grandfather.'

Three nights later Old Mrs. Forbes died in her sleep, as she had hoped she would; and it was when she was leaving her grandmother's house to go back to her own, after the funeral, that Emily remembered what Sister Mary Theresa had said—that the chapel at St. Margaret's was always open. She wondered now why she had never thought of it before—how she could have helped not thinking of it before. She walked slowly across the Square and went up the steps.

When she reached the little chapel and knelt down, she did not try to pray; it was so long since she had really prayed that she knew she could not do so now. But gradually the sense of peace and the awareness of Divinity which had come to her so many years before, in this same place, permeated her being again. She raised her eyes to the crucifix on the altar.

'I have to go along alone,' she murmured. 'There isn't anyone left to go with me now. Unless You will.'

The terrible loneliness which had engulfed her after David's marriage and Old Mrs. Forbes' death lasted a surprisingly short while. Emily realized that this was partly because she was so busy that she had no leisure whatsoever for introspection, and very little for reflection; she believed it was also because she resolutely kept her mind on the manifold tasks which confronted her while she was performing them, and did not permit herself to dwell on personal problems, except in connection with these. The periods that she did give over to deliberation were definitely set apart from her numerous and varied activities: some time in the course of every day she went to St. Margaret's Chapel, if only for a few minutes; and every night, before she went to bed, she devoted a few minutes more to quiet meditation. She made no attempt to force herself to utter prayers which did not come naturally from her heart to her lips. But almost immediately after her desperate avowal that she had only one possible source of communion left, the conviction that she was wholly alone began to lose its terrors and its strength. It appeared that there were, after all, a number of persons to whom she mattered and who mattered to her; in the preoccupation of her thoughts which centred on David and in the companionship with her grandmother, she had underestimated the importance of these other persons in her life.

Elizabeth was now very near her time, and though her condition gave no cause for actual alarm, certain aspects of it, including her age, indicated caution and care. She was easily annoyed

291

and upset, which was wholly uncharacteristic of her; the discussion of details regarding her mother's estate, and the management of her house fatigued and troubled her out of all proportion to their urgency and importance.

When Emily offered to take over the case of Elizabeth's household, her reply was definite, 'I'd really rather have you take Archie to your house than to have you and Deirdre come back here. Not that I don't love you both dearly, you know that. But just having so many people around——'

'I know. And it's what I'd prefer too—to stay where I am, I mean. Now be a good girl and try to take a nap. If you don't, we'll have to hustle you off to the hospital after all.'

The revision of a design for family living in the immediate future consumed a good deal of Emily's time; but it was accomplished with such surface smoothness that Elizabeth was both placated and deceived by its apparent simplicity. The other domestic problems were solved with almost equal dispatch, some of them more or less automatically. Doris, weeping bitterly, came to Emily and said it was all too evident that Mrs. Merriweather did not want a personal maid; indeed—if Mrs. Field would excuse the liberty—that Mrs. Merriweather did not know what to do with one. But perhaps Mrs. Field herself ... Emily did not want a personal maid, either, but she thought she would know what to do with one, if such a maid were willing to undertake chamber work also. Clark and Pearson, encouraged by the success of Doris, were the next to tell a masculine version of her story and invite a correlative response. Emily had no special use for a butler or a chauffeur, and no desire to build up an establishment into a semblance of what her grandmother's had been. But again she rose to the occasion, and the old men moved their belongings, as Doris had already moved hers, to the top floor of the Joy Street house with an air of importance, not to say triumph.

The rest of the staff was content to remain on Louisburg Square, particularly as the grim and capable Jenny was now doing most of the work; and everyone, but most especially Elizabeth, was delighted with the turn of events. Emily secretly derived less satisfaction from it; nevertheless, she did not fail to see that it had some rather amusing aspects.

'Talk about Victorian relics,' she said to Brian one day, when he had come to confer with her about her grandmother's will, 'I'm probably the only woman left in Boston who's living all by herself in a big house, except for five servants.'

'May I remind you that you're not living all alone, except for five servants. How could you forget dear little Archie?'

'I can't imagine. But I did, temporarily. Deirdre's got him so well under control that I'm hardly conscious of him.'

'Why don't you bring him out and park him in South Boston once in a while? My sister Katie would never notice the difference, if she had one more kid to look after, any more than my mother used to. As far as that goes, Mother'd be tickled to death to have him too.'

'All right. I'll bring him with me the next time I come over to supper.'

'Would that be tonight?'

'Why—it could be, I suppose.'

'Fine. I'll telephone her in a few minutes and break the good news. Meanwhile, let me remind you that you may find those five servants handy after all. You're taking over the second breakfast for Pell and Simonetta, aren't you?'

'Yes. I knew that was what Grandmamma would want me to do. I've already told Simonetta there won't be any change at all in the arrangements, except that they'll be carried out here, instead of on Louisburg Square.'

'And what about the first breakfast at Old Venice? Are you going to that?'

'Oh, yes! Simonetta specially asked me to. Didn't she specially ask you?'

'Indeed, she did.... And are you still planning to stand up with her?'

'Of course. Aren't you still planning to stand up with Pell?'

'Sure and why not? So it looks as if you and I'd be seeing quite a good deal of each other, first and last....'

Simonetta had already been informed of Pell's imminent arrival; but instead of 'telling her good news, she brought it', because he arrived the very next afternoon, and thereafter, preparations for an immediate wedding were the only order of the day. It was not until Brian lingered on, after the second breakfast, that Emily spoke to him of her own accord, about her grandmother.

She had been greatly moved by the significance of the marriage service which had been so long deferred, and this ultimate union of the two who had steadfastly loved each other for years poignantly recalled the solemn betrothal ceremony which had

293

taken place in her own drawing-room. But her emotions had been tinged throughout with joyousness; it had been impossible to escape the contagion of the conviviality which had pervaded the Italian breakfast at Old Venice; and the spectacle of the Joy Street house, decorated throughout with white flowers and thrown open to receive a large and festive gathering, had the effect of raising her spirits still further.

When Pell and Simonetta had finally gone over the crest of the Hill to their own little house, and Brian still showed no inclination to take his departure, even with the other last remaining guests, Emily found herself saying, 'Do you want to sit in the garden with me and listen while I "tell sad stories of the death of kings"?'

He did not instantly recognize the quotation. 'You know I'm always tickled to death to sit in the garden or anywhere else with you,' he answered. 'But as to sad stories and kings—isn't this a day for stories with happy endings? I should think it was. And stories about conquering heroes rather than dead monarchs!'

'You're right, in a way. But there's a story I think you would like to hear.'

He gave her a quick look. 'You mean about that Russian stuff your grandmother left you? Was that really given to her by a king?'

'No, he was only a grand duke. But I gather he was quite a regal person, just the same. I'm sure Grandmamma always thought of him as a royal lover.'

'A royal—— Good God, of course I want to hear it!'

It was very late when he finally left the garden. After Emily finished telling him the story of Feodor, in so far as she knew it herself, it seemed natural for them to go on talking of other things, and eventually he spoke to her about his campaign.

'It isn't going to create any awkwardness for you, is it, Emily?'

'No, of course not. Except that I think Uncle Russell may be here a good deal. He's taking it more or less as a personal insult that he can't use Grandmamma's house for his official headquarters. I suppose his official headquarters will be in some hotel.'

'Yes, inevitably. But he wants to sleep and eat here, he wants a private secretary and a private telephone installed, he wants you to do his entertaining for him? Is that the idea?'

'More or less, I think. And I don't like to say no. I want to do everything this summer, as Grandmamma would have done it, if she'd been alive, as she'd want it done.'

'And I say more power to you! ... Didn't I tell you you'd find a use for all those five servants yet?'

'Yes, you did. You're quite often right, Briny, about a number of things.'

'Thanks for those kind words.... Well, just let me know when you're about to begin your role as official hostess—for your uncle, I mean. Then I'll fade out of the picture, with my usual tact and grace.... I suppose you can sneak over to South Boston once in a while, even if I can't come here?'

'I'd feel terribly sorry if I thought I couldn't.'

'And what about the love nest on the other side of the Hill as a meeting place for us?'

Emily laughed. 'I imagine the bridal couple would like that entirely to themselves for a little while, don't you?'

'Yes. But the campaign isn't going to begin right away. And after all, we can sit in the garden and they can go to bed.'

Emily laughed again. 'Brian, you're incorrigible!'

'Would you like me any better if I were different?'

'No, I like you the way you are.'

'How much?'

'Very much.'

'Enough to marry me after all?'

'Certainly not. Go home, Brian, and stop talking nonsense.'

'Good night. Thanks a lot, Emily, for telling me the sad story about the death of a king.'

The next time he came, she told him something quite different. She could not have said why she wanted to, but the fact remained that she did. She told him how she had gone, not habitually, but frequently, before her marriage and in the period immediately thereafter, to St. Margaret's; and how she had stopped going, at first because of Homer Lathrop's cynicism and later because she found that a like cynicism had crept through her own being. Then she told him how she had gone there again, the day after her grandmother's funeral, for no other reason than because she felt entirely alone in the world and because she could think of no other place to go. Brian did not jest with her this time, or ask her inopportune questions. He listened attentively and gravely until she had finished telling him everything there was in her heart to say.

'And do you know, Briny, before I left there, I realized I wasn't alone. I don't mean—just on account of God. Of course I do believe again that His Spirit is always with us, wherever we go and whatever we do, that if we seek Him we shall find Him. But I mean it was just as if He had shown me, right then, that I'd keep more than I'd lost that there were any number of places I could still go, if only I would. *Earthly* places. *Pleasant* places. Places where I was wanted and needed, places where I wanted and needed to be, all of them with people in them who loved me and whom I loved. Do you understand what I'm trying to say?'

'I think so. Yes, I'm almost sure I do.'

'It doesn't trouble you, does it, because I've found such peace and comfort in a form of faith that's different from yours?'

'I don't believe it's so very different. Why don't you talk to Mat about that some day, if it's worrying you? He knows more about such things than I do. But, if it were different—no, that wouldn't trouble me. Even though I don't know much about such things, I do know they have a way of working out.'

They sat in companionable silence for some moments. Then Emily realized that Brian was not grave any longer, that he was grinning again and that there was a twinkle in his eye which was not without a spark of harmless malice.

'Do you remember that the day you took such exception to my technique as a suitor, I asked you whether you were troubled about the possibility that I might drink too much, and you said it really wasn't any affair of yours?'

'Yes, I remember.'

'Well, you tempt me to make a similar answer. Why *should* I be troubled about your religion—unless it is some affair of mine? Why should you think I would be, unless you're ready to admit that it is?'

She rose hastily and walked away from him, conscious of a flaming face. He caught up with her and put his arm around her.

'Sure and it's all right, mavourneen,' he said lightly. 'And I was a low dog, and all the rest of it, to trip you up like that. But this time, I'm going to have just one wee kiss and nothing you'll say will stop me, either.'

She did not see him alone again for some time, partly because her Uncle Russell moved in upon her almost immediately thereafter and practically took over the house, and partly because she and Brian were both so preoccupied in different directions. Brian won, hands down, in the primaries. The only other contestant for the nomination was an old ward heeler whose bosses belonged to a now-discredited political machine; and, as he himself admitted, the cards were stacked against him from the beginning—what could he do against a rising young lawyer, whose own political backing was powerful, and who was himself a recently returned 'hero' into the bargain? Russell Forbes had no opponent at all in the primaries; but when these were over, the pre-election campaign began in earnest, and both candidates were swept into the usual whirlwind of charges and counter-charges, slogans and speeches, rallies and parades. As Election Day approached, it became more and more evident that the contest would be very close; and Russell Forbes, who had hitherto been content to have Emily remain in the background, capably providing the setting for small private gatherings, urged to appear more frequently with him in public.

'I'm sorry, Uncle Russell. I don't feel that I can.'

'You don't feel you *can*! May I ask why not?'

'Because I'm not at all sure I believe in the principles you stand for and the way you interpret them. If I went to big public banquets with you and sat on the platform with you at rallies, it would give the impression that I did. Of course I don't suppose I could really help you anyway. I don't think I'm important enough to change a single vote. But you must think so, or you wouldn't ask me to come with you. So I'll have to ask you to excuse me.'

'You don't mean to tell me you'd sit back and see that flannel-mouthed Mick from South Boston take my seat away from me, without so much as lifting a hand?'

'I'm sorry, Uncle Russell, that you feel you have to talk about Brian Collins to me that way. I suppose it's part of the game to do mud-slinging in public. But Briny's a very good friend of mine. He's not coming to the house just now because he realizes it would create a certain awkwardness if he did. I realize that too. And I felt you had a prior right here, at present, on Grandmamma's account. But, as soon as the campaign's over——'

'I'm very much disappointed in you, Emily, and the company you keep. So are all your other relatives. So, incidentally, is Homer Lathrop.'

'I'm sorry about you and Uncle Homer. But I honestly don't

think the others are disappointed. I know Papa isn't.'

'Unfortunately, your father has never seen fit to show an intelligent interest in public affairs. And lately, he's become a very doting parent. Everything you do apparently seems perfect to him, just because you do it.'

'I'm very pleased and very proud that it does. I don't think I ever appreciated Papa until after Roger died. As to the other relatives, Uncle Sherman's a good deal more interested in his cranberry crop than he is in who wins the election—he claims it's unusually poor this year. Of course that's what he's been saying ever since I can remember, but still. . . . And Elizabeth's so wrapped up in the new baby, she doesn't even know there's a campaign on.'

As soon as she could, Emily left her uncle to cope alone with his dissatisfaction and walked over the crest of the Hill to see Pell and Simonetta. Despite what she had said to Brian, about their natural wish to have their house to themselves at first, they had made her extremely welcome from the beginning, and when she reached there, after the scene with her uncle, Pell flung open the door, not only with every evidence of great cordiality but with obvious excitement.

'I'm so glad you've come. We were just going to telephone and ask if you wouldn't sit in on a conference.'

'I'd be glad to. . . . What kind of a conference?'

'Well, Brian's had a brainstorm. He thinks that he and I ought to break away from Cutter, Mills as soon as we decently can. Of course we wouldn't leave them in the lurch; but the situation's beginning to ease with lawyers, just as it is all along the line. They wouldn't have too much trouble now filling our places.'

Brian rose from the depths of a cavernous wing chair at the farther end of the room and came towards them. 'You see what I mean, don't you, Emily? It isn't just that we'd get a lot of satisfaction out of being our own bosses, instead of being shoved around indefinitely by the Ruddy Oarsman and the Artful Dodger. It isn't even that eventually we'd make a lot more money than if they kept on taking most of the gravy. If we had our own firm we wouldn't just represent an experiment in better understanding between alien groups, the way we have so far. We'd represent an accomplished fact.'

'Yes, I do see what you mean. And I think it's a grand idea—from every point of view.'

All three went on to the rear of the room, where Simonetta was sitting with a bit of fine sewing in her hands and, for the next half-hour the question of a partnership was discussed, with the shared feeling and expression that, in principle, one had been started already. But it was Brian who made the most significant contribution to the conversation.

'You'd never guess who came into the office this morning and asked to see me—Priscilla's brother, Donald. He said he'd made up his mind to be a lawyer.'

'Why, the poor kid hasn't even got through the local high school yet, has he?'

'Yes, he has. More through good luck than through good management, if you don't mind my saying so, Emily. What's more, he's somehow got enough points to get into Harvard.'

'He hasn't!'

'I tell you he has. And now his idea is that he might cram a four years' college course into three years and that after that ... Well, to make a long story slightly shorter, I told him there'd be a place waiting for him with Collins and de Lucca any time after '52 that he was ready for it. So eventually, we will be having a Forbes in the firm, too.'

Yes, there would be a Forbes in the new firm, too, and she was glad of it; she would have been sorry not to have her family, or one like it, represented. But she recognized that it was not a Forbes, or anyone like a Forbes, who was to head the firm, to lend it prestige or to assure it sound financial standing. This was to be done by two men named respectively Brian Collins and Pellegrino de Lucca, whose immediate forbears came from groups long misprized and long underestimated. The days of such discrimination were numbered; and though the part she had played in bringing about this change was small, it was not negligible. She was not a failure after all. ...

As the campaign advanced, Emily formed the habit of going to the de Luccas' house whenever she could slip away from her own, in order to listen with them to the political news as it came over the radio. Pell had suffered no compunctions in telling Brian of his arrangement, and not infrequently the latter eluded his lieutenants and also put in an appearance at the 'love-nest'. Emily had come to recognize the probability of such brief visits, which she neither fostered nor discouraged; but it had not entered her head that Brian would make one on election night, or that she would hear from him directly until the following morning. However, when the returns began to come in, he called her over a private wire, and told her that the contest was 'too close to be comfortable'. An hour or so later he telephoned again and said he wanted to see her at once.

'You can't leave headquarters now, can you?' she asked, genuinely puzzled.

'I don't know how anyone's going to stop me, if I just walk out. Nobody's put a ball and chain on me yet.'

'But——'

'Stop saying "But"! As I've told you before, I wish it weren't such a favourite word of yours. I'm coming to Pell's, *but* you're right, I haven't got much time to spare, and the longer we talk over the telephone, the less time we'll have to talk face to face. Good-bye.'

Within five minutes, he appeared, in the whirlwind fashion which had always been more or less normal for him, but which had been intensified by his recent violent activities. Pell and Simonetta, simultaneously murmuring something incoherent about another radio upstairs, disappeared after the briefest of greetings. Brian was apparently quite oblivious of them in any case. He went up to Emily and put his hands firmly under her elbows.

'Listen,' he said, 'this thing is getting closer and closer. I still think I'm going to win. I meant to ask you, again, to marry me, after I was sure I had. But I changed my mind. I decided I'd rather ask you before I was sure. I decided I'd got to find out whether you had enough faith in me to believe that, even if I lose now, I'll win some other time.'

'I've got all kinds of faith in you, Briny.'

'Don't you dare add "but" to that! Have you got enough faith in me to tell me, this minute, that if I lose you'll come and live with me in South Boston until I can take you to a bigger and better place? You know I'd never come and live in your house. You can carry along as many of your trappings as you like, but you've got to let me provide the place for them—and for you. See if Pell wouldn't like to take over your house—of course he'll be the real head of the new firm because he'll stay in Boston all the time and I won't. He'll need a house like yours. Besides, this one won't be big enough for him and Simonetta very long. And they belong on Joy Street. You don't any longer and I never have. I won't pretend to that or anything else. I don't want *you* to pretend. I know you don't care for me the

300

way you cared for Roger, much less the way you cared for David. *I know you never will.* But you care in another way and it's a good way. Since you've got so much faith in me, you ought to be able to take my word for it that I'm right again. And you know I love you with all my heart and soul. Will you marry me whether I win or lose? Yes or no?'

'*Yes!*' Emily said.

It was two o'clock in the morning when he came back for her. They did not say much to each other in the course of their drive to South Boston. Brian had given his lieutenants the slip again, with great difficulty this time, and he knew he would have to drive fast to get home before they caught up with him. But they still had not done so when he opened the door of his father's house and all the family rushed forward to meet him. He waved his hat with his free hand and shouted a joyous greeting.

'Emily and I are on our way to Washington!' he cried. 'But we thought we'd stop in here first to say hallo and let you know we're going *together*!'

ALSO BY FRANCES PARKINSON KEYES

DINNER AT ANTOINE'S

Antoine's was New Orleans' most exclusive and gracious restaurant. The men who dined there were rich and successful, the women beautiful, vivacious, and talented. Orson Foxworth's party on 2nd January, 1949, was as glittering a company as any the restaurant had seen.

But the evening, on the surface so gay, was fraught with tensions and jealousies . . . all centring around Odile St. Amant, the young bride with the handsome but inattentive husband . . . the bride in the white dress. And when the dress was suddenly stained with the mark of red wine, it seemed a foreboding of the passion and death and drama that was to follow . . .

0 552 08834 X—40p

By Ernest Raymond

A GEORGIAN LOVE STORY

Set in London during the Edwardian and Georgian years, Ernest Raymond relates the simple and moving love story of a young boy and girl separated by background and birth but joined by a deep love.

Stewart O'Murry, whose family lives in respectable Hollen Hill, longs to know what goes on in the disreputable Hollen Dene area a few streets away. In his search for the unknown, he follows a seductive girl into a tobacconist's shop, and there, the first of many great surprises awaits him . . .

0 552 09125 1—40p

By Diane Pearson

THE MARIGOLD FIELD

Set amongst the poor but high-spirited people rooted in the farming country of southern England and in the bawdy streets of the East End of London, *The Marigold Field* is peopled by characters such as Jonathan Whitman, his cousin Myra, and Anne-Louise Pritchard of the Pritchard clan; and takes place in a changing era of social reform, straw boaters, feather boas, the Music Hall and, of course, the Boer War.

0 552 08525 1—30p

A SELECTION OF FINE READING
AVAILABLE IN CORGI BOOKS

Novels

☐	552 08651 7	THE HAND REARED BOY	*Brian W. Aldiss* 35p
☐	552 09018 2	A SOLDIER ERECT	*Brian W. Aldiss* 35p
☐	552 09218 5	A SEASON WITH EROS	*Stan Barstow* 35p
☐	552 09156 1	THE EXORCIST	*William Peter Blatty* 40p
☐	552 07938 3	THE NAKED LUNCH	*William Burroughs* 45p
☐	552 09217 7	THE DWELLING PLACE	*Catherine Cookson* 45p
☐	552 09160 X	BLONDE GENIUS	*J. T. Edson & Peter Clawson* 30p
☐	552 09174 X	A CHEMICAL ROMANCE	*Jenny Fabian* 35p
☐	552 09121 9	THE DAY OF THE JACKAL	*Frederick Forsyth* 50p
☐	552 09158 8	THE GOD BENEATH THE SEA	*L. Garfield & E. Blishen* 30p
☐	552 09221 5	BOYS AND GIRLS TOGETHER	*William Goldman* 75p
☐	552 09201 0	ALL EARTH TO LOVE	*Phyllis Hastings* 45p
☐	552 09125 6	CATCH 22	*Joseph Heller* 40p
☐	552 09127 8	HOUSE OF LOVE	*Ka-Tzetnik 135633* 35p
☐	552 09019 0	THE CONCUBINE	*Norah Lofts* 35p
☐	552 09173 1	HER OWN SPECIAL ISLAND	*Norah Lofts* 30p
☐	552 09176 6	HELL HOUSE	*Richard Matheson* 35p
☐	552 09139 1	RINGS FOR HER FINGERS	*Nan Maynard* 35p
☐	552 08791 2	HAWAII	*James A. Michener* 75p
☐	552 08124 8	LOLITA	*Vladimir Nabokov* 35p
☐	552 09219 3	THEODORA	*Jack Oleck* 45p
☐	552 09220 7	JOY STREET	*Frances Parkinson Keyes* 40p
☐	552 09140 5	SARAH WHITMAN	*Diane Pearson* 35p
☐	552 08887 0	VIVA RAMIREZ!	*James S. Rand* 40p
☐	552 08930 3	STORY OF O	*Pauline Reage* 50p
☐	552 08597 9	PORTNOY'S COMPLAINT	*Philip Roth* 40p
☐	552 08945 1	THE HONEY BADGER	*Robert Ruark* 55p
☐	552 08372 0	LAST EXIT TO BROOKLYN	*Hubert Selby Jr.* 50p
☐	552 09050 6	PASSIONS OF THE MIND	*Irving Stone* 75p
☐	552 09159 6	BLACK SEA FRIGATE	*Vivian Stuart* 30p
☐	552 07807 7	VALLEY OF THE DOLLS	*Jacqueline Susann* 40p
☐	552 08523 5	THE LOVE MACHINE	*Jacqueline Susann* 40p
☐	552 08384 4	EXODUS	*Leon Uris* 50p
☐	552 08866 6	QB VII	*Leon Uris* 50p
☐	552 08481 6	FOREVER AMBER Vol. 1	*Kathleen Winsor* 40p
☐	552 08482 4	FOREVER AMBER Vol. 2	*Kathleen Winsor* 40p

War

☐	552 09179 0	PRISONERS OF HOPE (illustrated)	*Michael Calvert* 40p
☐	552 09223 1	365 DAYS	*Ronald J. Glasser M.D.* 40p
☐	552 09161 8	INSTRUMENTS OF DEATH	*W. A. Harbinson* 40p
☐	552 08874 9	SS GENERAL	*Sven Hassel* 35p
☐	552 09178 2	REIGN OF HELL	*Sven Hassel* 35p
☐	552 09144 8	THE STRAITS OF MESSINA	*Johannes Steinhoff* 40p
☐	552 08986 9	DUEL OF EAGLES (illustrated)	*Peter Townsend* 50p
☐	552 09092 1	WEREWOLF	*Charles Whiting* 35p
☐	552 09222 3	BEYOND THE TUMULT (illustrated)	*Barry Winchester* 40p

Romance

☐	552 09198 7	A HOUSE FOR SISTER MARY	*Lucilla Andrews* 30p
☐	552 09207 X	THE GREEN EMPRESS	*Elizabeth Cadell* 30p
☐	552 09208 8	BRIDAL ARRAY	*Elizabeth Cadell* 30p
☐	552 09228 2	THE SEVEN SLEEPERS	*Kate Norway* 30p

Science Fiction

☐	552 09184 7	SATAN'S WORLD	*Poaul Anderson* 35p
☐	552 09229 0	STAR TREK 7	*James Blish* 30p
☐	552 09167 7	THE ALIEN WAY	*Gordon R. Dickson* 30p
☐	552 09149 9	STURGEON IN ORBIT	*Theodore Sturgeon* 30p

A SELECTED LIST OF FINE
NOVELS THAT APPEAR IN CORGI

*All these books are available at your bookshop or newsagent: or can be ordered direct
from the publisher. Just tick the titles you want and fill in the form below.*

CORGI BOOKS, Cash Sales Department, P. O. Box, Falmouth, Cornwall.
Please send cheque or postal order. No currency, and allow 6p per book to cover the
cost of postage and packing in the U.K., and overseas.

NAME ....

ADDRESS ....

(May 72) ....